Praise for *New York Times* bestselling author Diana Palmer

"Diana Palmer is an amazing storyteller, and her long-time fans will enjoy *Wyoming Winter* with satisfaction!"

—*RT Book Reviews*

"The popular Palmer has penned another winning novel, a perfect blend of romance and suspense."

—*Booklist* on *Lawman*

"Palmer knows how to make the sparks fly.... Heartwarming."

—*Publishers Weekly* on *Renegade*

Praise for *USA TODAY* bestselling author Delores Fossen

"Clear off space on your keeper shelf, Fossen has arrived."

—*New York Times* bestselling author Lori Wilde

"Fossen certainly knows how to write a hot cowboy, and when she turns her focus to Dylan Granger...crank up the air conditioning!"

—*RT Book Reviews* on *Lone Star Blues*

"An amazing, breathtaking and vastly entertaining family saga, filled with twists and unexpected turns, cowboy fiction at its best."

—*Books and Spoons* on *The Last Rodeo*

A prolific author of more than one hundred books, **Diana Palmer** got her start as a newspaper reporter. A *New York Times* bestselling author and voted one of the top ten romance writers in America, she has a gift for telling the most sensual tales with charm and humor. Diana lives with her family in Cornelia, Georgia.

www.DianaPalmer.com.

USA TODAY bestselling author **Delores Fossen** has published over one hundred novels with millions of copies of her books in print worldwide. She's received the Booksellers' Best Award, the RT Reviewers' Choice Best Book Award, and was a finalist for the prestigious RITA® Award. In addition, she's had nearly a hundred short stories and articles published in national magazines. You can contact the author through her webpage at www.deloresfossen.com.

New York Times **Bestselling Author**

DIANA PALMER

COURAGEOUS

HARLEQUIN® BESTSELLING AUTHOR COLLECTION

ISBN-13: 978-1-335-01567-9

Courageous

First published in 2012. This edition published in 2019.

Copyright © 2012 by Diana Palmer

The Deputy Gets Her Man
First published in 2003. This edition published in 2019.
Copyright © 2003 by Delores Fossen

Recycling programs
for this product may
not exist in your area.

Printed in U.S.A.

www.Harlequin.com

CONTENTS

COURAGEOUS 7
Diana Palmer

THE DEPUTY GETS HER MAN 271
Delores Fossen

Also available from Diana Palmer

Long, Tall Texans

Fearless
Heartless
Dangerous
Merciless
Courageous
Protector
Invincible
Untamed
Defender
Undaunted
Unbridled
Unleashed

Wyoming Men

Wyoming Tough
Wyoming Fierce
Wyoming Bold
Wyoming Strong
Wyoming Rugged
Wyoming Brave
Wyoming Winter
Wyoming Legend
Wyoming Heart

The Morcai Battalion

The Morcai Battalion
The Morcai Battalion: The Recruit
The Morcai Battalion: Invictus
The Morcai Battalion: The Rescue
The Morcai Battalion: The Pursuit

For a complete list of books by Diana Palmer, please visit www.dianapalmer.com.

COURAGEOUS

Diana Palmer

To Mel and Syble with all my love

PROLOGUE

PEG LARSON LOVED to fish. This was like baiting a hook. Except that instead of catching bass or bream in the local streams around Comanche Wells, Texas, these tactics were for catching a large, very attractive man.

She missed fishing. It was only a couple of weeks until Thanksgiving, and much too cold even in south Texas to sit on a riverbank. It was wonderful, in early spring, to settle down with a tub of worms and her tried-and-true simple cane fishing pole. She weighed down her line with sinkers and topped it with a colorful red, white and blue bobber that her father had given to her when she was five years old.

But fishing season was months away.

Right now, Peg had other prey in mind.

She looked at herself in the mirror and sighed. Her face was pleasant, but not really pretty. She had large eyes, pale green, and long blond hair, which she wore in a ponytail most of the time, secured with a rubber band or whatever tie she could lay her hand to. She wasn't really tall, but she had long legs and a nice figure. She pulled off the rubber band and let her hair fall around her face. She brushed it until its paleness was like a shimmering curtain of pale gold. She put on a little lipstick, just a touch, and powdered her face with the birthday compact her father had given her a few months earlier. She sighed at her reflection.

In warm weather, she could have worn her cutoffs—jean shorts made by cutting the legs off an old pair—and a nicely fitting T-shirt that showed off her pert, firm little breasts. In November, she had fewer options.

The jeans were old, pale blue and faded in spots from many washings, but they hugged her rounded hips and long legs like a second skin. The top was pink, made of soft cotton, with long sleeves and a low, rounded neckline that was discreet, but sexy. At least, Peg thought it was sexy. She was nineteen, a late bloomer who'd fought the wars in high school to keep away from the fast and furious crowd that thought sex before marriage was so matter-of-fact and sensible that only a strange girl would feel disdain for it.

Peg chuckled to herself as she recalled debates with casual friends on the subject. Her true friends were people of a like mind, who went to church in an age when religion itself was challenged on all fronts. But, in Jacobsville, Texas, the county seat where the high school was located, she was in the majority. Her school had cultural diversity and protected the rights of all its students. But most of the local girls, like Peg, didn't bow to pressure or coercion where morality was concerned. She wanted a husband and children, a home of her own, a garden and flower beds everywhere, and most of all, Winslow Grange to fill out the fairy tale.

She and her father, Ed, worked for Grange on his new ranch. He'd saved the wife of his boss, Gracie Pendleton, when she was kidnapped by a deposed South American leader who needed money to oust his monstrous nemesis.

Grange had taken a team of mercenaries into Mexico

in the dead of night and saved Gracie. Jason Pendleton, a millionaire with a real heart of gold, had given Grange a ranch of his own on the huge Pendleton ranch property in Comanche Wells, complete with a foreman and housekeeper—Ed and his daughter, Peg.

Before that, Ed had worked on the Pendleton ranch, and Peg had spent many long months building daydreams around the handsome and enigmatic Grange. He was tall and dark, with piercing eyes and a nicely tanned face. He'd been a major in the U.S. Army during the Iraq war, during which he'd done something unconventional and mustered out to avoid a general court-martial. His sister had committed suicide over a local man, people said. He was a survivor in the best sense of the word, and now he was working with the deposed Latin leader, Emilio Machado, to retake his country, Barrera, in the Amazon rain forest.

Peg didn't know much about foreign places. She'd never even been out of Texas and the only time she'd even been on a plane was a short hop in a propeller-driven crop duster owned by a friend of her father. She was hopelessly naive about the world and men.

But Grange didn't know what an innocent she really was, and she wasn't going to tell him. For weeks, she'd been vamping him at every turn. In a nice way, of course, but she was determined that if any woman in south Texas landed Grange, it was going to be herself.

She didn't want him to form a bad opinion of her, of course, she just wanted him to fall so head-over-heels in love with her that he'd propose. She dreamed of living with him. Not that she didn't live with him now, but she worked for him. She wanted to be able to touch him whenever she liked, hug him, kiss him, do…other things with him.

When she was around him, her body felt odd. Tight. Swollen. There were sensations rising in her that she'd never felt before. She'd dated very infrequently because most men didn't really appeal to her. She'd thought something might be wrong with her, in fact, because she liked shopping with girlfriends or going to movies alone, but she wasn't really keen on going out with boys like some of the girls did, every single night. She liked to experiment with new dishes in the kitchen, and make bread, and tend to her garden. She kept a vegetable garden in the spring and summer, and worked in her flower beds year-round. Grange indulged her mania for planting, because he enjoyed the nice organic vegetables she put on the table. Gracie Pendleton shared flowers and bulbs with her, because Gracie loved to garden, too.

So Peg dated rarely. Once, a nice man had taken her to a theater in San Antonio to see a comedy. She'd enjoyed it, but he'd wanted to stop by his motel on the way home. So that was that. The next man she dated took her to see the reptiles at the zoo in San Antonio and wanted to take her home to meet his family of pythons. That date had ended rather badly as well. Peg didn't mind snakes, so long as they weren't aggressive and wanted to bite, but she drew the line at sharing a man with several of them. He'd been a nice man, too. Then she'd gone out with Sheriff Hayes Carson once. He was a really nice man, with wonderful manners and a sense of humor. He'd taken her to the movies to see a fantasy film. It had been terrific. But Hayes was in love with another local girl, and everybody knew it, even if he didn't. He dated, to show Minette, who owned the local weekly newspaper, that he wasn't pining for her. She bought it, but Peg didn't. And she wasn't about to fall in love with a man whose heart was elsewhere.

After that, she'd stopped dating people. Until her father accepted this job working for Grange. Peg had seen him around the ranch. She was fascinated by him. He rarely smiled, and he hardly ever talked to her. She knew about his military background, and that he was considered very intelligent. He spoke other languages and he did odd jobs for Eb Scott, who owned and operated a counterterrorism school in Jacobsville, just up the road from Comanche Wells where Grange lived. Eb was an ex-mercenary, like a number of local men. Rumor was that a number of them had signed on with Emilio Machado to help him recover his government from the usurper who was putting innocent people in prison and torturing them. He sounded like a really bad sort, and she hoped the general would win.

But her worry was about Grange heading up the invasion army. He was a soldier, and he'd been in the thick of battle in Iraq. But even a good soldier could be killed. Peg worried about him. She wanted to tell him how much she worried, but the timing had never been right.

She teased him, played with him, made him all sorts of special dishes and desserts. He was polite and grateful, but he never seemed to really look at her. It was irksome. So she planned a campaign to capture his interest. She'd been working on it for weeks.

She waylaid him in the barn, wearing a blouse even more low-cut than this one, and made a point of bending over to pick up stuff. She knew he had to notice that, but he averted his eyes and talked about his new purebred heifer that was due to calf soon.

Then she'd tried accidentally brushing up against him

in the house, squeezing past him in a doorway so that her breasts almost flattened against his chest on the way. She'd peeped up to see the effect, but he'd averted his eyes, cleared his throat and gone out to check on the cow.

Since physical enticements didn't seem to be doing the trick, she tried a new tack. Every time she was alone with him, she found a way to inject sensual topics into the conversation.

"You know," she mused one day when she'd taken a cup of coffee out to him in the barn, "they say that some of the new birth control methods are really effective. Almost a hundred percent effective. There's almost no way a woman could get pregnant with a man unless she really wanted to."

He'd looked at her as if she'd grown another pair of eyes, cleared his throat and walked off.

So, Rome wasn't built in a day. She tried again. She was alone with him in the kitchen, her father off on his poker night with friends.

She'd leaned over Grange, her breasts brushing his broad shoulder, to serve him a piece of homemade apple pie with ice cream to go with his second cup of black coffee. "I read this magazine article that says it isn't size that matters with men, it's what they do with what they've got... Oh, my goodness!"

She'd grabbed for a dishcloth, because he'd knocked over his coffee.

"Did it burn you?" she asked hastily, as she mopped up the mess.

"No," he said coldly. He got up, picked up his pie, poured himself a fresh cup of coffee and left the room. She heard him go into his own room. The door slammed behind him. Hard.

"Was it something I said?" she asked the room at large.

THAT TACTIC OBVIOUSLY wasn't going to attract him, either. So now, she was going to try demure and sensuous. She had to do something. He was going away with the general, soon, to South America. It might be a long time until she'd see him again. Her heart was already breaking. She had to find some way to make him notice her, to make him feel something for her. She wished she knew more about men. She read articles in magazines, she looked on the internet, she read books. Nothing prepared her for seduction.

She grimaced. She didn't really want to seduce him completely. She just wanted to make him wild enough to feel that marriage was his only option. Well, no, she didn't want to trap him into marriage, either. She just wanted him to love her.

How in the world was she going to do that?

Grange didn't even date. Well, he'd gone out a time or two with a local girl, and there was gossip that he'd had a passion for Gracie Pendleton which was unrequited. But he was no rounder. Not in Comanche Wells, anyway. She imagined that he'd had plenty of opportunity to get women when he was in the military. She'd heard him talk about the high-society parties he'd been to in the nation's capital. He'd been in the company of women who were wealthy and beautiful, to whom he might have looked as attractive and desirable as he did to poor Peg. She wondered how experienced he was. More so than she was, certainly. She was flying blind, trying to intrigue a man with skills she didn't possess. She was stumbling in the dark.

She gave her reflection a last, hopeful look, and went out to impress Grange.

He was sitting in the living room watching a television special on anacondas, filmed in the Amazon jungle, where he was going shortly.

"Wow, aren't they huge?" she exclaimed, perching on the arm of the sofa beside him. "Did you know that when the females are ready to mate, males come from miles around and they form a mating ball that lasts for..."

He got up, turned off the television, muttering curses under his breath, walked out the front door and slammed it behind him.

Peg sighed. "Well," she mused to herself, "either I'm getting to him or I'm going to end up under a bridge somewhere, floating on my face." That amused her, and she burst out laughing.

Her father, Ed Larson, came in the door, puzzled. "Winslow just passed me on his way to the barn," he remarked slowly. "He was using the worst range language I ever heard in my life, and when I asked him what was wrong, he said that he couldn't wait to get out of the country and that if he ever got his hands on an anaconda, he was going to pack it in a box and send it home to you special delivery."

Her eyes popped. "What?"

"Very odd man," Ed said, shaking his head as he went into the house. "Very odd indeed."

Peg just grinned. Apparently she was having some sort of effect. She'd aroused Grange to passion. Even if it was only a burst of anger.

SHE MADE A coconut cake for dessert the following day. It was Grange's favorite. She used a boiled icing and sprinkled coconut on top and then dolled it up with red cherries.

After a quiet and tense dinner, she served it to the men.

"Coconut," Ed Larson exclaimed. "Peg, you're a won-

der. This is just like your mother used to make," he added
as he savored a bite of it with a smile and closed eyes.

Her mother had died of cancer years before. She'd
been a wonderful cook, and one of the sweetest people
Peg ever knew. Her mother had the knack of turning enemies into friends, with compassion and empathy. Peg
had never had a real enemy in her life, but she hoped that
if she ever did, her mother's example would guide her.

"Thanks, Dad," she said gently.

Grange was digging into his own cake. He hesitated
at the red candied cherries, though, and nudged two of
them to one side on the saucer while he finished the last
bite of cake.

Peg looked at him with wide, innocent eyes. "Don't
you like…cherries?" she asked, with her lips pursed sug-
gestively.

He let out a word that caused Ed's eyebrows to reach
for the ceiling.

Then he flushed, threw down his napkin and got up,
his sensuous lips making a thin line. "Sorry," he bit off.
"Excuse me."

Ed gaped at his daughter. "What in the world is wrong
with him lately?" he asked half under his breath. "I
swear, I've never seen a man so edgy." He finished his
own cake, oblivious to Peg's expression. "I guess it's this
Barrera thing. Bound to make a man worry. He's having to plan and carry out an involved military campaign
against a sitting dictator, with a small force and out of
sight of most government letter agencies," he added.
"I'd be uptight, too."

Peg hoped Grange was uptight, but not for those reasons. She blushed when she remembered what she'd said
to Winslow. It had been a crude comment, not worthy of

her at all. She'd have to be less blatant. She didn't want
to drive him away by being too coarse. She cursed her
own tongue for its lack of skill. She was making him
madder by the day. That brought to mind another possible complication. She could cost her father his job here
if she went too far. She was going to have to rethink her
strategy, once again.

So she puzzled on it for a couple of days and decided
to try something a little different. She curled her hair,
put on her best Sunday dress and sat down in the living
room to watch a recording of *The Sound of Music* when
she knew Grange was due in from riding fence lines.

He walked in, hesitated when he saw her sitting in
his place on the sofa and paused beside her.

"That's a very old film," he remarked.

She smiled demurely. "Oh, yes. But the music is wonderful and besides, it's about a nun who has a fairy-tale
romance with a titled gentleman who marries her."

He lifted an eyebrow. "Isn't that a little tame for your
taste?" he asked, and in a rather sarcastic manner.

She looked up at him with wide green eyes. "Why,
whatever do you mean?"

"Whatever happened to balls of anacondas and birth
control?" he asked.

She gasped. "You think that anacondas should use
birth control?" she asked, aghast. "Good heavens, however in the world would a male anaconda use a prophy-
lactic… Hello?"

He left the room so quickly that she imagined a trail
of flame behind him. But just as he went out the door,
she could have sworn she heard a deep, soft chuckle.

CHAPTER ONE

"I DON'T WANT to go to the Cattleman's Ball." Winslow Grange was emphatic about it. He glared at the other man. His dark eyes were hostile. Of course, they were usually hostile.

His boss just smiled. Jason Pendleton knew his foreman very well. "You'll have a good time," he said. "You need the break."

"Break!" Grange threw his big hands up in the air and turned away. "I'm going to a South American country with a group of covert ops specialists to retake a country under a bloodthirsty dictator..."

"Exactly," Jason said blandly. "That's why you need the break."

Grange turned back to him, with his hands deep in his jeans pockets. He grimaced. "Listen, I don't like people much. I don't mix well."

"And you think I do?" Jason asked reasonably. "I have to hobnob with heads of corporations, government regulators, federal auditors...but I cope. You'll be able to deal with it, too."

"I guess so." He drew in a long breath. "It's been a while since I led men into battle."

Jason lifted an eyebrow. "You went into Mexico to liberate my wife when she was kidnapped by your current boss."

"An incursion. We're talking about a war." He turned back to the fence, leaned his arms on it and stared blindly at the purebred cattle munching at a rolled-up hay bale. "I lost men in Iraq."

"Mostly due to your C.O.'s idiotic orders, as I recall, not to your own competence."

Grange said grimly, "I loved his court-martial."

"Served him right." Jason leaned against the fence beside him. "Point is, you lead well. That's a valuable ability to a deposed head-of-state who's fighting to restore democracy to his country. If you succeed, and I believe you will, they'll erect a statue of you somewhere."

Grange burst out laughing.

"But the ball is a local tradition. We all go, and donate to important regional causes at the same time. We get together and dance and talk and have fun. You remember what that is, Grange, don't you? Fun?"

Grange made a face.

"You ex-military guys, honest to God—" Jason sighed.

"Don't start with me," Grange told him. "You just remember that my military experience is why Gracie isn't lying dead in a ditch somewhere."

Jason shook his head. "I think about it every day." He didn't like remembering it. Gracie had almost died. Their courtship had been rocky and difficult. They were married now, and expecting their first child. Gracie had thought she was pregnant soon after their marriage, only she'd been mistaken. She wasn't this time. She was six months pregnant and beaming. They were happy together. But it hadn't been an easy path to the altar.

"I was going to ask her out, just before you married Gracie," Grange said to irritate the other man. "I even bought a new suit."

"It wasn't wasted. It's still in style. You can wear it to the Cattleman's Ball. Besides," Jason added with a grin, "you have no cause for complaint. I gave you a tract of land and a seed herd of purebred Santa Gertrudis."

"You really shouldn't have done that," Grange told him firmly. "It was overkill."

"It wasn't. You're the most valuable employee I've got here. It was a bonus. Well deserved."

Grange smiled. "Thanks." He made another face. "But you didn't have to throw in Ed Larson and his daughter."

"Peg's sweet, and she cooks like an angel."

The dark eyes glared. "She's after me. All the time. She says things…"

"She's barely nineteen—of course she says things…"

"She's trying to seduce me, for God's sake!" he burst out, and his high cheekbones flushed.

Jason's eyebrows lifted. "You do know that the Victorian Age is over and done with?"

"I am not about to start playing games with a nineteen-year-old," came the curt reply. "I go to church, pay my taxes and give to charity. I don't even drink!"

Jason shook his head. "I give up. You're a lost cause."

"You want to see a lost cause, look around you," Grange began. "We have the highest divorce rate, the ugliest economy and the greediest corporate entities on earth…"

Jason held up a hand. "I'm sorry, but I'm due in New York the week after Thanksgiving," he said drolly.

"I wasn't going to take that long to get my point across."

"You'll have to plant your soapbox someplace else. As to the ball, if you don't take Peg, who will you take?"

Grange looked hunted. "I'm going alone."

"Oh, that's going to put you on everybody's front page for a month."

His sensual lips made a straight line. "I'm not taking Peg! Her father works for me! So does she, while we're on the subject!"

"I can list all the people who took employees to past balls, if you like," Jason mused.

Grange knew already what a list that would be, and many of those couples ended up married. He didn't want to open that can of worms.

"It's only for about three hours," Jason continued. "What's the harm? And aren't you leaving the country two days later?"

"Yes."

"Think of it as a happy memory to take with you."

He shifted and averted his eyes. He ran a hand through his thick, black hair. "Peg won't have the money for a party dress."

"We have a new boutique in town. The designer, Bess Truman, is trying to drum up business, so she's outfitted half the town's eligible women with her stock. Remember Nancy, our pharmacist? She's got a green gown that she wore for an event that was filmed on the local television station. Bonnie, her assistant, has a red one that stopped traffic. Literally. Even Holly, who works with them, got a gold one. So Bess, she's the designer, she gave Peg one to wear also."

"Going to tell me what color it is?" Grange drawled sarcastically.

"You'll have to wait and see." Jason grinned. "Gracie said it's the most gorgeous of the lot."

Grange still hesitated.

"Ask her," Jason said, and he was solemn. "You've

been walking around alone for a long time. You don't date anybody. It's time you remembered why men like women."

His eyes narrowed. "Gracie put you up to this. Didn't she?"

Jason shrugged and pursed his lips. "Pregnant women have cravings. Strawberry ice cream with pickle topping, crushed ice with mango, their friends getting asked to holiday balls..." He glanced at Grange with twinkling eyes. "You wouldn't want to upset Gracie?"

"Yeah, hit me in my weak spot, why don't you?" Grange muttered.

Jason grinned wider.

He shrugged, "Okay. I should be testing weapons and drilling men. But I'll take the evening off and escort Peg to a ball I don't want to attend. Why not?"

"And be nice, could you?" Jason groaned. "Just once?"

He snarled. "I hate nice. I'm not nice. I was a major in a forward company in Iraq."

"It will be good practice for when you have to charm insurgents to surrender to your boss, the general."

Grange smiled coldly. "I won't need charm. I have several retooled automatic weapons and a few grenades."

Jason just shook his head.

PEG WAS IN the kitchen when Grange walked through the door of his ranch house. Jason had given him the house with the property, against his protests. Grange was still, technically, Jason's foreman on the huge Pendleton Comanche Wells property. But when he had free time, he could build up his own herd and renovate the huge white elephant of a house. Jason was paying Ed's salary. Grange was paying Peg's.

He never failed to appreciate Jason's generosity. The older man was a fanatic about repaying debts, and he felt that he owed Grange a lot for saving Gracie. Grange refused money, so Jason had found another way to repay him: the land, the house and the seed herd. It was worth a small fortune, but it was impossible to get around Jason when he was determined. Gracie had also been determined. In the end, Grange gave up and accepted with whatever grace he could manage. It was a hell of a reward. But it had been a desperate and dangerous mission. He could have died, so could his men. He'd managed the rescue in short time, and with no serious casualties. He hoped, he prayed, he'd be able to do the same with Emilio Machado's invasion force the week after Thanksgiving, when they went to South America to liberate Barrera from a merciless dictator who had led a coup against Machado.

Peg was nineteen, vivacious, with long blond hair and green eyes and a wicked smile. She and her father had been alone for five years, since the death of her mother from an aggressive, vicious cancer. The two of them had ended up working for Jason Pendleton, but his obligation to Grange had settled them here, in this old house.

Neither of them minded. Ed loved being foreman of Grange's small operation. He got the same salary he'd drawn from Jason at the Pendleton ranch property, but the duties were less rigorous and he had more free time. Peg, on the other hand, only had to cook for the three of them, and she was good at it. Not that the bunkhouse cook at Jason's place didn't stop by frequently to beg pies and cakes from her, because he couldn't do those. Peg never minded. She loved to cook.

"You should be in college," Grange said without preamble when he walked into the kitchen where she was just putting a meatloaf into the oven.

She glanced at him, laughed and stirred her potatoes, which were boiling. "Sure. I'll go to Harvard next semester. Remind me to ask Dad for the tuition."

He glared at her. "There are scholarships."

"I was a straight-C student."

"Work-study."

She turned around and looked up at him. It was a long way. She only came up to his chin. Her long, light blond hair was in two pigtails and her sweatshirt was spotted with grease. So were her jeans. She never wore an apron. She pointed the spoon at him. "And what would I study, exactly?"

"Home economics?"

She glowered at him. "Do you really want me to go to college and live in a coed dorm?"

"Excuse me?"

"A dorm that has men and women living in the same rooms, when they don't even know each other? Do you think I'm undressing in an apartment with a man I don't know?"

He gaped at her. "You have to be kidding."

"I am not. They have dorms for married couples. The rest have no choice about whether their dorm mates are male or female." She glared harder. "I was raised to believe that things work in a certain way. That's why I live in a place where people think like I do." She shrugged. "I read this old book by a guy named Toffler. Thirty years ago, he predicted that there would be people out of step with society and who couldn't fit in." She turned to him. "That's me. Out of step. Can't fit in. Doesn't belong anywhere. Well, anywhere except Jacobsville. Or Comanche Wells."

He had to admit, he didn't like the idea of her living in a dorm with male students she didn't know. On the other hand, he wouldn't like being forced to live with some woman he didn't know. How the world had changed in a decade or so!

He leaned against the wall. "Okay. I guess you're right. But you could commute to a college, or through the internet."

"I've thought about that."

He studied her pretty bow of a mouth, her rounded chin, her elegant neck. Her eyes were her finest feature, but the pigtails and lack of makeup did nothing for her.

She saw where he was staring and grinned. "Deterrents."

He blinked. "Excuse me?"

"My pigtails and my lack of makeup. They keep suitors away. If you don't care about fancy clothes and makeup, you're smart, right? So men don't like smart women."

He cocked an eyebrow. "If I wanted a relationship, I'd like a smart woman. I have a degree in political science with a double major in that and Arabic language studies."

The fork she was testing her potatoes with was suspended in midair. "You speak Arabic?"

He nodded. "Several dialects."

Her eyes fell. "Oh." She hadn't realized that he was college educated. She felt suddenly inadequate. He'd said that she needed to go to college herself. Did he find her unattractive because her mind wasn't developed like his? Or did he want her to leave?

He frowned. She looked worried. He recalled what Jason had said about that designer gown she'd been loaned. He grimaced. Well, he didn't really have any plans to take another woman...

"How about going to the Cattleman's Ball with me?" he asked bluntly.

She went from doubt and misery to euphoria in five seconds flat. She gaped at him. "Me?"

"Well, I don't think your Dad would look very good in a ball gown," he replied.

"The ball," she said, confused.

He nodded. "I hate parties," he said flatly. "But I guess I can stand it for a couple of hours."

She nodded. She looked blank.

"If you want to go?" he asked, because she looked... He wasn't sure how she looked.

"Yes!"

He laughed. The fork had flown out of her hand in her excitement. It landed, oddly, right in the sink. He laughed harder. "Nice toss. You might consider the NBA."

"Oh, I don't play football."

He started to tell her it was basketball, but she was beaming, and she looked really pretty. He smiled. His dark eyes sparkled. "Just a joke."

"Okay."

He shouldered away from the wall. "I'll get back to work. We'll leave about six on Saturday. They're serving canapés and whatnot. I don't think you'll need to cook supper, except something for your dad."

She nodded. "Okay."

He smiled and walked out.

Peg barely noticed the potatoes until water splashed out onto the stove. She tested them with a clean fork and moved the pan off the burner. She was going to the ball. She felt like Cinderella. She'd fix up her face and hair and make Grange proud. It would be the happiest night of her entire life. She felt as if she were walking on air as she started to mash the potatoes in a big ceramic bowl.

"I HEAR YOU'RE going to the ball," Ed Larson teased after they'd shared supper with Grange.

She blushed. She'd been doing that all through the meal. It was almost a relief when Grange went out to check the livestock.

"Yes," she said. "I was shocked that he asked me. I'll bet Gracie had her husband goad him into it, though," she added sadly. "I'm sure he said already that he wasn't going."

"I'm glad he is," Ed said. His face was solemn as he took a sip of coffee. "Rumor is that his group is leaving with Emilio Machado very soon. Revolution is never pretty."

"So soon?" she blurted out. She knew about the mission. There were no secrets in small towns. Besides, Rick Marquez, whose adopted mother Barbara ran the Jacobsville café, had turned out to be General Machado's son.

"Yes," her father replied.

"He'll die."

"No, he won't," he said, and smiled. "Winslow was a major in the army. He served in spec ops in Iraq and he came home. He'll be fine."

"You think so. Really?"

"Really."

She sighed. "Why do people fight?"

His eyes had a faraway expression. "Sometimes for stupid reasons. Sometimes for really patriotic ones. In this case," he added, glancing at her, "to stop a dictator from having people shot in their own homes for questioning his policies."

"Good heavens!"

He nodded. "General Machado had a democratic government, with handpicked heads of departments. He toured his country, talked to his people to see what their needs were. He set up committees, had representatives from indigenous groups on his council, even worked with neighboring countries to set up free-trade agreements that would benefit the region." He shook his head. "So he goes to another country to talk about one of those agreements, and while he's away, this serpent brings in his political cronies, has them put in charge of the military and overthrows the government."

"Nice guy," she said sarcastically.

"The general's right-hand man, too, his political chief, Arturo Sapara," Ed continued. "Sapara takes over the government then he closes down the television and radio stations and puts a representative in each newspaper office to report directly to him. He controls all the mass media. He puts cameras everywhere and spies on the people. Somebody says, anyone he doesn't like…they disappear, like two internationally known college professors disappeared a few months ago."

"Ouch."

"People think things like that can't happen to them." He sighed. "They can happen anywhere that the public turns a blind eye to injustice."

"I didn't realize it was that bad."

"Machado says he's not going to stand by and let the work he put into that democracy go down the drain. It's taken him months to mount a counteroffensive, but he's got the men and the money now, and he's going to act."

"I hope he wins." She grimaced. "I just don't want Grange to die."

He chuckled. "You underestimate that young man," he assured her. "He's like a cat. He's got nine lives. And he thinks outside the box, which is what makes him so invaluable to Machado. Example," he added, his eyes twinkling as he warmed to his subject, "North Africa in the early days of the North African campaign in World War II. The commanding German field marshal, Rommel, had only a handful of troops compared to the British. But he wanted them to think he had more. So he had his men march through town in a parade, go around the corner and march through again several times to give the appearance of numbers. He also had huge fans, aircraft engines, hooked up behind trucks to blow up the desert sand and make his column appear larger than it really was. By using such tricks, he psyched out the opposition for a long time. That's what I call thinking outside the box."

"Wow. I never heard of that German officer."

He gave her a blank stare. "Excuse me? Didn't you study about World War II in school?"

"Sure. We learned about this general called Eisenhower who later became president. Oh, and this guy Churchill who was the leader in England."

"What about Montgomery? Patton?"

She blinked. "Who were they?"

He finished his coffee and got up from the table. "I'll quote George Santayana, a Harvard professor. 'Those who cannot remember the past are condemned to repeat it.' And for the record, high school history needs retooling!"

"Modern history." She made a face. "A lot of dates and insignificant facts."

"The stuff of legends."

"If you say so."

He glared at her, grimaced and gave up. "We're leaving the world in the hands of shallow thinkers when we old ones die."

"I am not a shallow thinker," she protested. "I just don't like history."

He cocked his head. "Grange does."

She averted her eyes. "Does he?"

"Military history, especially. We have running debates on it."

She shrugged. "I guess it wouldn't hurt to check it out on Google."

"There are books in the bookcase," he said, aghast. "Real, honest to goodness books!"

"Dead trees," she muttered. "Kill a tree to make a book, when there are perfectly good ebooks for sale all over the web."

He threw up his hands. "I'm leaving. Next you'll be telling me that you agree with all the bookstore and library closings all over the country."

She hesitated. "I think it's very sad," she said unexpectedly. "A lot of people can't afford to buy books, even used ones. So the library has all that knowledge available for free. What are people going to do when they don't have any way to learn things except in school?"

He came back and hugged her. "Now I know you're really my daughter." He chuckled.

She grinned. "Aw, shucks." She lowered her head and scuffed her toe on the floor. "Twarn't nothing," she drawled.

He laughed and went away.

"Pie?" she called after him.

"Wait an hour or so until dinner has time to settle!" he called back.

"Okay."

SHE HEATED UP a cup of coffee and carried it through the house, out the back door and into the barn. Grange was sitting out there in an old cane-bottom wooden chair with a prize heifer that was calving for the first time. He wouldn't admit it, but he was attached to the Santa Gertrudis first-time mother, whom he called Bossie. She was having a hard time.

"Damned big bull that sired this calf," he muttered, accepting the coffee with a grateful smile. "If I'd known who the sire was, I'd never have let Tom Hayes sell me this pregnant heifer."

She grimaced. She knew about birth weight ratios. A first-time mother needed a small calf. The herd sire who bred this one was huge, which meant a much higher birth weight than was recommended. It would endanger the mother.

"I hope she'll do okay."

"She will, if I have to have the vet come out here and sit with her all night and pay him."

She laughed. "Dr. Bentley Rydel would do it for free. He loves animals."

"Good thing. His brother-in-law sure is one. An animal, I mean."

"You really have it in for mercenaries, don't you?" she asked, curious.

"Not all of them," he replied. "Eb Scott's bunch is a notch above the rest. But Kell Drake, Rydel's brother-in-law, was a career military man and he threw it all up to go off searching for adventure in, of all places, Africa!"

"Is Africa worse than South America?" she asked, making a point.

"Much worse, because you have so damned many factions trying to get a foothold there," he replied. "Most of the aid that's sent never reaches the starving masses, it goes to sale for the highest bidder and the money goes in some warlord's pocket." He shook his head. "Guns don't really solve problems, you know. But neither does diplomacy when you have two religions slugging it out in the same region, plus class warfare, tribal conflicts, greedy corporations…"

"Is there anybody you like?" she asked pointedly.

"George Patton."

She laughed, remembering her father had mentioned the name. "Who's he?"

His eyes almost popped.

"Well, I'm young," she muttered. "You can't expect me to know everything."

He drew in a long breath. She was. Very young. It made him uncomfortable. "He was a famous general in World War II. He served in several theaters of operations for the Allies, predominantly the North African and European campaigns."

"Oh, that Patton!" she exclaimed. "My dad was telling me about a German general named Rommel in North Africa. Then there was this movie I watched…did Patton really do those things?"

He chuckled. "Some of them. I went through West Point with a distant cousin of his."

"Neat!"

He finished the coffee. "You should go back in. It's getting cold."

She took the cup from his outstretched hand. "It is."

"Thanks for the coffee."

She shrugged. "Welcome." She glanced at the heifer, who was staring at them with wide brown eyes. "I hope Bossie does okay."

He smiled. "Me, too. Thanks."

She nodded, smiled and left him there.

THE NEXT MORNING, the veterinarian's truck was sitting at the barn. Before she even started breakfast, Peg ran out the back door and down to the barn. She'd worried about the mother cow all night.

Grange was leaning against a post, talking to the vet. They both turned when she walked in.

"Well?" she asked a little hesitantly, because she was concerned.

Grange smiled. "Bull calf. Mother and baby doing fine."

She let out a sigh. "Thank goodness!"

Grange grinned at her obvious relief.

"If you'd like to stay for breakfast," she told the vet, "I'm making biscuits and fresh sausage and eggs. We have hens and he—" she pointed at Grange "—bought us a freezer full of pork sausage and ribs and loins." She grinned. "We're rich!"

They both laughed.

"You're very welcome to stay," Grange told him. "She cooks plenty. And she's a good cook."

Peg blushed. Her eyes sparkled. "Nice to be appreciated."

"In that case, I'd love to join you, thanks."

"I'll get busy." She ran all the way back to the house. Grange liked her cooking. She could have floated.

CHAPTER TWO

"WHAT'S YOUR BROTHER-IN-LAW up to these days?" Grange asked their guest.

He got a droll look in reply. "Kell Drake always changes the subject when I ask. But he and one of his cronies were reportedly up to their ears in some project in South Africa that involves guns. I don't bother to ask," Bentley Rydel added when Grange started another question. "It's a waste of breath. He was working on something with Rourke, but I hear he's going overseas with you," he added with a pointed look.

"Rourke," Grange sighed, shaking his head. "Now there's a piece of work."

"Who's Rourke?" Peg wanted to know.

"Somebody you don't even need to meet," Grange told her firmly. "He's a..."

"Please." Bentley held up his hand, chuckling. "There's a lady present."

"You're right," Grange agreed, sipping coffee, with a smile in Peg's direction.

Peg laughed.

"Well, Rourke's in a class all his own," Grange continued. "Even our police chief in Jacobsville, Cash Grier, avoids him, and Grier's worked with some scoundrels in his time. Word is," he added, "that Kilraven, who used to work for some federal agency undercover in Grier's department, almost came to blows with Rourke over the woman he married."

"A ladies' man, is he?" Ed asked.

"Hard to say," Grange replied. "He thinks he is."

"He's definitely got the connections," Bentley mused. "Rumor has it that he's the illegitimate son of billionaire K.C. Kantor, who was once at the forefront of most conflicts in the African states."

"I've read about him," Ed replied. "A fascinating man."

"He never married. They say he was in love with a woman who became a nun. He has a godchild who married into a rich Wyoming ranching family."

"Well!" Ed exclaimed. "The things you learn about people!"

"True." Bentley checked his watch. "Gotta run, I'm doing surgery at the office in thirty minutes." He got up. "Thanks for breakfast, Peg," he added with a smile.

"You're welcome. Tell your wife I said hello. Cappie was a few grades ahead of me in school, but I knew her. She's a sweetie."

"I'll tell her you said so," he said with a grin. "See you."

The men walked him out to his truck while Peg cleared away the breakfast dishes. She put everything in the dishwasher and went upstairs to see what she had in the way of accessories for her big night at the ball. Cinderella, she thought amusedly. That's me.

PEG LOVED TO plant things. Especially bulbs. She knew that next spring, the hyacinths and tulips and daffodils and narcissus bulbs that she was planting now would be glorious in color and scent. Hyacinths, she mused, smelled better than the most expensive perfume. She knew about expensive perfume; she spent a lot of time at cosmetic counters sniffing it. She'd never be able to buy any of that for herself. But she loved to sample the luxurious scents when she went to the mall in San Antonio. She couldn't go that often, but she always made the most of each trip.

She finished putting the last of the hyacinths in, and got up from the ground. Her white sweatshirt was streaked with dirt. Probably her hair was, too. But she loved to play in the dirt. So did Jason Pendleton's wife, Gracie, who'd sent her the bulbs. Gardeners were almost always friends at first sight. There was a kinship among people who loved to plant things.

Grange drove up at the barn, cut the engine and got out. He walked up to Peg and stared at the long rectangular flower bed she'd put right next to the barn. He frowned.

"It's convenient to the source of my best fertilizer," she pointed out.

It took him a few seconds to puzzle that out. She was talking about animal waste, which was organic and quite effective. He chuckled. "I see."

"Mrs. Pendleton sent me the bulbs. They're nice ones, from her own garden. You don't really mind…?"

He shook his head. "Amuse yourself. I don't care."

"Dad's gone to the market," she said, wide-eyed. "Would you like to ravish me while he's away?"

He glared at her. This was her usual way of teasing, and it was beginning to get to him in ways he didn't like. "No, I would not," he said firmly.

She glared back. "Honestly, you're stuck back in the ice age! Everybody does it these days!"

"Including you?"

"Of course, me," she scoffed. "I've had sex continuously since I was fourteen."

His eyes were growing darker. He was shocked and trying not to show it. Peg didn't appear to him as a rounder. Was he that bad a judge of character?

"It's no big deal!" she exclaimed. "You are such a throwback!"

He turned on his heel and stormed off into the barn. He didn't like thinking that Peg was promiscuous. He was too old-fashioned to think it was a laudable lifestyle, regardless of how many people did.

She followed him into the barn, waving her trowel in the air. "Listen, people don't have to abide by ancient doctrines that have no place in modern society," she burst out. "There isn't one show on television that has people getting married before they indulge!"

He whirled, glaring. "That's exactly why I don't watch television."

"You're just the kind of man who thinks women should be saints and go around in frilly clothes and be seen yet not heard!"

"And you're the sort who thinks they should dress like streetwalkers and throw out profanity with every other breath!"

She tossed the trowel away and went right up to him. "I threaten you, don't I," she teased. "You're mad for me, but you think I'm too young and innocent...!"

The sudden pause was because, in a lightning-fast move that she hadn't anticipated, he backed her right into the barn wall, slammed his powerful body down on hers and kissed her with an expertise and insistence that made her heart stop dead.

"Damn you," he ground out against her mouth, and

both hands went to her hips, grinding them into the sudden arousal that was as unexpected as it was painful.

She was sorry she'd made such claims. She was scared to death. She'd never even been kissed except once by a boy who was even more bashful than she'd been, and the kiss had been almost repulsive to her. Since she'd had feelings for Grange, she hadn't even dated.

Now here he was taking her up on her stupid offer, and thinking she was experienced and she didn't even know what to do. Worse, he was scaring her to death. She'd never felt an aroused man's body. It was oddly threatening, like the lips that were forcing hers apart in a kiss that was years too adult for her lied-about worldly experience.

Her small hands were against his shirtfront, pushing. She tried to turn her face aside. "Ple…please," she choked out when she managed to escape his devouring mouth for a few seconds.

His head was spinning. She tasted like the finest French champagne. She felt like heaven against him. She was soft and warm and delicately scented, and she aroused him as no other woman ever had in his whole life.

She'd had men. She bragged about it. But as sanity came back in a cold rush, he became aware of her nervous hands on his chest, of her whispered, frantic plea. He lifted his head and looked point-blank into her wide, soft green eyes. And he knew then, knew for certain, that she'd never had a man in her young life.

"Stand still!" he bit off when she tried to move her hips away from the press of his.

The urgency in his tone stilled her. She swallowed, hard, and swallowed again, while he slowly moved back from her, his hands clenched as he turned away. A visible shudder went through his straight back.

She barely registered it. She was shaking. She leaned back against the barn wall, her arms crossed over her breasts. They felt oddly tight and swollen. She felt swollen someplace else, too, but she didn't know why. She should have listened more carefully in health class instead of reading books on archaeology while the teacher droned on and on about contraception, and the clinical details. Boring. Theory and practice, she decided, were sometimes unrelated, it seemed.

After a minute, Grange drew in a long, steadying breath, and turned back to Peg.

She couldn't meet his eyes. She was flushed and nervous and shattered.

Her vulnerability took the edge off his temper. He moved back to her, cupped her oval face in his big, warm hands and forced her eyes to meet his.

"You little liar," he chided, but he was smiling. He didn't even seem to be mad.

She swallowed once more.

He bent and kissed her eyelids shut, tasting salty tears. "Don't cry," he murmured tenderly. "You're safe."

Her lips trembled. The caress was out of her experience. It was so much more poignant than the hard, insistent kiss that had come without respect or tenderness. This was a world away from that.

Her hands flattened against his soft flannel shirt, feeling the muscle and warmth and heavy heartbeat under it. She savored the feel of his lips on her skin.

"And now we know that making false claims and being aggressive can lead to misunderstandings, don't we?" he murmured.

"Yes, well, we should have paid more attention in health class instead of covertly reading archaeology journals," she said unsteadily.

He lifted his head. "Archaeology?"

She managed a weak smile. "I like to dig in the dirt. Planting things, digging up artifacts, it's sort of similar, isn't it?"

He laughed softly. "If you say so."

She searched his eyes, feeling vulnerable. "You're not mad?"

He shook his head. "Ashamed, a bit, though."

"Why? It was my fault," she pointed out bluntly. "I was really out of line. I'm sorry."

He sighed. "Me, too."

She peered up at him. "You still want to take me to the ball, don't you?" she worried aloud.

His eyes narrowed. "More than anything," he replied, and his voice was like deep velvet.

She flushed. She smiled. "Okay!"

He kissed her nose. "Get out of here. I've got to check on my heifer."

"Cow," she corrected. "She's a cow, now that she's a mother."

His eyebrows arched.

"Sorry."

He chuckled. "I have to check on my cow," he corrected.

She grinned and started to leave.

"Peg."

She turned. Her name on his lips had a magical sound.

"My father was a minister," he said quietly, and watched her flush as she recalled the things she'd spouted off to him.

"Oh, gosh," she groaned.

"He wasn't a fanatic," he added. "But he had a very solid take on what life should be, as opposed to what other people thought was permissible. He said that the only thing that separated human beings from animals was the nobility of spirit that went with respect for all life. Religion, he said, along with the arts, was the foundation of any civilization. When those two things fell, so did society."

She searched his face. "One of my archaeological journals talks about the Egyptian civilization," she said, moving back to him. "The arts went first, followed by the religion that had been practiced for centuries. Or like Rome, when it absorbed so many other cultures and nationalities and they couldn't mix, so they ended up dividing the nation and it fell to internal conflict."

He smiled. "You should go to college and study anthropology."

"Chance would be a fine thing."

"Jason Pendleton endows scholarships at several universities. If you really wanted to go, he'd send you."

She flushed. "Wow! You think so?"

"I do."

She grimaced. "Well, there's that living in coed dorms thing," she said reluctantly.

That was when he remembered their talk on that subject earlier, before she'd claimed experience she didn't have. He should have remembered that while she was making her outspoken claims. A woman who didn't want to live in a coed dorm obviously wouldn't approve of sleeping around. He'd forgotten.

He touched her hair. "You could live off campus."

She looked up at him, searching his dark eyes. "Who'd take care of you and Dad?"

He felt a jolt in his heart. It hadn't occurred to him until then how well she took care of him. Freshly washed linen on his bed, dusted surfaces, little treats tucked into his saddlebags when he went riding the fence line, his coat always prominent in the front of the closet so that he had easy access to it.

"You spoil me," he said after a minute, and he wasn't smiling. "It isn't wise. I've lived hard most of my life in the military. I don't want to get soft."

"That won't ever happen," she assured him. "You have that same refined roughness that Hannibal was supposed to have when he fought Scipio Africanus, the famous Roman general, in the Punic Wars."

He blinked. "You know that, and you don't recognize the names of Patton and Rommel?" he exclaimed.

She shrugged. "You like modern military history. I like ancient history." She grinned. "One of Hannibal's strategies was to throw clay pots of poisonous snakes onto the decks of enemy ships. I'll bet the crew jumped like grasshoppers to get into the water," she countered.

"Bad girl," he said, shaking a finger at her. He pursed his sensual lips, still a little swollen from the hard contact with hers. "On the other hand, that's not a bad strategy even for modern warfare."

"Oh, it would never do," she replied. "Groups of herpetology advocates would march in the streets to protest the inhumane treatment of the snakes."

He burst out laughing. "You know, I can believe that. We live in interesting times, as the Chinese would put it."

She raised both eyebrows.

"An old Chinese curse. 'May you live in interesting times.' It means, in dangerous ones."

"I see."

He sighed, smiling as he studied her face. She wasn't pretty, but she had regular features and beautiful green eyes and a very kissable mouth. He stared at it without wanting to. "No more teasing," he said unexpectedly. "I have a low boiling point and you're not ready for what might happen."

She started to protest, but decided against it. She grimaced. "Rub it in."

He moved forward, and took her by the shoulders. "It wasn't a complaint," he said, choosing his words. "Look, I don't indulge. I was never a rounder. I don't like men who treat women like disposable objects, and there are a lot of them in the modern world."

"In other words, you think people should get married first," she translated, and then flushed, because that sounded like she wanted him to propose. She did, but she didn't want to be blunt about it.

He shifted a little. "Marriage is something I'll eventually warm to, but not now. I'm about to be involved in a dangerous operation. I can't afford to have my mind someplace else once lead starts flying, okay?"

Her stomach clenched. She didn't want to think about the possibility that he might get hurt and she wouldn't be there to nurse him. She wouldn't think about worst-case scenarios. She wouldn't!

"Don't go getting nervous," he chided. "I'm an old hand at tactics and, not to blow my own horn too much, I'm good at it. That's why General Machado has me leading the assault."

"I know," she said quietly. "Dad thinks you have great

skills at leadership. He said it was a shame you got forced out of the military."

He shrugged. "I believe, like my father did, that things happen for a reason, and that people come into your life at the right time, for a purpose."

She smiled gently. "Me, too."

He touched her soft mouth with his forefinger. "I'm glad that you came into mine," he said, his voice deep and soft. He drew back. "But we're just friends, for now. Got that?"

She sighed. "Should I get a refund on my prophylactics, then?" she asked outrageously.

He burst out laughing, shook his head and walked away.

"Is that a 'no'?" she called after him.

He threw up a hand and kept walking.

She grinned.

THE DAY OF the Cattleman's Ball, she was so nervous that she burned the biscuits at breakfast. It was the first time since she started cooking, at the age of twelve, that she'd done that.

"I'm so sorry!" she apologized to her dad and Grange.

"One misstep in months isn't a disaster, kid," Grange teased. "The eggs and bacon are perfect, and we probably eat too much bread as it is."

"Frankenbread," Ed muttered.

They both looked at him with raised eyebrows.

He cleared his throat. "A lot of the grains are genetically modified these days, and they won't label what is and what isn't. Doesn't matter much. Pollen from the modified crops gets airborne and lands on nonmodified crops. I guess those geniuses in labs don't realize that pollen travels."

"What's wrong with genetic modification?" Grange asked.

"I've got a documentary. I'll loan it to you," Ed said grimly. "People shouldn't mess around with the natural order of things. There's rumors that they're even going to start doing it with people, in 'in vitro' fertilization, to change hair and eye color, that sort of thing." He leaned forward. "I also heard that they're combining human and animal genes in labs."

"That part's true," Grange told him. "They're studying ways to modify genetic structure so that they can treat genetic diseases."

Ed glared at him. He pointed his finger at the younger man. "You wait. They'll have human beings with heads of birds and jackals and stuff, just like those depictions in Egyptian hieroglyphs! You think the Egyptians made those things up? I'll bet you ten dollars to a nickel they were as advanced as we were, and they created such things!"

Peg got up and glanced around her worriedly.

"What are you doing?" Ed asked.

"Watching for people with nets," she said. "Shhhhh!"

Grange burst out laughing. "Ed, that's a pretty wild theory, you know."

Ed flushed. "I guess I'm getting contaminated by Barbara Ferguson who owns Barbara's Café in Jacobsville. She sits with me sometimes at lunch and we talk about stuff we see on alternative news websites."

"Please consider that those websites are very much like tabloid newspapers," Grange cautioned. "I do remember that Barbara was saying that electrical equipment could sustain an electromagnetic pulse by being stored in a Leyden jar. It's a Faraday cage," he explained. "She was very upset when I corrected her, but I pulled it up on my iPhone and showed her the scientific reference. She quoted a source that was totally uninformed."

"Dang. I guess I'll have to toss my Leyden jar, then," Ed said with twinkling eyes, and grinned.

"If you can build one, let me know," Grange requested.

"Don't look at me," Ed replied. "I took courses in animal husbandry, not physics."

"I flunked physics my first three weeks in the class in high school, and had to transfer to biology." Peg sighed. "I loved physics. I just couldn't wrap my brain around it."

"I took courses in college," Grange said. "I made good grades, but I loved political science more."

"You might end up in Machado's government," Ed mused. "As a high official. Maybe Supreme Commander of the Military."

Grange chuckled. "I've thought about that. Plenty of opportunity to retool the government forces and make good changes in policy."

Peg felt her heart drop. That would mean he might not come home from South America, even after the assault, if it was successful. She might never see him again. She studied him covertly. He was the most important thing in her life. She hadn't slept well since that unexpected, passionate kiss in the barn. He wanted her. She knew that. He hadn't been able to hide it. But he wasn't in the market for a wife, and he didn't do affairs.

Her sadness might have been palpable, because he suddenly turned his head and looked straight into her eyes. There was a jolt like lightning striking her. She flushed and dragged her gaze away as quickly as she could, to avoid tipping off her father that things were going on behind his back.

Her father was pretty sensitive. He looked from one to the other, but he didn't say a word.

LATER, THOUGH, HE cornered Peg before she went into her room to start dressing for the ball.

"What's going on between you and Grange?" he asked quietly.

She sighed. "Nothing, I'm afraid. His father was a minister and he doesn't sleep around."

Ed, shocked, let out a sudden burst of laughter. "You're kidding."

She held up both hands. "Hey, I'm just the messenger. He doesn't drink, he doesn't smoke and he doesn't… well, indulge. He thinks people should get married first. But he doesn't want to marry anybody."

Ed's expression lightened. "Well!" Grange went up very high on his respected list.

"So he's taking me to a ball but not to a motel afterward, in case you were worried, I mean," she added with twinkling eyes.

He shrugged. "I'm out of step," he confessed. "I don't know how to live in this world anymore."

"I guess you and I live in the best place for dinosaurs," Peg pointed out. "We have plenty of company."

He grinned. "Yes, and we all live in the past. Look at the town square, all decked out for Christmas, with lights and holly and Santa Claus and his reindeer."

"With decorated trees in every public and private office, too," she added, laughing. "I love Christmas."

"So does Gracie Pendleton," Ed reminded her. "She's

got their place in San Antonio decked out like a light show, and the ranch here is sparkling with seasonal color as well."

"I'm going to be sparkling tonight, in my new borrowed designer evening gown," she said. "I had the beauticians teach me how to do my hair, and I've got Mama's pearls. I thought I'd wear them." Her face was sad. Her mother had died five years past. They both still missed her.

"She loved parties," Ed recalled with a sad smile. "But only occasionally. She was like me, a misfit who never belonged anywhere. Except with me."

She hugged him. "You've still got me."

"Yes, and you've still got me." He hugged her back, and then let her go. "I hope it's the best night of your life."

She smiled with breathless anticipation. "I think it might be."

THE GOWN WAS silver, with black accents. It draped across her pert, firm breasts from one shoulder, leaving the other arm bare. It was ankle length, with a tight waist and flaring skirt, in a clingy fabric that outlined every soft curve. The bodice was bow-shaped across with the drape from her upper arm diagonally to her other breast. The effect was exquisite, displaying her creamy skin to its best advantage.

The pearls were a single strand, off-white, with matching stud pearl earrings on her small ears. She put up her pale blond hair in a bun with little tendrils escaping, and a set of pearl combs, artificial but pretty, to keep it up. She used a minimum of makeup, just powder and lipstick, no eyeliner or messy mascara. Fortunately the nice boutique owner had even loaned her a pair of pumps to wear with the gown. Peg's shoes were mostly sneakers and an old pair of scuffed loafers. Her budget didn't run to fancy clothing.

Finished, she looked in the mirror and beamed at her reflection. She was never going to be beautiful, but she had good teeth and pretty lips and eyes. Maybe that would be enough. She hoped she could compete with all the really pretty women who would be at the ball. But most of them were married, thank goodness, so there shouldn't be too much competition there.

She had a nice coat that her father had bought her last winter, but when she looked at it in the hall closet she grimaced. It was a shocking pink, hardly the thing to wear with a couture gown. It was very cold outside today, with a high wind. She'd need something to keep her warm.

In desperation, she went through her own closet, looking for something that might do. It was useless. Except for a sweat jacket and a short and very old leather jacket, there wasn't anything here that matched her uptown outfit.

While she was agonizing over her lack of accessories, there was a knock at the front door. She went to answer it when she remembered that her father had gone out to the barn to check on the new calf and its mother, Bossie.

When she opened the door, she got a shock. It was one of Jason Pendleton's cowboys with a garment bag over his shoulder.

He grinned. "Got something for you, Miss Peg," he said, offering it. "Mrs. Pendleton said you'd need a coat to go with that dress, so she's loaning you one of hers.

She said it might be just a little long, but she thinks it will do nicely."

Peg was almost in tears. "Oh, it's so kind of her!"

The cowboy, an elderly sort, smiled. "You sure do look pretty."

She flushed. "Thank you!" She took the bag and opened it. The coat was black, long, with a mink collar. Real mink. She stroked it with breathless delight. "Please tell Mrs. Pendleton that I'll take great care of it. And thank her very much for me!"

"She said you're welcome. You have a good time tonight."

"Thanks," she said, beaming at him.

He grinned and went back to the ranch pickup he'd driven over in.

PEG WENT BACK inside and tried on the coat, with its fine silky lining. She looked at herself in the mirror and couldn't believe that the pretty woman there was actually plain Peg. She just shook her head.

"I feel like Cinderella," she whispered. "Just like her!"

Only she was hoping against hope that her carriage wouldn't turn into a pumpkin and that her gorgeous clothing wouldn't melt into rags at the stroke of midnight.

CHAPTER THREE

GRANGE CAME HOME to dress about a half hour before it was time to leave. Peg stayed in her bedroom. She didn't want him to see her until they were ready to go. She heard the shower running upstairs and sat down to watch the news on her small television while she waited for him. The news was too depressing, so she turned over to a documentary on the history channel instead. It was about the development of weapons, and how the spear of Paleo-hunters turned into the bow because of the speed of whitetail deer—which was the anthropologists' take on the innovation.

She was so engrossed in it that she forgot the time. A tap on her door startled her. She glanced at the clock and grimaced as she turned off the television and ran to answer the door.

She opened it, flushed and pretty with breathlessness. Grange, in a dark suit with a bow tie, stared at her with flattering speechlessness.

"Will I do?" she asked hopefully.

"Honey, you'll more than do," he said in a soft, deep tone which, combined with the unexpected endearment, almost burst her heart with joy. He smiled. "Ready to go?"

"Yes!" She grabbed her coat and started to slip it on. Grange got behind her and helped, letting her slide her arms into the silky fabric underlay of the rich wool coat with its mink collar.

"Mrs. Pendleton sent it down," she said. "I guess she knew that I wouldn't have a coat fancy enough to go with this dress."

He didn't let go. His big hands contracted on her shoulders. "That was nice of her."

"Yes. She's a sweet person."

"So are you." As he spoke, his thumbs eased the coat back. His head bent and he kissed her, tenderly, right on her neck where it joined her shoulder. He felt her shiver, heard her shocked intake of breath. "You taste like candy," he whispered, and his lips opened on the soft, warm flesh.

She leaned her head back, her breathing unsteady, her eyes closed. His hands moved to her waist. He turned her, ever so gently, and his mouth traveled to her throat, past the pearls, down, slowly, down to the very edge of the fabric over her breasts, and moved there in a sensual caress that shocked a defenseless little moan from her throat.

"I could pull the bodice down," he whispered, his head spinning, "and slide my lips over your breasts until I found that sweet hardness hiding there."

She shuddered. She arched back, helpless, hopeful, breathless with anticipation as he began to move the softly shaped fabric out of his way. She felt his mouth open, felt the warm moistness of it pressing against the swell of her breast. She moaned. Her body trembled as she arched again, pleading for relief from the tension that grew to unbearable need in seconds.

"What the hell," he ground out.

His hand came up and found the zipper, eased it

down. He pulled the fabric away and looked at the rosy, hard tips of her pretty breasts for just an instant before his mouth went down and covered one of them.

She cried out helplessly, which only made him more hungry. His mouth opened on the sweet flesh, his tongue traced the nipple, dragging against it to produce sensations Peg had never felt in her life.

Her nails bit into the fine fabric of his suit jacket. She was spinning like a top, burning, aching with desire that she'd never even dreamed of before this.

Somewhere a truck engine sounded loud even in the heated silence of Peg's room. She heard a door slam.

"It's... Dad!" she exclaimed hoarsely.

He barely heard her. He lifted his head, his eyes riveted to the stiff nipple. He cupped her breast and bent his head again to explore the soft flesh with his mouth. "Dad?" he whispered.

"Dad," she managed to say, and moaned.

His hand contracted gently around her soft breast. "Damn."

"Damn," she echoed with a shaky laugh.

He lifted his head with a steadying, deep sigh. He held the bodice away from her breasts, smiling warmly at the faint red marks he'd left there in his passion. "Beautiful," he whispered.

She flushed. Her body felt stiff and swollen. She wondered if his did, too.

With a rueful expression, he reached behind her and reluctantly zipped up the dress, hiding what he'd done to her. Fortunately no marks showed over the bodice.

She looked at him with awe.

He touched her soft mouth with his forefinger. It wasn't quite steady. "We'd better go," he said huskily.

She nodded.

He went out of the room and she came out behind him, retrieving the small evening bag the designer had also loaned her from her dresser on the way.

They were in the hall on the way to the front door when Ed came in. He looked from one of them to the other. They looked oddly flushed, but quite presentable.

"What a pair," he mused, smiling. "You look like socialites."

"Thanks, Dad." She grinned.

Grange chuckled. "Well, like impostor socialites, maybe. None of us working stiffs are likely to be mistaken for the real thing."

"I like us just the way we are," Ed replied. "Have a great time."

"We will," Peg assured him. "See you later."

"We'll be home by midnight," Grange said complacently, smiling at Ed. "I've got a lot to get done tomorrow."

Ed nodded solemnly. "Even more reason to enjoy tonight."

"Yes." He took Peg's arm. "Let's go. We don't want to be too late."

Peg winked at her dad on the way out.

GRANGE DIDN'T SPEAK on the way to the civic center in Jacobsville. He'd lost control of himself entirely back there. It had been a very good thing that Ed had come home when he did. Only a few steps to the bed, and he'd gone without a woman for a long time, a very long time. Added to that were Peg's visible feelings for him, and his weakness for her. All that, with her bedroom door standing wide-open and so inviting. Just as well that Ed had saved them from themselves, he thought.

PEG WAS NERVOUS. His silence did that to her. She had no resistance to him. She wanted him desperately. But he wasn't a playboy and he didn't want to get married, so where did that leave them? He was going away in a few days. She might never see him again. It was devastating, after what had happened back at the house. Her breasts were still tingling.

She glanced at him covertly. Had she made him mad? Was she too responsive? Should she have protested? But, why? He was experienced enough at least to realize what she felt for him. But he kept saying she was young. Did he mean, too young for him? Was her age the barrier to anything more serious than some heavy petting?

"Stop torturing yourself over there," Grange mused, glancing at her with twinkling dark eyes.

She jumped, and then laughed. "How did you know?"

"You're twisting that evening bag into a very odd shape."

"Oh!" She laid it flat and smoothed it, grimacing. "It's a loaner, too."

"A loaner?" he inquired.

"Yes. Like the dress and shoes. Cinderella gear." She leaned toward him as far as the seat belt would allow. "It transforms at midnight into rags. Just so you know."

"You'd be pretty even in rags."

She flushed. "Really?"

He glanced at her warmly. "Really." He forced his eyes back to the road.

She watched him, worried and curious. "Do you guys have automatic weapons and rockets and stuff, like in those merc movies?" she asked suddenly.

He glanced at her and chuckled. "Yes. But intelligence

gathering and coordinating native groups with ours are my stock-in-trade."

"Oh. Then you don't have to, well, go in shooting, right?" she asked, just to clarify the point.

Why worry her unnecessarily? he thought. So he smiled. "Of course not."

She relaxed.

And it was that easy. He didn't tell her about the after-hours training he and his major assault team had been doing over at Eb Scott's place, with state-of-the-art weaponry and some new toys that could be deployed at long range. It was going to be a bloodbath, even at its best, and a lot of his men weren't going to come home. He was in it for noble reasons: to depose a dictator who was torturing innocent people. But there was a substantial cash reward in the offing as well, and he had plans for his cattle ranch. He wanted a grubstake to get him started, something that he earned and not something that Jason Pendleton out of gratitude had given him. He wanted to build an empire of his own, with his two hands. That would mean a great risk. But without great risks, there were no great rewards. Besides that, Machado had hinted about a cabinet position if and when he regained power. That would be something to consider as well, although Grange hadn't thought about relocating to another country, in another continent.

"You're very solemn," Peg said, jolting him out of his mental exercises.

He glanced at her with something like consternation. Where would Peg fit into his plans? She was very young, at nineteen; perhaps too young. And taking her out of the country she'd lived in her whole life, to a new and very dangerous environment—it didn't bear thinking about. Besides that, there was the possibility that this might take months or even years to accomplish. He was gathering intel even now on the opposition forces and their capabilities. His men were good, but he would have to ally with groups that had boots on the ground in Barrera and coordinate them for an attack. It meant a lot of work.

"I was just thinking," he said after a minute.

She smiled. "Don't," she advised. "We're going to the ball and there is no tomorrow. Okay?"

"Okay."

THE JACOBSVILLE CIVIC Center was decorated for the holidays, with holly and tinsel, golden bells and a huge Christmas tree with ornaments made by the local orphanage and the friends of the nearby animal shelter. The Cattleman's Ball would benefit both charities.

The town citizens were decked out in their finery as well. Bonnie, who worked as a clerk at the pharmacy, was dressed all in red, one of the couture gowns provided by the local designer, and she was on the arm of a visiting cattleman who had arrived in, of all things, a Rolls-Royce. He was tall and dark and middle-aged, but very appealing.

He paused by Grange and seemed to know him. They shook hands. "Maxwell," he introduced himself. "I'd like to speak to you before you leave."

Grange nodded solemnly. "I'll make a point of it."

"Where did you meet him?" Peg asked in a hurried whisper.

Bonnie, blond curls very elegantly arranged, and grinning from ear to ear, said, "He came into the pharmacy to get a prescription for a friend, can you believe it? We started talking and he loves sixteenth-century Tudor history! So here I am."

"Good luck," Peg whispered.

Bonnie just shook her head. "I think I'm dreaming."

The visiting cattleman took her hand, smiled at the others and led her onto the dance floor.

Nancy, the pharmacist, dressed all in green, was standing with Holly, her clerk, dressed in gold, and they were shaking their heads at Bonnie and her escort.

"I wonder if he has a couple of nice friends," Peg whispered wickedly.

They both laughed.

"Well, it's that sort of night." Nancy sighed, looking down at her elegant green gown. "Can you imagine, all of us decked out like this?"

"It attracts men, too," Peg murmured under her breath as one of the local ranch foremen, a real dish, came forward, actually bowed, and led Nancy onto the dance floor.

Nancy just shook her head.

"What were you talking about?" Grange asked Peg as he led her out to dance.

"Loaned dresses and holiday magic," she whispered, smiling up at him. He was so handsome. She was amazed to find herself at a dance with him, when all her flirting had only seemed to chase him away. Now, here he was, holding her on a dance floor, and looking as if he couldn't bear to leave her.

In fact, he danced with a couple of the elderly women present, but otherwise, only with Peg.

"People will talk," he said with a wry smile, noting the interest from the other couples.

She shrugged. "People do. I don't care. Do you?"

He shook his head. "I don't care at all. But I'll be gone." Her face fell.

He pulled her close. "Don't think about it. There's no tomorrow. We agreed."

"Yes." She pressed close and shut her eyes. But already she felt the separation. It was going to be agonizing.

THEY STAYED UNTIL the last dance. He left her with Justin and Shelby Ballenger while he went outside with the visiting cattleman in the Rolls-Royce.

"Something big's going on, huh?" Justin asked Peg.

"Something," she agreed, with a shy smile. Justin and Shelby were co-owners, with Justin's brother Calhoun, of the enormous Ballenger Brothers Feedlot. They were millionaires many times over, and Shelby was a direct descendant of Big John Jacobs, the founder of Jacobsville, Texas. It had been an epic courtship, not without its agonies. But the couple was very happy and had grown children.

Grange was back shortly, and he looked pleased. "Time to go. It was a great party. I hope we made lots of money for the orphanage and the shelter."

"We did," Justin said with a smile. He put an arm around Shelby and held her close. "Record sums, I hear."

"Good, good."

"You be careful where you're going," Justin said, extending a hand to shake Grange's. "Noble causes are noble, but they come at a price."

"Yes, I do know. Thanks."

"We'll keep you in our prayers," Shelby said gently. "Keep well."

Grange nodded, smiled and tugged Peg out the door.

They watched Bonnie drive off in the Rolls-Royce.

"Will she have stories to tell!" Peg exclaimed. "I have to get a prescription refilled so I can get all the news!"

Grange laughed. "You women and your gossip."

"Hey, men gossip, too," she pointed out.

He made a face.

She had hoped that he might stop along the way, maybe park on some lonely back road. But to her disappointment, he drove right up to the front steps. And her father was inside, with the lights blazing.

He walked her onto the porch. His face was very solemn. "We've already jumped the gun, Peg," he said gently. "No need to make things more complicated. Not right now. I have to have my mind on where I'm going, and what I have to do. Distractions can be fatal."

The reality of the future caught her by the throat. She'd tried not to think about it, but now she had to face facts. He was going off to war, even if it wasn't some officially declared one. He might not come back. The panic was in her expression.

"Hey." He put his forefinger over her lips. "I made major before I mustered out of the military. You don't get those promotions unless you know what you're doing. Okay?"

She swallowed, hard. "Okay."

He smiled gently. "You have a wonderful Christmas."

"You, too." She grimaced. "I didn't get you anything yet. Can I send you something? Warm socks, maybe?" she tried to joke.

"I don't think warm socks and tropical jungles are a good mix, do you?"

She sighed. "Mosquito repellant and snake pellets?"

"Better. I'll try to get word to your father about our

progress, but it's going to be slow. I'll have phones with me, but they can be used by the enemy to call down air strikes. The military we're up against isn't going to be a pushover. Machado trained most of them, and we have to consider that only a few are likely to defect to our cause. People generally don't like sudden change."

"I don't like it at all," she agreed. "Stay here."

"People don't make history by staying home. Not my nature."

She sighed. "I know. Well, be careful."

"Count on it."

He bent, regardless of her father's presence in the living room, and kissed her with breathless tenderness. He looked into her eyes for a long time, until she felt shivers down her spine. "You're the most special person in my life. I'll come home. I've been alone for a long time. I don't want to be alone anymore, Peg."

She gasped at the way he was looking at her. "Me... me, neither," she whispered.

He kissed her eyelids, touching them with the tip of his tongue. "My sweet girl. I'll be back before you know it."

She nodded, forcing a wobbly smile. "Okay. I'll hold you to that promise."

He smiled. "Good night, Cinderella." He bent and kissed her one last time, hard, before he turned and she went inside.

Her eyes followed him with aching longing. She was the most special person in his life. He didn't want to be alone anymore. That had to mean something. It sounded like a commitment. It gave her hope. Great hope.

THE NEXT MORNING, Grange was in Emilio Machado's camp, gathering gear and talking to his men. Peg was as far from his thoughts as ice cream sundaes and television sports, because he couldn't afford the distraction of remembering her soft, eager mouth under his.

Machado was grim. "We have men, and equipment," he told Grange. "We have more financing, thanks to your efforts and those of Mr. Pendleton. But we have no air force and no carrier group…"

"Revolutions can succeed without either, as long as they have dedicated people and good intel," Grange reminded him. "Military intelligence is my strong point. I know how to organize a resistance movement. I did it in Iraq with local tribesmen. I can do it in Barrera."

Machado smiled. "You give me confidence. I know that the cause is good. I made a mistake. I left my country in the hands of a power-hungry traitor and many lives have been lost because of it. I worry for Maddie," he added heavily. "She was my friend, an American archaeologist who had made a very important discovery in the jungle near the capital. I do not know her fate. If they caught her, she is most likely dead. That will be on my conscience forever. There were also two professors at the university, my friends, who have gone missing and are also probably dead. It has been a hard thing, to lose so many people because I was careless."

"Don't dwell on the past or anticipate the future," Grange counseled. "Take it one day at a time."

Machado sighed. "You are right. Oh. I have a communication from an American journalist with one of the slick magazines. She wishes to accompany us…"

He handed the magazine to Grange. "Her name is Clarisse Carrington…"

"Oh, God, no!" Grange ground out. "No! How did she find out about our mission? She's like the plague!"

"Excuse me?"

"That damned socialite met me in the Middle East, when she was doing a piece for her magazine," he muttered. "I wouldn't fall at her feet at some damned cocktail party in Washington, and I guess it hurt her ego. So four months ago she started chasing me, after I went to a social gathering in Washington with some friends from the military. I gave her the cold shoulder. She was livid. After that, I couldn't go to a damned hotel anywhere that she didn't show up at."

"I see."

"She thinks she's irresistible," Grange said coldly. "She's not."

"She may have her ear to the ground about you. There must have been a leak. I will of course refuse the offer."

"Thanks."

Grange was looking at the magazine and he frowned at one of the cover stories. He opened it to a certain page, and grimaced. "Damn!"

"What?"

"You remember I told you about the officer who claimed my battle strategy was his own and got me court-martialed? The one I testified against?"

"Yes."

"He committed suicide."

"Goodness!"

"This is the story that hit the wires. I'd hoped it wouldn't, for his family's sake. He was caught out in another scandal involving blackmail and stolen funds earmarked for equipment," Grange read. "But his son states here that the officer who testified against him is responsible for his death—me." He sighed. "I know about the boy. He's been in and out of therapy all his life. His father said he was bipolar, but his drug problems seemed to me to be the worst of them. His mother was rich. She died and the son inherited it all. She didn't leave her husband a dime." He put down the magazine. "So the kid is filthy rich and blames me for his father's suicide. The socialite thinks she can seduce me over war coverage." He looked at Emilio Machado with wide eyes. "Perhaps I'm more of a liability than you can afford."

Machado just smiled. "My friend, we all have our burdens. I think you can bear these. Now, let us speak with your men and finalize our departure."

THEY HAD ARRANGED passage for Grange's handpicked fighters. Machado had a friend with an old DC-3 who transported the core body of mercs to a small city on the coast of South America, a transit point to Barrera, which was north of Manaus, in Amazonas, a city in the Amazon jungle. Other troops were massing inside the border of Barrera, organized in small groups by Machado's friends in the resistance. It wasn't a battle group by any stretch of the imagination. But, then, small forces with the will and means could often overthrow countries. As Machado reminded the others, a handful of his men, defecting to the political leader, Sapara, had overthrown him by stealth and surprise. They could do the same thing to his former lieutenant. It would just require precise planning and good strategy.

On the DC-3 plane, bound for a small covert airstrip in Barrera, Grange outlined his plan of battle to Machado.

"A surprise attack is going to be the most effective means of recapturing your government," he told the general. "Here—" he pointed to the very small capital city,

Medina "—is the heart of the military, in the underground HQ in the city. We have an ally with bunker-busting bombs, but we only have two of them. It means that if we have to go with an all-out military assault, we'll have to coordinate the strike at the military communications and tactical network with the simultaneous capture of all news media outlets, airfields and the three military command centers in Colari, Salina and Dobri, here, here and here." He pointed to red marks on his waterproof map. "These cities are smaller than Jacobsville." He chuckled. "So taking out those command centers could be accomplished by one man with a .45 Colt ACP," he added.

Machado sighed. "The element of surprise will be difficult, my friend," he said. "My adversary has agents. He is no fool."

"I know." Grange straightened, very somber. "The hardest part is getting everyone familiar with his own role in the attack. I've already done that. I sent two of my men ahead to contact your former military commander, Domingo Lopez, in Medina. They're disguised as farmers, and yes, they'll pass muster," he added. "They're Tex-Mex, some of my best men, and two of them are masters of demolition. They're ex-Navy SEALs."

"I am impressed," the general said.

"I also sent one of my former company commanders, who's proficient in scrounging equipment and arms from unlikely places, along with a South African merc who's one of the best I've ever seen, to set up a base camp. We've got a Native American tracker named Carson, a merc with a bad attitude who can speak all the native dialects. They're accompanied, among others, by an Irishman who knows electronics like his own fingerprints. He can do anything with computers, and he's a past master at writing virus codes."

Machado's eyebrows arched. "Virus codes?"

Grange grinned. "O'Bailey belonged to the British military before he found his way to Eb Scott's group. He shut down the entire military communications network in an outlying area of Iraq with an old PC running obsolete software," he informed. He shook his head. "Got a medal for it, in fact."

"You have good people," Machado said. "I hope that our endeavor will not result in injury or death to any of them."

"So do I, but most wars cost blood," Grange said. "We'll all do the best we can. Thing is, we may not have an immediate victory. So our priority has to be taking out their communications, their SAMs and the national media."

"Surface to air missiles." Machado sighed. "I got them from Russia. They're state-of-the-art," he added grimly. "I thought they would give us protection from dangerous enemy states nearby. It was a lack of foresight on my part, as I never dreamed they might be used against my own people." His expression was solemn. "My former commander will not hesitate to destroy whole city blocks, along with their inhabitants. He will kill anyone to keep power."

Grange laid a big hand on the other man's shoulder. "We'll do what we have to do. Just remember that many innocent people have already died. If we don't act, many more will."

"I know that." Machado smiled sadly. "I know it too well."

One of the other soldiers came down the narrow steps

from the deck above. "We'll be landing in about an hour, captain said," he told them. "It's a few miles from a quiet little village on the river. Nothing much is there in the surrounding area except for a small landing strip just big enough to accommodate our plane. Our intelligence indicates that Sapara built the strip to accommodate landings by an oil corporation doing preliminary investigations in advance of setting up operations."

"Yes," Machado said grimly, "and Sapara began killing natives to force them out of the area. Some remain, despite his depredations…a situation I hope to resolve. However, it is a good place to land," Machado said, and his dark eyes flashed with another brief smile. "It was where I landed on the day I invaded Barrera the first time. The nearby people are sympathetic to our cause."

Grange shrugged. "So lightning will strike twice, in this case."

"My friend, I sincerely hope so."

THEY LEFT THE plane quickly, under cover of darkness, and sent it off to Manaus for the time being, with other members of the group. Grange hadn't fought a jungle war in some time. His last theater of operations had been the deserts of the Middle East. But his men had the newest camouflage uniforms, and the computer-generated pattern blended perfectly with their surroundings.

They set up a base camp with tents and built a small fire for cooking. They weren't expected, so there was not much danger of discovery at this point in time. Coffee was made, to exclamations of joy from the men in camp, and ration packs were passed around. The jungle sounds were alien, but the men would adjust.

Grange finished his meal and coffee and rose. "I'll

get in touch with my forward platoon and see what intel they've gathered," Grange said, excusing himself.

He contacted Brad Dunagan, his former company commander who had gone with the other party to Manaus and made his way to the outskirts of Medina to set up a second camp. He was by now coordinating the small units of the invasion force. Grange used a scrambling device and a frequency that was unlikely to be monitored by the enemy forces.

"What's up?" he asked quietly.

"We have two tanks, a couple of SCUD missile launchers, several rocket launchers, a truckload of munitions and about fifty natives who hate the government and know the layout of the city well enough to help us with an incursion," he answered.

"I'm impressed."

"I hope so…"

"Tell him what I did, sir," O'Bailey called from the campfire with a laugh in his voice.

"O'Bailey wants me to tell you that he got his hands on a gaming computer and he's reworked it to engineer a Stuxnet-type virus. He's going to give it to the Barrera military."

"Good man!" Brad exclaimed. "Tell him we'll buy him a truck."

"No!" O'Bailey complained. "I want a Jag!"

"Son, I can't afford a Jag myself." Grange chuckled. "When I can get one, you can get one."

"Okay, sir, I'll settle for a nice truck with a good music system."

"Deal." He turned back to the radio. "Brad, I'll give you the signal when O'Bailey is ready to upload the virus. I want everyone in place, all the troops massed and personnel deployed on site before we start. Nobody moves a muscle until they have the word. Got that?"

"Got it, sir," Dunagan agreed.

"This is going to require pinpoint accuracy," Grange said. "We can't afford to make a single slip."

"I know that. We'll be ready."

"I'll be in touch."

He turned off the unit and sat back, frowning. It was going to be a difficult operation. There were too many things that could go wrong. He wished they'd been able to persuade one of the friendly governments to loan them a support group, but that had been out of the question. Nobody wanted to risk riling up Barrera's neighbors, given the world economy and the threats still prevailing in the Middle East. They had well-wishers and offers of help once the mission was a success. But a lot depended on Grange's battle plan and the quality of his ragtag army. He hoped it would be enough.

CHAPTER FOUR

THE PROBLEM WITH such a complex assault, Grange mused, was coordination and intelligence gathering. There were so many variables, not the least of which was knowing the terrain, the weather, the threats from wildlife and other humans, and the advance knowledge of people in power in Barrera. The resistance did have some artillery support, and limited air support capability. It would have to be perfect timing to avoid civilian casualties that might antagonize those who were on Machado's side at the present time.

Machado, fortunately, did have people on the inside in positions of power with whom he was in communication. One of his former lieutenants, General Domingo Lopez, who had been his military chief of staff, was now Dictator Arturo Sapara's supply chief. It was a position of humiliation for one of the government's premier strategists. But Lopez supported Machado and was willing to do whatever it took to help with turning the military against the stringy little dictator Sapara, including swallowing a demotion. He knew Machado would come back, and he was going to be in a position to help. He'd managed to sneak that message out.

"We do, unfortunately, have a timetable to follow," Machado told Grange during one of their brainstorming sessions in their base camp. "The weather. Next month, which is only days away, the rainy season begins." He glanced at his military chief. "I need not tell you what miseries our troops will face if we cannot bring this campaign to a quick conclusion. We cannot move men and materiel through tropical rain forests during monsoon season."

"I know." Grange sighed. "I did train in jungle warfare, and I have experts on my staff," he replied. "I handpicked men who'd fought in South Africa and in Central and South America in local campaigns. The biggest problem I have is with the few who have never been in a jungle." He threw up his hands. "Two men came in with machetes...!"

Machado laughed richly. "My friend, in most American cinema, we always see men crashing through the jungles wielding machetes."

"True, but even experts miss," Grange said, "which means you'd better have medical support and a nearby hospital, because infection is epic down here. When I told them that we used secateurs—pruning shears— to cut through undergrowth, they thought I was kidding. Then I started explaining snakes." He shook his head. "Rourke was down here with a team not too long ago. We have this one guy, Sean O'Bailey, who was in his group. O'Bailey had never seen a snake before he went to Iraq, anyway. Irish, you know. So down here in South America, he came face-to-face with a *surucucu*," he added, giving the native word for a bushmaster, "and had to change his pants later. Lucky for him the snake didn't attack. I've heard of them chasing men into villages during breeding season, and attacking people without provocation. I'm keeping him here on the computer, where he's safer. And we're safer, too," Grange advised.

"Yes, a scream carries for great distances, even in the jungle. You were able to procure the weapons I requested?"

Grange nodded. "RPG-7 rocket launchers and AK-47s and UZIs." He shook his head. "All these advances in modern weaponry, and look what we're still using. My God."

"Old weapons, true, but durable and easy to learn and hard to disable," Machado said. He grinned. "I conquered Barrera the first time using such weapons, and only a minimum of light artillery and two tanks."

"Yes, but that was before we could call down weapon strikes by F-22s and Apache helicopters."

"We will, alas, have few of those at our disposal. I am hoping for the element of surprise," Machado said.

"As am I. We've managed to get inside the border with boots on the ground, without being detected, thanks to some great work by our pilot. And fortunately we didn't have to use a chopper for transport. That can be a real pain."

"I did not understand this 'chalk' scenario, used by the chopper pilots," Machado said. "Do I understand that the pilots would not permit troops aboard until they inspected each soldier they transported?"

"Absolutely correct," Grange said grimly, and explained why the process was so vital.

Machado sighed. "I understand. I never had such pilots. I am impressed."

"So was I, when Eb Scott suggested them to me," Grange said with a smile. "But they'll be used only as a last resort. I still think it may be possible to bring down the government from the inside, with minimum force."

"General Lopez—whom my enemy Sapara demoted to colonel—has access to top-secret reports of troop movements. He will be able to make certain suggestions to the other military leaders, to help conceal our position when we go in."

"Lucky that he survived the first purge," Grange agreed.

"Many did not." Machado's face set in hard lines. "I will avenge them, given the opportunity. Our greatest asset for the moment is Sapara himself. He has become addicted to gifts from his close neighbors—the coca leaf. As his addiction grows, he becomes more and more divorced from reality and less able to comprehend how hated he has become among his citizens."

"Addictions are unwise," Grange replied. "Hell, I don't even smoke or drink."

"I did notice," Machado said.

He shrugged. "It was an economic thing for many years, I couldn't afford it. Then it grew to be a habit. Now it's an obsession."

"Alcohol can be a menace, especially in an operation such as ours."

"Which is why I've banned it. I tried to ban cigarettes, but there was almost a mutiny," Grange explained. "So I specified times and places where men can smoke. The smell could give away positions. Just like men talking, guns being loaded…"

"We take great risks." He put a hand on Grange's shoulder. "But I assure you, the rewards will be great, if we succeed."

"When we succeed, chief," Grange replied with a grin. "No pessimistic thinking here."

"As you say. When we succeed."

O'BAILEY WAS DRINKING coffee and looking around himself uncomfortably. "Sure, and now I'll be seeing snakes in my dreams," he muttered, glaring at Grange.

"Rourke told you there were snakes here, the first time you had a mission in South America," Grange told him.

"I thought he meant wee garter snakes, like my sister has in her garden in York, not sea serpents!"

"It was a bushmaster, you toad." Rourke chuckled, his one brown eye twinkling as he sat down beside the Irishman, running a hand through the long blond ponytail he wore to check for bugs. "I bet it wasn't even a big one."

"I saw a bushmaster, once, and begging your pardon, sir," another recruit piped in, "the damned things are huge!"

"It's huge when it's about to strike at you, for sure!" O'Bailey retorted.

Rourke grinned. "I read this book, about this explorer who got lost in South America in the early part of the twentieth century," he recalled as he spread out a cloth and cleaning kit and polished up his .45 Colt ACP. "Guy named Fawcett. He was a surveyor for the Royal Geographic Society. He took a party of men into places where no white man had ever gone, and wrote about his adventures. He was told a story about this guy who was washing at a stream when he felt somebody tap him on his shoulder, first one side, then the other. He thought it was his imagination. He turned around and looked right into the eyes of a *surucucu*. Said he screamed and ran, because the snakes have a reputation for being aggressive and lethal, but it didn't follow him. Seems this one had a sense of humor."

Grange laughed. "I heard one, too, but a little worse—a bushmaster ran amok and attacked a camp of people, bit half of them."

"I hate snakes!" O'Bailey said angrily.

"You're in the wrong business, mate," Rourke advised. "Best you go back to Dublin and sell used cars again."

O'Bailey made a face. "Can't make any money selling cars. This, however, will make me a legend in me hometown and a wealthy bloke if we can pull it off. General Machado's offering us a hell of a bonus if we win."

"If?" Rourke asked, his eyebrows lifting, moving the black eye patch over his bad eye just a hair to adjust it more comfortably. "Bite your tongue!"

"Sorry, sir," O'Bailey said with a grimace. "I forgot we was on the winning side, but just for a minute. Honest."

Grange shook his head and walked away.

He looked out over the jungle with apprehension. So many dangers, not the least of which were jaguars and snakes. But there were smaller dangers, the mosquitoes that carried dengue fever and malaria—thank God it was the dry season and they weren't prevalent now. But in a month that would change and they would face insect and waterborne diseases along with swampy conditions as the rains moved in. If they couldn't succeed in less than a month—and that was wishful thinking—the campaign would have to be discontinued until the rains ended, which would give the coca-soaked madman running Barrera plenty of time to get help from some of his sympathizers. It was a risk they couldn't afford. So Grange was determined that they would succeed in the time allowed.

His greatest hope was for a bloodless coup in the capital, Medina. He and Machado had plenty of men, good air support and decent light artillery. But if Machado's friend Lopez had influence and could use it, help sabotage things inside the military headquarters, and if Grange could deploy specialized teams inside the city, and do it with pinpoint accuracy—and use his jungle fighters as support to encourage help from the native populations nearby—they might pull it off.

What he wanted first was to send in teams of advisers to drum up support among the indigenous tribes. They lived on the outskirts of Medina and most of them had helped Machado gain power in the first place. Intelligence indicated that their numbers had been decimated as Sapara took power and that they were keen on revenge. Rourke would go in with several other men, in disguise, and try to enlist help. At the same time, Machado and several other men would air-drop into Medina near the military quarter, where men would meet them and provide support.

If all else failed, it would mean a campaign fought in the jungle near Medina, and it had to be a quick one, with immediate success. There were so many factors, so many things that could go wrong. Grange felt sick to his stomach thinking about how many of his men, his friends, he might lose in a firefight. But he'd sent men into combat to die. It was something every commander in wartime had to do. It was never easy.

That brought to mind his commanding officer in Iraq who had committed suicide after his court-martial.

Grange felt guilty about it, but he didn't know what he could have done differently. If he'd followed the man's orders, his whole platoon would have died. His quick thinking and strategy had saved them, but his commanding officer had forced him out of the service with an honorable discharge as bait to spare him a court-martial. Grange had taken the deal, but the commander's own right-hand man had gotten drunk and spilled the beans, so the officer was himself court-martialed. Except that, unlike Grange, he'd been dishonorably discharged. He couldn't take the loss of face, or probably the loss of the high salary he'd been getting. His gambling debts, allegedly, had been immense. So he killed himself and now his mentally challenged drug-using son was gunning for Grange as the author of the tragedy.

Grange shook his head. As if he'd have pushed any man to do such a drastic thing as taking his own life. And he'd had his own tragedy from using drugs, when he was barely into his teens. His own sister had taken her life, when her boyfriend's father threatened to have Grange arrested and charged in a murder that his friends had committed. She'd died to save her brother. It had saved him, in one respect. He'd cleaned up his act and gone on to become an exemplary citizen. But it could have gone another way. He was sorry for the officer's son. At least, the boy wouldn't be over here trying to kill him, he thought.

Nor would the Washington socialite, Clarisse, be able to hang around him, thank God, since Machado was going to refuse to allow her to go with the troops. That brought to mind Peg, waiting back home in Jacobsville for word of him. He didn't dare phone her, but there were other ways of communicating that wouldn't allow someone to eavesdrop and pick up their location. His friend Rourke knew all the tricks of the trade and he had a little ham radio kit that he carried everywhere with him.

PEG WAS WASHING dishes when the telephone rang. Her father was out doctoring one of the cows with an eye infection, so she dried her hands and went to answer it. They had a dishwasher, one of many appliances that Grange had purchased for the house, but Peg didn't like to use it for just two plates, cups and saucers. It seemed a waste of both water and electricity, so she did just the few things by hand.

"Hello, Grange residence," she said politely.

"Miss Peg Larson?" an unfamiliar voice replied.

"Uh, yes…"

"I'm Bill Jones. You don't know me. I'm a ham operator. I've just had a communication from a gentleman on another continent. He wanted me to pass along a message for him. I'm to tell you that a gentleman named Grange is enjoying his vacation, but misses you very much."

She caught her breath. "He's all right?"

He laughed. "I assume you were waiting to make sure he got to his destination. I can assure you that he arrived in perfect health. He also said to tell you that he might not be able to contact you directly, but to wish you happy holidays and to say he hopes he'll see you in a few months. He says he misses you very much," he repeated.

"Thanks," she said fervently. "Oh, thank you. I… We were worried."

"I'll pass that along."

"And please wish him happy holidays also and tell him, well, tell him to be careful. And tell him I miss him more than he knows."

"I'll do that. Have a good evening."

"Thanks, you, too."

She hung up, delighted that Grange had thought to relay a message so far, and under such dangerous conditions.

She went out the back door and down to the barn. Ed had just finished smearing salve into the cow's eyes. He turned and smiled.

"Something up?" he asked.

She grinned. "Grange sent us a message. He says he got to his destination okay and he's doing well, and he hopes we have a happy holiday season."

"That's a relief," Ed said, standing. "I was getting a bit concerned. He told me before he left that he'd try to get word to us, but I wasn't sure… I mean, it's a hell of a trip, and there are plenty of dangerous places along the way. Not that he isn't good at what he does," he added firmly.

"I know that. I was worried, too," she confessed after a minute.

They walked back toward the house together. The leaves on the oak trees were mostly gone by now, but a few still clung to the pecan trees. The nuts were long gone. Squirrels had carried them off, mostly when they were still green.

"I should load my shotgun and stand guard over that tree," Ed remarked of the largest and oldest of the nut trees. "Maybe you'd get a handful of nuts to make cakes with."

"You have to sleep sometime," she reminded him. "They'd find a way to sneak in after dark. You can't defeat squirrels. They're too smart."

"I guess you're right."

"Barbara always orders the raw nuts and gives me

some," she said, referring to the owner of Barbara's Café in Jacobsville. "Not to worry, Dad, you'll get your Japanese fruitcake this Christmas. Honest." It was a yellow cake, made in three layers, with one spice layer that contained nuts and a boiled white sugar frosting on which coconut and nuts and red and green candied cherries were sprinkled.

He let out a sigh of relief. "Can't live without that cake. Your mother, God rest her soul, made one every year. So did her mother."

"Yes, but Granny used those tiny thin cake layers and made six of them. Mom didn't have the patience. She reduced it to three layers and taught me, so the recipe goes on. I gave it to Barbara. She said it's one of her bestsellers in the café. Mom would have loved that."

He nodded. "She was a great cook. So are you, sweetheart."

"Thanks. But it's mostly just basic stuff with me. I'm not inventive."

"Inventive is not always good," he reminded her with a twinkle in his eyes. "I haven't forgotten the Danish potato recipe."

She grimaced. "Neither did the boss," she said, referring to Grange. "He tasted it, looked at me, asked if we'd ever had that before. When I said no, he said, 'Well, let's never have it again, either.'"

He chuckled. "Wasn't so bad. It's just the idea of a sweet Irish potato that upsets men. It's unnatural."

She rolled her eyes. "Meat and potatoes. That's all men ever want on the table."

"Best food in the world is simple food."

"Yes, but it's not a bad thing to try new stuff."

"Try new meat and potato recipes."

"I did!"

He glowered at her. "Not that new."

She burst out laughing and went back into the house.

THE NEXT MORNING, she had to pick up a prescription for her father. He tended toward high blood pressure, so Dr. Copper Coltrain had him on a medication that combined a water pill with something to stabilize blood pressure. The pharmacy had a nice generic drug that they could afford, even on their tight budget.

Nancy filled it and Bonnie brought it to the counter.

"Have you heard from him?" Peg asked excitedly, because Bonnie was grinning from ear to ear. She'd gone to the Cattleman's Ball with a man driving a white Rolls-Royce. It had been the talk of the town.

"In fact, he phoned me day before yesterday," she confessed as she rang up the prescription. "From Paris!"

"Wow," Peg said, all eyes.

"He's coming back to the States in about three weeks, and he hopes he'll have time to stop by and take me out to dinner in San Antonio." Bonnie shook her head. "Imagine that, a millionaire likes me."

"Everybody likes you," Peg pointed out. "I think it's great!"

"So do I. I just hope it isn't really a dream that I'll wake up from."

Peg leaned toward her. "Want me to pinch you?"

Bonnie made a face. "Shame on you."

Peg grinned. "Just trying to help."

SHE STOPPED BY Barbara's Café afterward. Barbara had a bag of fresh pecans for her. "I always order them for

Christmas cooking, it's no big deal to get an extra bag for you," Barbara said firmly when Peg tried to pay for them.

"Well, thanks a lot," Peg told her.

"You shared that great cake recipe with me," Barbara reminded her with a smile. "It's been a big hit with the customers."

"We love it, too," Peg confessed.

Barbara lowered her voice. "Heard from Grange?"

She nodded, looking around cautiously. "Just that he got where he was going. Nothing else."

Barbara bit her lower lip. "I see."

"What do you know that I don't? Come on, please?"

Barbara drew her back past the kitchen, where two women were working at the stove and the counter, onto the back porch.

"Do you remember that officer who got in trouble for claiming Grange's battle strategy as his own, the one who got Grange kicked out of the army?"

"Yes."

"Well, he killed himself."

"Oh, my gosh!" Peg exclaimed.

"That's not all," Barbara continued grimly. "He's got a son who's not all there, if you know what I mean. And he's sworn that he's going to make Grange pay for it."

"Good luck to him, trying to find Grange," Peg said, trying to ignore the sudden coldness in the pit of her stomach.

"I hope you're right. But his father had friends and they might know something about where Grange has gone, and why," Barbara continued. "Rick heard from his father, General Machado," she added under her breath. "He said the general had to refuse to allow a journalist along with his invasion force because she turned out to be some socialite who was pursuing Grange."

Peg's heart did a flip. "A socialite?"

"Don't worry," Barbara assured her with a warm smile. "The general said that Grange threatened to quit the job if Machado let her accompany them. He hates her."

Peg relaxed. "Well, that's something. You had a distinguished guest for Thanksgiving, we heard."

"Yes. Rick's wife's father. He's a general, too. Has sort of a bad attitude, but a warm heart," she added. She laughed. "He likes to cook."

"Now that's interesting," Peg mused with a wicked smile.

"He also knows almost everything that's going on in the military," Barbara continued. "So if Grange's commanding officer's son has plans to go overseas, we'll know. Try not to worry. I just thought you should be told."

Peg hugged her impulsively. "I do, too. Thanks."

"It's all very worrying," Barbara said. "I totally agree with what General Machado wants to do. But it's so dangerous."

"Tell me about it." Peg sighed. "It must be terrible for Rick, too, since he only just found out who his father is."

"Absolutely. He's afraid that he'll lose him before they really get to know each other."

"We'll just hope and pray that everything works out," Peg replied.

"They have good help," the older woman replied. "Most of the men that went with Grange are Eb Scott's."

"He's fussy about the men he trains, I've heard," Peg said.

"Very fussy. They eat in the restaurant, so I know a lot of them. One of the best is a South African named

Rourke." She frowned. "I don't think I've ever heard his first name." She laughed and shook her head. "It wasn't until recently that I knew Grange's was Winslow."

Peg nodded. "Everybody just calls him Grange."

"Even you?"

Peg flushed. "Even me."

"He doesn't date anybody locally," she pointed out. "I mean, he was taking Tellie Maddox out for a while, before she married J.B. Hammock, but they were only friends. And since then, he hasn't dated at all." She laughed. "We were all pretty shocked when you showed up at the Cattleman's Ball with him, let me tell you."

"So was I," Peg replied. "I never dreamed I'd get to wear such clothes, either. That was such a sweet thing our local designer, Bess Truman, did, so sweet! And Mrs. Pendleton loaned me a coat!"

"I heard about that, too. Gracie's a doll. We've been friends for a long time." She shook her head. "I could have slugged Jason Pendleton for the way he treated her. Let me tell you, that was a rough courtship."

"They seem so happy together."

"They are, now. And they were good friends before he got mixed up with that model. But that's another story." Barbara hugged her again. "Take your pecans and go home and make your dad a nice cake. I've got to get back to work!"

"I will. Thanks again for the pecans." She started to leave, turned around and walked back, her expression worried. "If you hear anything from Rick's father-in-law, you know, about that officer's son who wants to hurt Grange—you'll tell me, yes?"

"Yes," Barbara promised. "But don't you worry, young lady. Grange can take care of himself."

Peg smiled. "Of course he can. But if you knew he was headed for trouble, you could have Rick's father-in-law, the general, warn him. Couldn't you? They're friends, aren't they?"

"They are, and I will."

Peg relaxed a little. "I know I don't need to worry. But I do."

"We all worry, when the people we care about are in danger," Barbara agreed quietly.

Peg nodded. She clutched the package of pecans. "Thanks again."

Barbara smiled. "My pleasure."

PEG DROVE BACK to the ranch, distracted. So many complications were cropping up. She had deep feelings for Winslow Grange. She thought that he had some for her as well. It had pleased her to learn that he didn't date anybody, and that it had only been friendship between him and Tellie. In fact, she knew Tellie: they'd been at school together. She'd assumed that Grange had feelings for the other girl. Now she felt better.

Except for that socialite. Grange didn't like her. But the woman was obviously persistent. What if she ignored the general's permission and went anyway? What if she showed up in Grange's camp and vamped him?

"Vamped," she muttered to herself. "Peg, you need to get a grip. Nobody talks like that in the twenty-first century!"

She turned onto the ranch road, but she was still frowning. Men in desperate situations sometimes did desperate things. Grange might not be as cautious as he usually was, and if the woman was a sophisticate and aggressive, she might push her way into his life.

Peg was poor and not beautiful. She didn't know how

to behave in high social circles; she didn't even know how to do a proper place setting. That woman would be experienced and chic and knowledgeable about such things. Grange might compare them, and Peg might come off in a less than favorable light.

She tormented herself with those thoughts all the way into the house, and bumped into her father because she wasn't looking where she was going.

"And what's wrong with you?" he teased.

Her face screwed up. "I can't even set a proper table, and I don't know how to behave in high society."

He looked shocked. "Excuse me?"

"There's this Washington socialite who's after Winslow," she muttered. "She tried to get signed on with the expedition as a journalist. She's chased him everywhere. What if she shows up in his camp...?"

"Peg, get a grip," he said gently. "So what if she does? Grange is no schoolboy. He took you to the Cattleman's Ball, you know."

Peg sighed. "Yes, but she's probably beautiful and has gorgeous clothes."

"If he doesn't want her, that won't matter."

She searched his face quietly. "Really? You think so?"

"I know so." He glanced at the bag of pecans in her hands. "Go make a cake. It will help."

She blinked. "Help who? Me, or you?"

He chuckled. "Both of us. You'll be diverted while you're cooking it, and I'll be rapturous while I'm eating it."

"Oh, Dad." She hugged him. "Thanks."

"Stop worrying. Grange isn't an idiot. You'll see."

She nodded. "Okay."

THAT NIGHT, SHE dreamed. There was a jungle and Winslow was lying in a huge jungle hammock, stretched out in only a pair of Bermuda shorts, with his broad, hair-covered chest bare, his hair mussed as he smiled up at her.

"Come here, baby," he whispered.

She went to him. She was wearing a red sarong, something more Polynesian than South American, with white flowers on it. He deftly untied the sarong and tossed it out of the hammock. His lean, strong hands smoothed over her breasts hungrily and he bent to kiss them. She moaned in her sleep, shifting restlessly as she felt his body grow hard and taut and swollen against her hips. She felt him move, felt the shorts go over the side of the hammock as he shifted her suddenly under him and began kissing her in earnest.

"Oh, Winslow," she whispered, shocked, as she felt him begin to penetrate the soft warmth of her. She arched up to the pleasure, her body shivering. She heard him laugh tenderly at her frantic motions as she tried to bring him even closer.

She was burning. She was on fire. The heat and the tension combined to make her crazy. She couldn't get close enough. She wanted him, so much!

And then she realized that they were in a hammock. She looked up at him in all seriousness, and said, "But we can't do this in a hammock!"

All at once, she woke up.

She shivered, because it had seemed so real. She licked her dry lips and looked at the pillow she'd been clutching to herself. If only she'd kept her mouth shut in her dream, she muttered. She closed her eyes, rolled over and tried to go back to sleep.

CHAPTER FIVE

GRANGE HAD DUNAGAN send the two scouts into Medina under cover of darkness, to contact Machado's friend Domingo Lopez.

It would be a race against time, especially if they had to fight a heated battle to gain entrance to the city. There was a chance, just a small chance, that they could pull off a bloodless coup by taking all the key positions in the government before fighting broke out. If they could control the communications centers, the military computers, the media and all the bridges leading into the city, there might not be a fight. It would depend on many factors. But as Grange had been taught, you hope for the best, and you always prepare for the worst.

If it came down to it, they had contacts who might persuade the governments nearby to help. And the United States had spec ops people in the vicinity who would liaise with them if needed. It would be a black operation, one of many that went on and were never reported, but it could happen.

Grange knelt down beside Rourke, who was checking his radio and listening to local media.

"All government propaganda," Rourke said in a disgusted tone. "This most recent newscast deals with two professors at the local university who were arrested and put in prison for speaking out against the nationalization of the foreign oil companies here and the oppression."

"Oil," Grange replied heavily. "The blessing and curse of the past three generations. Or is it four? Our whole damned society runs on oil."

"And we pay for it with periodic ecological disasters," Rourke replied.

"Yes."

"I had this amazing anthropology professor in college," Rourke began, still fiddling with the radio. "He told us that any society which finds itself a niche that's dependent on one exhaustible commodity is doomed to extinction."

"Don't tell the oil executives that. They'll protest in droves."

Rourke made a sound deep in his throat. "Probably true. But we're in a hell of a mess globally, you know. The top one percent of the world controls the ninety-nine percent. The average citizen can't even afford decent shoes for his kids."

"Or find a job."

Rourke nodded.

"You're South African. Don't you have a better society with all the changes?"

"We still have regional conflicts. Some of the tribes don't get along with each other, much less with most of the rest of us. But let an outsider make a remark, and we're one united bunch of sinners." Rourke chuckled. "It's our Africa. We don't like people hitting on her."

"Her?" Grange pursed his lips. "Sexist."

Rourke roared.

"How much media are we up against here, in this part of South America?" Grange asked, suddenly somber.

"Locally, just one television station, two radio stations, and three newspapers. Excuse me…two newspapers. They firebombed the third for printing an article El Presidente didn't like."

Grange frowned. "That's about the size of the media you'd find in a small American city, like with 20,000 or 30,000 people."

Rourke nodded. "That's the size of Medina. This is a very small country, and it's surrounded by big and powerful neighbors. It has newly discovered oil reserves, and rumor has it that an American anthropologist dug up proof of a civilization older than the Egyptian pyramids; interestingly, right in the midst of the potential oil field region. She's gone missing since the coup, however. Presumed dead." He leaned closer and nodded toward the distant general, Machado. "He was sweet on her. He really wants a shot at Sapara now. Pure revenge, as much as the desire to save his country."

"I hope we can. I've been thinking about this. If we can find a way to infiltrate the most important objectives, we may be able to avoid a long ground assault. With the rainy season at the door, it could be a disaster, which puts us in a very dangerous position strategically. Quite frankly, I don't see bombing the city into submission. If we make enemies of the locals, we'll never get the usurper out."

"I agree," Rourke said. "We need intelligence. Lots of it. And we need our reserves hidden."

"I thought the same thing, so I've shipped our largest force over into a friendly country, so to speak, near the Mato Grosso area."

Rourke raised his eyebrows. "The Mato Grosso?" he said. "A bad place. A very bad place. Isn't that near where Fawcett and his son and his son's best friend went missing in 1925?" he asked, alluding to a mystery that had never been solved, the fate of a British explorer, Colonel Percival Fawcett, and his two young companions, one of whom was his son. Even in modern times, it prompted people to go into the jungles to solve the eighty-plus-year-old mystery; many never returned.

Grange smiled. "Near the Mato Grosso. While they're not occupied with war, they might find someone who knows about Fawcett's fate. Who knows? But at least we'll avoid the appearance of an insurrection. They'll stay out of sight until we need the firepower. I'm banking on taking the city without bloodshed, through the back door, with spec ops."

"My idea as well."

"Now all I have to do is convince El General," Grange said, nodding toward the brooding ex-patriot, who was sitting alone.

"It won't take much convincing. He doesn't want bloodshed, either," Rourke replied. "I think he's seen enough of it in his time."

"Who hasn't?" Grange said on a heavy breath. "I'd like to grow old without ever hearing gunshots again."

"Then you're in the wrong business, mate," Rourke told him. "You need to give up jobs like this."

Grange made a face. "Can't afford to. Jason Pendleton made me a gift of a house and land and purebred cattle, not to mention a foreman whose daughter is the best cook I've ever known. I have to support them all now. I get paid a small fortune to ramrod Pendleton's Comanche Wells ranch, but it's not enough for upgrades and new bulls. So here I am." He frowned, studying Rourke. "Which brings to mind a reverse question. Do you really need the work? You've got that incredible animal park and your father…"

Rourke's one dark eye flashed dangerously. "Don't," he said in a tone that was deadly soft, like the uncoiling of a poisonous snake.

Grange held up a hand. "Sorry."

Rourke averted his gaze to the radio. "My fault. I'm sensitive on certain subjects."

"I know. I shouldn't have said anything."

"No harm done." He forced a smile. "Go convince our fearless leader to try this the easy way, upending the government from the inside."

"I'll do my best."

Rourke smiled. "I know you will."

GRANGE COULD HAVE bitten his tongue. He knew, as only a few others did, that Rourke was allegedly the illegitimate son of K.C. Kantor, the ex-merc billionaire. But Rourke never mentioned his parentage, never talked about Kantor, even though he'd worked for the man for years. It was an open secret, but it was tricky to mention it to Rourke. Very tricky. And this wasn't the time to throw salt on old wounds.

He sat down next to Machado. "I sent the reserves down to Casera, in the Mato Grosso, in the DC-3. We have people in Manaus, but we couldn't afford to send a group of mercs there. We have friendly ties in Casera from Rourke's last incursion here," he said. "Rourke and I want to try infiltration—cutting up Sapara from the inside, using his own people against him. The same thing he did to you, El General, but in reverse," he added with a smile.

Machado sighed. "I, too, would prefer a bloodless

revolution." He shook his head. "These poor people have suffered enough already, because I was careless." His face set into hard lines. "That will never happen again."

"We have two men inside the city," Grange continued. "Those who we sent to seek out your former commandant and see if he'll help us. I believe he will."

"Yes. So do I." He sighed again and sipped strong coffee. "Certainly he has suffered under my adversary. Fortunately for us, he was too valuable to kill or imprison. He knows the workings of the military and the location of all the strategic computers in the military headquarters. He will be our greatest asset if he can be convinced to risk his life in this endeavor."

"I agree. Now, we just sit back for a few hours and hope for the best."

WHILE THEY WERE hoping for the best, a jeep came driving up into the compound. The driver, a local tour guide who was friendly to Machado and knew of his camp from the natives, had a passenger.

"Good God!" Grange exclaimed with barely leashed fury. "I don't believe it!"

Machado was also surprised.

The passenger climbed lazily out of the jeep. It was an American woman in her mid-twenties, with short, wavy blond hair, blue eyes, dressed like a debutante on safari in khakis with a camera slung around her neck.

"I came anyway," she announced haughtily. She walked up to Grange and touched his chest, almost purring. "I can't keep away from you, dear man!"

"*¡Alto!*" Grange called in Spanish to the driver, who had reversed the jeep and was about to leave. He took Clarisse by the arm, walked her, protesting, back to the jeep, opened the door and put her inside. She almost fell. Her expression was one of dazed disconnection. Was she drunk?

"I'm not leaving…!" she protested.

"Like hell you're not leaving," he said through his teeth. "Of all the repulsive women I've ever known, you take the cake. What do I have to do to convince you that I don't want you? You think you're irresistible to any man you meet? Lady, you have the morals of an alley cat," he added with contempt. "I wouldn't lower myself to sleep with you if you were the only damned woman left on earth! Does that make it any clearer?"

Rourke had spotted her, too. He came forward, unnaturally hostile, even for him, and glared at her. "What the bloody hell do you think you're doing here, Tat?" he asked coldly.

She was shocked, not only to find Rourke in the camp but to hear the old nickname he'd called her long ago when she'd lived in South Africa briefly, near his home. They'd been playmates once, even friends.

She lifted her chin pugnaciously. She felt very combative. She was taking antianxiety meds, probably too many, since the recent tragedy that had robbed her of her entire family. Nobody knew. Nobody except Rourke. He'd actually come to the funerals. He'd been kind. Sort of…

"I'm a photojournalist," she told him icily. "It's my job."

"Na," he said sarcastically. "Your job is seducing men, isn't it? And Grange is on your list? It's a long list, too. Everybody's fair game."

Clarisse, who never reacted to criticism, just stared

at him. What she was feeling inside was her own secret pain. She wouldn't reveal it.

"Yes, I seem to be at the top of the list," Grange muttered coldly. "But it's no use, and I've been telling you that for months!" He wondered why Rourke looked almost relieved. "Listen, lady, I have a woman in my life," he snapped. "A sweet, young, innocent woman who would be appalled if she ever had to actually meet you. The contrast is absolutely epic."

Clarisse swallowed. Her face flamed.

"Now get the hell out of this camp and don't come back," Grange said furiously. *"¡Vaya!"* he called to the driver. *"¡Vaya ahora mismo!"*

"I'll make you sorry for this," Clarisse said, her usual flirtatious manner in eclipse. "I promise you I will!"

"Do your worst," Grange shot back, angry out of all proportion. *"¡Vaya!"* he told the driver once more, and banged on the hood with his flattened hand.

The jeep roared off into the distance. Grange watched it go, more furious than he'd been in years. The damned, persistent woman, showing up here...!

Rourke glanced at him. "How long has she been after you?"

"On and off since I was in Iraq," Grange replied. "She was following my unit for a magazine story. But she's turned up the heat in the past four months. She's been a hell of a nuisance."

"I see." Rourke went back to his work, deep in thought.

Grange caught his breath and leashed his temper as Machado joined him. "I'm sorry," he told his boss. "I just lost it. She'll go to Sapara and we'll all die because of my stupid mistake."

"Not likely, my friend," Machado said with a gentle

smile. "I know women. That one will not betray an entire platoon of men to get even with just one. But I would sleep with one eye open from now on."

"Yeah." He turned. "Sorry."

Machado studied him. "She is practiced and sophisticated, and you find her unappealing. You like innocence I think."

Grange nodded. "There's a girl back home. My foreman's daughter." He shifted and averted his eyes. "She's like a breath of spring."

Machado chuckled and clapped him on the back. "Now I understand. Come. Forget about the mad socialite and have coffee with me. Soon, we shall hear from our contacts in the city."

CLARISSE FLEW BACK to Manaus on the small airplane of a man she knew and put one of her contacts in Texas to work. An hour later, she knew who Peg Larson was and where to find her. Grange was going to be very, very sorry that he'd ever said such insulting things to her. She only wished she could do something to hurt Rourke as well, but Rourke was made of steel. A bomb wouldn't damage him.

Grange, however, could be hurt. She was the descendant of one of the founding fathers of the country, from a powerful family. She had money and charm and she knew how to use both. Grange was going to pay for his insults, and pay big.

She looked out the balcony of her hotel room overlooking the large jungle city of two million souls, her eyes lingering on the opulent Opera House built in 1896. Back during the rubber boom of the early twentieth century, Manaus, called the "Paris of the Tropics," had been the center of a thriving industry that made millionaires of men willing to brave the jungle with its precious rubber trees. The boom had fallen by the 1920s and only regained some success with the advent of World War II and its need for rubber. But canny biologists had taken rubber tree seedlings out of South America and transported them to plantations in Ceylon and the Orient, thus breaking the monopoly. Thereafter, Manaus settled back into its jungle and the era of great fortunes carved out of wilderness were at an end. But the city was a phoenix, destined to rise again.

In 1967 with the passage of the Manaus Free Zone, the city became an important center for the manufacture of electrical and electronic goods, and also a beautiful resource for ecological tourism, preserving the beauty of the Rio Negro, on which it was situated, and its biological diversity.

Manaus had a grandeur all its own. Portuguese, not Spanish, was spoken here, which was technically Brazil, on the black waters of the Rio Negro. Where Grange and his men were camped just inside the border of Barrera, the language was Spanish. Comfortable in either language, Clarisse had no problem communicating what she wanted. And with that in mind, she picked up the phone and reserved two business class round-trip tickets from the United States to La Paz, and then booked passage on a flight to Manaus, also for two. She wasn't going to take no for an answer. She was going to convince Peg Larson to come down here. Then, she had darker plans for the woman who had taken Grange. Very dark plans. Her conscience pricked her. She wasn't usually this devious, and she didn't hurt people deliberately. She took more of the antianxiety meds and lay down on the bed and closed her eyes. She shouldn't feel guilty. Grange had it coming.

She shivered as, in her mind's eye, she saw the Rio Negro flowing, remembered what had happened here four months ago. She closed her eyes and shuddered. It was too soon. She shouldn't have come back. She went looking for the antianxiety meds and frowned when she noted that the bottle was almost empty. No matter. She had a friend, a doctor, who lived in the city. She'd call him and get more.

She went back to Washington, D.C., the next day. She was furious and taking far too many drugs. Her mind was clouded by a damaged ego and shredded pride. All she could think about was getting even. Grange would pay and so would his American love interest. They would all pay.

PEG WAS FEEDING the small flock of Rhode Island Red chickens that she and her father kept for fresh eggs when a silver Mercedes-Benz pulled up in the driveway. She put down the bowl of chicken feed and went out to meet it.

At first she thought it might be Gracie Pendleton, but the Pendletons drove Jaguars. In fact, Gracie had a racing-green one, her favorite color.

It wasn't Gracie.

A beautiful woman with short, wavy honey-blond hair got out of the car. She was dressed in immaculate khaki slacks with what looked like a blue silk blouse. Over it was a khaki vest with a hundred pockets, or so it seemed.

"Hi!" she called in a friendly tone, and smiled. "I'm looking for Peg Larson."

Peg blinked. "That's me."

"I'm Clarisse Carrington," she replied, offering a hand to shake Peg's. "I've just come from South America." She moved closer, looking around warily to make sure nobody was close enough to overhear. "I've just seen Winslow Grange."

"Is he all right?" Peg asked, her face frozen with fear.

"Perfectly all right." Clarisse hated that look on the younger woman's face. It was obvious how she felt about Grange, and for just an instant, Clarisse felt a pang of guilt for what she planned to do. It didn't last long. She smiled again. "They're waiting for things to come together before they go in. He wants to see you."

"Is he coming home?" Peg asked, excited.

"No. That isn't possible." She looked at her expensive tan loafers. "But he wants me to bring you over to his camp. I'm a journalist, so I can go anywhere I like. I have a private plane and a jeep with a driver. I purchased tickets from San Antonio to Atlanta, where we'll fly to Miami for the nonstop flight to Manaus. I also have two business class round-trip tickets on the flight to Manaus from Miami. I've booked a hotel suite for us in Manaus. It's not too far from where Grange and his men are camped."

The woman was speaking rapidly. Her eyes didn't look quite right. Peg began to hesitate. "It's so expensive. How would I pay it back?"

"Are you joking?" Clarisse cleared her throat. "You don't have to pay it back. I'm independently wealthy. I work as a journalist for fun, not profit."

"Why would you do this?" Peg persisted.

Damn, Clarisse thought, the woman was smart. Maybe too smart. But she forced another smile. "I'm doing an article on the assault," she said, "for a well-known magazine." She named it. It was one of the more famous glossy ones, so Peg recognized it from doctors' waiting rooms. "This is a human-interest piece, about the people behind the people who are fighting. I'd planned to do one about another man in the party, but I couldn't get his sibling to agree to fly there." She averted her eyes, telling the lie with a straight face. "It's quite dangerous. Not really," she amended quickly. "But the girl is afraid of snakes. There are snakes in this part of South America…"

Snakes. It seemed a thin excuse. Peg would have gone anywhere to see a brother if she had one. She'd go anywhere to see Grange. He'd sent her the shortwave message, but he hadn't mentioned this woman. Wasn't there something about a socialite who was chasing him?

"Please. The story will be so good for the coup effort. It will only take a couple of days," Clarisse said quickly, because Peg was wavering. "I'll have you back home by the weekend. I promise." The smile was beginning to chafe. "Winslow really wants to see you," she added. "He misses you terribly."

Peg's heart jumped. She forgot everything she'd heard. Grange wanted to see her. She'd missed him so much that it seemed her heart had been torn out of her. She retraced places he'd been, sat in his bedroom and stared at the bed where he slept. She mooned around her own bedroom where he'd kissed her and touched her with such passion. She went over and over their last meeting, when he'd kissed her again, but with aching tenderness. She had torrid, erotic dreams about him almost every night. She knew he felt something for her. But she hadn't realized how powerful it was. If he wanted to see her so badly that he'd asked a journalist to bring her over, to another country, just for a couple of days...perhaps he wanted to propose?

"Oh, my," Peg exclaimed, with a hand at her collarbone.

"The fighting may be intense, when they go in," Clarisse said grimly. "He's a good soldier, but what if something happened and you didn't go? What if you never got to see him again, because you were afraid of the jungle?"

"I'm not afraid of the jungle," Peg muttered, and her green eyes flashed at the other woman. "I don't like snakes, but I don't have any phobias of them."

"Brave girl." Clarisse chuckled. "Okay, then, what's your problem?"

"If you write the story, won't it give away what General Machado is trying to do?"

"Dear girl, I won't publish until after General Machado is back in power." Clarisse laughed at the other woman's lack of knowledge. "I'd never betray them. It isn't my nature. Not even if I were tortured."

Peg still hesitated. She should call somebody and check this woman out, before she ventured into the jungle with her.

Clarisse almost saw that thought in her mind. She checked her watch and grimaced. "The plane leaves from Atlanta for Miami in four hours," she said. "We'll have to rush to the airport in San Antonio to make connections. The Miami flight is nonstop. And the tickets are nonrefundable," she added with just the right worried expression.

Peg groaned aloud. Tickets to South America. Grange waiting to see her before a bloody assault that might fail. No time, no time!

"I'll pack something," Peg said. "I have to tell my Dad…"

She was already running for the house. "Come on in," she called to Clarisse. "You can sit in the living room, I won't be long, I promise."

"Pack lightweight things, like silk," Clarisse advised as she walked into the house.

Peg stopped short and gaped at the older woman. "Silk?" She waved her hands around. "You think I can afford to buy anything made of silk? I can't even afford a silk scarf!"

Clarisse bit her lip. She hadn't realized that the other woman was wearing cotton because it was all she had. She looked around her at the cheap furnishings. Poverty row, she thought with guilty contempt, and then remembered the role she was playing. "Just pack something comfortable. And make sure you take a raincoat or a slicker. The rainy season is just getting started. You'll need sunblock, too, but Manaus is a large city. We can buy toiletries when we get there," she said. "You'll have trouble getting them on a plane, so just bring clothes. Not cotton," she added firmly. "Cotton gets wet and stays wet. Something drip-dry. And make sure you have a pair of boots and some pants made of synthetic fiber."

"Oh. Okay. I'll hurry." Actually she had lots of poly-cotton stuff, because it was cheap. Silk, on her budget! That was a hoot.

Clarisse wandered around the living room. Her eye caught on a painting above the mantel, of running horses against a cloudy sky. "Who painted this canvas over the mantel?" she called to Peg.

"A local artist, Janie Brewster Hart," she called back. "She's exhibiting in San Antonio right now, along with her sister-in-law, the wife of our state attorney general, who sculpts."

"Nice work," Clarisse murmured. The painting was really good. The woman had talent. She had a sudden thought. This was Grange's house. He owned it. He lived here. She frowned. It had echoes of his personality. It was Spartan and bare-bones comfort. Scattered around were souvenirs he'd brought home from the Middle East. There were a couple of small paintings, along with some fossilized stones and a bone-sheath knife. There were framed photos of him with his Green Beret unit in Iraq. That brought back painful memories of Clarisse's attempts to flirt with him. She'd been less aggressive in those days, almost painfully shy. She'd had to force herself to be forward. Nobody knew the truth about her. Not even Rourke.

"I'm almost ready, I just have to call Dad and tell him where I'm going."

"Don't tell him more than you have to," Clarisse called back grimly. "The phone might be tapped."

"You're kidding!"

Yes, she was, but she didn't want Peg's father to catch on. She didn't want any hitches in her plans.

"No, I'm not kidding. This is a covert military operation and this is Grange's home. It's not impossible." Even as she said it, she realized that she might accidentally be telling the truth.

There was a pause. "Okay. He's over at the Pendletons' ranch. I'll just call him and say I'm going out of town for a couple of days with a school friend who wants company in Atlanta."

"Good girl."

For just a few seconds, Clarisse almost had a change

of heart. This was cruel. She wasn't born a cruel person. She'd been made cruel by her past. Grange thought she was some sort of man-eater. It was funny. She was as innocent as Peg. She just knew how to act. Except that it wasn't an act with Grange. She really wanted him. He reminded her of Rourke...

She swallowed, hard, and went to the neat, tidy kitchen to get a bottle of water. There wasn't any, so she had to drink from a glass filled from the faucet. She winced. She took the pill bottle out of her fanny pack and swallowed two pills. She hated flying. But she had to get used to it. The meds helped with that. They helped with everything.

Funny, she'd never been really attracted to any man except Rourke. Grange had come into her life at an outpost in Iraq, where he was with a spec op group, Green Berets. She'd followed them, with permission from the military because she had friends high up in the Pentagon, to do a story. Grange had suddenly become her main objective. She'd tried every way she knew to attract him but nothing had happened. He'd been polite enough while she did the story, but once he was out of the military he disappeared. She'd seen him again at a party in Washington, D.C., just after the greatest tragedy in her life. That was after she'd started taking meds for the nightmares and anxiety. Her whole personality had changed. She'd been aggressively flirtatious for all she was worth. It was useless. He'd given her the cold shoulder. She'd become obsessed with getting him to notice her, followed him around every time he came to a city, showed up in restaurants, even in hotels. He hadn't said much, but he'd suddenly stopped going to hotels where she could bribe employees to tip her off.

That had only spurred her determination. Funny, he wasn't at all her type. She sighed and put the glass in the sink. The water didn't taste half bad. Much better than bottled.

Her mind went back to her last meeting with Grange in Barrera, to the insults he'd shouted that all the men had heard...that Rourke had heard. He didn't want her. He thought she was repulsive. That word went through her like a hot lance. What did he know about her, about her past, about her suffering? He didn't want to know. He had this sweet, innocent girl who didn't even look to be out of her teens, and she had no money, no connections, no nothing. Whereas Clarisse had everything, but she couldn't get Grange.

"I must be mad," she told herself in a whisper. "Totally mad!"

"What was that?" Peg asked from the staircase.

"Your water tastes good," Clarisse said.

"Thanks. We have a well. The water is always cold and good." She came into the living room with a ratty suitcase, wearing high heels and her best Sunday dress. "Is this okay?" she asked about her ensemble.

Clarisse was struck dumb. She blinked. "Have you ever flown on an airplane?"

"Well, no. Yes. I mean, I got to fly in a crop duster plane, once," Peg replied. "It's a little two-seater airplane. We spray big crops with insecticide from them. I mean, we don't. Some people do."

Clarisse took a deep breath. There were few places on earth she hadn't been. She'd flown in everything from passenger planes to military aircraft. This child had never set foot on an airplane and thought you needed to wear your Sunday best to get aboard. High heels in the

Hartsfield International Airport in Atlanta would be a disaster, where passengers had to walk vast distances between the ticket counter and the concourses.

"You need to wear slacks and a lightweight shirt and boots with socks. Carry a sweater onboard. You can't walk through an airport in high heels. You'll have blisters. They can cause infection and be fatal in tropical rain forests. Blood poisoning sets in."

"Oh." Peg flushed.

Clarisse moved closer. "It's okay," she said gently. "I wasn't born knowing these things, either. I had to learn."

Peg smiled shyly. "Thanks. I'll go change."

She rushed back to her room. Clarisse felt as if a house had fallen on her. Peg was so much like Matilda. Not in looks, but in attitude and grit and innocence. She closed her eyes on a wave of pain. Her fault. Her fault. She'd insisted that Matilda go on the native boat with their father to sightsee in the jungle outside Manaus, a great adventure, while she interviewed the chief through an interpreter. It was a family outing, a working one for Clarisse. But Matilda, sweet Matilda, had paid for her shortsightedness! Now she was going to put another child in danger, deliberately, for revenge...!

"I'm ready," Peg announced.

Clarisse looked at her with wide, hesitant eyes. "I don't know. Maybe this is a bad idea," she said, thinking aloud.

"Please, I want to go," Peg pleaded. "I'd do anything to see him. Anything!"

Clarisse set her teeth firmly. Grange had insulted her in front of Rourke, who hardly needed a reason to hate her more. Grange made her feel cheap and small. The insult drove the kindness right out of her. She forced a smile. "Well, then, let's be off!"

PEG HAD NEVER been in an airport terminal, except once when she went with her father to meet Jason Pendleton when he needed a quick ride to the ranch. San Antonio's was big and the place was crowded with people. She glanced at the palm trees outside and shook her head. "That always amazes me," she murmured. "Palm trees. It's like Florida, I guess. I've never been to Florida, though."

Clarisse just nodded. The girl was clueless.

They got aboard after an hour's wait. It wasn't called first class anymore, it was business class. The compartment held only about four people, men with cell phones and laptops, connected to the internet and totally oblivious to their surroundings.

Peg was fascinated with everything. When the flight attendant went through her ditching routine, explaining the vest with an accompanying video, Peg paid rapt attention.

"That was totally cool," she told Clarisse excitedly.

"Oh, yes, like a waterproof vest is going to be a lot of help on land."

Peg blinked.

"The only water we fly across is rivers and lakes," came the droll reply. "If we go down, believe me, a vest is the last thing we'll need."

"Oh." She toyed with the controls on her seat. "Well, we'll fly over the ocean going to South America," she said brightly. "If we had to ditch there, they'd come in handy."

The plane, if it fell, would hit the ocean at several

hundred miles an hour, at which speed the water would be like a brick wall, Clarisse thought. The plane would disintegrate, along with the passengers. Even if they weren't in pieces, sharks would certainly find them filling. But she didn't say any of that to Peg. She took another one of her pills, prescribed for extreme anxiety, and went to sleep so she wouldn't have to think about the horrible revenge she was taking on a man who didn't want her.

GRANGE SAT WITH Rourke in the darkness, his conscience bothering him.

"I shouldn't have been so vicious to Clarisse," he muttered. "That was wrong. I just lost my temper. She's been dogging me for years. I'm tired of it. Especially now."

Rourke played with his coffee cup. "You don't know much about her, do you?"

Grange's eyebrows arched. "I know that for the past couple of months she's been an unbelievable pest."

Rourke stared into his coffee. "About six years ago, her father won appointment to the staff of the U.S. State Department. Four months ago, they sent him to talk to the Barrera government about an oil contract. To maintain appearances, because he was already finding ways to kill natives who opposed oil exploration in their territory, Sapara sent him out to one of the native villages to discuss a treaty. This is always done with the chief of the tribe involved or with many chiefs if territories overlapped." Rourke sipped coffee. "Near Manaus, there are luxurious riverboats for tourists, but if you want to go see a group of natives, far back in the jungle here, you take a guide who knows the country and you travel in a local boat." He set his lips. "To make a long story short, the boat was in need of repair and going over a rapid, it capsized. Where it capsized, there were piranhas."

Grange was almost frozen in place. He waited for the rest.

Rourke made a face. "Her father had cut himself shaving. It wasn't a bad cut, but it was enough. He probably drowned before the piranhas got him, but they pretty much stripped him below the waist. He'd brought both his daughters with him. He thought it would be a lark. When the youngest, Matilda, saw her father go under, she swam back from safety to save him. She died, too. Clarisse had been interviewing the native chief. She watched in horror from the bank. She lost her whole family." He shrugged. "I heard from a mutual friend that she's been on anxiety meds ever since. Sometimes, when the memories get bad, really bad, she takes more than she should and they affect her judgment. She does crazy things." He sighed. "I don't care for her. In fact, I find her utterly offensive. But after the tragedy, her mind snapped. How do you fix that, eh?" he asked, noting the paleness of his companion's face. "How do you fix a broken mind?"

"If I'd known that," Grange said quietly, "I wouldn't have been so brutal. I should never have been so blunt." He shrugged. "I'm missing Peg, badly, and worried about the assault." He looked Rourke in the eye. "If we have to go in with all our artillery, lots of people are going to die. Maybe even him." He nodded toward Machado, who was bent over, discussing something with two of their comrades. "I've gotten fond of him."

Rourke nodded. "Ya. Me, too." He patted Grange on the back. "Don't worry so much. Clarisse will get over it. She's gotten over worse." He was recalling an intimate incident with her, when she was much younger, one that had alienated him forever. He wondered if she remembered. He tried not to.

"It would be nice if we could take back things we said in anger."

Rourke chuckled. "And if dirt had nutrition, we'd never starve. Get some rest. We'll have a big day to-morrow, one way or the other."

"A big day," Grange agreed.

CHAPTER SIX

PEG COULDN'T STOP staring as the cab took them into Manaus, en route to the hotel Clarisse was staying at. She had a huge suite, plenty of room for the other woman to share, because it would take a day or two to make arrangements for the trip into the jungle. Clarisse would have to have a guide she could trust completely, one who could get them to their destination through back ways.

That meant tracking down Enrique Boas, who was a tour guide with much experience of the jungles. Clarisse would also need a hired car better than the lumbering piece of metal that Enrique usually drove, preferably a Land Rover.

There was a village about an hour's ride from the place where the American group was camped, also inside Barrera near the border with Amazonia, a small native village with people who spoke only Portuguese. There were no outsiders there. Enrique's mother lived in the village, so it was the perfect place to leave the young woman beside her. Then she would go to Grange's camp and tell him what she'd done.

She wondered if he might attack her. She didn't care. Her plan was well thought-out and flawless. She was going to ditch her rival in a place from which there was no escape, and tell Grange only that she'd taken the woman into the jungles and left her.

The pills made her mind foggy. The woman could die. Tourists frequently died here, from lack of knowledge. Insect bites could cause disease. Snakes could kill. Rivers had piranhas...

She felt sick. Matilda, frantically swimming to try to save their father while Clarisse stood helplessly by in total shock and did nothing. Nothing! Dear God, she had loved their father and her sister, why hadn't she done something? Matilda, brave Matilda, had died...

She shivered. The memory was still too close, too near, too horrible. Four months. Yesterday. Why had she ever come back down here? Following Grange. And for what? He didn't want her, he'd never wanted her! He'd gone to a little dried-up Texas town and found this petunia, this violet, this unbelievably naive child of nineteen. Peg. Peg, whom she was going to punish for Grange's betrayal. She blinked. Why was it Peg's fault? She looked at the younger woman and was again haunted by the memory of her beloved sister. She took a deep breath, trying to focus through a drugged haze as the car pulled up in front of the hotel.

"This is it," she told Peg. Her face felt numb. How odd. She handed the driver a bill. He got out, bowing, and went to fetch their bags from the trunk, to carry them inside for the two American women. It was a very nice tip the older woman had given him.

Clarisse faltered on the way to the curb and would have fallen face-first if Peg hadn't caught her.

"Careful," Peg said, concerned. "You don't want to break a leg or anything."

Clarisse bit her lip. She blinked. "Thanks, Matilda."

Peg looked at her with clear green eyes. "Who's Matilda?"

It came rushing back. The thrashing in the water, the screams, almost inhuman screams, the horror, the blood…

Clarisse caught her breath and swallowed again, hard. She stood very still, her face white as a sheet. This wasn't Matilda. This was Peg. Try to remember. No! Try not to remember…!

"We'd better go in," she told Peg.

"Here, lean on me," Peg said gently. "You're not well."

Clarisse felt a pain like a knife through her chest. She looked at the younger woman, her clear eyes, her kind expression, and almost hated her. Did she really believe that a benevolent stranger had come halfway across the world to do her an expensive kindness? She was so trusting. Matilda had been trusting…

"I'm okay," Clarisse said heavily. "I'm okay. But… thanks."

Peg just smiled. "I'll take care of you. Don't worry."

The pain grew worse. Peg was years younger than her companion, but she had character and grit. Clarisse felt the comparison keenly.

"The food here is very good," Clarisse said.

"Great. I'm starved."

Clarisse looked at her watch. "We'll have to get something from room service for now. They eat very late, compared to hotels in the States. Nothing will be open before seven, maybe eight."

"Tonight?" Peg exclaimed.

"I'm afraid so."

She sighed. "At least I can get a sandwich, right?"

Clarisse laughed. "Cheese and crudités, perhaps."

"What's a crudi…crude…that thing?"

"Raw veggies with a dip."

"I think I had that once."

"You'll have many new experiences in this country." Some of them would be unforgettable and terrible. Clarisse turned away with new guilt. "Let's go upstairs. I'm very tired. I imagine you are, too."

"Not so much. When will we go to see Winslow?" she added hopefully.

"It will take a day or two to make the arrangements, it's not so very far from here, but transportation is a pain in the rainy season. We can't go by boat, so we have to use the so-called roads. There's a paved one that runs from Manaus to the capital of Amazonia, but we have to go north. The roads are dirt and some of the bridges get washed away. Usually, though, not this early in the season."

Peg's heart sank. "Oh."

"We don't want any accidents," Clarisse added. "It would worry him. This is a crucial time for them all."

"Yes. Of course. I wasn't thinking. Can we call him?"

"That would be unwise."

Peg bit her lip. "I'm sorry. I'm just not thinking clearly. I think I have that thing, what's it called…jet lag?"

"I should have given you melatonin to cope with that, along with the quinine." Clarisse had been pumping quinine into the other girl since they got on the plane at San Antonio, to cope with mosquitoes. There were almost none in Manaus, but where they were going, there would be plenty. For some odd reason, she'd felt protective of the girl from the start.

"The important thing is to go by the time it is when you arrive," Clarisse continued. "We'll sleep when it's bedtime in this time zone, and get up when it's morning. You'll get used to it."

"You must travel a lot," Peg said as they paused outside the door to the suite.

"Yes. A lot." Trying to run away from my memories, Clarisse could have said. But she didn't. She only smiled. "And here we are!"

She opened the door.

Peg walked inside gingerly. She'd never been anyplace really fancy in her life, except to a big restaurant in San Antonio that Grange had taken her and her father to, just after they came to work for him. But that was nothing compared to this.

Everything was luxurious. The fabric was rich, the double beds, both of them, had satin covers of spotless white with green trim. The curtains matched. There was a phone and a computer and a fax machine. There was a little refrigerator with drinks and snacks. The carpet was exquisite. The paintings on the wall looked real, like the ones Grange had at the ranch back home.

Peg felt a twinge of guilt. She hadn't told her father much; just that a school friend was taking her to Atlanta on a real airplane for a couple of days to shop and was paying for their hotel. If she'd told him the truth, he'd never have let her go without an argument.

"Don't you like it?" Clarisse asked, noting the frown.

"The room is beautiful," Peg told her. "I've never been anyplace so fancy. It's like a dream. But I was thinking about Daddy. I lied to him. I never did that before."

"He'll forgive you. Just remember how much Grange wants to see you."

Peg sighed. "I'll try." She looked around again. "It's so exotic. Are there really parrots and iguanas here," she asked, "like those pictures in the magazine I read on the plane?"

"All sorts of wildlife in the Amazon," Clarisse said, getting drowsy. "Most of it is lethal if you don't know where you're going."

"I'm glad I have you." Peg grinned. "It's nice to have a traveling companion who knows the location."

Clarisse sighed. "Yes." She threw herself onto the bed and closed her eyes. "Just going to nap, for a minute." She opened her eyes. "Don't go out of the room. Promise me."

Peg was disappointed, but she felt the older woman was protecting her. "Okay," she said reluctantly.

"Tomorrow we'll go sightseeing," Clarisse murmured. "I'll show you the zoo."

"There's a zoo?" she exclaimed.

But Clarisse had fallen asleep.

PEG WANDERED AROUND the room and ended up on the balcony overlooking the city. She wanted to know everything about this place. She'd never dreamed she'd actually be able to go to a foreign country. But now that she was here, she had misgivings. She'd lied to her father. She'd come a thousand miles or more with a woman about whom she knew absolutely nothing except that Clarisse had claimed that Grange wanted to see Peg, that he was desperate to see her.

That had been enough to convince her to go. Now, she was worried that she'd been too impulsive and put herself at risk. She had her passport, but weren't you supposed to get shots and stuff before you went into another country? Clarisse had given her pills to prevent malaria, but she hadn't had any immunizations except for a tetanus shot the year before in Jacobsville. She didn't have any money, except for a couple of dollars. She didn't have any medicine. She hadn't brought a phone.

The more she thought about it, the more worried she became. Added to that, she was starving. Clarisse had said they'd order food, but she'd fallen asleep.

Out of curiosity, Peg opened the room service book. It did have food listed in several languages, none of which she recognized except the English and Spanish. She wasn't fluent in Spanish, but she could understand it and speak a little. Reading it was more difficult, despite years of study in high school. In the two years since graduation, she hadn't paid much attention to written Spanish, other than the signs that appeared locally in Jacobsville. Now, she wished she'd studied more. Manaus was in Brazil, where the language was Portuguese. Good luck trying to read that, she thought, much less speak it. She wondered if Clarisse understood the native tongue.

Hesitantly she picked up the phone and dialed room service.

"*Sí?*"

She swallowed. "Do you have fish?" she asked hesitantly.

There was a pause and a low, delighted chuckle. "Yes, we have fish," came the amused and pleasant reply. "English, yes? I speak it. You want fish—we have every variety you can think of!"

"How wonderful!" She hesitated. "Can you recommend a kind? I've never been to South America before. I want to try new things."

He laughed joyfully. "I will send up a platter of several varieties for you to sample. And how would you like it cooked?"

"Fried?" she asked. "And potatoes, also fried, and with ketchup?"

He laughed. "Coming right up. Would you like something to drink?"

"Oh, yes, please, do you have hot tea?"

"Jasmine, perhaps?"

"Yes!"

"With sugar?"

"Please! I'm so hungry!" She glanced at Clarisse. "My traveling companion went to sleep… I guess I'd better not order for her until she wakes up."

There was a pause and a coolness in the tone now. "That will probably not be until morning. The *señorita* will sleep a great deal now." There was a pause. "You are her friend?"

"Well, I don't know her, really," Peg faltered. "She came to get me and said that my, well, my boss wanted me to fly over with her. He's…" She hesitated; she couldn't give anything away about the military operation. "He's working over here. Research," she added quickly.

There was a pause. "If you need anything, the concierge downstairs can direct you. Also, the American Embassy has a consular office here."

"You're very kind," Peg said. "Thank you."

"It is no difficulty to be kind, *señorita*," he said softly, in a very pleasant deep tone. "The food will be there in less than a half hour."

"Thank you. *Gracias*," she faltered again.

He chuckled. "Here, it is *obrigado*. Portuguese."

"*¡Obrigado!*" she repeated, laughing delightedly. "My first Portuguese word!"

"You will learn others, I am certain. *Boa tarde*." He

laughed again. "That means 'good afternoon.' A phrase for you to remember."

"Boa tarde," she replied.

"Boa tarde." There was another laugh in his tone as he hung up.

WHILE SHE WAITED for the food, she went to the computer, presumably Clarisse's, and turned it on. She hoped the other woman wouldn't mind. She started to go to the web browser when she noted an odd file. It seemed related to the country around them so, impulsively, she brought it up and opened it.

It was a memo, dated four months ago. It dealt with a foreign visitor, a federal employee of the United States Embassy, with Clarisse's last name. He had fallen into the river while on the way in a small canoe to visit a local Indian tribe, negotiating an oil lease, which would be beneficial not only to Brazil, but also to companies in the United States. The story said that a cut on his face had bled into the water and attracted piranha. They were not always dangerous, the reporter imparted, but apparently these had not fed for some time, so they attacked the man. A young girl, his daughter, had jumped in, attempted to save him and they had both died. The child's name was… Matilda. One daughter had been left behind, watching horrified from the shore. The story implied that she had suffered a nervous collapse afterward and been taken to a local hospital, where she remained, undergoing therapy.

Appalled, Peg closed the file and shut down the computer. She stood over Clarisse with an aching heart. The poor woman, to suffer the loss of her family and to watch it happen. No wonder she'd collapsed. Peg was shocked that Clarisse could even bring herself to come here at all, after the tragedy.

With her eyes closed, and her face relaxed, the lines of strain and grief were even more pronounced. Peg sighed. Poor, poor thing, to have to deal with such a horrible thing. It was even more amazing that she could be so generous to another person, a total stranger. The tragedy would have made most people withdraw into themselves. Peg thought she would have reacted that way. But then you never really knew how anyone would behave in a situation until they were facing it, she thought.

She went to the window and looked out. This luxury hotel, one of the finest in the city, according to the brochure on the table, was located on a white sandy beach. It had surprised Peg to find a modern metropolitan city rather than a few shacks in the jungle with jaguars and snakes prowling outside the village.

In fact, Manaus was called the "Paris of the Tropics." It was a beautiful city, full of light and color, with modern buildings mixed with the older colonial architecture, with everything that New York or a European major city could offer in the way of amenities. Peg had been fascinated when they flew in to see an ocean liner sitting at the harbor. Yes, Clarisse had told her, the Amazon River was navigable all the way to Manaus by ocean liners. They called here frequently. There was also the national airline, TAM, which offered international flights to and from Manaus as well as other South American locations.

From the balcony, Peg could see the white beach and palm trees and the shimmering water. It looked more like an ocean than a river, she thought, and wished so much that she could go out there and see it up close. She hoped that in the two days Clarisse planned to use making arrangements to get to Grange, she really would take Peg sightseeing. It might be the only time in her life she'd get to see a foreign city. Not that she wouldn't have forsaken all of that just to see Winslow again. Her heart raced at the thought of his face when he saw her. She couldn't wait!

THE WAITER BROUGHT a huge tray with fish and tea and an incredible dessert with all sorts of decoration.

"Raoul thought that you might like to sample one of our specialties, also, for dessert," he told Peg, smiling. "It contains many of the local fruits, including coconuts. If you need anything else, you need only ask."

She hesitated, looking worried. "I don't have a tip," she said uncomfortably.

He smiled kindly. "*Señorita,* it is nothing. Believe me. The thought means much."

"*Mil gracias,*" she said in her gentle Spanish.

He was delighted. "*De nada,*" he said to her surprise. "You will find that if you can understand Spanish, you can understand much Portuguese. It is a mystery, you see, but it is true. You will see. *Bom dia.*"

She grinned from ear to ear. "*Bom dia.* And *obrigado.*"

He bowed, still smiling, and left.

Peg gave a guilty glance toward Clarisse, who was snoring. Well, the older woman could order something when she woke. She hoped she had enough in her small savings account to pay for her part of this lovely meal. She was going to offer, anyway.

She sat down at the window, so that she could look down on the beach, and dug into her food.

SHE COULDN'T EAT it all. The fish was delicately breaded and fried, delicious. The potatoes were seasoned perfectly. There was a small fruit salad and the indescribable dessert that made Peg close her eyes in ecstasy. She'd never tasted food like that. She wished she spoke enough Portuguese to beg for the recipes. But surely they were a hotel specialty, so they wouldn't share them, probably. What a shame. Her father would be overwhelmed if she presented him with such a meal.

She grimaced. She hoped she wouldn't have to tell him where she was. He was going to be very angry. She'd never lied to him before. But she wanted to see Winslow, so badly. It would be all right. Surely it would!

BY BEDTIME, MANAUS time, Clarisse still wasn't awake. Peg looked out over the city, which was dressed in a million colorful sparkling lights. It was the most beautiful city Peg had ever seen, and it was huge. At night, it was possible to see how far the city boundaries extended. She hadn't dreamed of finding something like this in the mysterious and dangerous Amazon. How incredible!

She opened the hotel booklet and read, in English, about the founding of the city and its history.

By the time she finished absorbing it all, she was drowsy. It had been a very long day, and Clarisse still wasn't awake.

With a sigh, she went to take a shower and put on her long cotton gown. Half an hour later, she was sound asleep.

SHE WOKE TO the sound of a suitcase opening. Clarisse was replacing cosmetics and toiletries. She was wearing a different outfit, still khaki, but this time with a blue vest of many pockets and blue kid boots to match.

She glanced at Peg rubbing her eyes. "Awake at last." She laughed. "Did you sleep well?"

"Very, thanks. I ordered supper last night. I'll pay you back…"

Clarisse waved a hand. "My treat. I'm sorry I conked out on you, but I was really worn to the bone. I've done this flight twice in three days without a break. Jet lag catches up. Are you hungry? I've ordered breakfast. The coffee here is incredible, do you drink it?"

"Yes, I love coffee."

"I wondered. Raoul said you ordered tea last night."

"I didn't think they had coffee."

"Child!" Clarisse exclaimed. "This is South America! They practically invented it here!"

Peg laughed. "Sorry. I was really tired. I've never been anywhere. This place is fantastic!" she added as she got out of bed. "It looks like pictures of New York City at night! I never dreamed it was so big."

"It's big, all right. There's an opera house that was built during the rubber boom, not to mention some of the most modern skyscrapers in the country, and plenty of cathedrals."

"Will we have time to go explore?"

"Certainly. First you have to have some jabs. I've had a doctor friend of mine come over to do the honors. I've already started you on a course of quinine, as a preventative. Malaria is rampant down here, although not on the Rio Negro, and we're in the very beginning of the rainy season."

"Jabs? Shots?"

Clarisse nodded. "Injections. Hepatitis A and B, malaria, yellow fever—Winslow would never forgive me if you went down with some vicious tropical fever," she added, and wouldn't look at Peg. She hadn't planned on this sort of protection for the younger woman, but her conscience was already killing her. She wasn't going to let the girl go out into the jungle without vaccinations, at least.

"I hate shots."

"You'd hate diseases more," Clarisse assured her.

She sighed. "I guess so."

There was a knock at the door. "Breakfast," Clarisse announced, and forced a smile.

THEY ATE AT a leisurely pace, and then the doctor arrived. He brought along prescription medicines that he'd had filled for them, including Levaquin for traveler's diarrhea in case Peg, unused to the area, contracted it.

Peg thanked him profusely, because the shots hadn't hurt.

He smiled, bowed and walked out with Clarisse into the hall. She came back a couple of minutes later. "It's all right to eat or drink anything here in the hotel," she told Peg, "but don't even think of drinking water or eating food from any of the villages outside the city. And for God's sake, pay attention to insect bites…they're dangerous if they're not dealt with at once."

"Okay," Peg said.

Clarisse turned away. "We should go. I'm going to take you around town. You have to see Manaus. It's unbelievable."

"I don't know how I'll ever be able to pay you back," Peg said miserably.

Clarisse looked at her with shock. She'd taken people around the world with her from time to time, and nobody yet had offered to pay for so much as a napkin!

"Pay me back?" she asked, obviously surprised.

"It's so kind of you, to do this for me," Peg replied. "I

don't like to take things from people unless I can offer something back."

Clarisse swallowed. She didn't know quite what to say, and the guilt was growing. "I like Grange," she said after a minute. She lowered her eyes. "He asked me to bring you."

Peg wanted to ask her about the rumors, that some society woman was chasing Grange. She wondered if Clarisse knew the woman. It couldn't be Clarisse herself, she was sure. This woman was kind and generous. She wasn't the sort of coldhearted person that Peg had heard about. But she was hesitant to bring up an unpleasant subject, especially now.

"Then thanks very much," Peg said. "But if I can do anything for you, ever, I'll do it. Whatever it is."

Clarisse didn't look at her. "We should go."

THEY DID THE rounds of the city. The opera house was a holdover from colonial times, with huge columns and pink surfaces. Inside, they were given slippers to go on over their shoes, because the floors were old and very slick. Peg wandered through the opulent building with pure wonder in her eyes. She'd heard opera coming out of Grange's room from time to time. Once he'd let her listen to one of his DVDs by a celebrated opera star whose name was Plácido Domingo. There was a particular song that she'd loved, called, in English, "No One Sleeps," or something like it.

"I heard an opera song once. It was set in China and there was this song about nobody sleeping…"

"That would be *Turandot*. The aria is 'Nessun Dorma,'" Clarisse said in a haunted tone. "Yes. It's one of the most beautiful I've ever heard."

"This guy named Plácido Domingo sang it. I got goose bumps."

Clarisse turned to her. "Have you ever been to an opera?"

Peg laughed softly. "I've never been anywhere," she confessed. "Until now."

"You should go to an opera. At least to one. It's an experience you'd never forget." Like this one, she was thinking, but she bit her tongue. Poor Peg would never forget what was about to happen. Clarisse moved a little aside, took out another couple of antianxiety pills and swallowed them quickly with the bottle of water she carried. Pills. Pills to wake her up, to put her to sleep, to block out the memories, the horrible memories…

"We'd better go," she told Peg after a minute. "We don't have a lot of time."

"Oh. Sure!"

Clarisse took her out of town on a bus tour that went to a local zoo. There were all sorts of animals that could be found in the Amazon, including monkeys and iguanas and tapirs. There were also piranhas, in a huge aquarium they visited.

"We shouldn't have come here," Peg said quickly, when she saw Clarisse's expression as she looked at the fish with their huge jaws and sharp teeth. "Let's leave."

Clarisse seemed to turn in slow motion. She stared at Peg. "What?"

"You shouldn't have to look at them…" She bit her tongue.

Clarisse's blue eyes flashed fire. "You've been snooping!" she said coldly. "You've been looking at my computer, haven't you?" she demanded, while Peg went white as a sheet.

CHAPTER SEVEN

PEG DIDN'T KNOW what to say. The other woman looked wild, out of control, as if she were on drugs. Peg knew what that was, because one of the ranch hands at the Pendleton ranch had briefly had a fling with illegal substances. It had been Ed Larson who'd confronted the boy, who'd made some uncomfortable advances toward his daughter. The boy, fortunately, had gotten treatment, compliments of Jason Pendleton, and was now back on the job and behaving himself. But Peg had never forgotten the look on his face, in his eyes, or the way he acted.

"Yes," Peg said heavily. "I was looking for information about Manaus and there was a file with a newspaper clipping. I thought it was about a tourist attraction. I'm so sorry. So very sorry. Your sister and your father... how horrible!"

Clarisse felt as if she'd sustained a body blow. She'd had no comfort. Rourke had been at the very secretive funeral, but she hadn't dared ask him for comfort. He'd offered to do anything she needed. She'd refused very formally and moved quickly away.

She'd never wanted close friends. Her time at an exclusive girls' school in Switzerland had left her isolated and uncomfortable, because her mother had been deeply religious and had taught Clarisse to respect herself and her body, not to play sexual games with her friends and get drunk and use drugs. Those things were wrong. Animals mated without discrimination. People held out for love.

Not that she hadn't been tempted. There was a professor. She'd had a violent crush on him. But he liked other men. Clarisse hadn't known why the other girls were giggling at her blushing confusion when he was near her. It had unsettled her sense of who she was. She hadn't gone near another man, except for some heavy social flirting to make her friends think she was normal. And Grange thought she was a party girl. It had been laughable.

Yes, she'd gone off the deep end when he wouldn't respond to her. Grange hadn't cared about her wealth. He didn't want her.

And here was the reason, right here. This sweet, innocent, empathetic child who was looking at her with an expression of such compassion that Clarisse actually broke down, for the first time since the accident.

"Oh, no, it's all right," Peg whispered, gathering the older woman up close. "It's all right. You have to let the grief out, or it will fester, like an infected wound." She hugged her, rocked her. "It's all right. It's all right."

Clarisse sobbed like a child. To find comfort in such an unexpected place, in an enemy, a woman who was a rival, whom she meant to harm. It was unbearable.

She succumbed, but only for an instant. She jerked back and dug into her fanny pack for one of the Belgian lace hankies she carried. She wiped her eyes and her nose. She felt sick.

"You haven't even talked about it, have you?" Peg asked quietly.

"Who would I have talked to?" Clarisse asked bluntly.

"My mother died years ago. My father and my sister..." She swallowed. "They were all I had. I have no other family, and the only friends I have need encouragement, like expensive evenings on the town or private flights to resorts or holidays at five-star hotels abroad..."

"Those aren't friends," Peg replied.

Clarisse drew in a long breath. "I've never had a friend."

Peg grimaced. "I've never had a really close friend. I have friends," she added. "But it's not quite the same."

"No. It's not."

"You okay?" Peg asked gently.

Clarisse took another breath. "Yes." She put away the handkerchief. She glanced at Peg and then averted her gaze. "Thanks," she said awkwardly.

Peg smiled. "We all need a hug sometimes."

Clarisse laughed unsteadily. "So they say."

Peg wanted to mention the pill bottle and the frequency with which Clarisse dug into it. But she didn't. They barely knew each other. But in a few days, when they got to Grange's camp, she was going to. She liked the older woman. She didn't want her to end up like that boy on the Pendleton ranch.

"We'd better go back to the hotel. I still have arrangements to make, and your arm may be sore from those immunizations," she added, noting the swelling where Peg's tank top left her arms bare.

"I feel a little sick," Peg confessed. "Thanks."

"You can lie down for a while. I'll get the ball rolling."

Peg stopped as they left the aquarium. "I wasn't snooping. Honest. I was really only looking for stuff on Manaus. I wanted to know where to ask you to take me."

"It's all right," Clarisse said. But she didn't say anything else.

PEG WAS VERY sick. The immunizations combined to give her a fever. Clarisse sat up with her, confounded by her own concern for her rival. She wet washcloths and bathed the other woman's brow. In the end, she phoned a doctor she knew and asked him to come over.

"It's only a reaction," Dr. Carvajal assured Clarisse as he started to leave. His eyes narrowed. "You take too many of those pills, my friend," he added, concerned.

She averted her eyes. "Only when I need them. Really."

"You can take too many. They compromise your judgment."

"Do they?"

He sighed. "Why is she here?" he asked abruptly. "The little one. Why did you bring her to Manaus?"

"To see her friend," she replied, lowering her eyes. "A man she knows, who works over here."

He wasn't blinking. "And you do this for charity, yes? The child has obviously never been out of her own country."

She glared at him. "This is my business."

"Yes," he said after a minute. "It is. But you have not been back here since the tragedy, and I think the past is haunting you. Like the pills, the memories are making you reckless." He laid a hand on her arm. "You must promise me not to do anything dangerous, especially with the child in your care. Another tragedy would finish you, my girl."

She went pale. "What do you mean?"

"I mean your hold on reality is fragile, like your emotional state. You are not strong. Not anymore. You must not take chances. Amazonas is a dangerous place, full of peril, and that child in there has no knowledge of those dangers. You will not risk her life, will you?"

Clarisse was wondering if he was right, if her judgment was really compromised. She didn't seem to be acting in character at all lately. This trip was insane. What she planned to do with Peg was even more insane. But it had seemed quite rational before...

"I'm giving her a treat. I won't hurt her," Clarisse promised him.

"You are not a cruel person," he replied. He smiled. "I remember your mother. Such a sweet and kind lady. She was always the first to go when anyone was sick... She lived for the Holy Church, for the Holy Virgin. She was a great lady."

Clarisse's eyes closed. "My world died with her. Dad and Matilda never understood."

"Your father carried your family around Africa and South America, wherever the American Embassy sent him, so that you had little time to form friendships. You had only your mother as an anchor. Your father was forever away on embassy business and Matilda was a child. You and your mother, you were like twins. I know you miss her."

She drew in a long breath. "Thank you for coming over."

"The little one will be all right." He smiled. "You make a good nurse."

Clarisse laughed hollowly. "No. Not a good one."

"She will be better in the morning. You will see."

"Thanks."

"Stay out of the jungle," he admonished.

She crossed her heart playfully.

He made a face and left.

Clarisse went back to the bed, her eyes on the flushed

face of the sleeping girl, her tousled blond hair spread over the pillow. She dampened the cloth again and laid it over Peg's forehead. This plan was looking stupider by the day.

She wondered if perhaps the doctor was right. The antianxiety meds did seem to be compromising her judgment. She was uncertain of her ability to do without them. Which was why she took the bottle into the bathroom, saved enough to ensure that she could wean herself off the pills slowly, then emptied the remainder into the toilet, and flushed it.

"Now we see if he was right," she murmured to herself. She grimaced. How would she live without pills?

She swallowed her fear. She'd lived without them before the tragedy. If her judgment was really being compromised, and she thought perhaps it was, she could prove the theory this way. And if she had a meltdown for lack of them, well, she could always have them refilled. It would mean a call overseas for the pharmacy to do so, but she was rich, wasn't she?

She went back into the bedroom. Peg had just opened her eyes.

"I feel terrible," she murmured weakly.

"Yes. A reaction to the injections. I'm so sorry."

"Not your fault," Peg murmured and forced a smile. She frowned as she felt the cloth on her head and knew that Clarisse had been doing it to take down the fever. "Do we have aspirin?" she wondered aloud.

"Aspirin? Of course!" Clarisse could have thumped herself for not thinking of it. She went to her luggage and drew out a bottle. She got bottled water from the small fridge, making a mental note to ask housekeeping for more water. They were going through it quickly.

"You aren't allergic to aspirin?" she asked before she opened the bottle.

"No," Peg said.

She shook out two tablets into Peg's hand and stood over her while she swallowed them.

"I had the doctor come and check you a few hours ago," she said surprisingly. "He said that it was just reaction, nothing dangerous, and you'd be better in a day or two. But the aspirin will help bring down the fever. I'm sorry I didn't think of it sooner."

Peg was staring at her curiously. "You've been up with me all night."

Clarisse looked embarrassed. "I was afraid to go to sleep," she confessed. "You looked very ill."

"And you called a doctor?"

"He's a friend. A very good one."

Peg was still looking at her. "Thank you," she said hesitantly. "Except for my dad, nobody ever stayed up all night with me when I was sick. My mother did, but she died years ago."

"So did mine." Clarisse sat down on the bed. "She was born here," she said surprisingly. "Her mother was German, her father was from Madrid. She worked tirelessly on committees to help the church."

"The Catholic church?" Peg asked.

Clarisse nodded. "She was a saint." She lowered her eyes. "Not like me at all. I'm not a good person."

Peg laid a hand on her arm. "Yes, you are," she said firmly. "You sat up with me all night and got a doctor for me. Would a bad person do that?"

The guilt was even worse. Clarisse wanted to confess, but the younger woman's admiration was new and sweet, and it made her happy for the first time in months.

She squeezed Peg's hand. "You rest. I'm going to order breakfast. Think you could eat some eggs?"

Peg sighed. "I'll try, but something light, please. My stomach's upset, too."

She smiled. "I'll see what they suggest."

THEY HAD A light breakfast and Peg went back to sleep. By the next day, she was up and dressed and feeling much better. The swelling on her arm had gone down, too.

Clarisse had been edgy for the first few hours after she flushed her pills. She took just the prescribed amount, avoided caffeine and drank water and juice. Her doctor had told her how to wean herself off them, and she remembered the instructions and followed them. By the next day, she, too, was feeling better.

She dressed and had a good breakfast with Peg in the restaurant downstairs. Outside, they could see colorful birds and hear the sound of the jungle so close, near the river.

"The floods come soon," Clarisse said. "Sometimes the hotel floods, but it's in a beautiful place. I used to love to come here, when I was a child. We lived in Washington, D.C., most of the time, with my father's people. But Momma missed her home, so we'd come here to visit."

"Do you have friends or family here?" Peg asked.

"Not anymore," she replied. "I had an aunt, my mother's sister. She died about the same time my mother did."

"It's sad, not to have family. All I've got is Dad."

"No aunts or uncles?" Clarisse asked curiously.

Peg shook her head. "Both my parents were only-children."

Clarisse grimaced. She sipped coffee. It was only the one cup, which she hoped would last the day. Caffeine would make her nervousness worse.

Peg was watching her. "I haven't seen you take any of those antianxiety pills," she commented gently.

Clarisse laughed. "I'm weaning myself off them, and flushed the majority down the toilet," she murmured. "The doctor thought I was taking too many of them. I didn't think so. But it seems he was right. My mind is clear, for the first time since Dad and Matilda...since the accident."

Peg smiled. "I'm sure the anxiety meds served a useful purpose, at the time."

"They did." Clarisse finished her coffee with a sigh. "But life has to be faced squarely, and with clear eyes, as my mother used to say."

"Good advice."

Clarisse shrugged. She smiled. "So, what do you say we get my driver and go out to the native village near Grange's camp? I phoned Enrique earlier. He's just back from São Paulo, so he's free to chauffeur us out of the city. I'll leave you at the village and go and get Grange. I have to have the driver to find his camp—it's not in an obvious place."

"Today?"

Clarisse laughed again. "Today."

"Couldn't I go with you to his camp?"

Clarisse sat back in the chair and looked thoughtful. "Peg, dear, I haven't been honest with you. I want to be, but you're going to hate me when you know what I did."

Peg searched the woman's drawn face with soft green eyes. "You're my friend now," she said quietly. "I won't hate you, no matter what you've done."

Clarisse fought tears and lost. She pulled out the Belgian lace hanky and wiped her eyes. "It's pretty bad."

"Tell me. You'll feel better."

Clarisse took a deep breath. It was really going to hurt if Peg started to hate her. "I had a crush on Grange," she said. "I don't even know why. He's not at all my type of man. But I fixated on him after we met in Washington, D.C., after the…tragedy. I was taking a lot of pills and the fact that he didn't want me was a lure. I developed an obsession to make him want me." She hesitated. Peg didn't look angry yet. "Grange thinks I'm a playgirl… that I go around seducing men. My mother was deeply religious and she taught me to respect myself and my body. I've never even…" She cleared her throat. "Well, you know."

"Actually I do know," Peg confessed with a shy laugh. "I got teased about it at school, but I just told the other girls that I'd grow old without having to worry about STDs or some of the other life-threatening illnesses, and that I'd have some self-respect. It's amazing how many of them gave in to boys just because it was expected." She made a huffy sound. "I live by my own rules, not anybody else's."

"Good girl," Clarisse said with affection. She sighed. "But to continue, I went to General Machado's camp and told him I wanted to travel with the troops and do a story about them. I really am a photojournalist," she added quietly. "I even have credentials. But Grange knew I was also feeding my obsession for him, and he ordered me out of the camp. He called me a party girl, a prostitute. He did it in front of a man I've known all my life, a man I…respect." She winced, recalling the way Rourke had looked at her when Grange called her the next best thing to a prostitute. "I was half out of my mind on those stupid pills and I wanted to get even with Grange." She looked at Peg with wild, wounded eyes. "I brought you over here to put you in harm's way. I'm so ashamed, Peg. You've been kinder to me than anyone ever was, outside my own family. I'm so ashamed!"

Peg unexpectedly got up, went around the table and hugged the other woman. "You stop right there. People do stupid things, and they make mistakes. That's why they put erasers on pencils, isn't it, because nobody's perfect?"

Clarisse hugged her close. "I've never known anybody like you."

Peg smiled. "Lucky you."

"No, I mean it!" She pulled back, red-eyed and teary. "I'll make this up to you if it's the last thing I ever do," she said firmly. "No matter what. I'm going to take you to the village. They're good people, you'll be safe there. It's where Enrique's mother lives, just inside Barrera, in a native settlement. It wouldn't be possible for Grange to be seen in Manaus, Sapara has agents here. It's best to do it out of the sight of any possible spies, and the village is very secure. Enrique will guide me back to Grange's camp—I'd never find it on my own and I'd be scared to try, with the rainy season starting. So I'll go to Grange and tell him what I've done and hope he'll forgive me, too. Then I'll bring him to you. When he goes back to his camp, I'll get you back to Texas, safe and sound."

Peg brushed back the disheveled blond hair that had fallen into Clarisse's eyes. "He's a good person," she said softly. "He'll understand."

"You think so?" She wiped her eyes. "He might have me shot, so if I don't come back, you'll know what happened. Which reminds me..."

She reached into her purse and pulled out a wad of large bills. Glancing around to make sure nobody was watching, she stuffed them into the pocket of Peg's jeans. "That's a fail-safe," she said under her breath. "You've already got a round-trip return ticket, but the cash will ensure that you can get back to Manaus if something goes wrong. You take the ticket and the money with you, in your fanny pack, along with your ID and a change of clothing."

Peg felt chills run over her. "What could go wrong?"

Clarisse frowned. "I don't know. I get these…feelings sometimes. It's probably nothing, but just in case, you have enough cash to take care of you." She got up and picked up the bill. "Peg, I'm really, really sorry I got you into this," she said. "Part of it was ego, but a large part was the pills. I didn't realize what they were doing to me."

"We had a guy on the ranch who got hooked on pre-scription meds," Peg replied surprisingly. "He ended up in rehab. I was actually trying to get up enough nerve to talk to you about those pills you were taking so many of," she added after a minute.

"You sweetie," Clarisse said, and meant it. "You're so much like my sister." She bit her lip and turned away. "We'd better get cracking."

"Yes." Peg followed behind her. She had more respect than ever for the tortured woman.

THEY PACKED EVERYTHING, but left the suitcases at the hotel. They only took what would be needed for one or two days' travel.

"This driver knows Amazonia like the back of his hand," Clarisse told her on the way out of the hotel. "He belongs to one of the local tribes."

"Do they speak English?" Peg worried.

"No, but they understand Spanish and Portuguese." She smiled. "Your Spanish will work very well, even if you only use the verbs and don't conjugate them."

"They speak three languages?" Peg was impressed. "We get these ideas about people in primitive places," she tried to explain.

Clarisse laughed. "Yes, we do. And then strange women take us to foreign places where we're forced to learn things against our will," she said wickedly.

It was the first time she'd joked with Peg, who laughed. "Well, I'm not complaining. I'll get to see Grange and that will be worth everything."

"He'll kill me," Clarisse said cheerfully. "I've always wanted to know what it was like to stand up against a wall with a blindfold and a cigarette."

"You don't smoke," Peg pointed out.

"Don't mess up my imagination with a lot of irrelevant facts, if you please."

She laughed.

THE DRIVER'S NAME was Enrique Boas and he was tall and good-looking, with wavy black hair and large dark eyes. He had a wonderful smile.

"I am honored to escort two such lovely women," he said, bowing.

Peg was entranced. "Thank you!"

He took her hand and kissed it. "Such a delightful smile," he said. "You have eyes like the jungle itself, of the purest green."

"Stop that, she's spoken for," Clarisse said with unexpected protectiveness.

"Spoken for?"

"She has a *novio,*" Clarisse explained. "We're going out to his camp to bring him to her."

"Ah. Such a lucky *hombre,*" he exclaimed, with eyes that adored a blushing Peg. "Then we should leave quickly, yes?"

"Yes," Clarisse said. "We need to leave Peg at your mother's village, where she'll be safe."

"Near the ruins." Enrique nodded, opening the doors for the women. "An American archaeologist said they would upend old theories about South American civilization. She told us that the ruins predated the Egyptian pyramids, can you imagine?"

"Ruins?" Peg asked. "Wow! I'd love to see them."

"First things first," Clarisse said as she climbed in next to Enrique and let him close her door. She chuckled as she looked over the seat at Peg. "First Grange shoots me, then you see him, then we can climb the ruins."

"He can't shoot you. Tell him I said so," Peg told her firmly.

"I will. I just hope it works!"

Peg grinned. Enrique climbed into the Land Rover, started it, and they were off.

THE VILLAGE WAS very small. There were bread-loaf-shaped houses with thatched roofs in an oval pattern around a huge cleared area. The people were small and dark, with black hair. Both sexes wore dresses that resembled Roman togas. They came out shyly as Enrique stopped at the entrance to the clearing and called out to them in his own language.

An elderly woman approached the two women alone, slowly and with suspicion.

Enrique said something to her. She replied in a questioning tone. He smiled and gestured at the two women and said something else.

"Ah," the elderly woman said, nodding.

She approached Peg and studied her, fascinated with her blond hair and her green eyes. She asked Enrique something.

He burst out laughing. "She wants to know what tribe you come from, that has green eyes," he said.

She grinned. "Tell her it's a tribe called Texas."

He laughed heartily and repeated the words to the woman.

She grinned.

"This is my mother, Maria," he told the two women. "That's not her birth name, but we have a priest who comes frequently to the village, and she has a name that was given to her by him when she was much younger."

"Maria," Peg said. She studied the elderly woman. *"Me gusta ser aqui,"* she said in Spanish. "I'm happy to be here."

"¿Se habla espanol?" the old woman declared, and suddenly embraced her. *"Bienvenidos."*

"Gracias."

"Well, I can see that you'll be in good hands," Clarisse said with a smile. "Give me a hug, too, and then Enrique and I will be off. I want to get this over with," she added, grimacing. "The sooner the better."

Peg hugged her back. "It will be all right. How long do you think it will take?"

Clarisse turned to Enrique and raised her eyebrows.

"A couple of hours to drive there, if they haven't moved the camp, and if the tributaries haven't risen enough to destroy the bridges," he replied. "If they've moved camp, I will have to track them. It's easy to lose even a large force of men in the jungle if you don't know where to look. After we find them, it will take a couple of hours to get back. We should be here by dark."

Peg nodded. She looked from one to the other. "Be careful out there, okay? I know you're experienced," she told Enrique, "but I've only just learned how dangerous this place is. Be safe. Both of you."

They smiled. "We're old hands at this," Clarisse assured her. "I spent a lot of time doing feature material on the jungle for European magazines. And Enrique here—" she smiled at him "—was my guide each time. I daresay I know almost as much as he does."

"Except for the tracking part." Enrique chuckled.

Clarisse waved a hand. "Hardly necessary. I won't have to find my way through the jungle. That's why I have you along."

He grinned, hugged his mother, spoke to her for a minute and then started toward the Land Rover.

Clarisse hugged Peg again. "You be careful. Don't, for God's sake, go out of the village for any reason. There are all sorts of dangerous things—insects, snakes, even jaguars. Promise me."

"I promise."

"Wear rain gear." She looked up and grimaced. She pulled her slicker over her head as an unexpected downpour landed on them. Peg did the same. "And use that money if you have to," Clarisse said grimly.

"You and your 'feelings,'" Peg scoffed. "Everything's going to be fine."

Clarisse nodded. But she didn't smile. She took one last look at Peg and turned around to follow Enrique. She didn't look back.

PEG SMILED AT Enrique's mother, Maria.

"¿Puede muestrame su ciudad, por favor?"

"¿Como no?" the old woman replied. *"¡Venga!"*

Maria took her from one thatch-covered loaf-shaped dwelling to another, introducing her to the people inside. Peg noted that hammocks were slung everywhere for people to sleep on. There were many children, all of whom seemed fascinated with the American woman with the long blond hair and green eyes. They followed her when Maria went from house to house.

Maria explained the native foods to her. Peg worried about eating anything outside the city, or drinking the water, but she wasn't about to offend these kind people who welcomed her as a member of the family. She asked about the reason some of the houses beyond the village, closer to the river, were built on stilts, and they explained that the rivers could rise many feet and flood, especially in January through June, the dreaded rainy season. These loaf-shaped homes could be easily and quickly replaced after a flood. They had been built exactly in this fashion since the earliest days of the tribe's existence.

She sat down with them in the center of one large dwelling where a huge cooking fire was going strong. Two women smiled at her from nearby. They were roasting some sort of meat. There was a pot of something that looked curiously like tapioca. Near the central supporting pole that held up the roof, a woman worked tirelessly at a loom with a baby on a blanket nearby.

She was offered a gourd of liquid, which she thought was water until she took a sip. She gasped and grabbed her throat. It was alcoholic. Very alcoholic. The women burst out laughing.

"Don't be offended," Maria said in Spanish, but she laughed, too. "We offer you hospitality."

"I'm not offended, not at all," Peg assured her. She laughed. "I never drank alcohol in my life."

"No? Here in the jungle many people do. This is made from the leaf of a coca plant, one variety which is not used to make the evil narcotic that the militias sell to make a lot of money," Maria said. "There are other beverages made from fruit. Alcohol is a curse among many of our native tribes, because it steals the brain and makes people very lazy."

"It's the same in my country," Peg told her. "In most countries, I think."

Maria nodded. "Here. You must try this." She pulled meat from the spit and offered it on a woven dish.

Gingerly Peg took a piece of it and chewed. She blinked. "It tastes just like chicken."

Maria and the other women almost rolled on the ground with delight.

"Why, that's because it is chicken!" Maria replied finally. "Did you not see the hens and roosters running around in our village?" she laughed, but not in a demeaning way. She was amused.

Peg flushed, but she laughed, too, and dug into the delicately salted meat. She learned later that the natives didn't use salt, but they knew that Europeans did and they thought Peg would like it. She was destined to learn a lot about the tribe. Quite a lot, and very soon.

CHAPTER EIGHT

CLARISSE WORRIED ABOUT whether or not they could find Grange and General Machado, even though Enrique was pretty sure he knew where the camp was. The rainy season was just beginning, but the waters of the tributaries were already starting to rise.

The part of Barrera where Grange was camped was on the other side of a difficult crossing over one of the tributaries of the mighty Amazon. Clarisse held on for dear life as Enrique rolled the tough Land Rover over a bridge that moved alarmingly as they traversed it, and along roads that seemed to have been meant for people on foot, not in vehicles.

"This machine lives up to its good reputation," Enrique called out to her.

"Yes, it does," Clarisse agreed. She ran a hand through her short, wavy blond hair and grimaced. "Are you certain we're going the right way?"

He pulled out a GPS unit from the console and glanced at it. "Yes, according to this we are."

She sat back, sighing. "Grange is going to be very angry."

"Why?"

She laughed. "Don't you remember him throwing me out of camp last time we were there? But I brought him a peace offering, his friend from America." She smiled.

"It's nice of your mother to shelter her. She's a lovely person. Really lovely."

"My mother or your young friend?"

She smiled. "Both."

He glanced at her. "You seem… I don't know…different this time."

"No meds," she said on a ragged breath. "I've given them up."

He nodded. He didn't say anything.

"When people drown, is it quick?" she blurted out.

He slowed down to look at her. "You are remembering the boat that capsized with your family."

"Yes. The piranhas…" She swallowed hard.

"Drowning is very quick in that river," he assured her quietly. "And the piranhas would have gotten them only when they had already passed into the next life. You understand?"

"You mean they wouldn't have felt it…?"

"That is what I mean. It would have been quick. It is of little comfort, I am certain…"

"It is of much comfort. Thank you, Enrique."

"De nada." He looked at the map and stood up in the Land Rover, to look through the roof. "I think I see a road." He started to sit down again.

She drew in a slow breath. "Well, at least…!"

A gunshot shattered the windshield and penetrated Enrique's body. He cried out and collapsed against the seat, bleeding from the chest.

"Enrique!"

Before Clarisse could cope with the shock, or move to help him, the windshield shattered on her side of the Land Rover and something hit her head, hard. The last thing she saw was a band of men in government military uniforms running toward her...

CLARISSE'S HEAD FELT as if it might explode. She was sick to her stomach, but the two soldiers escorting her only stopped when she had to bend over and vomit in the street. The minute she was finished, they pulled her roughly along toward a large building. She'd been unconscious for a while. She remembered an explosion. She couldn't remember anything else. Her mind was foggy.

They were in a city. She didn't know for sure, but she thought it was Medina. Only the capital was this big, and it wasn't a large city by American standards, either. Nor was it particularly modern. Some of the structures dated back to colonial times, primarily the cathedral. She wasn't surprised to see armed soldiers in camo standing idly at the front doors. It had been rumored that Sapara had closed the churches against massive protests. The protestors had been gassed and then shot. It had made international headlines. Soon afterward, the state had denied access to all foreign journalists.

Clarisse knew that she was going to be interrogated. No matter what happened, she must not give away the real reason she was in the country. She wasn't going to betray Grange or Peg even if they killed her.

But she could claim credentials as a journalist. That would be plausible and explain her presence here. She remembered the explosion and then she remembered what had happened. They'd been shot! Poor Enrique was likely dead. She'd seen him jerk back under the impact of the bullet, seen the blood. He hadn't moved. His poor mother! And Peg—Peg would believe that Clarisse had deserted her. Grange wouldn't know that Peg was even in the country. God, what a mess, and all her fault!

Her first thought was that someone had betrayed her location to the authorities. She hadn't told anyone where she was going, except Peg, who would never talk about it. On the other hand, Enrique knew, and he might have spoken to someone about taking an American on a trip. Hopefully he hadn't divulged any more than that.

Her escort pulled her into a room in a stone building with the national flag flying outside, past more armed guards, into a central office. There, behind a desk, sat the narcissistic little madman who had overthrown the government and taken power. Arturo Sapara himself, the snake.

Arturo Sapara was forty-six years old, bald, mustached and fat. He had tiny little eyes in a fat face, and his teeth were yellow.

He looked her over with cold eyes. "Ah, Señorita Carrington," he said, reading from her unfolded passport. He put it on the desk. "How kind of you to come and visit me."

"It wasn't voluntary." She was fighting another round of nausea. She groaned and went white.

"Quick, get her the trash can," Sapara snapped at her guards. "Do not let her soil the carpet. It is imported from Morocco!"

They produced a trash can. Clarisse bent over and deliberately missed it.

"Damn you!" Sapara burst out. "You witch!"

She stood erect again, almost reeling from the headache and the nausea combined. "I thought the money would be worth it," she said insinuatingly.

"Money?" he queried, forgetting his rage.

"The wire services offered me a small fortune to sneak in here and look for two missing foreign professors." She was making it up as she went, but it looked as if it might work. "I thought with the help of a native guide, I might be able to find a back way into the city and get a disguise."

"So that is why you had the driver, eh? Well, he is dead." He waved a hand. "My men left him where he was, sitting in the Land Rover. Someone will find him." He smiled with contempt. "Perhaps not until it is just bones in tattered clothing, however. You were not coming in this direction."

"We took a different route because the rivers are rising."

He hesitated. But the excuse convinced him. The rainy season made river crossings tricky from time to time. His little eyes narrowed. "Why do they want news of the teachers?"

"Professors," she replied coldly. "They have family in the United States. Family with influence in the media."

His eyebrows lifted. "Do they, indeed?" He smiled. It was a terrible smile. "I am gratified to know this. Perhaps it would be as well to put them to death soon."

"Why?" she burst out. "What have they done that deserves death?"

"They have been teaching treason at the local college," he said icily, "and having their students send messages, lies, about my government to enemy foreign nations. They call me a dictator. I am President of the People's Republic of Barrera," he said in a grand-sounding tone. "My government will serve the people..."

"The people are starving," Clarisse said. "They have no money because you tax everything. You've appropriated businesses, you've nationalized private corporations, even foreign ones, and you've closed the doors of the churches…!" she continued, her voice gaining strength.

"Churches have no place in a civilized society," he said curtly. "They should all be removed."

She gave him a long, cold stare. "Over the millennia, many governments have conspired to close churches and ban religion. France comes to mind, just after the revolution in 1792." She smiled coldly. "I believe that in France, today, there are many, many churches of all denominations?"

"Bosh." He stood up. "Since she is so interested in the incarcerated professors, you may escort her to a cell beside them," he told the officers in Spanish. "She is to be given water, but water only. Take her away."

Sapara still had her fanny pack on the desk. Her heart sank. Her passport, her return ticket to America, her credit cards, the little cash she hadn't given Peg, all there. She would have nothing, even if she could find a way to escape. It truly looked like the end of the road. Well, she told herself, I've had a good run. But she worried about Peg. The poor young woman would think the worst, that Clarisse had deliberately deserted her and left her to her fate. It wasn't true. But she had no way to contact Peg and tell her so. And what about Grange? He was so close to Peg, but he would never know it. The girl would face all sorts of dangers…

"Take her away," Sapara repeated, waved his hand and sat back down.

The soldiers took Clarisse by the arm, overstepping the place where she'd thrown up on his majestic carpet, and escorted her out of the room.

THE TWO PROFESSORS were Julian Constantine and Damon Fitzhugh. They taught, respectively, South American history and botany at the small college in Medina.

Dr. Constantine was in very bad shape. He was tall and pleasant looking, with graying dark hair and eyes. He was thin and pale and unshaven. His clothing looked as if it hadn't been washed in months.

Dr. Fitzhugh was elderly. He had white hair and blue eyes, and he was as sickly looking as his colleague.

The cell door was locked and the guards left her. The cell was small. There was a bed, of sorts, with a tattered blanket. There was a bucket which was, presumably, used for relieving oneself. There was a pan of water on a small table. Nothing else. The prison was from the colonial era, as near as Clarisse could tell, and had never been upgraded. Machado had planned a renovation here, but his work on the small country's economy had taken precedence.

Clarisse lay down on the bed, doubling over. She was so nauseated she could barely stand it, and her head hurt.

"American?" Dr. Fitzhugh asked from the next cell.

"Actually, yes," she said, happy to hear that he spoke with a crisp and pleasant British accent. "I'm Clarisse Carrington."

"I'm Damon Fitzhugh. Dr. Damon Fitzhugh. The gentleman in the next cell is Dr. Constantine. Are you all right? You seem quite pale."

"I've been unconscious. I think I was shot," she said, feeling her scalp. She found a wet, tender spot and pulled her hand back. It was coated in blood. She winced. "No wonder I have a headache." She felt the spot more carefully. The bullet had apparently grazed her, but in the tropics, that was dangerous enough. If infection set in, she was fairly certain Sapara wouldn't put himself out trying to find her a doctor.

"If I had the means, I could make you a poultice," Dr. Fitzhugh said kindly. "My field is botany. I came down here to teach because it afforded me the opportunity to research the local native medicine preparations. They are without peer in all the world."

She managed a smile. "Thank you for the thought."

"I'm here," Dr. Constantine told her, "because the history of South America fascinates me, especially the period of rubber plantations in the early part of the twentieth century." He shook his head. "Not our finest hour, to be sure. Many atrocities were perpetrated on the native people here."

Clarisse lay back down. "I know something about the opera house in Manaus."

"Yes, they brought it down the river in pieces at a cost of millions of dollars and put it back together, didn't they? No expense was spared in its construction."

"Yes. Opera companies came down to Manaus to perform," she said, glad of the conversation that took her mind off how sick she felt.

He nodded. "But it ended many times in tragedy when the singers contracted yellow fever or malaria. A number of them died later from infections they picked up down here."

Clarisse grimaced. She was thinking of Peg. She'd cautioned her about not going into the jungle, but what if Clarisse didn't show up and Peg, valiant Peg, decided to try to find her? It didn't bear thinking about!

"You two are professors. Why are you in here?"

Dr. Fitzhugh's mouth made a thin line. "When Emilio Machado was deposed, we were furious. His replacement is a cheap little rat who indulges his taste for fast cars, fast women and expensive new homes, while the native people go hungry. He's thrown out all foreign journalists, closed the embassies of foreign nations, nationalized utilities and now he's planning a huge operation with some oil company to start drilling here."

"Yes," Clarisse said quietly. "My father was helping to negotiate terms with the local chiefs for the oil company in question. He was with the American Embassy office in Manaus. That was four months ago."

"Well, Sapara gave the green light to oil exploration. Many of the tribes were intimidated into signing an agreement. But one of the native tribes protested." His face tautened. "They live apart from civilization, in one of the thickest parts of the Barrera jungle. They use the weapons of their ancestors, blow guns with poison darts, and practice herbology to treat all sorts of diseases. They threatened an attack. It's almost humorous in a dark way, because Medina does have some modern weapons. But Sapara decided to make an example, in case any others considered revolution. He had mercenaries go into the jungle and kill dozens of them, terrify them, until they fled from the land where he planned to locate the oil explorations."

Clarisse was remembering Enrique and his mother, whom she'd known for many years. "Money makes me sick."

"It isn't money. It's the greed for it, the obsession with it that causes many of the problems in life." Dr. Fitzhugh drew in a breath. "To make a long story brief, Dr. Constantine and I were creating propaganda leaflets and organizing our students to make large-scale peaceful protests and publicize the plight of the native tribe. This was, of course, before Sapara threw out all the foreign journalists who would have spread the story around the world." He smiled sadly. "All our plans fell when we were arrested, in the middle of the night, by Sapara's City Guards."

"Sapara thinks he's creating Nazi Germany here," Dr. Constantine added in a soft, weary tone. "He has his version of the storm troopers, complete with fanatical overlord and bone-breaking training. How do you fight a man like that?" he added heavily.

"I don't know. But I hope someone can." While she spoke she was looking around at the tops of the cells.

"Oh, there are no cameras here," Dr. Constantine said. "We checked that out the minute we were installed here, several months ago. They don't have the money for surveillance, or for most city services, since Sapara is building his new mansion. Every penny goes to its construction. It looks like a palace, which is probably what he had in mind."

"Yes, we have one guard. He's old and fat and he doesn't like his job. He does like us," Dr. Fitzhugh added with a chuckle. "I think he'd let us out if we had anyplace to go. We don't, of course, except to our homes, where they'd pick us up in a minute as soon as they realized we were gone." He glanced at Clarisse. "As revolutionaries, I'm afraid we leave a lot to be desired. Health concerns kept us both out of the military, so we have no training whatsoever."

"That makes three of us," Clarisse said quietly. "I do wish my head would stop hurting."

Dr. Fitzhugh frowned. He asked her several questions about her symptoms, but finally he smiled and nodded. "Only a mild concussion, I think, although we'd need an MRI scan to be sure." He shook his head. "I did study medicine in my youth, but I thought I'd like sleeping nights, so I switched to botany. No emergencies, you see."

Clarisse smiled. "I don't have any meds with me. They took my ID, my credit cards, cash, everything I had on me, including some meds for nausea and headaches."

"Lovely man, Sapara," Dr. Constantine said pleasantly. "I hope we can repay his hospitality one day." He looked around. "At that, this place is far more grand than the room I lived in while I was at university."

Clarisse laughed. So did Dr. Fitzhugh.

"When I feel better," she said finally, "perhaps we could discuss travel plans?"

The two men looked at each other. "Travel plans?"

She smiled. "I have friends."

They turned to her, curiously.

"We might wish to pay them a visit," she clarified. "I don't know the way, but I think I can find someone who will. Would it be possible for you to speak with some of your students if we managed to escape?"

Dr. Fitzhugh chuckled. "Oh, yes. I memorized the phone numbers. If the phones still work," he added blithely. "Since Sapara nationalized the phone company and put his own people in charge, it only works sporadically. Like his military communications, from what I've been told. His computers are still running outdated programs," he said, and burst out laughing. "Amazing that they haven't been hacked, like those in Iran."

Dr. Constantine shrugged. "As if any true hacker worth his salt would lower himself to hack an obsolete computer system."

Dr. Fitzhugh pursed his lips. "In fact, one of my students is a hacker with imagination and style. He actually suggested putting a virus into the military computer system here. I denied him the effort, thinking it would get us all arrested." He gave Clarisse a wicked grin. "I do believe it might be warranted, now, however."

Clarisse brightened. Grange would love it! "In that case, we must get out of here and give him the opportunity to practice his craft."

"It's a 'she,' actually," he said, laughing at Clarisse's consternation. "One of the only female hackers I've ever known. Her parents sent her down here in a last-ditch effort to keep the FBI from putting her in prison in America. She was quite obnoxious. Hacked into the Secretary of State's computer and published one of the more secretive, gossipy emails all over the web. Her parents promised to get her out of the country, or she'd be in prison now, I expect. Like us," he added ruefully.

The others laughed. The two men seemed suddenly less lethargic and far more energized.

"You think it's possible, really possible, that we might be able to get out of here?" Dr. Fitzhugh asked slowly.

"Not only possible, dear man. Probable." She felt her head again and winced. "And I want a bat, a very big bat, to hit Mr. Sapara in the head with, next time I see him."

"I'll provide one myself," Dr. Fitzhugh assured her. He grinned. "I have a very old cricket bat, you see. Used to play when I was a boy. It's quite heavy, made of good wood. It would make a lovely knot on his head."

"How kind of you," she drawled and then winced, because every facial movement only aggravated the headache.

"Do try to sleep for a bit," Dr. Fitzhugh said gently. "The two of us will discuss some hypothetical situations and have plans ready when you wake up. We can formulate a revolution while we're incarcerated."

"Many famous and infamous plans and books have come from people imprisoned for various reasons. The famous novel *Don Quixote* was written by Miguel de Cervantes in the sixteenth century, after he was put in debtors' prison in Spain." She sighed. "I loved *Don Quixote*. What a noble cause, to restore honor and morality to a decadent world." She closed her eyes. "We could use him today."

The two male doctors looked at each other and nodded. They began to throw out suggestions for an escape. Clarisse drifted off to sleep, at last. But Dr. Fitzhugh woke her up at odd intervals, just to make sure the concussion wasn't severe enough to cause unconsciousness or something more deadly.

PEG HADN'T BEEN worried until the sky began to darken and people started going into their huts. Maria tugged her back inside. The rain came and went, in spurts. It was fascinating to Peg.

"My son and your friend will return soon," she assured the American woman in her halting Spanish. She was far more at home in her native tongue or Portuguese.

"I hope so," Peg said. "It's dark."

Maria nodded. "It is not easy to find men who do not wish to be found, especially in the jungle. They will be here soon," she added, smiling. "You will see."

Peg sighed. "I'm sure you're right. Soon."

BUT THE HOURS passed. The village went to sleep. Peg lay in a hammock in the palm-roofed hut, listening to the rain. Every so often, droplets would find a way through the roof and drip on the floor nearby. She smiled, thinking of houses she and her father had lived in over the years, where she'd had to find pots and pans to contain the drips.

Her eyes were wide-open in the darkness, worrying. What had happened to Clarisse? At first, to her shame, she thought the other woman might have followed through on her initial impulse, which was to strand Peg in the jungle to get even with Grange for rejecting her.

However, that theory fell through when she considered Enrique. This was his village, and his mother lived here. Even if Clarisse left the country, Enrique knew where Peg was and he would come back and say something. He would do it because of his mother, if not because of Peg herself.

But Enrique didn't show up. Neither did Clarisse. Peg spent a sleepless night, worry torturing her.

By the time morning arrived, suddenly and brilliantly, she was convinced that something terrible had happened.

"Have you heard from your son?" Peg asked Maria hopefully. A runner could have come to the village during the night, while she was fitfully sleeping.

"No," Maria said. She looked very concerned. "I do not wish to add to your worry," she said hesitantly, "but Enrique said he would come back on his way to the city. He keeps his word. He is like his father, who never told a lie all the time we were married."

Peg bit her lower lip.

Maria touched her arm gently. "We must have hope," she said. "Perhaps there was an accident with the vehicle. A flat tire? An engine fault? Who can say? We must wait and hope for the best."

"I guess so. But I'm a little worried."

Marie nodded. "Yes. So am I. This is not like my son."

Peg learned how to cook the special dishes they liked in the village, while the women laughed with delight at her obvious pleasure as she succeeded. She'd read travel brochures in the hotel where she and Clarisse had stayed, advertising tours into the jungle with overnight stays at selected native villages. All sorts of requirements had to be met, including proof of immunization, which were provided to the native people by the tour guides. Considering the horror of the past, during which many indigenous tribes had been utterly destroyed by disease to which Europeans were immune, it was a logical and wise step.

But Peg hadn't been required to do those things, most likely because Enrique had spoken with Clarisse, or possibly because he had taken care of the details. He was, after all, a tour operator himself. Clarisse had mentioned that he infrequently allowed a guest to stay in this village where his mother lived, as a courtesy, only if he trusted the visitor. Local natives were quite distrustful of outsiders.

Maria had mentioned that to Peg in one of their conversations. "We keep to ourselves," she explained in her slow Spanish. "We do not like outsiders here. You laugh. Why?"

"Because my little town in America is just the same," she explained, smiling. "It's a very small place, not a lot bigger than your village. When new people come in from the cities, we're suspicious. We have to get to know them before we feel comfortable even talking around them."

Maria's bright eyes smiled. "We have many things in common."

"Including chicken." Peg said it with a rakish grin, and Maria burst out laughing.

BUT THE DAY passed quickly. After they finished the evening meal, and walked outside to listen to the night sounds around a central fire where people were sitting and talking, Peg's mind began to wander again, and she was very worried about Clarisse. She was worried about Enrique, for Maria's sake.

She had to consider what she might have to do about her own situation. She didn't have a visa. She had a passport, because Jason Pendleton had helped her get one a year ago, in case he had to send her father overseas to talk a deal for him in, of all places, South America. It had been a rare bit of foresight, because Peg hadn't had any problem getting through customs. But her passport required the airport, which was in Manaus. There were no vehicles here. There wasn't even a phone. She'd counted on Clarisse and Enrique to take her to Grange, who would presumably find a way to get her back to Manaus. She seemed to be stranded, with the rainy season already making things very wet.

As she darted into a hut to avoid being soaked, again, she recalled Clarisse's teasing tone about the cottons she'd planned to pack. In the jungle during rainy season, cotton got wet and stayed wet, it didn't dry in the humidity. People here wore synthetic fabric because it had the virtue of being quickly dried.

The rain ceased after a couple of minutes and she stuck her head out again. Two children, brown and beautiful, stopped to flash her shy grins with perfect white teeth before they ran off. She laughed delightedly. In its own foreign way, this village was very much like Comanche Wells. She'd have to try to remember it so that she could share her trip with her father.

Meanwhile, she was growing more concerned than

ever about the possibility of never seeing Comanche Wells again. If Clarisse and Enrique didn't come back soon, she was going to have to figure out what to do. Maria would help, she was certain. But what if Maria lost her son? What if he and Clarisse had met with some terrible accident? What if…?

SUDDEN CRIES CAUGHT her attention. It seemed that the whole village was running toward the road that led into the jungle. Something must be happening. Peg ran toward the source of the commotion.

Two native men were carrying a man on a makeshift litter. As Peg got closer, she heard Maria cry out.

There was a man on the pallet, very pale, unconscious, with blood all over the front of his shirt.

"Is he dead?" Peg asked in English, and then had to repeat it in Spanish so that Maria would understand.

Maria had her hand in her son's shirt. Her face was wet with tears. She drew in a harsh breath, but then she relaxed a little. "He is alive," she said. She opened his shirt and used it to clear away the blood so that she could see the extent of his injury. There was a wound just under his rib cage. A bullet wound.

"He's been shot!" Peg burst out. She looked around. "Where is Clarisse?" she asked frantically.

"That we must wait to know, until he can tell us. If he can ever tell us," Maria said with heavy practicality. "Bring him," she told the others in Portuguese. "I will send for the doctor."

CHAPTER NINE

PEG WAS ALMOST frantic. Here she was, stuck in a foreign country, in a native village with no transportation to an airport, with no way to contact Grange, with only one change of clothes and no idea what to do next. Now Enrique had been injured and Clarisse's whereabouts were unknown. If the driver had been shot, Clarisse might have been wounded also, or killed.

"Where did they find Enrique?" Peg asked Maria when her son was being carefully placed on a pallet of woven palm leaves in Maria's hut.

She asked the men who had brought him into camp. "Across the river," she said, giving the natives' name for it. "The vehicle was on the side of the road. The windshield was broken. On both sides," she said worriedly. She looked at Peg, whose face showed her concern. "There was also blood on the passenger seat, where your friend's head would have been. They did not find her body," she added. "But one of our hunters said there were tracks from another vehicle nearby and footprints of two men wearing boots. It was most likely the military. They patrol these roads. The madman who has charge of our country now likes to use us for targets if we get in his way," Maria added coldly. "Many of our cousins have died for his new oil site."

"I'm so sorry," Peg said. "I knew it was bad, but not anywhere near this awful in Barrera."

"If you stay here for very long, you will learn much." Maria called for water, in a ceramic bowl, and she bathed her son's brow with it. "He has fever. I hope the doctor comes soon."

"You can get a doctor to come from Manaus?" Peg asked.

Maria glanced at her. "No. It is too far on foot, although we will send a canoe to the city to bring back a doctor. Enrique might die in the meantime. We have a friend who has medical training, who was working nearby at the ruins when Sapara took over our country. The friend had to hide to avoid being killed, as a friend of Emilio Machado."

"I know of the general," Peg said. "He's something of a legend back home. People love him."

Maria was impressed. "Here, too, he has many friends. We are hopeful that one day he will return and hang Sapara."

Peg only nodded.

There was a flurry of activity outside and a visitor entered, dressed in soaked khakis and heavy boots, with a wide-brimmed safari hat over what looked like short dark wavy hair.

"Are you the doctor?" Peg asked in her Texas drawl.

The hat came off and a tall, muscular woman in her late twenties with an astonished expression stared back at her from pale blue eyes. "Good Lord, are you from Texas?" she asked in a similar drawl. "It's been so long since I've heard an accent from back home!"

Peg laughed. "I'm from Jacobsville."

"I know that one." She chuckled as if at some private

joke before she turned to the patient. "Oh, dear. That looks very much like a gunshot wound."

"Someone shot my son," Maria said worriedly. "We think it was soldiers of Sapara. Can you do something?"

"Been a while since I've extracted a bullet, but I think I can manage." She pulled the pack off her back and started to unload it. "I'm trained in anthropology," she said, "but I was a medic in the army for a couple of years and I did mercenary work afterward."

Peg was astonished. "Mercenary work?"

She nodded. "Yes. I'm a black belt in karate and tae kwon do, and several other martial arts. I palled around with a guy named Colby Lane."

"I know him!" Peg exclaimed. "Well, I sort of know him. He's married and has two children. His wife is a DEA agent, and he works private security for the Ritter Oil Corporation in Houston."

"I heard he got married," the woman said quietly. "I had a case on him once, but he wasn't interested in me. At the time, he liked the soft, feminine sort." She sighed. "Not my thing. I like adventure. Maria, can they boil some water for me?" she added as she took out what looked like a small case of surgical instruments. "And I'll need something astringent."

Maria nodded and got up to fetch the supplies.

"Infection is very dangerous here, isn't it?"

The other woman nodded. "Very." She looked up and her blue eyes smiled. "We haven't introduced ourselves, have we? I'm Maddie Carlson."

"I'm Peg Larson," came the smiling reply. "Nice to meet you. I'm so glad you know how to treat bullet wounds."

"I've had a lot of practice," Maddie said. "One of

our group was a doctor, well, a resident, named Micah Steele..."

"Good Lord!" Peg burst out. "He lives in Jacobsville."

"Working with Eb Scott?" Maddie asked, surprised. She was pulling back clothing to examine Enrique's wound.

"Oh, no, working as a partner with two local doctors, and at the hospital."

Maddie stopped what she was doing and just stared.

"And he's married. He and Callie had two children, a little girl and a boy two years old."

Maddie caught her breath. "If they'd taken bets on that guy ever getting married, I'd be poor now." She shook her head. "Go figure. Colby Lane is married, Micah Steele—not Eb Scott and Cy Parks, though, surely?"

Peg chuckled. "Yes, and they both have kids."

"Well, I never!" Maddie exclaimed. She nodded and smiled comfortingly at Maria as she brought the things Maddie had asked for. "Eb still have the counterterrorism training facility?"

"Oh, yes. In fact, some of Winslow's men got their training there."

Maddie frowned. "Winslow?"

"Winslow Grange. He's working with General Machado."

"Grange. I don't know him."

"There's another guy, Rourke..."

Maddie shook her head. "Don't know him, either. I've been out of merc work for several years. I'm doing archaeology exclusively now, and I'm on the verge of a world-shaking discovery near here. Damned poor timing, Sapara's coup. I had all the help I needed when Machado was in power." She hesitated for a minute to wash and use an antibacterial substance on her hands before putting on disposable rubber gloves. "He was kind to me. I had sort of a case on him," she said with an odd shyness. "I'm not his type, though. Too tough. I think he likes more feminine women. I can't change my spots at this age."

"You shouldn't have to," Peg said gently. "People have to be themselves to live in the world."

Maddie glanced at her with a smile. "Smart girl."

She went back to work by the light of a lantern. She was skilled. She probed gently for the bullet, which was lodged in the lower portion of Enrique's chest. She pulled it out almost at once. "There are glass fragments in the wound," she said, frowning.

"The runners said the windshield was shattered on both sides," Maria commented.

"The windshield saved him," Maddie mused. "Stopped the force of the bullet so that it didn't penetrate too far. It did collapse the lung, though. That's what knocked him out. I don't have the equipment to reinflate it, damn it. The most I can do is give him an antibiotic and let them send for the doctor in Manaus. He'll manage until then, I think. Maria," she called, "you need to send a canoe to Manaus…the fastest you have, and get a doctor out here to finish what I started. This is just field dressing."

"The canoe has already been sent. Thank you for what you have done," Maria said. "You can stay with us. I have told you many times."

"Sapara is after me," the woman said heavily. "He doesn't want to risk his new oil operation, and if I get word to the outside about the major find here, he'll have the international community breathing down his neck.

He doesn't want that, not with his delicate negotiations going on. He's quietly clearing out all the native tribes in the way of the oil fields, and not telling his potential new partners about it."

"Do you know which oil company he's negotiating with?"

"Yes. Ritter Oil, out of Houston."

Peg caught her breath. "Oh, we all know about that one," she said. "Eugene Ritter would have Sapara for breakfast if he knew what was going on here."

"He would?" Maddie asked, surprised. "An oil magnate with a conscience?"

"Count on it. And Sapara had better be careful. Colby Lanc works for Mr. Ritter."

"Colby." Maddie smiled. "He'd put together a team and wipe out Sapara's men in a heartbeat. Damned idiot, Sapara," she muttered while she finished bandaging Enrique, who was breathing roughly. "I wish somebody would make hash out of him."

"Plans are in motion for that, so I hear," Peg said, her voice sad. "General Machado is mounting a coup attempt."

"Emilio?" Maddie was washing her hands, but she stopped. "He's here?"

Peg nodded. "Grange is head of his commando forces. I wish I knew where they were, so that I could find Grange. A friend brought me over to Manaus to see him. Now she's vanished. I'm afraid she may be dead. She was in the Land Rover with Enrique, and Maria's friends said that both sides of the windshield were broken and there was blood on the passenger seat. Her name is Clarisse. She's been so good to me…"

Maddie dried her hands. "She wasn't found?"

"No. They said it looked as though the military had taken her away."

Maddie's expression was taut. "Did she know anything about the general's plans?"

"She knew that he was here with an invasion force."

Maddie didn't say anything. She turned away quietly.

"They'll torture her, won't they?" she asked. "Won't they?" she added insistently when the other woman didn't answer.

Maddie turned around. "If she has information vital to Sapara, yes, they'll torture her."

"Oh, no!"

"I was in Africa a few years ago, with a merc group that planned to overthrow a very nasty dictator. I got sloppy and got caught." She unbuttoned her shirt and exposed her shoulder. There was a large, white scar. "One of the dictator's men put a knife right through my shoulder. He smiled while he did it. He said that if I didn't talk, he'd put it through my breast."

"What happened?!"

She laughed and rebuttoned her shirt. "The last thing he heard was UZI fire. The last thing he saw was Colby Lane's face over it."

"In the nick of time!"

She nodded. "Micah Steele patched me up while Colby cursed. Colby didn't feel anything romantic for me, but he was always my friend. I'm sure he still is."

"You've had some adventures!" Peg exclaimed. "I've never been anywhere in my life or done anything dangerous, until now." She laughed softly. "I'm sorry to tell you that I'm quite enjoying it. Well, except for poor Enrique." She glanced at him. "And Clarisse, wherever she is."

"Enrique will sleep now," she said. "I gave him an injection to help the pain. By the time it wears off, hopefully the doctor will be here." She then glanced at Peg. "You said that you came to see this Grange fellow. Are you engaged to him?"

"No. But I think he likes me." She smiled shyly. "He took me to a yearly ball in Jacobsville, and he doesn't date anybody, you see. Well, neither do I."

Maddie smiled. "I get the picture. So you came here to see him, in this dangerous place?"

"Clarisse came to get me," she explained, leaving out the reason, because Clarisse had already paid a high price for what she'd planned. "We came out here because she was going to leave me in a safe place while she and Enrique brought Grange back here. She said it wasn't far. Only Enrique knew where to find his camp," she said sadly. "I guess Grange has no idea that I'm even in the country now, and poor Enrique got shot and Clarisse got kidnapped because of it."

"Life happens," Maddie said philosophically. "But things will work out. You'll see."

"At least Enrique will live. But Clarisse," Peg said worriedly. "I wonder where she is?"

CLARISSE WAS SHIVERING in her cell. Her perfect skin had been marred by a knife. She was bleeding under her silk blouse, under her bra. Only a vicious man could have done to her what that animal had done in his effort to extract further information from her about Machado. He'd even threatened rape, but another soldier had snapped at him that she was rich and had powerful friends. The barbarian had satisfied himself with cutting her.

She had told them nothing. She remembered her

childhood, playing with Stanton Rourke when they were children, and once he'd held her head underwater for a childish prank and tried to make her apologize. She'd held her breath and refused to give an inch. His brown eyes had been eloquent, although he hadn't voiced any admiration for her fearlessness.

For a brief time, Clarisse and her parents had lived in Africa, when her father had been a minor diplomat for the U.S. State Department, early in his career. Rourke had lived nearby with his mother.

He was older than Clarisse by five years, but at ten, she'd been precocious and adventurous. She and Rourke had gone exploring and gotten into trouble often. Rourke's ability to speak Afrikaans and several native dialects had come in handy. He was a past master at explaining his way out of difficult situations. But once they'd encountered a vicious adder. Clarisse had been bitten because she hadn't seen it. Rourke had carried her in his arms to the doctor and waited while she was given an injection. He sat by her, along with her mother, while she recovered. She hadn't realized how kind a person he was.

Then she'd heard the rumors and, being too young to understand, she'd blurted out that people said he was the illegitimate son of the millionaire K.C. Kantor. Rourke had walked away and never spoken to her again even when her father was reassigned and they were leaving. They did meet occasionally many years later at society functions in Washington, and he was pleasant. But then they'd met once in Manaus just after her mother's death, years ago. He'd been insulting and cold and sarcastic, because she'd made an utter fool of herself with him. It was still horribly embarrassing to remember what she'd done. Now she avoided him.

The thoughts made the pain easier to bear, for some reason. Perhaps it was the memory of those events early in her childhood that gave her strength. Rourke had been her idol when she was a child. He was utterly fearless. He knew people who fought in revolutions. He'd told her about them, about the ordeals of capture. It helped her cope, now, when she herself was a victim. She wasn't going to tell Sapara anything. Not if they killed her. She owed Grange, for what she'd done to poor Peg. Dear Peg, who would hate her, who would believe she'd betrayed her. And what of Enrique, dead on her account? Poor Maria!

"Miss Carrington," Dr. Fitzhugh called gently. "Miss Carrington!"

She fought down nausea and managed to sit up. "I'm okay," she whispered, and even dragged up a smile.

He looked at the blood on her blouse and seemed to grow taller with rage. "I will see that man dead if it's my last act on this earth!"

"Thanks," she said. "But we really need a plan, and soon. He won't stop until they make me tell what I know. I can't do that. I'd have to let them kill me."

Dr. Fitzhugh grimaced. "Dear God. How did we end up like this?"

"Blame greed."

He nodded. "I wish I could dress those wounds for you. Perhaps we could demand a doctor."

"That would amuse him."

"I suppose so. My dear woman," he said, words failing him.

"What's happened?" Dr. Constantine asked from his cell on the other side of hers.

"I think they call it torture."

Dr. Constantine cursed roundly and then apologized. She smiled. "Thanks. I think you were eloquent."

He laughed despite the gravity of the situation.

Dr. Fitzhugh moved closer to the bars. "I've been thinking about what you said. That native village, we could get to it if we had transportation. Our jailer here has a cousin with a wagon and two mules. He often drives supplies down to the village where you left your young friend."

"He does?" she asked, suddenly hopeful and afraid to hope.

"Yes. The jailer might help…"

There was the sound of heavy feet moving closer. The jailer, a heavy, mustached man of sixty or so years, stopped at the cells and gaped at Clarisse, at the blood on her blouse. "*Señorita*. Oh, *¡Dios mio, Señorita! Lo siento. Lo siento. ¡Los animales! ¡Puede que se vaya al infierno para siempre!*" He was actually sobbing.

Clarisse, touched by his compassion, moved to the front of the cell. *"¿Nos puedes ayudar?"* she asked softly, using the familiar term deliberately, because a family member would be that upset at her treatment more than any stranger.

He hesitated. But then his face set, and he nodded curtly. "*Sí*. I can do that. But you have no place to go…"

"Yes, we do," Dr. Fitzhugh said. His Spanish was dreadful, but he made himself understood.

"Yes," Clarisse agreed quietly. "A village south of here. Not so very far, if we had a way to get there."

The jailer came closer. "My cousin, he has mules and a big wagon. He goes to south villages to take supplies every Friday. That is tomorrow. I will get you out before the shift changes. You," he told Dr. Fitzhugh, "must hit me in the head with something, so they will not kill me."

"Dear old fellow, I'd rather die!" Dr. Fitzhugh said fervently.

He spoke in English, but the jailer read his consternation and smiled. "You are kind. But this must be done. I have a wife, very ugly but she loves me." He shrugged. "I am her only support, so I must not die. You must hit me. It will be all right. I have a very hard head." He laughed and tapped it.

"I don't want you to be hurt," Clarisse said, her expression troubled.

"It will be all right," the jailer said in a tender tone. "I had a daughter…she would have been your age if she had lived. The fever took her, when she was just a small child." He wiped away more tears. "My wife is Dutch. The child was blonde, like you." He smiled. "If you stay here one more day, Sapara will kill you. You must go now."

"All right, then. But if we all live, I'll make sure you never want for anything again as long as you live. And I'll take care of your wife, too."

The tears fell even harder. He swallowed hard. "My name is Romero Coriba."

"Mine is Clarisse."

He smiled. "Clarisse." He nodded. "I will make the arrangements. I must bribe a guard."

"I have money, but it's in Sapara's possession," she said miserably.

"Oh, that is no problem. I know where he keeps things." He grinned wickedly. "And the bribe is rum. The guard outside has a big thirst for it. I have a bottle of it that El Presidente Machado gave me before he was ousted by that impostor, Sapara," he added coldly. "Anyway, I have saved the rum for a special occasion. It seems I have found one!"

Clarisse laughed through the pain. "When Sapara is ousted, I'll buy you a case of the best rum I can find."

"*Señorita,* you are an angel from heaven. And I am sorry, so sorry, for what was done to you. Those two animals that work for Sapara... I could strangle them. Especially Miguel. He likes to hurt people."

"I have a friend who likes to hurt people, too," she said coldly. "I'll make sure he knows who Miguel is."

He nodded. "That will be a pleasure. Now I must go and make arrangements. I wish I could do something for you."

"Romero, you're giving me my life," she said solemnly. "What is more important than that?"

He smiled and went away.

"At last." Dr. Fitzhugh sighed and sat down on his ragged bunk. "Hope!"

"Yes," Clarisse agreed. She lay back down, too, wincing as her blouse pulled against the cuts. "Hope."

ROMERO CAME IN the early hours before dawn with the keys to their cells and carrying a baseball bat.

"I have everything arranged. The other guard has fallen asleep from drinking the whole bottle of my good rum, and my cousin is waiting at the door with ponchos to cover you three. He will drive you to the village. He has two strong sons who will go also, just in case of trouble. The family has cousins in the village."

"I can't repay you now, but I will. I promise," Clarisse said, and hugged the old man, despite the sting of the cuts on her chest.

He patted her awkwardly on the back. "You be safe, my friend," he said softly.

She smiled through tears of gratitude. "I'll see you again."

"Now," Romero said, handing the bat to Dr. Fitzhugh, "you must hit me."

Dr. Fitzhugh took the bat and grimaced. "Well, at least I've had medical training," he said in his crisp British accent. "I know where to hit you to least affect your poor brain. But you'll have a hell of a headache."

"Better a headache than to die," the jailer said in halting English and grinned.

"Very well," Dr. Fitzhugh said. "Thank you with all my heart for your help. Please close your eyes."

"*Sí,* I can…!"

The jailer fell with a *whump.* Dr. Fitzhugh felt for a pulse and listened to the other man's breathing. "God, I hated doing that!" he exclaimed. He laid the bat nearby, so that it could be found.

"I know. Let's go!" Clarisse said.

The three of them ran for the back door, down the long hall, hoping, praying, that there wouldn't be a squad of soldiers outside to meet them. The jailer had sounded confident, but Clarisse was terrified. She would be shot if they caught her. Shot, or worse. It didn't bear thinking about. She stifled her thoughts and just ran.

But at the back door, there was no sign of anyone. There was a guard, slumped against the wall, unconscious and breathing loudly.

Clarisse bit her lip almost through. "Oh, my God," she groaned, almost sobbing.

"*Pssst! Señorita!*"

Her heart jumped. She looked toward a load of what

looked like munitions just behind the jail. She ran, motioning the two men to follow.

"I am Jorge," a small, dark man told her, doffing his sombrero. "These are my sons, Rafael and Sandrino."

"I'm Clarisse. These are my friends. You are Romero's cousin?"

It impressed him that she used the jailer's first name, a grand lady like this who was obviously American. He grinned. "Yes, I am his cousin. Here."

He had one of his sons hand out ponchos, made of woven fabric that would cover them to the knees. He also had big hats that would conceal their faces.

"We must go. But do not run. Walk. Slowly."

Clarisse ground her teeth together. He was right. But that long walk across the plaza, past the fountain, to the outskirts of the military complex was the longest walk of her entire life. They met only one guard. Jorge said something to him and pointed at his companions. The guard gave them an odd look. But then, sleepy and apathetic, he waved them on. They continued the walk to Jorge's wagon.

Clarisse climbed into the back, on top of several bushels of some sort of grain, and collapsed. The men did likewise.

"And now we go," Jorge said, his sons sitting on the wide wooden seat beside him. He whipped the mules with the reins and the wagon began to move, jerkily at first, and then smoothly. Except for the bouncing.

CLARISSE'S FRIEND, DR. Carvajal, came into the hut hours later, soaking wet in spite of his raincoat, carrying his medical bag.

"Hello, again," Peg greeted him.

He smiled. "Hello. Where is Clarisse?"

"She was in the Land Rover with Enrique," she told him as he put down his bag and started to examine Enrique. "We don't know what happened to her, but we think the military kidnapped her."

"Dear God," he exclaimed heavily.

"She must have been alive," she pointed out. "Or they'd have left her, like they left poor Enrique."

He looked up at her and managed a smile. "You make sense. Yes. Perhaps that is what happened."

He started to work, inserting a tube through a slit that he made with a scalpel where the bullet had been extracted. "This is good work. Who operated on him?"

"I did," Maddie said, coming in the door. "I was an army medic for a few years."

"You should have studied medicine."

"Not me," she declared. "Too tame. I like exploring."

"You are the archaeologist," he exclaimed.

She nodded grimly. "Please don't pass that information around. I'm hiding from Sapara and his thugs. They'd kill me on sight. What I know would deprive him of his new oil lands."

"You have discovered something?" he asked.

She nodded.

He looked grim. "Listen to me, you must get to the capital and tell someone in the government what you know."

She laughed. "It's in Barrera. And Sapara is the government."

The doctor cursed under his breath. "That little worm!"

"I can think of much worse things to call him," Maddie agreed. "I hope General Machado kicks his butt."

"Machado? He is here?" he exclaimed.

"Yes," Peg said. "Here and close by. He's going to kick Sapara all the way to the Atlantic Ocean."

"I will gladly loan him a pair of boots," the doctor said so fervently that everyone laughed.

But Peg was still worried about Clarisse, and nothing eased her fears.

"She will be all right," Maria said softly. "I promise. And I have a surprise for you."

"A surprise?"

"Sim."

Maria went outside and motioned to a man. *"¿Ahora?"*

He chuckled. "Yes. They are coming down the road now."

"They?" Peg went outside and looked. There was a jeep approaching, an American jeep. As she looked, a tall, dark-headed man wearing camo gear got out and came marching straight toward her.

He stopped, gaping. "Peg?" he exclaimed.

His expression sent her running right into his arms, to be lifted and kissed and kissed and kissed until her mouth hurt, and still she kissed him back with all the passion she'd saved up since their parting.

"They said there was someone here who had important information for me," he exclaimed. He kissed her eyes. "They didn't say who!"

She smiled as he kissed her again. Her arms tightened around him. "I'm so happy."

His mouth burrowed into her soft neck. "How the hell did you get here?"

"Clarisse brought me."

"Clarisse…!" He started to speak but she covered his mouth with her soft palm, which he kissed involuntarily.

"She brought me here when she was taking drugs.

She was literally out of her mind with grief. She had me immunized and she nursed me all night long. Then she told me about her father and sister—" she stretched the truth a little "—and how tragically they died four months ago. We became friends. She said she was going to tell you what a horrible thing she'd done and you could shoot her if you wanted to. She left me here where I'd be safe and went to look for you with Enrique. He's inside. He's been shot."

"Shot?" he exclaimed.

"Yes. And Clarisse was taken away by Barrera military. If she isn't dead, they're probably torturing her to make her talk," she said grimly. "I should never have let her go. I should have asked Maria to send a tracker to find you!"

"Hell," Grange said heavily. "What a mess!"

"Come on inside, out of the rain," Peg said, tugging at his hand. "I have a lot of friends here. I want you to meet them."

He shook his head, smiling. Trust Peg to make friends in a foreign country without any trouble at all. He was scared to death to find her here, but so happy that he didn't have the will to fuss at her for coming. He put his arm around her and hugged her close as they went into the dwelling. He felt her soft breast pressing against his side, under his arm, and almost shivered with desire. All those heated dreams that ended in cold reality, and here was his Peg, in his arms, again, at last! He couldn't even manage to be angry at Clarisse.

Peg moved closer to him and looked into his eyes as they entered the enormous thatched hut, inside which a small campfire burned. The look she gave him was even hotter than the fire.

CHAPTER TEN

GRANGE WAS INTRODUCED to the people inside the hut. Maddie made him smile. She knew the old group of mercs trained by Eb Scott, and she'd done merc work before going back to college to finish her degree. She was the missing archaeologist.

"I've heard a lot about you," he commented with a wry smile.

"I've heard quite a bit about you as well," she replied with a speaking glance at Peg. "From this amazing young woman."

"I'm not amazing at all," Peg protested.

"Yes, you are amazing," Dr. Carvajal told her. "You broke our mutual friend of a very uncomfortable affection for anxiety drugs. You may have saved her life in the process."

"Only to help risk it here," Peg said sadly. "God knows what they're doing to her right now!"

"We'll find a way to get her out," Grange promised. "I swear it."

"Thanks," she replied softly, worshipping him with her eyes.

He touched her hair gently. She was so lovely, he thought.

"Has the fighting started?" she asked.

He grimaced. "We're having some issues right now. The general thinks we can do this from the inside. But we had two men sneak into the city to talk to one of his former generals, and they haven't been heard from again. So either Sapara found and killed them, or they haven't been able to make contact."

"Bad news," she said.

He nodded. "So now we're working with locals who are fed up with Sapara and his men, training them to fight and shoot. It's going to be messy."

"Oh, dear."

He sighed. "Every battle plan has its limitations. This was a lot easier on paper." He smiled at her.

"I guess so."

There was a cry from the center of the village.

Grange and Peg went outside, leaving the doctor and Maddie to work on Enrique, with a worried Maria standing close by.

A mule-drawn wagon pulled up at the entrance to the village.

"It is just supplies," Maria said, poking her head out the doorway. "It comes every Friday to bring us grain."

"Oh," Peg said, disappointed.

As they watched, three poncho-covered people joined the three men and moved into the village. One, shorter than the others, was walking very slowly, as if he was ill.

They came closer, removing the hats that covered their faces. It was Clarisse, with two men.

"Clarisse!" Peg exclaimed, and ran to hug her close and rock her and weep. "Oh, Clarisse, I thought you were dead! I'm so happy!"

That hug hurt like hell, but Clarisse didn't say a word. It was so nice to have a friend. She hugged Peg back. "I'm okay. I've been shot, cut up and threatened, but I'm still going strong. I'm just…" There was a little rush of breath and she slumped to the ground.

Grange picked her up and carried her into the hut. Maria slung a hammock quickly for him to put her into.

He removed the poncho and gasped. Her blouse was soaked in blood. "Good God, what have they done to her?" he exclaimed.

"She was tortured, young man," one of the men, the shorter one, said heavily. "We've all been through hell in Sapara's asylum. We hope to pay him back very soon for his hospitality. I'm Damon Fitzhugh. This is Julian Constantine. We teach at the Barrera University. At least, we did. This brave young woman helped us escape. I do hope her injuries aren't too bad. She was shot and had a mild concussion, before they did this to her. But we couldn't do anything to help her, and Sapara wouldn't even call a doctor. The animal!"

"Here," Dr. Carvajal said, moving to the hammock. "Let me wash my hands. Maria, if you please, bring water and a cloth."

"At once. My son?"

He smiled wearily. "He will be all right now. The lung is inflating. It will take a little time. The field dressing was quite impressive," he said with a grin at Maddie.

"Thanks," the archaeologist replied.

He washed his hands and turned back to Clarisse. He gave Grange and the two men a speaking look.

"We'll wait outside," he said gently, and smiled at Peg, motioning to the two professors, who followed him to another building nearby, where they were offered food and water around the central fire, which they accepted gratefully.

The doctor peeled back Clarisse's blouse, wincing at

what he saw. There was a deep slash on her arm, which had cut a vein. Fortunately it had coagulated, but she was in bad shape. "Dear God. What sort of man could do this?"

"Someone who needs a dose of lethal lead poisoning," Peg said in her slowest drawl.

"I do agree."

The cuts were profuse, and quite deep.

"She will need plastic surgery when this heals," he said as he stitched them. "There is no way it can be done now, she has lost much blood and most of these wounds will require stitches." He winced. "I would not have had this happen to her for the world."

"Nor I," Peg said heavily. "Poor Clarisse!"

"She has a wound on her head also," Maddie noted. "The blood's caked there."

"Yes." He examined it when he finished the stitches. He bandaged the lesser wounds after treating them with an antiseptic powder. He shook his head. "So much damage."

"They tried to make her talk," Maddie said coldly. "I'll bet she didn't tell them anything."

Maria came back into the hut. "That is true. I have been speaking to the *arriero*—the mule driver. He says she told him that she never said a word, no matter what they did to her. They were going to take her back to be tortured some more this morning. A friend helped them escape. The men say that they will not tell me who, so he must be a relative." She smiled. "He has to be a kind person."

"There are a few in the world," Peg agreed.

"This was a deep wound. But the bullet only grazed her head. How fortunate that the soldier's aim was off."

"Will she be all right?" Peg asked worriedly.

The doctor nodded. "She is tired and she seems dehydrated."

Clarisse stirred. "So sleepy," she murmured. She winced. "Sorry, I must have nodded off. They tortured me, but they didn't get zilch," she said with flashing eyes. "There's a man who works for Sapara, Miguel something. If I ever see him again, I want to be packing a gun."

"I'll find one for you, somehow," Peg said, and smiled. "I'm so glad you're all right."

"I thought I saw Grange," Clarisse whispered weakly.

"You did. He carried you in here. You passed out."

"Lack of sleep, lack of food—they didn't even give us much water. I'm so thirsty!"

"Here. It is all right?" Maria asked the doctor as she handed a small ceramic bowl to Clarisse.

"Yes. It is what she needs."

Clarisse tried to take in the contents at once, but the doctor restrained her. "Too much will make you sick. Slowly."

Clarisse nodded. She winced as she lifted her arms again to drink from the bowl. "Thanks, Maria. I'm so sorry about Enrique. We got lost and he stood up to get his bearings. That's when the shooting started. Will he be all right?"

"Yes," the doctor said with a smile. "Like you, he will need a few days to heal. But he will be fine. You can come back to the city with me…" the doctor began.

"I'm not leaving," Clarisse said coldly.

"Excuse me?"

"I'm not going anywhere," she said icily. "I know the layout of the headquarters building, the shift change times, and I have a friend inside. I'm the most valuable asset General Machado has at the moment. I'm going in with them."

"My dear woman," the doctor began to protest.

"In that case," Peg began, "I'm going, too."

"No, you're not," Clarisse said firmly.

"She's right." Maddie stepped in, her face grim. "You're a liability in the field. You'd get people killed. Which brings us to you," she told Clarisse, and turned to her.

"Never mind arguing," Clarisse told her. "I've won the right to help. I'm going." She held up a hand. "I'll stay outside the action. But I can help. I have a photographic memory, and I can draw."

Maddie sighed. "Okay. I won't argue. I'll let him do it." She pointed to Grange as he entered the hut.

Grange looked grim, and angry.

"Tell her she can't go," Maddie said firmly.

"Get a rope and tie her up," Clarisse added with a faint laugh.

Grange was looking at Clarisse with a mixture of irritation and respect.

"What's wrong?" Peg asked.

"Rourke's on his way," he muttered. "Damned fool, I tried to stop him but I couldn't."

"Why is Rourke coming?" Clarisse asked. Her expression was complicated. Peg couldn't read it, but she seemed flushed and excited as well.

"I told him you'd been tortured," Grange said heavily. "I guess his conscience is as guilty as mine. I shouldn't have been so hard on you. Neither should he."

Clarisse managed a weary smile and lay back down, wincing. "I've got a guilty conscience of my own, for involving Peg in all this. She's such a sweetie," she added, looking at Peg with real guilt. "She's so much like my sister…" She stopped because tears were welling up in her pale blue eyes.

"It's all right," Peg said gently, smoothing back her hair. "It's all right."

The tears overflowed.

Grange had never seen Clarisse cry. He thought she was tough as nails, totally without morals. His Peg, he thought with genuine pride, was one woman in a million. She'd cracked through Clarisse's hard shell.

He wanted to tell Clarisse she was staying out of the action, but Rourke had a history with her. Since he was disobeying orders to come here anyway, he could deal with Clarisse.

THEY WERE ALL sitting around the fire, eating a small meal, when the jeep came roaring up to the edge of the compound. A tall, angry man with blond hair and a black eye patch over one eye came striding toward them.

His sensual lips were set in a thin line and his face was harder than stone. As he drew closer, Peg noted that his one eye was an odd shade of brown. He didn't hesitate, or wait to be introduced to the other people; he went straight to Clarisse and knelt beside her.

His practiced gaze went from her badly stained blouse, betraying the blood even after Maria's attempts to wash some of it out, to the place where the doctor had to cut away a little of her hair to treat the bullet wound.

"Who did this to you, Tat?" he asked her with ice in his tone, and a sort of accent that Peg had never heard before.

She drew in a long breath. Well, at least he wasn't calling her names or being sarcastic. If she'd been more gullible, she might even believe that he cared. "One of Sapara's men," she said quietly. "A butcher named Miguel who works in the military headquarters building adjacent to the prison."

His face was like granite. "He'll pay for it. I promise you. We won't leave anything alive in the whole damned place!"

"You make sure you don't hurt Romero," she replied quickly. "He saved us. I'd be dead if not for him. He's the jailer. An old man, fat and dirty and sweet."

"Romero." He gave her a long look. "So you like older men, do you?"

"He's married."

"Why would that stop you?" he teased, and then saw the expression cross her face just before her eyes dropped. She wouldn't look at him again.

"Tat…" he said slowly, regretfully.

"I'm okay," she said quietly. "I'll have a few battle scars, but I'll be fine."

He looked again to her stained blouse and winced. He remembered her skin, her soft, beautiful creamy skin; her breasts like smooth seashells with those delicate pink nubs…

He stood up, shaking off the memory.

"Hell of a place for scars," he said icily.

"Hey, nobody wants me," she replied with a self-deprecating smile. "Nobody will see them except me."

He might have challenged that another time. He knew she slept around. Everybody knew. But he couldn't snipe at her; not now, when she was hurt, when some damned animal had savaged her like that. With a knife, the brute. Rourke had gone crazy when Grange had told him what happened. Nothing would have stopped him. All he'd wanted in life at that moment was to get to her, to see her, to make sure she was all right. He could never have her, but nobody was going to hurt her if he could prevent it. He hated what was done to her.

"At least it was nothing worse, thanks to Romero," Clarisse said heavily. "They'd have killed me if we hadn't escaped. Have you met the professors?" she added quickly and introduced them to Rourke.

"She's the bravest woman I've ever met," Dr. Fitzhugh said as he shook hands. "What a trouper!"

"Brave, and lovely," Dr. Constantine added with a smile at her.

"Not so lovely now," she said with a sigh. She smiled back. "But it doesn't matter in the least. Now that I've had a taste of Barrera under its new management, I can't wait for some payback. I memorized the layout of the military headquarters," she added. "I don't know, maybe it's the same as it was when the general had power, but I kept my eyes and my ears open and I asked questions. Our jailer was very kind. He told me a lot."

Rourke's eyes narrowed. "We'll look out for him," he promised.

"Sapara's computers are still running the old systems," Dr. Fitzhugh offered. "I have a student who can hack anything. I thought of using something like the Stuxnet virus…"

Grange burst out laughing. "Great minds running in the same direction," he replied. "We have an Irish computer whiz kid with our unit who just engineered a similar virus using an old gaming computer, one of the tower ones. He's ready to introduce it to Sapara's military computers. And we have another group poised to sabotage the media."

"I do love a good fight!" Dr. Fitzhugh chuckled. "By

the way, some of our students have been helping fight the oppression. Most of them are taking final exams now, but they'd help if we asked them. They know the city very well."

"I'd rather not involve innocent civilians right now, unless I have to," Grange replied. "I'm grateful for the offer, though, and we may have to resort to other methods. Battle plans change quickly."

"Indeed they do, young man." He looked around at his companions. "I must say, we look quite the band of ragamuffins," he joked.

"We survived," Clarisse reminded them, smiling as she sipped broth. "It doesn't matter how we look."

"I suppose so, but I should love a change of clothing." Dr. Fitzhugh sighed. "I fear I may begin to offend olfactory senses soon." He sniffed his sleeve and made a face. Everyone laughed.

Grange looked at Peg. "You should go home."

"Yes," Clarisse said.

"Absolutely," Maddie agreed.

Peg gave them all a long, stubborn stare. She folded her arms and sat down.

Grange shook his head. "That's my girl," he said, and she blushed, because he really meant it. She laughed and the way he looked at her made her heart soar. Here they were, together at last, and surrounded by a whole army of people in a place where *privacy* was an unknown word. She could have groaned out loud.

Grange saw that frustration, and shared it. But his pride in her was visible. Like his hunger, burning in the back of his dark, intent eyes. "Okay, baby," he said in a velvety tone that sent warm shivers down her spine.

"You stay. But you stay here with Maria," he said emphatically. "You aren't going to war."

She grinned at him. "Whatever you say. As long as I get to stay."

He smiled back. "What a woman," he murmured, and his eyes stared into hers for so long that she blushed. She was having uncomfortable sensations in a place she couldn't talk about. Her body seemed to have a whole knowledge of things her mind had never experienced. She wanted nothing more than a big wide hammock with Grange in it, like in that erotic dream she'd had back home. She wondered if she dared tell him about it? Well, she had time to think about that. Thinking was the only thing she could do at the moment, since she seemed to be living in the Grand Central Station of Barrera, she mused, and smiled warmly at the people around her. She did seem to have a knack for making friends, she thought.

GRANGE SCROUNGED A pencil and scraps of paper and had Clarisse draw the approximate positions of the guards in the headquarters building. She and the two professors discussed the changing of the guard and the equipment in Sapara's office. The men knew more than Clarisse, because they'd been incarcerated for several months.

"He had a lot of radio equipment in his office, I remember," Clarisse said, a little wearily. "A wide-screen television, entertainment system, even a gaming computer."

"Manaus is the center of the electronics industry in this part of the continent," Dr. Fitzhugh remarked. "I love fiddling with computers. It's a free-trade zone, so taxes aren't high and the equipment is reasonably priced."

Clarisse had her hands wrapped around a warm ceramic bowl of herbal tea. The scent of it was calming. She listened to the conversation of the people around her as if in a fog.

Rourke sat down beside her. He took out his pocketknife and began to whittle at a thick piece of wood he'd found.

"You used to do that in Africa, when I was a child," Clarisse said quietly. "I still have the swan you carved for me when I was ten."

"You were a game kid, Tat," he mused. "You followed me places where some of the other boys wouldn't even go. Never lagged behind, never complained. Not even when I let you get snakebitten..."

"I walked right into it," she interrupted. "You couldn't have stopped it."

He whittled some more.

It was a companionable silence for a minute or two.

"The doctor said you'd need plastic surgery on those cuts. They must be deep." His voice was angry.

"Battle scars," she said, noting his eye patch. "You won't wear a glass eye, I won't have plastic surgery."

He raised both eyebrows.

"I earned my scars," she said, and her face set in hard lines. She looked down into her tea. "I've spent my life playing at reporting, doing lighthearted interviews with men in the field, emphasizing the human interest bit." She drew in a breath. "But now I have some idea of what it's really like, behind the scenes." She looked up at him. "It's a nasty business."

He nodded slowly. "They give AK-47s to boys ten years old, drug them up and send them out to kill and die. That's the real world."

She shivered.

"Good reason to go back home and write a gossip column from now on."

She sipped tea. "No. I'm going to find a way to do some good in the world with my life."

"You're a bit old to study nursing."

She glanced at him coolly. "I'm a photojournalist. You may think I don't take it seriously. I do. I could get on with one of the wire services, Reuters maybe, and do some in-depth coverage of issues like those soldier children."

He actually seemed to go pale. "That's insane. Do you have any idea what might happen to you under combat conditions?"

She pulled aside her blouse and showed him one of the scars above the cup of her bra, an angry red with the black stitches. "Yes," she said. "As a matter of fact, I do."

He winced. It hurt him, in ways he could never reveal to her, to see those wounds. He'd pushed her away, ridiculed her and verbally attacked her for years. He pretended to hold her in utter contempt for her rich lifestyle and her morals. The truth was that he didn't dare get close to her. He knew things that she didn't. There was a secret. He couldn't bring himself to disclose it. But it meant that he could never be anything except a casual friend, or an enemy. Given the choice, it was easier, much easier, if she hated him. So he used hostility to keep her from seeing through the mask.

He went back to his whittling. His expression was harder than ever. "Suit yourself. I don't guess it would bother you at that, being assaulted by men. Not with your history."

She was too worn, too sick, to strike back. It was a

vicious remark. Once, she'd have hit him for that. But she was tired and depressed, still shivery from her ordeal. "Think what you please, Rourke."

He hated himself for what he'd said to her. She'd been savaged and he hadn't been able to save her. He closed his eye briefly and then went back to work on the piece of wood he was carving. He didn't say anything else.

Clarisse wondered at his odd behavior. He couldn't go five minutes without offering her some terrible insult. But let something bad happen to her, the death of her family or her capture and torture by a madman, and he was first on the scene. It had always been like that. It made no real sense. He did hate her. It was impossible not to know it.

While she was puzzling out those things, the roar of another jeep sounded in the pleasant silence. It pulled up beside the other jeep and three men got out.

One was tall, with a broad face and wavy black hair. He was in front. All three wore army fatigues.

Rourke and Grange were on their feet in a flash, and armed, but they reholstered their weapons as General Emilio Machado walked into camp.

"Have we moved our headquarters here?" he asked in a pleasant, but exasperated, tone, spreading his hands expressively.

There was a faint gasp. "Emilio?" Maddie went forward, hesitantly.

The look on the general's face was indescribable. "Maddie! You're alive!"

She was going to make some laughing comment when he shot forward and scooped her up against him, going around and around with her, laughing as he hugged her and hugged her.

"*¡Dios mío!* I thought they'd caught you and killed you!" he exclaimed, breathless with relief. He put her down and framed her face in his big hands. "How happy I am to see you," he whispered. He bent, as if he might kiss her, but aware of his surroundings, he drew back, quickly. "Thank God you escaped."

Maddie managed a weak smile. Her knees were weak from his enthusiastic greeting. Perhaps he did feel something for her!

She laughed. "Yes, I'm alive. I've been hiding at another village, closer to the ruins. Maria sent for me when Enrique was shot. I took out the bullet. That old military training comes in handy when you can't get a doctor on the spot. A runner brought Dr. Carvajal here from Manaus, so he was on hand to patch up Clarisse."

"Clarisse was shot?"

"No," Maddie said with anger in her clear voice. "She was tortured."

Machado ground his teeth together. "Atrocities. More atrocities. Is there no end to Sapara's brutality!"

He joined the others at the campfire. "Four of you?" he exclaimed, noting the two professors, Peg, and Clarisse.

"The two missing professors," Clarisse said, introducing them with a smile.

"Poor little thing. What did they do to you?" he asked her, noting the bloodstains on her blouse.

"A bit of torture," she said, shrugging it off and trying not to break down again under that obvious compassion. "Nothing serious. Sapara wanted to make sure I was only here to do a story about the missing professors and that I wasn't harboring any other secrets." She smiled with pure malice. "He didn't get a word out of me about you."

"How did you escape?" the general wanted to know, and dropped down to sit beside them.

"With the help of an old jailer…"

"Romero." Machado sighed. "One of my good old friends. They will kill him for helping you…"

"Not bloody likely," Dr. Fitzhugh remarked smugly. "I hit him with a baseball bat and left him lying unconscious half in my cell. It's all right," he added, holding up a hand for Machado's protest, "I studied medicine before I switched to botany. I knew where to hit him to do the least damage. Better a headache than a bullet."

"I agree," Machado said. "He is a good and kind man. I am surprised that Sapara allowed him to remain."

"Couldn't get anybody else to do the job," Dr. Constantine said grimly. "He went through ten jailers and finally brought Romero back in desperation. He's made so many enemies that he can't keep staff."

"That is good news for us," Machado said.

"Very good news," Grange agreed. "We need to find some way to make contact with those two men you sent into the city to seek out Lopez."

"Perhaps the doctor might have an idea," Clarisse piped in, smiling at the doctor from Manaus. "Don't you have a cousin in Medina?"

Dr. Carvajal responded, "Several cousins. I will get word to one of them whom I can trust not to talk. He will find out for us."

"He will need to contact General Domingo Lopez," Machado informed him. "And tell him to come back to the village here. That should not arouse suspicions. Domingo will help. I had plans to get him out of the country, fearing that Sapara would kill him. But Domingo knew so much about the military operation that he was indispensable. Sapara is a politician. He has never even shot a gun. When he helped me take Barrera, he stayed behind the lines to speak to reporters," he added coldly. "I even made him my political leader. It never occurred to me that he would betray me. I didn't think he had the nerve."

"The new dictator has an affection for the coca leaf," the doctor said coldly. "He uses it more and more. This, also, can work to our advantage. My cousin can ask Lopez about the routine of Sapara."

"We know he's building some palatial mansion outside the city," Clarisse mused. "Presumably he visits it from time to time to see the progress."

"Brilliant!" Machado remarked.

She smiled. "I'm getting smarter all the time. Must have something to do with getting hit on the head with a bullet."

Rourke didn't comment. But his dark eye winced as he glanced at her.

WHILE THE OTHERS sat and talked, Grange went for a walk with Peg around the village clearing. It was dark and the sounds of the jungle were close. A sharp animal cry split the silence.

"Jaguar," Grange said easily. "It isn't likely to come into the camp. They don't like fire." He looked down at her, but it was so dark that he couldn't see her eyes. "Night is really night down here in the tropics," he whispered. He pulled her close. "That's a good thing and a bad thing," he murmured as his head bent. "The good is that nobody can see us do this…"

CHAPTER ELEVEN

PEG WENT UP on tiptoe, trying to get closer to Grange's devouring mouth. His arms were bruising, he held her so tightly. It was as if he couldn't get enough of her warm, soft lips.

"I missed you," he ground out. "More than I ever dreamed I could. And you show up here...!" He kissed her harder.

She sighed, smiling under the warm, soft crush of his lips. "Are you sorry?" she whispered, laughing faintly.

"My body isn't," he groaned. "Just my brain."

"Tell your brain to shut up," she suggested, and pressed closer.

His big, lean hands caught her upper thighs and tugged her hips against his. He shivered with the movement. His body was aroused, painfully aroused, and here they were in a native village with not one private place on offer to do something about his condition.

"If only," he growled, "there was a bed somewhere!"

"There's hammocks," she whispered, shivering along with him. She felt a hot, violent swelling in her body. She wanted to take her clothes off. What an odd feeling!

"I don't think you can make love in a hammock," he bit off against her eager mouth.

"Yes, you can," she whispered urgently as she felt his

hands slide over the tops of her thighs and rivet her to the growing hardness of his body. "I had this dream..."

"This dream," he repeated huskily. "Tell me about it."

"I don't know," she hesitated.

"There's nothing you can't tell me," he murmured against her mouth. "Come on."

"You were lying in a hammock in a pair of shorts and I had on this Hawaiian sarong thing," she said. She trembled as his hands pressed harder, grinding her against him. "You untied it and threw it on the floor and took off your shorts..."

"And then?" he whispered breathlessly, his mouth opening suddenly on an exposed breast.

She had to fight to think. "And then I said you couldn't do that in a hammock and I woke up," she said, flustered.

He chuckled.

"But I think I really woke up because I've never done, well, that, before and I don't know exactly what happens. I do, sort of, from books and movies. But not really."

"I'd love to show you exactly what happens," he whispered. "I haven't done it, either, but I'm absolutely positive that we'll do it right the first time."

She laughed delightedly through the shivers. "Are we going to?"

"Yes. As soon as we're married."

She drew back a breath and looked up at him with her heart in her eyes, only barely visible in the semidark night. "Married?"

He nodded solemnly. "It takes a brave woman to come into a combat zone just to see her man," he said huskily. "Besides all that, you cook like an angel and I want you so much that I can barely stand up and walk when you're around."

"Really?" she exclaimed happily.

He moved her hips against his. "Can't you tell?"

"Uh, yes, I did, uh, notice." She was flustered once more, and buried her face against him, laughing.

"Oh, God, I wish there was some horizontal surface I could lay you down on," he groaned, bending to her mouth in a fever of passion. "I couldn't stop. And here we are, surrounded by people…if we just had a hammock, even!"

"But there aren't any hammocks here that don't have people in them!" she added on what sounded almost like a sob.

His hands went under her blouse, pushing her bra out of his way so that he could feel the soft, warm flesh. There were hard, tight little nubs that excited him. His thumbs rubbed over them and Peg arched and gasped at the surge of pleasure his touch produced.

Her own hands tugged his shirt out from under his belt and found their way up to the thick mat of hair that covered his broad, muscular chest.

"Peg…" He tried to protest, but it felt too good. He slid her shirt up and pulled her against his bare skin. The result was explosive.

She could hardly breathe. All she could think of now was relief. There had to be some end to this painful tension, some way to end it, some way to make it never end. Her mind whirled around and around as his mouth opened over hers and forced her lips apart. His tongue delved softly inside, into that sweet, warm darkness even as his hands slid under her slacks in back and down to find other soft skin.

"Yes," she choked. "Yes, oh, yes, please…!"

"Yes," he groaned.

"No," came an amused voice from just beyond the darkness. "Absolutely not."

They froze in place. They looked toward the voice. A light was shining, thankfully, at their feet instead of any higher.

"You have to come back to the campfire. The children are getting an education that they're far too young for," Clarisse told them.

She turned the flashlight around. Where the two would-be lovers hadn't heard or seen anything, about ten children were in the brush just watching and giggling.

"Oh, my goodness," Peg said unsteadily. She moved back from Grange and righted her clothing.

"Talk about sex education in the raw," Grange muttered. He burst out laughing as he tucked his shirt back in. "Caught like deer in the headlights!" he declared.

Peg was flushed, but she laughed, too. "Blame it on the night," she murmured.

"You should come back to the campfire," Clarisse said in a gentle tone. "Maria said that one of the men was killed by a jaguar only a few days ago, and they couldn't find it to kill it. We don't want the commander of our troops eaten, now, do we?" she added with a wicked grin.

They moved back into view of the campfire so that their faces were visible.

"Sorry," Peg said, clearing her throat. "We were talking."

"In the oldest language known to man," Clarisse added with an amused glance at Grange, who actually flushed, high on his cheekbones.

"We are all human," Machado reminded Grange. He smiled as he looked at an embarrassed Peg. "Nothing to worry about, I assure you."

"Nobody's paying attention anyway," Clarisse told the couple in a low tone, nodding toward O'Bailey, who was telling an ancient tale from Ireland about the standing stones to a rapt two professors, plus Maria and Dr. Carvajal. "He's quite good at storytelling." She leaned closer to them, so as not to interrupt the flow of the story. "I'm also told that he's dangerous behind a computer keyboard."

"That's the one?" Peg asked. "The one who engineered the virus?"

Grange nodded. "O'Bailey is one of our best newcomers. Eb Scott trained him, too. He's quite good in the field, never gets rattled."

"I'll bet I'd go to pieces," Peg said, glancing at Clarisse. "I don't know that I could have done what you did," she added with affection. "You're so brave."

Clarisse hugged her gently. "My dear, you have a courage all your own, and a rare, rare ability to make friends with even the most hostile human beings." She pointed at herself. "Case in point."

"You aren't hostile," she protested.

"But I was." She smiled.

Peg stared at her for a minute and then said, "We can all be hard to get along with, when we live through tragedies," she said gently. "The important thing is to get through them without damaging ourselves too much in the process."

"Old thoughts for a young mind," the general said softly.

She grinned. "I'm an old mind in a young body."

"I must agree," the general said. "Is there coffee, do you think?" he added heavily. "It will be a long night. I fear for my scouts. It seems that Sapara may have captured them."

"They won't talk, if he did," Grange said quietly. "They're trained to resist even the most intense interrogation methods."

Machado didn't reply. He knew more about torture than even Grange did. His early life had been spent roaming the world, hiring out his talents to various governments. He didn't use torture as a tool in his presidency, but he'd had to speak harshly to Sapara for torturing a media person just before his political comrade usurped his government. Sapara and his people made an art of it.

A small, dark man wearing nothing except what seemed to be a spandex bathing suit came into the circle of light. His hair was cut in a circle high above his ears and he had tattoos on his skin, visible in the firelight. He was carrying a bow that was much taller than he was, with a handful of arrows that had to be five feet long each.

Maria glanced at Machado, who got up and went to talk to the short man. Incredibly Machado spoke the native tongue of the visitor. He spoke, listened while the other man talked, then spoke again. He smiled and nodded. The visitor left.

"Thank God and the Holy Mother and all the saints!" Machado exclaimed. "Our two missing scouts turned up at their village." He gestured toward the native who was already running out of the camp. "They did contact Domingo Lopez, but they didn't get back to us in the camp because they thought they were being followed. They diverted to escape their pursuers. They've become guests of the Yamami, another branch of Maria's tribe north of here, where they'll be safe until they're needed. I'm going there now."

"I'll come with you," Grange said.

"Me, too." Rourke got up.

O'Bailey started to rise, but they waved him down.

"The fewer of us, the better," Machado told him. "It will be difficult to get through as it is. We'll have to take a boat." He turned and spoke to one of the male village elders, who nodded and spoke. "It will be risky at night, but this man knows the river and the trouble spots. He'll get us through. It isn't that far."

"Here, then, take this," O'Bailey said, handing him a handheld shortwave radio. "We're using a frequency that they can't monitor. If you have to talk, limit it to one or two words and cut it off immediately so they can't track it." He grinned. "Phones would have to bounce off a satellite and they might monitor those. But they won't be able to monitor anything for long. I'm ready to introduce the virus, whenever you give me the word. After that, they won't be able to launch a missile, order an attack or even speak to one another."

"You're a wonder, O'Bailey." Grange chuckled.

"Here's a pad and pen, write me girlfriend and tell her!" O'Bailey drawled.

They all laughed.

"We'll give you the word as soon as we reach the outskirts of the city," Machado told the Irishman grimly. "There is a tunnel, one whose secret I never had occasion to share with nonmilitary personnel like Sapara, thank God. It was used for movement of troops and weapons, and only I have the codes to unlock it."

"That's a real blessing," Rourke said quietly. "I was wondering how you meant to get into the city undetected. I should have known you'd have something foxy under your sleeve, mate," he told Machado.

"I always play my cards close to the chest," Machado replied, flashing white teeth. "This one strategic secret may save us a bloody revolution inside Medina. Assuming that the electronic unit is still functioning," he added quietly. "It is well protected from the elements, though, so I am hopeful."

"If it doesn't work, however," Rourke said quietly, patting his sidearm, "we can handle it. Several of our men were in Baghdad during the war. They're familiar with urban combat."

"I hope they don't have to use it," Grange said. "But it's best to be prepared."

"You be prepared and come back safe," Peg said to him. "I wish I could come with you."

He kissed her forehead. "So do I, baby, but you'd be a liability."

"If it's any comfort, I can't go, either," Maddie told her, putting an affectionate arm around her. "I'm far too rusty to function in a combat group. Now I mostly just dig up stuff," she added.

"Very important 'stuff,'" Machado said, and looked at her with warmth and real interest. "When I regain power, you can go back to work."

Maddie smiled a little shyly. "I'll look forward to that."

"So will I," Machado told her, and his dark eyes stared into hers for so long that she blushed.

"Can I speak to you for a moment?" Clarisse asked Rourke quietly.

"For just a moment," Rourke bit off. "We're pressed for time." He followed her out of earshot of the others. "All right, Tat, what is it?" he asked impatiently.

She took off the cross she always wore under her blouse, reached up and secured it around his neck. "For luck," she said.

He frowned, fingering it. "You're not religious. You couldn't be, with your lifestyle," he said venomously.

"Think what you like. My mother gave it to me. I never take it off. It's saved my life in some bad places," she added, recalling once that a Christian general in a Muslim area had saved her from a bullet when he noted it, during an uprising she'd covered in Africa.

Rourke's lips made a thin line. "I don't believe in all that stuff," he said angrily, and went to remove it.

She put her hand on his chest, over the cross. "Just wear it. Would you? You can bring it back to me when you've secured the city." She didn't look at him as she spoke.

His dark eye stared at her bent head, shining like gold in the light from the campfire. She was incredibly beautiful. But her mother had told him something, years ago, when he started to become really interested in her. It had caused him no end of heartache. Clarisse didn't know, couldn't know. Her mother had sworn that she would never tell her daughter the truth. Clarisse was the one woman on earth he couldn't afford to encourage. He should take off the necklace and throw it at her. He almost did. But her concern, so curiously expressed, gave him pause.

"All right. I'll wear it."

She managed a smile. "Good luck."

He met her eyes for a split second, held them, and hated himself for doing it. The expression on her face made him want to hurt something. He turned away quickly and rejoined the others.

"We'll be back before you know it," Grange assured a worried Peg. "But no matter what happens, you stay put."

"Awww, shucks, foiled again. I thought I'd follow you on foot along the riverbank when you weren't watching."

"I can find some rope to tie you up, dear," Clarisse warned. "Even if I have to cut up a hammock."

Peg made a face at her. "Be careful out there," she told Grange and Rourke.

"I make friends everywhere I go," Rourke said with a rakish grin.

Clarisse didn't look at him. She turned her attention back to the campfire, where the professors were entreating O'Bailey to tell them some more Irish lore.

"We won't be too long," Grange assured Peg. He looked down into her eyes for a long moment. "You're my whole life now," he whispered so that no one else could hear. "Stay safe. If I lose you, I have nothing worth living for."

She sobbed against his mouth. "That goes double for me! Don't you dare get hurt!"

He laughed and hugged her close. "That's my girl."

He bent to kiss her, but very briefly, before he followed Rourke and Machado and the native villager into the forest.

IT WAS ALMOST dawn when there were sounds of movement in the distance.

Peg and Clarisse crawled sleepily out of their hammocks and went outside. Maddie and the two male professors were already in the clearing near the center of the village, listening. It wasn't a loud sound, but it was noticeable. The natives had alerted the visitors.

"Sapara's men?" Peg asked worriedly.

"It's coming from the river," Maddie said. "Sapara would be coming from the north, more or less."

"Could it be a riverboat?" Peg continued.

"A small one of some sort, possibly. I've seen some strange vehicles on the river," Maddie said.

Clarisse didn't speak. She just watched.

A few minutes passed before a tall, distinguished-looking man wearing khakis came walking into camp with a party of native people.

"So it is true," he exclaimed. "I didn't believe Garcia when he told me!"

The three women stood up, staring at the man curiously. But Maddie got up, smiling, and went to meet him. They shook hands.

"Good to see you again, Rev," she said. She motioned him into the circle. "This is Reverend Blake Harvey," she said, smiling. "He does missionary work here for a union of Protestant churches in America. This is Clarisse and that's Peg." She indicated the two women. "Clarisse is a photojournalist for one of the larger American newsmagazines, and Peg's here to talk to me about the ruins." She was concealing their true purpose, not to mention the upcoming revolution nearby.

"A dangerous place, this," Reverend Harvey noted. He sat down by the campfire, smiled at Maria and was given a bowl of the wonderful native soup she'd just prepared. He thanked her as he sipped it. "Compared to what I've been eating lately, this is a feast," he observed. "Garcia's people eat most of their monkey meat raw and what they drink isn't compatible with my stomach," he told them. "They give me the best they have, which is a marvelous testament to the kindness of strangers in a strange land."

"I've never met such generous people," Peg said in her soft drawl. "I've learned so much!"

"Ah, a student?" the reverend asked.

Peg hesitated, nervous of going further. She didn't want to say anything that might, even slightly, affect the success of Machado's mission.

"In fact, yes, she's a foreign exchange student of mine." Dr. Fitzhugh came to her rescue, coming forward with a smile to offer the smiling lie. "I'm Dr. Fitzhugh," he said, shaking hands with the missionary. "I teach in Medina. At least, I did. I was arrested for sedition." He chuckled. "But Dr. Constantine and I—he's sitting over there learning a new dialect—managed to escape, with some help from our friend." He pointed to Clarisse.

The reverend noted her stained blouse and frowned. "Young lady, have you been hurt?" he asked worriedly. "I do have some medical training…"

"Unnecessary, but thank you," Clarisse said with a smile. "Dr. Carvajal from Manaus treated me. He had to go back to the city for an emergency," she added.

"A good man," Reverend Harvey said, sipping more of the soup from the ceramic bowl in his hands. "He came to the village a few weeks ago to help a young woman in labor with her first child. A boy," he added. "Fat and healthy and beautiful."

"We have heard of you," Maria told the reverend. "They say you walked into bullets when the men from the Sapara government tried to take the land from the Yamami," she added, naming the tribe for only the second time in Peg's hearing. Later she would learn that they were an offshoot of another tribe, the Yanomamo. This splinter, largely family, group, and another offshoot of it where Machado's scouts were staying, had moved away from the main body of the tribe and set up house-keeping in Barrera two generations past. They still had trade with other native tribes, but they lived mostly to themselves. They preserved the ancient traditions of the forest people and resisted the attempts of modern industrialists to move them off their land in order to use it for oil extraction. Sapara had threatened to destroy Maria's entire tribe if they continued to resist. It was one more reason for Machado to get the usurper out of office.

Peg knew that Ritter Oil Corporation would never agree to the destruction of native people to bring about the oil development. So she told Maddie and Maddie told O'Bailey how to get in touch with Ritter's head of security, Colby Lane, in Houston. That process was underway. Once Mr. Ritter knew what was going on in Barrera, regardless of the outcome of the attempt to unseat Sapara, there would be no danger to Maria's tribe.

MEANWHILE, GRANGE, MACHADO, Rourke and the natives approached the outskirts of Medina quietly and under cover of darkness, through the jungle, to a makeshift camp with a large tent under heavy camouflage. There they met up with the missing scouts, two worn-looking men in camouflage gear. They were accompanied by what looked like twenty Yamami natives, all carrying extremely long bows and arrows, and painted for war.

"Budding commandos," one of the scouts said with a wide grin, indicating the natives. "They know the jungle intimately. We appealed to them for aid when we escaped from the city and they brought us here the long way around to throw Sapara's men off the scent. They say there's a tunnel nearby leading back into the city, but it has some sort of electronic lock on it."

Machado chuckled. "Indeed it does. I placed it there. The tunnel was built by my predecessor as president, and it's how I entered the city the first time to overthrow him. I never told Sapara about it. I kept it as one of my top military secrets. Only Domingo Lopez knows that it even exists."

"That's a stroke of luck," Grange said.

"A stroke of luck, indeed," Machado said grimly. "Because if we can get inside the city, to Sapara's office undetected, we can seize the government without having to fire a single shot."

"Well, maybe one or two shots," Rourke piped in as he joined them.

"This will work," Grange said. "I'm sure of it."

"My friend," Machado replied, "I am also sure of it. Now if the rain will just hold off for a few minutes…"

Even as he spoke, the rain started coming down in bucketfuls all over again. Machado laughed. Everyone ran inside to avoid being drenched.

THE HUT WHERE Maria and the three women were eating had a huge pole in the center holding up the roof, which was thatched with some sort of palm leaves. Peg had been fascinated with its intricate construction, and more fascinated with the fact that the women built a cooking fire on the dirt floor right inside the hut. It did get a bit smoky, but it was efficient and rather charming. Another native woman had a loom near the center pole, and she was working quickly and efficiently at a beautifully colored blanket.

"You look worried," Clarisse said, noting Peg's frown.

"It's my dad," she replied. "I told him I'd be away for a couple of days. He'll be worried."

"We'll talk to O'Bailey," Clarisse promised her. "He's a whiz with computers. He'll get word to your father."

"Okay!"

O'Bailey was sitting in front of his computer, which was powered by a small portable generator. He grinned at the women. "Wouldn't dare use this any closer to the command post. Sound carries in the jungle. Even two men talking in a whisper can give away a position." He indicated the computer screen. "I'm just waiting for the general to give the word, and Sapara won't be able to talk to anybody."

"Good man," Clarisse stated. "We're wondering if you can get a message to somebody in Jacobsville, Texas, for Peg. She thinks her father will be worrying, since he doesn't know where she is."

"In fact, I know a ham operator in Jacobsville. Grange used him to send a message to Peg once, I believe."

"Yes!" Peg exclaimed. "I'd forgotten. I never knew who the man was, but he told me that Winslow was safe and missed me." She laughed out loud. "Could you get in touch with him and have him tell my father that I'm all right and I'll be home soon?"

"I can do that. In fact, I'll do it right now while I don't have anything else to monitor."

He set up his equipment, made the call on scramble and told the man at the other end to contact Peg's father. "He'll be glad to do it, he said," he told Peg when he finished. He grinned. "Good thing we didn't tell him where you are, ya?"

She burst out laughing again. "Oh, yes. Although I'm going to catch hell when I get home," Peg said with resignation.

"I'll go with you and explain it myself," Clarisse said

firmly. "I'm the cause of all your recent troubles. I have to try to make it up to you."

"Are you nuts?" Peg exclaimed. "I've gotten to live in a five-star hotel, travel down the Amazon in a boat, live in a native village and see the culture firsthand, participate, sort of, anyway, in a revolution to restore freedom to an oppressed people—and you want to make it up to me?"

Clarisse hugged her warmly. "You make me feel as if I did something worthwhile, when I had really bad intentions. My only excuse is that I didn't know you at all." She looked at the younger woman with pure affection. "Nobody who knows you could ever hurt you deliberately. You're too sweet."

Peg grinned and flushed a little. "Thanks."

"Look!" Maddie said suddenly.

They all turned and Enrique came to the central campfire, wobbling a little. He smiled sheepishly. "Sorry about what happened," he told Clarisse, wincing when he saw her stained blouse. "I really messed up."

"No, you didn't," Clarisse said gently, and smiled. "You couldn't have anticipated a military patrol. We never even saw them."

"I would love to have a conversation with them," Enrique said as he sat down beside his mother and smilingly accepted a bowl of broth from the steaming pot over the fire. "A very intense conversation. So, could someone loan me a pistol?" he added to O'Bailey with a grin.

O'Bailey chuckled. "I'll be glad to. But I think we may have a change of government soon. Best to cross your fingers."

"Mine are all crossed," Peg said, and demonstrated. They laughed.

IT WAS A great relief to find that the tunnel's control unit was still functional. Machado remembered the electronic code that unlocked the massive steel door into the tunnel, although it had been years since he used it. He grinned at his men as the lock gave way and the door swung back.

"Amazing," Grange said admiringly. "I have trouble remembering my own phone number."

"Wouldn't have mattered if you'd forgotten," Rourke drawled with a smile. "There isn't a lock made, electronic or otherwise, that I can't get past. Where does this tunnel lead exactly?" Rourke asked. "And how far do we have to go?"

"It leads directly to military headquarters," Machado said, "and emerges into the basement through what looks like a solid wall. My predecessor had it built by German engineers. It's formidable, and deep enough to survive all but the newest bombs."

"I hope nobody knows we're coming," one of the scouts remarked. "General Lopez said that he was planning a diversion. When we're ready, I have the frequency to contact him."

"Which I sent to O'Bailey." Rourke looked at Machado in the darkness of the tunnel, lit only by a small flashlight after the gate was closed and locked behind them. "Whenever you're ready, I'll give him the code to fry Sapara's computer communications systems and send the signal to Lopez."

Machado looked at his men. Grange was as grim as he was, himself. Rourke never seemed to be rattled. Brad Dunagan, the second-in-command to Grange, was tall and blond and never seemed to speak unless asked about something, but he was a good man. The two scouts, Carson and Hale, were both of Native American ancestry, and Carson had black hair that came down to his waist in back. He'd loosened it when they came into the tunnel. Machado smiled. It was something he'd read about in books on Native American warfare of the past; Plains warriors going into battle always let their hair down.

"Are we ready?" Machado asked his companions.

The Yamami came forward, carrying their incredibly long bows and arrows. One of the scouts, who'd learned their dialect, passed along the question. They grinned and nodded enthusiastically.

"I'm always ready," Rourke said.

Grange smiled. "Same here. Give the word, General."

Machado smiled faintly. He drew his sidearm. "Gentlemen, *¡vámonos!*"

O'BAILEY HEARD A tone come over the computer. Grimly he started typing. A minute later, he hit Enter.

He wondered whether or not to tell the company around the campfire that all hell was about to break loose in Medina. Peg and Clarisse and Maddie were smiling as they listened to one of the reverend's stories about his first days on the Amazon as a young missionary. They looked at peace and happy. No need to turn those smiles upside down, he decided at last. He turned his attention back to the computer screen, wishing the invasion Godspeed.

THE STREETS WERE dark. Medina was, in many ways, more medieval than modern as a city. It was poverty-stricken—more so since Sapara had overthrown the existing government—and there was no money left for improvements to the city's utilities. There were no streetlights, no public buses, apparently no public transport of any kind. The small city had unpaved streets and they were a mess with rain coming down, sporadically drizzling and then in bucket loads. There were lights in some small houses and music and drunken laughter came out of a bar they passed.

"Don't they have a police force here?" Grange asked under his breath as they walked, single file, down an alley that led to the military headquarters building.

"It's in there," Machado said grimly, having glanced inside the bar. "Dead drunk."

"That's one thing in our favor," Rourke murmured quietly.

"Wait here for a minute," Machado said. He moved toward the rear door of the building, hesitated and opened it.

He eased through to the interior, going slowly. Grange, unasked, moved in behind him with his sidearm raised by his right ear and the safety off.

As they turned a corner, past two closed doors, an old, heavyset man came toward them.

He stopped, caught his breath and stood very still, waiting to be shot.

But Machado motioned to him quickly, urgently, and he moved forward into the dark hallway.

"It is you?" the old man exclaimed. "It is really you?"

Machado embraced the old man. "It is, old friend, and very soon you will be back in a position of authority. Where is Sapara?"

Romero looked around cautiously. "Upstairs in his office, with a woman," he said with disgust. "He has his two thugs, Jose and Miguel, standing outside to 'protect' him from intrusion."

"Hey, Carson," Grange called softly.

The man with long, loosened black hair came forward. He looked at Grange.

Grange only nodded grimly.

Carson showed a flash of white teeth and pulled an enormous Bowie knife out of its sheath.

"Not Miguel," Rourke bit off. "He's mine."

"He will be the bigger of the two men, *señor,*" Romero told the tall, lithe man in camo gear.

Carson glanced at Rourke. "Something personal?" he asked in a deep whisper.

Rourke nodded. "Tortured a woman. A friend of mine."

Carson's face hardened. "I understand. I won't be long."

He went around the corner and up a flight of stairs so silently that nobody heard him move.

Just then, two men came in through the front door of the building, the part that led to the jail. They were Sapara's men and they were running.

Romero went to meet them while the Americans melted against the wall.

"What is it?" Romero asked innocently.

"Our entire communications grid just went down," one of the men said in Spanish. "We have to tell the *commandante...!*"

CHAPTER TWELVE

"ACTUALLY, WE'D RATHER you didn't, mate," Rourke drawled as he dropped the first one to the ground with a hard right to the diaphragm.

"It's none of his business anyway." Grange chuckled as he dropped the second man.

Upstairs there was a sudden thud, followed by an even harder and louder thud that made several rhythmic thumps.

The Americans rushed into the hall to find the big man, Miguel, lying at the foot of the steps with a blank stare at the men just joining him.

He started to speak, but Rourke had him gagged and tied up in seconds. "I'll deal with you shortly," he said, and in a tone that chilled.

"Hurry," Machado said, taking the lead up the stairs. "We cannot afford to let Sapara escape."

But there was no hope of that. Carson, the Plains Indian, had the other guard hog-tied on the floor, the door open, and two dazed people, wrapped in a blanket, staring up at him over the sights of a .45 ACP from a thick llama skin on the floor of the massive, luxurious office.

"Carson, you're a wonder!" Grange exclaimed, patting the other man on the back.

"Tell Eb Scott," the tall man drawled. "I need a raise."

"Machado!" Arturo Sapara blurted out. His face was flushed and he looked stoned.

"You were not expecting me, I see," Machado said coldly. "The first lesson you should have learned is to expect retribution."

Sapara struggled to his feet, leaving the embarrassed woman to struggle into the furry llama skin he'd left behind. "I can explain!" he began, and moved toward the desk.

Grange was there first. "I'm afraid you won't be able to do that." He turned off the electronic communications equipment. "You see, we've fried your comms. There won't be any way for your military to respond. In fact, just about now, General Lopez should be telling the armed forces to stand down."

"You cannot do this!" Sapara said furiously. "I am the ruler of a sovereign nation!"

"Not really," Machado replied pleasantly. "You have just been deposed. You will, of course, be spending the next fifty years of your life in prison for high treason. Lopez and most of my men will be happy to testify to this."

"I will testify, too," the forgotten young woman wrapped in llama skins said furiously. "He has my father in jail. He said he would kill him if I did not do what he said. My husband is at home with our children, and I had to leave them weeping. He—" she pointed a shaking finger at Sapara "—came with that butcher Miguel to take me away to sleep with him!"

"I will have them all killed!" Sapara yelled at her.

"You won't be doing any more killing," Grange said quietly. "Carson, escort the former president of Barrera to our least comfortable cell downstairs, if you please. And send Romero to guard him." He smiled as he said it.

"Not that fat pig! I fired him tonight!" Sapara yelled.

"I have rehired him at a better salary and made him my chief of police," Machado said with a grin. "How unfortunate for you."

"I will reclaim my government! The people will rise up against you!" Sapara fumed.

"Not when they see your new palace that was built at their expense. Not when we open the jails and they see what has been done to their countrymen. Not when the world press is allowed into Barrera to see the atrocities you have committed here," Machado said, gathering steam as he spoke. "You will be fortunate not to be tried by the World Court on charges of crimes against humanity!"

Sapara, for once, shut up. He wrapped the sheet closer around his fat body.

"Take him away, please," Machado said, waving a hand. "The very sight of him offends me. And, Rourke, will you find this young woman's clothing, and a place for her to dress, and have one of our men escort her to her home, please?"

"My pleasure," Rourke said. *"Señora?"*

She nodded. "My things are over there." She indicated a door leading to an inner office. "I will be quick."

She went to dress. Machado turned on the communications station and called General Lopez. He was grinning from ear to ear when he finished speaking with him.

"The military massed behind Domingo and detained the handful of troops loyal to Sapara," he told his comrades as he rejoined them. "They are facing treason charges, along with Sapara. Even now, the men are going to secret detention centers to free protestors who have been detained without benefit of counsel." He laughed. "It will be a day for thanksgiving."

Romero came lumbering up the staircase and smiled. "The padre has come," he told them. "He would like permission to reopen the cathedral and say mass."

"He has my blessing," Machado replied. He clapped a hand on Romero's shoulder. "And thank you for your help, my new Chief of Police."

"Me?" Romero's face brightened. "You are serious?"

Machado nodded. "Such courage must be rewarded. You saved the life of a very brave young lady and helped her and the two professors to escape. They have sung your praises for many days."

"The young lady, she will be all right? They did monstrous things to her...!"

"She will be fine," Machado assured him. "She was concerned for you. We all were."

He laughed. "I have a hard head, and it does not hurt anymore. The teacher did know where to hit me." He frowned. "That man with one eye, he has taken Miguel away."

"Has he?" Machado asked nonchalantly.

"Should I inquire where he is going with him?" Romero added.

Grange moved forward and pursed his lips. "I've found that it's unwise to get in Rourke's way from time to time. I should say that this would be one of those times. Clarisse told him that a thug named Miguel was the one who cut her."

Romero nodded grimly. "That is so. He enjoyed torturing people. Especially women." He paused. "Do you think Miguel will be coming back?"

"I daresay he will be providing a meal shortly for one of Barrera's hungrier predators," Machado murmured quietly. "Sadly it is likely to have indigestion for the rest of the day."

"I totally agree," Grange said. He looked around at the motley group of men and smiled. "Great job, guys. Really great. I love a battle with no casualties."

"You will all be awarded bonuses as well," Machado told them, "and positions in my government for any who wish to have them."

One of the older mercs moved next to Carson. "I know of Eb Scott, but I just signed on recently. Didn't he have a kid?"

"Yes," Carson replied.

"Was it a girl or a boy?"

"Yes," Carson said, and walked off.

THERE WAS A lot of conversation after that. Machado and Grange just laughed. It was going to take some time to turn the government around and put things to right. But this was a good beginning.

"The longest journey begins with a single step, doesn't it?" Grange asked, nodding. "This has been one hell of a good step."

"Indeed." He studied the younger man. "I believe there is a young woman waiting for you back at Maria's village."

Grange nodded, his dark eyes sparkling. "How would you like to be best man at my wedding, as soon as we wrap things up here and I can find someone to marry us?" he added.

Machado smiled from ear to ear. "It would be my honor."

GENERAL DOMINGO LOPEZ presented himself in the presidential offices an hour later. He embraced Machado with enthusiasm. He had, in his wake, what seemed like an entire class of college students.

"We're so happy!" one of the girls, American, exclaimed, with a grin for Grange. "Can you help us find our missing professors? Sapara arrested them and put them in prison months ago—"

"Drs. Fitzhugh and Constantine?" Grange interrupted.

"Why, yes," she faltered.

He chuckled. "They're the guests of a Yamami village on the border between Barrera and Amazonas," he said. "In good health and good spirits."

"Oh, thank you!" She hugged Grange and looked up at him speculatively. "I was just wondering…" she began.

He held up a hand. "I'm engaged." He looked briefly uncomfortable, but he smiled to ease the sting of the blunt statement. "She came all the way from Texas just to see me. She's helping in the native village."

"A brave young woman," the college woman exclaimed.

"Very brave… I'm going to marry her to make sure she doesn't do it again."

"You might stay home," came the dry suggestion. "Then she wouldn't have to."

"Good point," he conceded.

"When are the professors coming back?" a male student asked. "And when will the troops get out of our college so that we have some freedom again?"

"Our men are sweeping the city now, to make sure of that," Machado told them. "We are restoring democracy, one building at a time. You should stay off the streets until we are confident that we have full control. There might yet be rebel elements bent on resisting," he added grimly. "I would not like any of you to be hurt."

"Thanks," one of the younger students said, with a flush. "Nice to have you back, General," she added. "It's been difficult since the coup."

"Things will change, and rapidly," Machado promised. "The reign of terror is over. The secret police will be running for cover themselves, now."

"If we see any trying to hide, we'll tell you where they are," the young woman near Grange promised. "Thank you for saving our professors."

"I didn't," Grange told them. "It was a young woman, a photojournalist. She was tortured by one of Sapara's men." There were gasps and murmurs. "She found a way to escape and got the professors out with her."

"I intend to award her a medal for it, when things are back to normal here," Machado said. "She contributed to our bloodless victory."

Rourke had rejoined them. He didn't comment. He was grim and quiet. Grange started to ask about Miguel, but thought better of it.

BACK AT THE village, everyone started running toward the dirt road when they heard the sound of vehicles approaching.

Peg was in the vanguard, her eyes bright with excitement, her heart pounding. When she saw Grange get out of the lead jeep, she ran toward him as fast as she could go. He caught her on the fly, wrapped her up in his arms and kissed her as if there would never be another day on earth for either of them.

She responded with her whole heart, opening her mouth eagerly under the warm crush of his, safe and secure in the embrace of his powerful body. She couldn't get enough of him. The waiting, the worry, combined to make her almost desperate to hold him and touch him, to know that he was still alive, unharmed.

"I was so scared," she whispered frantically.

He chuckled. "Lack of confidence, there," he murmured between kisses.

"Oh, not at all," she protested breathlessly. "I knew you'd never make a mistake, but we knew that Sapara had snipers…"

"They can't hit anything," he replied and kissed her again.

"Hey, get a room, will you?" Rourke cracked as he joined them.

Grange made a face at him. "I'm trying to propose marriage. Go away until you're needed as a witness."

Rourke made a face back then grinned as he left to give them some privacy.

"Marriage?" Peg asked, her eyes wide and soft. "You really meant what you said, before you left the village?"

"Of course," Grange said softly. "Marriage, kids, the whole nine yards. If you're willing—!"

She cut him off midword, her mouth so insistent that he groaned.

"Of course I'll marry you," she whispered, shaken.

"All we need now is a license and a minister…"

"There's a minister sitting by the campfire telling stories to the professors," she said. "He's been here for two days."

Grange blinked. "A minister?"

She nodded. "A missionary. He's very nice."

He smiled. "Trust you to find one in the middle of the jungle."

"I'm resourceful," she said.

"Very. Okay, you want to be married here in jeans

and a sweaty shirt instead of a white lacy dress back home?" he teased.

"I don't want to wait," she whispered again, and flushed as his eyes burned down into hers. "Sorry."

"Don't apologize," he said tautly. "You're not the only one hurting." To emphasize the point, he brought her hips gently against his and let her feel the effect she was having on him. She flushed, but she didn't drop her gaze. "I'm hungry," he whispered. "I've waited for you all my life."

She was breathless. "I've waited for you all mine."

He smiled slowly. "I hope it comes naturally," he murmured in a low whisper. "I suppose we'll learn together."

She pressed close and closed her eyes. "That's the way it should be."

He kissed her hair and took deep breaths until his body lost its tautness. "Let's go talk to that minister."

"Let's," she whispered back.

REVEREND HARVEY SHOOK hands with Grange. "I've heard quite a lot about you, young man. I'm grateful that you returned to this lovely young lady in one piece. Revolutions can be very messy."

Grange nodded grimly. "We were very fortunate. We had a couple of incidents while we were securing Medina, but we'll wrap it all up soon. Then we can empty the prisons of political detainees and let people get their lives back."

"We all owe you and your men a debt of gratitude," Reverend Harvey replied. "I've seen the result of Sapara's rule. It has been traumatic for everyone."

"Especially this oil exploration thing," Enrique said, joining them. He was still weak, but he was recovering nicely from his ordeal. "My mother was afraid the village would be decimated to remove opposition to the drilling."

"Oh, we took care of that," Clarisse said, smiling as she joined the little group. "Tell him, Peg."

"We had O'Bailey get in touch with one of his ham-operator friends in Texas. He called Eugene Ritter, who owns the Ritter Oil Corporation, in Houston," she said, "and told him what was really going on over here. He's got a moratorium on oil drilling in Barrera until General Machado—excuse me, President Machado," Peg corrected with a wide grin, "is back in power and contacts him directly."

"Good work!" Grange said. "Hey, O'Bailey, how would you like to be head of the military communications defense unit here?" he added, calling to the young man.

O'Bailey stood up. "Saints be praised, I'll not wither away in Eb Scott's training school!" he stated. "Truly, I'm flattered by the offer, but I have to think about it for a bit."

"No rush," Grange said. "El Presidente said to make the offer."

"Nice of him," O'Bailey added.

ROURKE PULLED UP behind Grange's jeep and got out. He approached the camp, still distant and grim. He went to Clarisse, unhooked the cross and put it in her hands.

"You look odd," she said, hesitant.

He lifted his chin. "I want you to go home."

She shrugged. "I was born in Manaus," she said. "Technically, South America is my home."

"You know what I mean. Go home to Washington

and give cocktail parties," he added curtly. "Stay out of combat zones."

She lifted an eyebrow. "You can't tell me what to do, Rourke."

His face hardened. "Fine. Get yourself killed."

"And I don't need permission for that, either, thank you." She shifted. "Did they find Miguel?"

His face went even colder. "I found him. He won't be torturing any more women."

"Oh." She didn't know what else to say, whether to thank him or question him or just walk away.

"I would never have wished that on you, Tat," he said in a low, quiet tone. "In spite of our differences."

She averted her eyes. "Thanks."

He drew in a long breath. "Ya."

"Are you going back to the States?" she asked after a minute.

"I don't know where I'm going. I don't plan ahead. It depends on what Mr. Kantor plans for me to do next."

She stared up at him. "You need to have a life that doesn't revolve around what Mr. Kantor wants, Stanton," she said daringly.

His one eye flashed dangerously. "Not your business."

She sighed. "No. You're right. Not my business." She turned away. She didn't speak to him again.

THE CEREMONY WAS short but sweet. Reverend Harvey produced a certificate of marriage, had it witnessed by Rourke and Clarisse and notarized by himself. He had Grange and Peg join hands and he began to read the familiar marriage ceremony from the Bible.

They got to the part about exchanging rings and the couple stared at each other with horror.

"We don't have rings," Grange groaned.

"Rings can come later," Peg said. "I'm getting married without a wedding dress, so we can get married without a ring."

"I'll buy you one the minute we get to a city," Grange promised her. "The best one I can afford."

She smiled up at him, beaming. "I'd settle for the band off a cigar, and you know it."

He chuckled and hugged her. He cleared his throat. "Sorry, Reverend," he said at once, and the amused clergyman finished the ceremony.

"I now pronounce you man and wife," he said at the conclusion. He smiled. "You may kiss the bride."

Grange turned to Peg and looked down at her with eyes that were at once darkly possessive and tender. "Mrs. Grange," he said very softly, and bent to kiss her with breathless tenderness.

She smiled back, kissed him tenderly and hugged him close. "Mrs. Grange," she repeated, tingling all over at the sound of her new name. She could hardly believe they were really married.

The men shook hands with Grange and kissed Peg on the cheek.

"President Machado wanted to come with us," Grange told his bride, "but he had a mess to straighten out in the presidential offices, and not much time to do it in. By the way—" he addressed O'Bailey "—thanks for giving us a quick fix on that mutant virus you created. I never want to get on the bad side of you. I'd lose my internet rights forever!" he joked.

"That you would, boyo," O'Bailey said with a flash of white teeth. "Computers are my life, sadly for old Sapara."

"Everything's back up and running, including communications. President Machado has announced his comeback to the world media," he added. He glanced at Rourke. "Did you tell her?" he asked, nodding toward Clarisse.

Rourke shook his head.

Grange smiled at the blonde woman in the stained blouse, her usually immaculate hair ruffled and unruly... her face showing the strain of the past days. "President Machado is going to award you a medal for bravery under fire."

"What?" Clarisse exclaimed, flushing. "Me? But I didn't do anything!"

"You escaped from prison and got your two fellow Americans out as well," Rourke said quietly. "As neat a job of it as I've ever seen. Sneaked yourself and the professors out of the city and kept your nerve, despite your injuries. The stuff of legends, Tat."

She flushed even more from the look in Rourke's dark eye before he averted his gaze and moved off, as if he hadn't wanted to make the comment in the first place.

"I don't know what to say," Clarisse faltered.

Peg hugged her. "Nothing to say. You did great!"

She hugged the younger woman back. "You have to come and visit me in Washington once in a while," she said. "Both of you," she added. "I'll get you the Presidential Suite at our local five-star hotel," she cooed. "And I'll take you shopping," she added to Peg. "Something to help make up for the way I behaved when we first met."

"I've already told you, there's nothing to make up for," Peg said gently. "I've had the greatest adventure of my life!"

"Well, not yet," Grange murmured with pursed lips

as he grinned at her. "Marriage is going to be the greatest adventure of both our lives."

"You know, he's right," Peg said, nodding enthusiastically. "Jungles are a snap compared to making a marriage work."

"We'll make ours work, baby," he told Peg, hugging her close.

She pressed against him and smiled. "Of course we will."

THEY LEFT THE village laden with presents. Maria gave Peg a woven bag and a blanket, the one the young woman had been working on at the loom in the central hut in the village. Peg cried and said she'd never forget any of them.

The professors were driven back to Medina, along with Rourke and O'Bailey and the reverend, who thought there might be people there in need of him after the bloodless coup. Enrique stayed in the village with his mother, to recuperate a bit longer.

Clarisse hitched a ride with Grange and Peg to Manaus, across bridges that were almost lost to the rising water. They arrived, ragged and stained and dirty, at the hotel where Clarisse and Peg had left the bulk of their luggage what seemed like so long ago.

The desk clerk, who knew Clarisse, stared at her with astonishment. "*Señorita,* your clothing…!"

She held up a hand. "Not to worry, Carlos, I've taken up mud wrestling with crocodiles. If you think I look bad, you should see the crocodile."

He hesitated, wide-eyed, and then burst out laughing.

She grinned. "I hope you haven't given up our room."

"Not at all. Anything you require will be provided."

"I'll need an additional room also. A suite. For my friends, who are newly married." She indicated Grange and Peg.

Grange started to protest.

Clarisse held up her hand again. "A wedding present," she told him. "The best I have to give. Please. Humor me."

Grange looked at Peg, who just smiled and shook her head.

"You can't argue with her," she told him, indicating Clarisse. "You can't win. Just give in gracefully and say thank-you."

"Thank you," Grange capitulated after a minute, and hugged Clarisse. "Thank you for everything."

"I'm trying to mend fences," Clarisse said. "With you and Peg at least. I can't mend them with Rourke."

Her face was sad.

Peg wondered what went on with those two, Clarisse and Rourke, but she wasn't going to pry. It was apparent that they had a long history together, but something kept them apart.

"Thank you for our wedding present," Peg said.

Clarisse smiled. "It's my pleasure."

THEY HAD A suite to themselves, one that overlooked the rising Rio Negro in the distance. The jungle canopy was just visible across the huge, beautiful metropolitan city of Manaus.

"I thought of villages in the jungle, not a major city like this, when I read about South America," Peg told her new husband as they stared out the window.

"It's actually the hub of the area," he said. "Cruise ships come to port here, and electronics are the major industry. It's a free port. No taxes."

She turned to him, looking up with soft, worshipful eyes. "It's been a very long few days," she said.

He nodded. He smoothed back her hair. "Well, I don't know about you, but I need a bath."

She laughed. "I do, too."

He waved her toward the bathroom. "Ladies first. Unless you want to share. To conserve water, I mean."

She hesitated, staring at him as she tried to comprehend whether or not he was teasing. Her blush grew redder and redder.

He saw her embarrassment, and felt the difficulty of this new relationship keenly. He framed her face in his hands. "It's all right," he said softly. "It's all as new to me as it is to you. We'll just take it one step at a time. You have a bath. I'll have a bath. We'll have a nice supper and a glass of wine—yes, I know, I don't drink, but a glass of wine isn't addictive," he added when she protested. "Then we'll go from there. Okay?"

She hugged him. "Thanks for understanding. I hate being shy. I should be all over you... I should know everything to do..."

He stopped the words with his mouth. "I love it that you don't know what to do," he said. "I don't know what to do, either, except for what I've learned from movies and books and listening to other men. So we start even. I like that."

"I like that, too." She moved back. "I'll go take a bath."

"Use soap," he directed.

She made a face at him.

"Use water," he added as she closed the door behind her.

She made a noise.

He chuckled and went to order supper from room service.

CHAPTER THIRTEEN

PEG HAD A gown, but Clarisse had insisted on taking her shopping before they parted to go to their respective suites. So Peg had a pink negligee that cost the earth, with a matching peignoir. The silk barely covered her small, taut breasts and lace hinted at the curves underneath. The gown went all the way to her ankles. She left her blond hair long as well, drying it in the bathroom so that it hung to her waist, in a soft thick curtain. She looked in the mirror with surprise. She looked older, more mature. She liked the way she looked.

She recalled an uncomfortable conversation with her father earlier, when she'd come back from shopping. He had been livid about her sudden disappearance.

"I called Cash Grier, and he started calling people," Ed Larson raged over a bad connection with static. "I was beside myself!"

"I'm really sorry, Dad. I'll make it up to you. I promise. I have so much to tell you. It's been the greatest sort of adventure and I got married…" She bit her lip. She shouldn't have blurted it out like that.

There was an ominous pause. "Who did you marry? Some South American smooth-talking Romeo with ten wives…?"

"I married Winslow Grange."

There was an audible intake of breath. "You married Winslow?" he exclaimed.

"Yes." She hesitated. "We'll be home soon, I promise. I have a new friend who's a photojournalist and she seems to be a millionaire as well. She got us a suite in the hotel for our honeymoon and took me shopping… She's been great."

"I'm just speechless," her father said. There was a thud, as if he sat down hard in the rocking chair he had in the living room. "Speechless!"

"I know it's a shock and I'm sorry I didn't tell you what was going on. But the upshot is that we won the war. General Machado is now back in power and ex-president Sapara is in a jail cell awaiting trial on charges of high treason. We didn't even lose a man, although we did have a few who were wounded in the street fighting after Sapara was captured."

"And where were you while all this was going on?" he asked, horrified.

"I was in a small native village just inside the border of Barrera. There was an anthropologist hiding out there… She's made an amazing discovery. And there were two college professors, a doctor, a Protestant minister…!"

"You're making this up!"

She laughed. "No, Dad, I'm not making it up. It will take days to tell you the whole story. But it's got a happy ending. Really."

He sighed. "Well, as long as you married someone sensible that I approve of, I won't fuss. When are you coming home?"

"It will be a few days," she said. She cleared her

throat. "Winslow and I want to see Manaus together. So far, all we've seen is jungle and rivers and crocodiles."

"Crocodiles?"

"It's okay, they didn't eat anybody," she said quickly. Then she remembered something she'd overheard about the man named Miguel, who had tortured Clarisse, having run right into a nest of crocodiles near the river. Odd. "I mean, they didn't eat any of our people," she amended.

"Well, I suppose if it ends well, it is well," he conceded. He laughed. "So you're married. Mrs. Grange. That's wonderful, Peg. I wish you could have been married here, though..."

"Not a problem. I'll get a white dress and we'll do it again when we get home," she added. "I wouldn't mind a church wedding. We had a simple civil service, although it was very nice. The minister is a brave man. He walked right into a hail of bullets trying to save the native people from a bunch of Sapara's thugs who were trying to run them off their land for oil exploration."

"Say, there was something in the news about that," he said quickly. "About Ritter Oil Corporation pulling out of exploration in Barrera because of serious disagreements with the existing government."

"I'll bet they go back, now. President Machado won't let anyone threaten the native tribes."

"I'll bet they do, too," her father replied. "Oil is the big deal right now. We need it badly, if we're to continue as a civilization."

"Don't start," she teased.

"Okay. Have a nice honeymoon and then please come back home and cook. I'm tired of eating charcoal." He paused again. "I need to find a house of my own..."

"You are not moving anywhere," Peg said firmly. "We're a family. We live together."

He chuckled. "Okay. But maybe I'll take a vacation when you two come home. Mr. Pendleton offered to send me out to Colorado for some ranching management seminar. Said he'd put me up at a five-star hotel and let me eat whatever I wanted. After cooking for myself all this time, it's tempting."

"Tell him you'll go," she advised. "You need some time off."

"Well, I'll go after New Year's," he said. "I've missed you, girl. And I've been worried out of my mind."

"I'm really sorry about that," she said softly. "Really."

"I guess it goes with the job when you're a father. So Machado's president again. That's really great news."

"Could you call Barbara Ferguson, do you think, and have her tell Rick that his father is now head of a sovereign nation again?"

"That would be my pleasure," he replied. "That general has been down here visiting, and taking her around town. Took her to the opera in San Antonio, I heard."

"Well!"

"Kind of sad, you remember that boy whose father just killed himself...the one that got Grange in so much trouble?"

Her heart skipped. She had visions of him lying in wait for them when they went home. She'd forgotten the threat until how. "Yes, I remember," she said solemnly.

"Jumped off the roof of a ten-story building two days ago," he continued quietly. "They said he was high as a kite and told his partying friends that he could fly. Then he offered to demonstrate. Pity that people let drugs get such a hold on them."

Peg was thinking of Clarisse and the danger she'd been in. That could easily have been Clarisse. "It's very sad," she said aloud.

"Well, I'll let you go. I know this call's costing a fortune. You come home. Let me know when and I'll meet you and Winslow at the San Antonio airport. Okay?"

"Okay, Dad!" she said brightly.

"And congratulations, to both of you. Can't think of anybody in the world that I'd rather you married."

"Thanks."

"I'll talk to you soon."

She'd had her bath and brushed her hair. She stood at the mirror and looked at herself with quiet wonder. She looked so different!

Winslow was just coming out of the bathroom. He was wearing silk boxer shorts and nothing else. He looked incredibly sexy, with his hair-covered chest bare, the muscles in his arms and legs displayed. Peg just caught her breath.

He pursed his lips. "Well, aren't you a beautiful sight!" he exclaimed, his eyes sketching her. "I like the gown."

She shrugged and managed a smile, although she was very nervous. "I like the boxer shorts," she said, flushing. "Room service brought food and a bottle of wine. I wore my raincoat until he left." She shifted nervously. "He laughed."

He made a face. "Let him. He probably has to spend his nights with a television set instead of a woman."

She laughed. "I was just thinking that. So we have food and wine, and will it hurt?" she blurted out suddenly, flushing again.

His eyebrows arched.

She turned redder and lowered her eyes. "Sorry, I just open my mouth and words pour out."

He moved closer, framing her face in his warm, gentle hands and searched her green eyes with his dark ones. "It might," he replied. "First times aren't easy, they say. But I'll be as careful as I can not to hurt you." He shrugged uncomfortably. "It's hard for me, too, Peg. I've never done it, either."

"Didn't you ever want to?" she asked in a whisper.

"Once or twice," he confessed. "But never enough to take the risks."

"You mean diseases and stuff."

"I mean that I believe sex and marriage go hand in hand," he replied. "It's an old-fashioned, out-of-date attitude, but I can't change. I won't change. The world may not recognize any difference between right and wrong, but people of faith do. There's a nobility, an idealism, about two people keeping themselves chaste until marriage, discovering all the wonders of being together for the first time." He smiled. "I think it's sexy," he said in a deep, velvety tone.

She laughed softly. "Me, too," she said.

Her hands tangled in the soft, thick hair over the warm muscles of his chest. "I think you're very sexy, too."

He tilted her face up to his and bent to smooth his sensual mouth over her soft lips. "Honey and sugar," he whispered as his tongue teased her lips.

She moved a little closer, warming to the slow, easy rhythm of his mouth on hers. She felt safe. Secure. Loved. She reached up and linked her arms around his neck while he kissed her. He brought her body completely against his and she gasped. It was like being nude. There was only a whisper-thin layer of silk between her breasts and his chest, and even that was suddenly far too much.

She made a sound in her throat and he reacted to it at once. His hands smoothed the tiny straps of the gown and the sleeves of the peignoir down her arms, baring her pretty, hard-tipped breasts to his hungry eyes. A flush ran down his high cheekbones as he looked at her with pure hunger.

She shivered and arched up a little. "It's okay, if you want to touch them. I want you to, so much!"

"Baby," he whispered as his big hands closed around her waist, disposing of the silky garments, "you can't imagine what I want to do to them."

As he spoke, he lifted her clear off the floor and buried his mouth against that soft, warm, firmly mounted skin. She gasped at the incredible surge of pleasure it brought, and her hands dug into the back of his head, coaxing him to keep doing it.

She felt him walk toward the bedroom, but she was too far gone to care what he did, as long as he didn't stop.

He slid onto the coverlet with her, one hand going urgently to the waistband of his boxer shorts. He kicked them out of the way while his mouth opened on her soft breast and took it almost completely inside. His tongue slid over it, teasing the nipple so that it went even harder and she moaned, almost in anguish, and began to move involuntarily against his body.

His mouth slid up her throat to cover her chin and then her lips, insistent and hungry as he nudged her legs apart with his knee and settled between them in stark intimacy.

She wanted to protest that she wasn't sure she was

ready, but his mouth was making her crazy. She felt him probe at the softness that had never known a man's touch. She opened her mouth, but his covered it again, devouring it, while his hand did something shocking to that part of her that he was touching.

Just as she started to protest, a flash of pleasure that was almost primeval lifted her hips completely off the bed. She followed his hand, trembling, aching, her eyes suddenly wide-open, looking straight into his as he moved onto her body with intent.

He pushed into her and made a rough sound, shuddering with his first taste of intimacy. His hands rested beside her head, his eyes probing hers as his body slowly merged with hers.

"Oh...my...goodness," she choked out, shivering with each slow, firm movement of his hips.

"It's not even going to be bad, is it?" he whispered unsteadily. "Here. This will make it easier," he added, when she grimaced as the barrier began to break. He touched her again, more confident now, and watched to see how her body reacted to the blatant intimacy. He looked down at her, saw her soft body open to him, saw himself going into her, slowly, slowly, slowly...!

He shuddered and groaned harshly. "Peg," he bit off. His eyes closed on a wave of pleasure unlike anything he'd ever known.

She gasped. "Gosh, you're...big," she whispered, her eyes wide and shocked.

"Yes, baby, and...getting bigger...by the second," he murmured as he pushed into her with a rhythm that was at once insistent and welcome. "Men swell...when they're excited."

"Are you...excited?" she asked bluntly.

"Yes. Yes, baby. Yes!" He was moving his hips as he spoke, shivering. One lean hand went under her hips to lift her up to the hard, deep thrusts. "No, don't close your eyes, Peg," he said huskily. "I want to watch."

She flushed. He was seeing her in an intimacy that she'd never shared with anyone, and it was so stark and earthy that she knew she'd remember it all her life. This first time. This first joining.

He nudged her legs apart even more and moved roughly between them, invading her soft flesh with deep, hard movements that made her cry out in a strange high-pitched tone. But it wasn't from pain. The pleasure was so keen that it almost hurt.

Her nails dug into his powerful arms. She looked straight into his eyes as the rhythm took on an urgency that lifted her hungrily toward every thrust. She shuddered and shuddered as the tension built like a wild thing, until she thought it would tear her apart.

He hesitated, poised above her, his manhood so aroused that he shook all over with the force of it. "Watch," he whispered in a deep, harsh tone. "Watch me do it."

And as he spoke, he plunged into her so deeply, so hungrily, that she felt the tension snap with the force of a tree falling.

She cried out, her voice shaking, her body shaking, as she felt the climax wash over her like a wall of lava. He blurred in her eyes, while she moved urgently under him, desperate to keep that pleasure, to hold on to it, to never let it stop, never, never, never...!

He arched down into her at last and cried out in a broken voice as his body, too, surrendered to passion and found fulfillment. He thrust down rhythmically, helplessly, trying to prolong the unbearable pleasure. But all too soon, it was gone, and nothing would bring it back. He collapsed onto her damp body, shivering with her in the aftermath.

She clung to him. Her lips pressed against his warm shoulder, feeling the moisture on it. She felt him, still deep inside her body, with a sense of wonder. So this was how it was, a man and a woman, joining, belonging to each other. She hadn't dreamed there would be so much pleasure in it.

"Sorry," he whispered after a minute. His chest rose and fell. "I lost it, there at the end. I didn't hurt you too much…?" he added worriedly as he lifted his head.

She pushed back the unruly damp black hair that fell onto his forehead. "I didn't notice," she said, and then laughed shyly.

He laughed, too. "I didn't realize it would feel like that," he confessed a little uncomfortably. "Reading about it and doing it are different things."

"I noticed." She touched his mouth with her fingertips. He was beautiful to her. So beautiful. "I couldn't believe you really wanted me for keeps. I'm not even pretty. And I'm small, here." She indicated her pert breasts.

"I like you small, here," he whispered, and bent to open his mouth and suckle her. She shivered.

He lifted his head. His body was swelling again. She felt it, and reacted to it with a slow, deep rotation of her hips.

He drew in a long breath. "Peg…"

She did it again. She watched him shudder. "I like that," she whispered. "I like making you hungry."

"I can't stop, if I start."

She smiled in a new way, a confident way, and thrust

her hips up against his, where they were still joined. "Promises, promises…!"

His mouth crushed down over hers. It was a long time, a very long time, before they remembered the cold cuts on ice in the living room, and the untouched bottle of wine.

THEY WANDERED AROUND Manaus three days later, hand in hand, visiting the zoo, and the Indian Museum, and speculating on what had happened to Colonel Percy Fawcett in 1925 when he went into the jungle with only his son and his son's best friend in search of El Dorado. None of the party of three was ever to be seen again. Books dealt with speculation, but the mystery was never solved.

"Perhaps that's why it fascinates people," Peg said as they strolled through the place where some of Fawcett's dispatches and artwork were displayed. "It's because we don't know what happened that we're interested."

He nodded. "It was sad for his family. He had a daughter and a son, and his wife, still living. Not knowing, hoping that he might still return. It wasn't much of a life for them."

"I remember reading that he felt his life's work would be a failure if he didn't find the lost city." She stopped and looked up at Grange. "But he gave his journals to the world. For eighty years, since his youngest son first published them, they've given adventure and romance to generations of people around the world. Armchair adventurers who can't delve into the jungle and learn its mysteries. Wouldn't you call that a life's work that had value, that was worthwhile?" she added. "Because I would. I think the insight he gave into the world he

discovered is a legacy even more powerful than finding a lost city."

He smiled. "It seems our friend Maddie may have
done just that," he told her. "Apparently those ruins
she discovered are going to rewrite Amazonian history. She's not the first to find remnants of a high culture here, either. There are several other archaeologists
down here digging, including a young man from the
University of Florida who's written a book about his
discoveries. There's also a female archaeologist who's a
direct descendant of President Theodore Roosevelt. The
ex-president spent weeks in the jungle here and wrote
about his own experiences just after he lost his bid for
reelection. Fascinating stuff. I'll have to lend you some
of my books."

She stood on tiptoe and kissed him. "We can read
them together," she whispered. "When we run out of
things to do at night."

He pursed his lips and his dark eyes twinkled down
into hers. "That might take a few years."

"Or a few decades." She laughed as she turned back
to the exhibit. "This is a honeymoon we'll enjoy telling
our kids about one day."

He was looking at her speculatively. "I wouldn't mind
kids, when we've had some time together to travel and
explore."

She smiled. "Me, either. Something to look forward to."

He nodded. "Yes, it is."

CLARISSE WENT WITH them to the airport. She'd had a
brief word with Rourke before they left the hotel, and it
hadn't been a pleasant conversation, from appearances.

She walked away from him white in the face, without speaking, and she didn't look back.

She forced a smile for Grange and Peg, though, and went through customs and passport control with the smile pinned to her face.

THE FLIGHT TO Miami was pleasant, but very long. Clarisse, Peg noted, slept most of the way. When Peg and Grange were ready to make the connecting flight to San Antonio, Clarisse said her goodbyes.

"I'm going back to Washington now," she said, "for a few weeks, while I get over the past ones," she added with a laugh that wasn't really humorous at all. "Then I'm going to find something worthwhile to do. Something that doesn't involve cocktail parties."

"Try to stay out of trouble, will you?" Peg teased.

Clarisse sighed and hugged her. "I'll do my best. Thanks for everything, Peg. I owe you a lot."

Peg kissed the other woman's cheek. "You don't owe me a thing. I can write my memoirs, now. I'll have some extraordinary stories to tell about life in the jungle!"

"Indeed you will." She shook hands with Grange. She'd tried to buy him a business class ticket home, but General Machado had taken care of that. "You take care of my friend."

He grinned. "I'll do that. Watch yourself."

Clarisse nodded. She gave them both a last look and walked away to baggage claim.

PEG AND GRANGE had time for a snack and a cup of coffee before their flight to San Antonio was called. They strolled through the airport hand in hand, looking in store windows and just enjoying their new relationship.

THE FLIGHT HOME was shorter than the others, thank God, but Peg was wilting when they walked onto the concourse. Her father was there waiting for them, looking worried and uneasy until he spotted them.

He burst out laughing and hugged Peg. "I love you. I missed you. If you ever do this to me again, I'll have him ground you." He pointed to Grange.

"Not to worry." Grange chuckled, embracing the older man. "I'll stay home for a while. She won't have any reason to go looking for me. Thanks for coming to meet us, Dad."

The word came out so easily that it seemed perfectly natural. Ed shook his head. "Always wanted a boy of my own," he mused, grinning.

"You can take me fishing," Grange promised. "But right now, I could do with a meal. How about you, honey?" he asked Peg.

"I could indeed. I'll cook us…"

"You'll cook nothing," Ed interrupted. "Barbara's got everything ready in the café. The meal's on her."

"Well!" Peg exclaimed. "How nice of her!"

"There's a price," Ed murmured. "She and Rick want to know all about the revolution, so you'd better be ready to talk. Rick's wife is interested, too. You know who she works for."

"Yes, we do," Grange replied with a smile. "She has some great connections. Including one of my best friends, her father, who's now head of the…well, that letter agency I admire so much."

They all laughed.

RICK MARQUEZ GREETED them like lost family. "How's my dad?" was his first question.

"Thriving, and up to his ears in business," Grange replied. They all sat down around a table against the wall while Barbara motioned to one of her cooks to start bringing out food. "Sapara's got a nice cell all to himself. Couldn't happen to a nicer guy," he added. He shook his head. "A man who'll order a woman tortured will do anything."

"A woman?" Barbara stared at Peg with horror.

"Not me," Peg said quickly. "A photojournalist who was with us in Barrera. She refused to tell Sapara's men anything she knew about a counterrevolution. Did it so well that she convinced him nothing was going on except that she was looking for two missing college professors for her newsmagazine."

"What a brave woman," Barbara said.

"You don't know the half of it," Peg said grimly. "Her driver was shot, the college professors had been almost starved during their imprisonment. She got the professors out and found a way to get back to the little native village where I was staying. Oh, corn on the cob! My favorite! And barbecue... I think I've died and gone to heaven," she exclaimed as food was placed on the table.

Barbara chuckled. "I know how much you like it. Dig in."

"This is really nice of you," Ed Larson commented.

"Yes," Grange agreed, and Peg nodded as she worked her way around a buttered ear of corn.

"I thought you'd be hungry. Besides, he wanted to know about his dad." She indicated her adopted son, Rick Marquez, who was hanging on every word.

"I've been concerned," Rick said.

"Everybody has, including my daughter-in-law." Barbara nodded. "She got called into the office an hour ago. Some new homicide. She's really good at her job."

"Yes, she is," Rick said, grinning. "Now I've got competition and in my own department!"

"That doesn't sound like a complaint to me," Peg teased.

"It's not," Rick replied. "She's great company. Finally I've got somebody to go to lunch with! When I'm not at home," he qualified, winking at his mother.

"One question," Barbara continued. "How in the world did you end up in the jungles of South America, Peg, dear?"

Peg hesitated, with the corn cob, half-finished, in midair while she tried to think of a way to explain her trip without incriminating her new friend Clarisse.

"Well, it's like this," Grange replied for her. "I know this woman who works for the wire services. She's independently wealthy and she owed me a favor." He held up a hand. "I know it was irresponsible of me to ask her to bring Peg out to South America, and I know it was dangerous. But honest to God, I missed her so much I was about nuts!" he added, and with such fervor that Peg couldn't believe he was acting.

There was a pause in the conversation while Grange looked at his new wife with eyes that almost consumed her face.

Ed picked up his cup, full of freshly brewed coffee, and laughed. "I guess I can understand that. Since it turned out well, and you came back married, I don't have any room to complain. So I won't."

"It must have been frightening, though," Barbara said. "That's still uncivilized country, isn't it? I mean, don't all the people live in grass huts in the jungle and hunt and fish...?"

"Barbara, Manaus is one of the most modern cities on earth," Peg commented. "It has over a million and a half citizens and it's the center of the area's electronic industry. Besides all that, it's a free port. Cruise ships come up to it from the ocean. It's called the 'Paris of the Tropics.'"

Barbara gaped at her. "Well, see, you don't learn that on the news."

"No, they're too busy telling you every facet of every celebrity's private affairs and posting chatter from social sites to tell you anything really informative," Ed Larson muttered.

"He doesn't watch television." Peg indicated her father. "He thinks it's evil."

"Actually it is evil," Barbara agreed. "Everybody on my conspiracy website agrees that the mainstream media makes up most of the news anyway. If you want to know what's going on in the world, we'll know it before it even flashes on the screen of a network television station. For example, when Anak Krakatau started erupting, did you hear that on TV? Or when they started having thousands of earthquakes on El Hierro, that volcano in the Canary Islands, was that reported until it had been going on for weeks?"

"Conspiracy nut, cough," Rick said facetiously, nodding toward his mother.

"I am not a nut. But there are conspiracies," she informed. "Ask your father-in-law." She frowned, staring at Grange. "I meant to ask, did you hear about what happened to the son of that man who forced you out of the military? He killed himself just after his father's suicide."

Grange nodded. "Peg told me. A sad business. Very sad."

"Yes. Drugs ruin so many young lives."

Peg, who had reason to know from Clarisse's experience, only nodded, too.

CHAPTER FOURTEEN

THE WEDDING WAS a town social event. All of Eb Scott's crew showed up, along with a number of other ex-mercs including Cash Grier and Colby Lane and his wife, from the Ritter Oil Corporation in Houston.

Peg, dripping white lace from a couture satin gown—courtesy of Gracie Pendleton, who refused to take no for an answer—walked down the aisle of the local Presbyterian church to the sound of the wedding march, smiling from ear to ear as she joined Winslow Grange at the altar.

The minister who'd known them both for years smiled benevolently as he read the service and, at last, pronounced them man and wife. This time there were rings exchanged. Ed had given his daughter a wedding ring that had belonged to her grandmother, a pretty thing that was a family heirloom. It was joined by a small diamond engagement ring that Grange had insisted on giving her. He, too, was wearing a ring, a simple wide circle of gold. They shared a second wedding kiss, much more relaxed than the last one in a jungle camp, and walked down the aisle to the congratulations and laughter of the wedding guests.

There was a reception at the church's fellowship hall, catered by many local women.

Colby Lane was introduced to Peg. He, in turn, introduced his wife, a pretty blonde woman who turned out to be a working DEA agent.

"We didn't mean to crash the wedding, but I wanted to thank you personally," Colby said, "for my boss, Eugene Ritter. He had no idea what was going on in Barrera, or that his project was threatening the native tribes. He was outraged."

"I knew he would be," Peg said simply. "Mr. Ritter has a reputation for fair play."

"It's well earned."

"Now that President Machado is back in the presidential building," Grange added, "he'd love to talk to you about that oil project. This time, it will be done right, with the consent of the native people and the government."

"I'll tell him," Colby said. He pursed his lips and his dark eyes flashed. "Rumor is that you may become the chief of staff of Machado's army."

Grange didn't let a hint of expression show. "That's the talk. Nothing's been decided, though."

"It would be a peach of a job," Colby commented.

"Yes. He's a great guy," Grange agreed.

LATER, WHEN THEY were alone together in the ranch house—Ed having discreetly left for the conference he'd told Peg about on the phone—Peg curled up beside Grange in bed.

"What about that job?" she asked.

He sighed. His fingers tangled in her soft blond hair, twining it around them. "I don't know, baby. It's a big change. It will mean living in Barrera for the foreseeable future. The hospital has gone downhill with Sapara's neglect, and many doctors left the country under his regime. It will take time to rebuild all that. There are some dangerous tropical diseases. Many of them don't show up for years, and they can kill you."

She rolled over against him, savoring the clean smell of his powerful body beside her. "Life kills you eventually."

He looked down at her solemnly. "It would be a risk. Especially if we had a child."

She smiled lazily. "We can have a child when we're ready. For a few years, we could help the general get his country secure and I could find a way to help, maybe in the orphanage. The reverend Harvey was telling me how desperate they were for someone to take charge of it. Nobody wants the job."

"You'd go?" he asked with a frown. "You're a homebody. You don't even like going up to San Antonio to eat out."

She smiled. "I think I'm learning how interconnected everything is," she said. "We all belong to this big family. Sort of like Jacobsville and Comanche Wells, but on a global scale. I like the general. I know there will be risks, but he's going to need all the help he can get. We don't want children right away, so we can wait until we're settled for them to come along. Dad can come and visit. We can come back and visit him. It's not that far away."

"You never cease to amaze me, baby," he said.

She sighed. "I've had an adventure. It's changed me, just a little. I wouldn't mind staying in Barrera for a few years. Then when you've had enough, when you have the army the way you think it needs to be, you can come home and be a rancher and I'll be a rancher's wife, if that's what you want. Dad can run the ranch while we're gone. He'll make it grow."

He rolled her over on the bed and looked down into her rapt eyes. "You've got all the answers tonight," he murmured with a soft smile.

"Well, not quite all." She shifted and tugged away the top of her gown, watching the way his dark eyes settled on her breasts with aching hunger. "I'm still working on the mystery of life. Want to help me further my education…?"

His mouth opened on the hard nipple, while his hands quickly removed all the fabric in the way. "This is one fun way to learn things," he murmured huskily. "Slide your leg around mine. That's it!"

She moaned as the changed position made the pleasure even hotter. She arched up to meet the hard downward thrust of his hips. It was so easy now; there was never any discomfort, only a delight that seemed to feed on itself.

"You're hot inside," he whispered into her ear as he shifted suddenly with a rough movement of his hips. "Soft, and hot!"

"Hungry…too," she gasped. "Oh, yes, do that…! Do it again!"

His hand slid under her and he shifted, laughing through his pleasure at the moan that tore out of her arched throat. "I never get tired of watching you," he whispered. "You never hold anything back. You give and give and give."

She was too breathless to answer him. She arched up again, looking into his eyes as the pleasure began to build in her, like little ripples that grew slowly, relentlessly, into riptides. "Oh, gosh!" she bit off.

"It gets better every time, doesn't it? Hold on tight," he ground out. "Tight, baby, tight, tight, tight…!"

She felt his hand under her, guiding her hips into the hard, rhythmic thrust of his body as he drove into her.

"I can't bear it," she sobbed.

"So good," he whispered brokenly. "So good, so good…!"

He cried out as the tension suddenly broke, leaving him shuddering over her. She wrapped her long legs around his hips and arched up to try to hold him there, keep the pleasure, never let go of it. But all too soon, her own tension snapped and she collapsed under his weight, holding him to her, shivering in the sweet aftermath.

"If I'd known how good it could really be," she whispered into his ear, "I'd have seduced you in the barn months ago!"

He burst out laughing. "It wouldn't have been this good. Not back then. And you wouldn't have liked to take that memory into old age."

She smiled into his throat. "No. I really wouldn't have. It's so much sweeter like this. My husband."

He hugged her close. "Don't ever expect to have another one."

She grinned and bit his shoulder. "You can't beat perfection," she said, and gave him a wicked grin. "Uh, you're not stopping already?" she asked when he lifted his head. "I mean, do you feel weak or something? Old age creeping up… Oh!"

He ground her down into the mattress and his mouth covered hers. "I'll show you who's old!" He laughed.

MUCH LATER, THEY raided the kitchen for cheese and crackers and cold milk. Peg gazed across the table at her husband, with all the love she felt in her soft green eyes.

"What are you looking at?" he teased deeply.

"The world," she said softly. "My whole world."

He couldn't manage a comeback. There was a lump in his throat.

"I've just remembered something!" she exclaimed.

His eyebrows arched.

"Christmas is next week and we don't have a tree!"

"I'll go right out and get us one tomorrow," he promised.

"I haven't bought presents!"

"There are stores open tomorrow, too."

She sighed. "What a Christmas this is going to be!" she exclaimed, her bright eyes sinking into the softness of his.

He laughed. "The best one ever."

She nodded. "Oh, yes. I can't wait!" she said breathlessly. And she smiled with her whole heart.

EPILOGUE

"GOSH, DAD, DID you really lead an army in here to get that bloodthirsty dictator out of office?" John Grange asked his father with wide, dark eyes.

Grange chuckled and ruffled the thick dark hair on his son's head. "I did," he confessed. "I'm just glad I don't have to do it again," he added with a gentle smile.

"I totally agree," Peg, his mother, said. She went close to her husband and pressed against him with a sigh, nuzzling his broad chest with her cheek. "I'm so tired," she murmured. "These overseas flights are getting harder and harder."

Grange smoothed back her long blond hair and kissed her forehead. "For me, too, sugar." He sighed.

"Why can't we just stay here all the time?" John wanted to know. "Mr. Machado—I mean, President Machado—wants to take me with him and his wife to those ruins they've finally finished excavating. I'm really keen to go!"

"He made a great decision, appointing Maddie head of his state archaeological service," Peg noted. "She's perfect for the job." She smiled demurely. "And it keeps her out of the digs, now that she and Emilio have a young son."

"Rick Marquez was over the moon about that announcement," Grange recalled. "He said he never liked being an only child. He comes over about twice a year to see the boy."

"I wish he was my age." John sighed. "All I have to play with lately are girls." He made a face.

"In about six years, you won't be complaining about that. Besides, my boy, you have the most wonderful manners and girls already love you," Peg said. "Mrs. Cates actually phoned me to say how much she enjoyed that bouquet you brought her when she was feeling bad. You have a tender heart."

"Takes after his mom," Grange said with obvious affection.

She made a face. "And his dad," she said with a twinkle in her green eyes. "But I promise never to mention that in the hearing of your department heads," she added, crossing her heart. "After all, it wouldn't do to lower the image of the chief of staff of the Barrera Republican Army."

"Big title, lots of work," he said. "Back home a ranch that needs me."

"My dad looks after the ranch, along with your new livestock foreman." She frowned. "That man has some personality issues. I mean, he can lead a mean bull across a pasture just by talking to it. But he can't manage more than two words when he's talking to people."

"He's Lakota," Grange said easily. "He thinks he has to be stoic and unapproachable. His grandfather told him that."

"Well, he's strange," Peg noted. "I guess he's good at what he does. His son, Carson, was with us during the invasion," she told John. "He had a way with words, too," she recalled with a chuckle.

"He's settled down now, too," Grange said, shaking

his head. "There aren't a lot of single men left in the army. Even O'Bailey's finally getting married—to that little techie who works for Professor Fitzhugh at the local college."

"I hope she doesn't keep snakes for pets," Peg said, tongue-in-cheek, remembering O'Bailey's terror of them.

"No worries there."

Peg looked at her watch. "We've just got time to eat before the plane comes to take us to Medina. Imagine having a real airport there now, complete with a runway that can accommodate baby jets!"

"Yes, very nice, now that Machado owns one," he quipped. "The people were so grateful to be out from under Sapara's rule that they voted to put on a special sales tax just to buy him one. But he had to promise never to leave the country for more than a week at a time," he added, recalling that one lengthy trip had led to Sapara's coup.

"Nice that he'll send the jet to bring the leader of his armed forces home after a trip abroad to see his father-in-law," Peg murmured dryly.

Grange drew himself erect. "That is no way to talk to the supreme commander of the army," he said with mock indignation.

She reached up and kissed him warmly. "Sorry," she purred.

He just laughed.

THEY HAD A nice meal at the airport concession and then filed out to await the arrival of Machado's jet. It landed promptly and the three Americans got inside. Minutes later, they were on the way to Medina, the capital of Barrera. It was a short flight in a jet.

A LIMOUSINE WAS waiting to take them to the presidential palace. Machado had felt guilty about living in it, since Sapara had robbed the populace to get enough money to build it. But the people said it was very impressive and would be good for diplomats from Western nations to see, because it represented the hopes and dreams of the Barrera people for modernization.

Ritter Oil Corporation had offices here. Old man Eugene Ritter had funded a trust for the indigenous people, to help send their bright young people to college and improve conditions for them. The oil discovery was discreet, and in no way interfered with the culture and traditions of the natives. Ritter had been given a ceremonial position in one tribe, due to his sensitivity for their customs.

"Barrera's come a long way in ten years," Peg remarked as they circled the airport's landing strip.

"It has indeed," Grange replied. "Those enormous oil reserves will make us formidable in international trade circles."

"Yes, indeed. And the discoveries in archaeology have put us on the map, too." She glanced at him. "I love having Barrera citizenship, but I'm glad we kept our American citizenship. We may want to go home to retire one day."

He smiled. "I know you miss Texas," he began.

"I do, of course I do, and I miss Dad," she said. "But we have Skype on the computer, so we can talk to him and see him on video at the same time. That means a lot. Meanwhile, we're both doing important work here.

You head the army and I head one of the larger charity organizations. We've been a part of the recovery effort. I'm very proud of that."

"Are we staying for a while?" John asked with a sigh. "I'm tired of flying."

"You? Tired of flying? Who wants to be a pilot one day?" Peg gasped.

"Well, I do want to be a pilot, but riding is boring," he muttered.

"Don't wish your life away," his father remarked. "Enjoy every single day as if it were your last."

Peg smiled as she listened to that remark, recalling her friend Clarisse and how that observation fit her. She heard from Clarisse on holidays. She was happy that the older woman, who began as an enemy, had found happiness after a tormented younger life.

"AND WE'RE HERE," Grange said, smiling as the limousine pulled up at the front door of the imposing building where Emilio Machado lived and worked.

Machado himself greeted them at the door, hugging Grange and kissing Peg's hand. He ruffled John's thick dark hair.

"You have grown even taller," he remarked. "I hope my youngest son will also have my stature. He is very short."

"He's five now," Peg said, laughing. "He'll start growing upward soon enough."

"Maddie continues to assure me of that," he noted. "Come, sit down and tell me all about your trip. Did you see my oldest son?"

"We did," Grange said. He pulled an envelope out of his pocket and handed it to Machado. "He and Gwen thought you might like a more recent photo of your grandkids."

There were two of them, both girls. Rick and Gwen were happy together, and they made good parents. Grange and Peg saw them often when they visited Texas.

"They have grown even since the last picture," Machado said, smiling at the images of one girl with dark hair like Rick and one with blond hair like Gwen. "A beautiful family." He glanced up. "You mentioned that Gracie Pendleton's little boy has a flair for piano."

"Indeed he does," Grange replied. "They say he's a child prodigy. If they ever have time to come over here, you should teach him to play the guitar."

Machado chuckled. "That would be a pleasure. I have too little time to practice these days. My life is rich and full."

"Papa!"

A little boy, dressed in jeans and a T-shirt, came flying into the room with his arms outstretched. Machado caught him in midleap and hugged him, whirling him around. *"Mi hijo."* He laughed. "And how are you today?"

"I'm learning Portuguese," he announced. "I can say *'obrigado!'* It means thank-you!"

"Very nice. You should talk with John to practice it," Machado said, putting the child down. "He speaks many languages, just like his father."

"Well, mostly just Spanish and Portuguese," John said modestly. "I'm trying to learn Farsi, but it's real hard."

"All the more reason to apply yourself to your books," Grange teased.

"I have a book in Portuguese! Can you read it to me? Please?" the boy asked John.

"Go ahead," Grange said, waving his hand. "We'll be right here."

"Okay, Dad." John went into the other room with the smaller child.

"Maddie would have been here to greet you, but an important member of the Egyptian antiquities division has come to visit. He wanted to see the newest finds. We are building a museum to house them," he reminded his friend.

"A grand museum," Peg said. "It will bring tourists from all over the world."

"We have come far, from a ragtag army trying to overthrow a tyrant," Machado said. "God has blessed us all."

"Yes." Grange sat down across from Machado in the sitting room. "Which brings to mind a subject I've been reluctant to pursue."

Machado cocked his head and smiled. "I can read minds," he teased. "I have some idea where your thoughts have taken you."

Grange nodded. He glanced at Peg. "She won't say a word," he continued. "She goes where I go and never complains. But her father is getting older. My ranch is growing bigger and requires more oversight than I can give it." He hesitated. "General Lopez has worked wonders with modernizing your armed forces, and he's been my right arm since I took over leadership here. But he's more than earned the right to be your military commander. And I really want to go home."

"Winslow!" Peg exclaimed. "You never said a word!"

He smiled gently. "I've had this on my mind for a long time," he replied. "I love Barrera," he told Machado. "But my heart is still in Texas. Peg and I are getting older now, too, and we're both homesick. I want to go back home. If you think you can spare me. I can stay on reserve status, if that suits you, and I'd certainly come back if you ever needed me."

Machado sat back in his chair, his dark eyes smiling. "I know that. General Lopez will be the happiest man on earth if I give him your position. But you must allow me to make you an allowance. I think you Americans call it retirement."

"That's not necessary..." Grange began.

"It is," Machado said firmly. "Without your assistance, I would never have been able to recover my position here. We both know that."

"Yes, well, it was your canny knowledge of tunnels and our ability to use surprise that did that, not any real military strategy of mine," Grange insisted.

"Still, I could not have done it alone. You must humor me." He leaned forward. "If you feel obligated to me, you might send me a shipment of prime beef once in a while," he added with a big grin.

"Done," Grange assured him, smiling back.

"You mean it?" Peg asked her husband, her heart racing. "We're really going home?"

"We're really going. We'll come back and visit from time to time, though. I promise," he told the general. "And we do have Skype on all our computers," he added. "We can talk over that connection, complete with video, and we can watch your son grow up."

"As I can watch yours grow up." Machado stood up and embraced Grange. "It has been an honor to have you in my government. I will truly miss you. All of you," he added with a nod at Peg.

He kissed her hand and she smiled. "I'll miss Barrera," she said softly. "But I have to admit, I'll be very happy to go home. No place, no matter how wonderful, is ever the same. I've made many friends here. I've learned a lot about South America and its culture, and about the world. I wouldn't take anything for the experiences I've had here."

"I am glad that your experience of Barrera is something you wish to recall," Machado said with a big smile. "So I wish you bon voyage and I hope to hear from you soon, when you are settled again in Texas."

"You can count on it," Grange assured him.

BACK IN THEIR hotel room, Peg kissed him and kissed him and kissed him. "What a wonderful surprise!" she exclaimed, and kissed him again.

Grange chuckled as he hugged her and returned the kisses. "You'd never have complained, but I know you miss your dad and your friends, and having your own space around you."

She nodded. "It's been great living here. John's learned more than I have," she added. "He'll miss his school friends. But he'll make new ones in Comanche Wells."

"He already has friends there," Grange reminded her. "Especially Rick Marquez's eldest daughter," he hinted. "They play video games together every time we're in town."

"That's true," she agreed. She sighed. "I'm very happy."

"I'm so glad. Hey, John, you packed yet?" he called to their child.

John poked his head out the door. "I never unpacked," he pointed out. "Now I can ride horses whenever I want, and listen to Granddad's stories about the old days in Texas...wow!"

"I thought you loved it here," Peg remarked.

John grimaced. "I do. But Texas is home. You know?"

Peg hugged him while he fidgeted. "I know."

"Let's get to the airport, then," Grange said. "We can phone your dad to meet us at the airport when we get in."

"What a surprise he's in for," Peg remarked.

They phoned Ed Larson from the airport. He drove in to get them, looking worried as he met them in the terminal.

"Something gone wrong in Barrera? Anybody hurt?" he wanted to know at once.

Peg hugged him. "We've come home for good. Winslow thinks we need to live in Texas now and raise our son and grow our ranch."

The old man bit his lower lip. His eyes were suddenly watery. He turned away for a minute, hands deep in his jeans pockets. "Imagine that."

"I missed you," Peg said gently.

He cleared his throat. "Missed you, too. All of you." He met Grange's eyes. "Big sacrifice for you, though," he said gently. "Not every man gets to be chief of the armed forces of a country."

"I get a pension, and I have great memories," Grange said warmly. "But I'm glad to be home. There's no place like Texas. Not in the whole world."

Ed shook hands with him, firmly. "I'll second that. No place at all." He broke into a huge grin, hugged Grange impulsively, then Peg, then swung John up in his arms and hugged him, too. "I could dance I'm so happy!"

Peg's eyes were watery. Winslow had sacrificed a career, an amazing job, a whole country just because his

THE DEPUTY
GETS HER MAN

Delores Fossen

To my editor, Kathryn Lye.
Thanks so much for everything.

PROLOGUE

"When in doubt, mumble."
　　　　　—Bumper Ditties by Evie E. Garrett

RAYANNE WATCHED WHILE her almost-lover tried to curse and zip his jeans at the same time. Apparently, the simple tasks were too hard for Rios McKay.

"Why?" Rios demanded. He barely got out that one word before swearing viciously as his zipper nicked his thumb.

Other than wishing his zipper had nicked some other protruding part of his body, Rayanne didn't think there was a lot she could do. She'd just had carnal fulfillment snatched away and had been embarrassed beyond belief. Yet Rios obviously thought *he* was the one who should be upset.

She was clearly missing something here.

"Why?" she mimicked, hoping he would clarify why at the last possible moment he had catapulted himself away from her as if she'd scalded him.

He looked at her as if her ears were on backward. "Why what? Why what! I can't believe you have to ask me that. Why didn't you tell me you've never been with a man?"

"I did." Trying to restore some shred of dignity, Rayanne got up from the saddle blanket and began to straighten her clothes. No easy feat considering her knit top and skirt were both around her waist. She had no idea where her brand-new midnight-blue lace panties were. The last time she saw them, Rios was twirling them around his finger.

"Yeah, you told me about a second before I almost found out the hard way. Good grief, Rayanne, you should have said something before I got you down on that ground. That's not something you keep from a man."

"I didn't tell you because we've been kissing for the last half hour. Hard to talk with your tongue in my mouth." Giving up on the panties, she wiggled the skinny skirt to its original place and did what she could to cover herself with the stretched-out top. "Besides, why would my, uh, lack of experience make a difference to you? . You've been with more women than you can count."

He hitched a thumb against his chest. "I wouldn't have touched you if I'd known." His gaze skated around the woods, looking at everything but her. "I don't mess around with innocent little girls."

Ouch, that stung. Rayanne scowled at him and turned her bra around so her breasts fit in the cups. Not that it made that much of a difference. "I'm not a little girl. I'm eighteen, and I wanted you to be my first."

There. She'd said it. And unfortunately, it was the truth. At least, it was the truth ten minutes ago. She'd longed after Rios for years. He was the bad boy of Longhorn, Texas. And the main character in dreams so steamy they made her blush. Now Rayanne was abundantly sure she wanted to pluck out every strand of his body hair with a pair of bent tweezers.

"Your first?" he repeated. He kicked at some dandelion fluff. Little white umbrellas scattered like snow around them. "Not this man. Not me. I don't want to be anybody's flipping *first,* got that?"

"Yeah, I got that."

Rayanne wanted to deliver a memorable exit line, one that he would remember for the rest of his life. A line like the ones her aunt Evie came up with for her bumper stickers. However, there were a couple of problems. She was so embarrassed she couldn't think of an exit line, and she had no way to exit since Rios was the one who had driven them to Whiskey Creek. Exiting now would mean a ten-mile jaunt on a country road at night.

Still, she considered it.

The distant sound of a howling coyote had her considering it just slightly less.

Mustering what pride she could muster, Rayanne hiked up her chin and looked Rios McKay right in the eye. "Home," she finally managed.

Home? She wanted to bop herself upside the head. She had just experienced the single most embarrassing event of her entire life, and all she could come up with was *home?* Rayanne tried but couldn't think of anything better. Besides, she really did want to get home.

She reasoned the only silver lining to this dreary cloud was that her aunt wouldn't know what a fool she'd made of herself. Rayanne soon learned she was wrong about that. The minute she walked inside the house and greeted Evie with a thin smile, her midnight-blue lace panties untangled themselves from her hair clip and dropped to the living room floor.

Evie arched her daffodil-colored eyebrows. "Something you want to tell me, huh, Rayanne?"

Because Rayanne knew she had to come up with an

explanation for the errant panties, she took some advice from one of her aunt's bumper stickers.

She mumbled.

CHAPTER ONE

"Wherever you came from, you're not there now."
—Bumper Ditties by Evie E. Garrett

New York City
Eleven years later

"YOU HAD NO CHOICE but to apprehend that chicken, Detective Garrett. It was definitely in the line of duty, and that's what I'll tell anyone who asks." The uniformed rookie tried to keep his deadpan expression but was failing miserably. Rayanne could see the corners of his mouth twitching.

"Well, yes," she agreed, hoping that was all he had to say on the subject.

It wasn't.

"I mean, it just kept flying up in your face while you were trying to…" And his serious expression went completely south. "Negotiate with it." He started to snicker as they made their way into the patrol room.

As his superior Rayanne supposed she should correct him, but she couldn't bring herself to do it. She, Detective Rayanne Garrett of the NYPD, had apprehended a chicken during a hostage standoff. Yes, it would be a hard thing to live down. And it had really put a damper on the day, which continued to be damper-riddled. Damper-riddled because Dr. Malcolm Keene, the precinct shrink and her often annoying friend, was waiting for her.

"Are you all right?" Malcolm asked. "Someone said there was a hostage standoff with a radical group."

Rayanne didn't like his edgy tone. The man always seemed to be on the brink of a nervous breakdown. Not a terribly good advertisement for a mental health expert.

"Yes, there was," she said. "But the standoff ended without major incident."

"Well, nothing major except for the chicken." The rookie again. "There was chicken ca-ca all over the back seat of the cruiser."

Rayanne thought he'd already left, and with one hard look, she let him know that's exactly what she expected him to do. He snapped his shoulders straight and walked away.

"A chicken," Malcolm repeated.

"Yes." She considered not adding anything to that sparse response, but then she figured it might sound better coming from her. "Members of an animal rights group locked themselves, some barnyard animals and a deli owner in the back of a semi. When I tried to get them to release the hostage, they let the animals escape. There was this chicken. It kept squawking at me, and it flew in my face. It was in my line of sight of the hostage so I caught the darn thing and put it in the squad car."

"A chicken," he repeated.

"A Rhode Island Red, I think."

"So that's why they're acting like children."

Rayanne was about to ask what he meant by that when the desk clerk handed her three message slips—all telling her that Rios McKay had called.

Definitely more dampers. Big ones. "You're sure about this name?" Rayanne asked.

"Positive." The clerk bobbed her head and cracked a wad of gum. "I even had him spell it."

"Did he say why he was calling?"

"Sure didn't. Said he'd stop by when he got a chance."

"Stop by? Here?"

The woman gave her a blank stare. "That'd be my guess."

Great. That meant Rios was probably in the city on vacation. Why had he picked New York of all places, and why had he felt the urge to drop by to see her? It wasn't as if they'd stayed in touch after the infamous debacle at Whiskey Creek so many years ago. Truth was, she'd just plain avoided him.

Rayanne crumpled the pieces of paper and tossed them into the trash. "If he phones again, tell him I don't want him stopping by and I'll return his call the first chance I get."

Yes, when the equator froze over. That would surely be soon enough. She definitely didn't need a visit from Rios, not after the feathered hostage incident. She needed some time to compose herself and make sure she didn't have any lingering aroma of poultry and poultry by-products on her clothes.

"Will do," the woman assured her after she gave her gum a few more annoying cracks. "Say, I heard about the chicken."

"Already?" Rayanne checked her watch. "It just happened an hour ago."

"News travels fast around here. Makes you wonder why we bother with faxes and stuff."

Rayanne glanced around the squad room. And

agreed. News did travel fast, and apparently so did people doing really stupid things. Malcolm's comment suddenly became crystal clear. *So that's why they're acting like children.*

Yes, that about summed it up.

Someone had taped a picture of a strutting chicken cartoon to the outside panel of her cubicle. A ribbon of ratty Christmas tinsel framed it, and underneath were the words Dangerous Fugitive Apprehended at Last.

"See?" Malcolm said, pointing at the picture. "This is exactly what I was talking about the other day. They're making fun of you. This is sexual harassment."

Rayanne rolled her eyes. "It's not sexual harassment." She tore the picture from the padded wall, squashed it into a ball and sent it flying into a nearby trash can. "Poultry harassment, maybe. They're not doing this because I'm a woman. They do this to everybody."

He made a sound to indicate he didn't agree. "You can't tolerate this kind of behavior. It's juvenile—"

Rayanne cut off what he was about to say with a gesture of her hand and looked at the clutter of desks in the squad room. The place buzzed with activity that seemed both routine and chaotic at the same time. Phones rang, people talked, and the smell of bad coffee and stale pastry hovered like smog.

Here, air quality was a contradiction in terms.

She quickly scanned the dozen or so people to locate Detective Steve Beech. The man was a master at pranks, and she could see his handiwork in this one. Besides, he was one of the few people who knew how to use the new copier.

"Beech?" she called, knowing she had to make an obligatory insult to the perpetrator of such a joke. If their situations had been reversed, Beech would have done the same to preserve the camaraderie of the office, and Rayanne would have plastered something equally amusing around the perimeter of his desk. In the grand scheme of things, sulking about it or whining would have been juvenile. A good insult, however, would keep the goodwill flowing.

"What?" Beech answered. He did his part. He at least tried to cover up his grin and look concerned about whatever she was about to dish out.

In turn, Rayanne tried to put some grit in her voice. "Put another picture like this on my wall, and I'll make you a soprano the hard way."

That brought on the expected round of laughter. "Sure. Whatever you say, Rayanne."

"And you think that'll do it?" Malcolm crisply inquired.

She fished through her pocket, located the last of her fruity-flavored antacid tablets and stuck it in her mouth. "Eventually. They'll get tired of it, trust me. I know you're trying to help, but I don't need a shrink, okay?"

Malcolm nodded, after a long moment where he just stared at her. "All right, we'll try it your way a little longer. Sheez."

Rayanne turned in the direction of his somewhat stupefied gaze and became a little stupefied herself. There wasn't an inch of wall paneling not covered with photocopies of cartoon chickens. Some of them even had little badges doodled onto their feathered chests.

"I'm getting the lieutenant in here right now," Malcolm informed her.

She sighed and caught his arm. "I don't want the lieutenant. Please, Malcolm, just go. I have reports to file. Calls to make. Chicken pictures to remove."

He hesitated, his jaw muscles working. "We'll talk about this tonight at dinner." He did an about-face to plow through the squad room.

"Dinner," Rayanne said under her breath.

Mercy, she'd forgotten all about that. She had agreed to meet with Malcolm to discuss an incident regarding one of the rookies. Rayanne had wanted to have the meeting in Malcolm's office, but he'd somehow managed to talk her into hashing through the details over dinner. She made a mental note—don't do that again. No sense encouraging a relationship with Malcolm that she didn't want encouraged. The man just wasn't her type.

In fact, Rayanne was still sorting out what constituted her type. Her notions were somewhat nebulous in that area, but she definitely didn't want a man like Malcolm who always seemed to be in the middle of a sedative-required moment. Nope. She was looking more for a calming influence in her life. Too bad she hadn't run across even a remote candidate in, oh, at least seven or eight years. If this went on much longer, she might have to lower her standards.

"Say, Rayanne?" Detective Beech called. "Did that guy ever get in touch with you?"

Bracing herself for another joke, Rayanne shrugged. "What guy?"

"He didn't give his name. Tall. Cowboy boots. Said he's been calling but hadn't been able to reach you. He was around here just a minute ago."

"Cowboy boots," Rayanne repeated. She didn't like that little shiver that went down her spine. No, she didn't like it one bit. It was her cop's shiver, the one that had saved her derriere and other body parts on numerous occasions. She cautiously looked in the direction of her desk. The shiver turned into a full quake when she saw the man.

"Rios McKay," she mumbled under her breath.

He sat no more than a few feet away from her. In her chair, no less. Well, perhaps he wasn't actually sitting. He lounged with one long jeans-clad leg stretched out in front of him. His other foot, black snakeskin boot included, was pressed flat against the center drawer on her desk. He looked as if he had spent half his life in that chair. In this office. With his foot on her desk.

The man had the audacity to smile at her.

Rayanne's stomach did a somersault. There was just something about Rios McKay and that cocky smile that made her stomach go into a tailspin. Of course, he did that to most women, she begrudgingly conceded. He oozed sensuality, and to top it all off, he was a cowboy, complete with jeans that were snug in all the right places and a natural ruggedness that only hours in the Texas sun could give.

He was hot stuff.

And he knew it.

Eleven years hadn't changed him much. That dark black hair was still a little too long. It wasn't effeminate, however. Nothing about Rios was effeminate. He could have been a poster model for elevated testosterone levels.

There were tiny lines touching the corners of his eyes. They didn't look like wrinkles, even though he was thirty-three. Character lines, people called them. As if Rios needed any more character on that face.

"What are you doing here?" Rayanne asked when she remembered she had the capacity to speak. She only hoped he didn't notice her voice was a little too breathy. It was definitely not her cop's voice.

"I came to see you."

She would not blush. Would not. Would not. Would not! She was beyond that. She wasn't eighteen now, but a mature woman. She wouldn't give him the satisfaction of thinking he'd embarrassed her all those years ago.

"Well, what can I do for you?" Rayanne gave herself a mental pat on the back when she managed to keep her expression blasé and her tone casual. She didn't feel even a splash of blush creep onto her cheeks.

The corner of his mouth kicked into a wider smile, causing his dimples to wink at her. "Same old Rayanne. You still do that little thing with your breath."

The mental patting stopped. "What little thing?"

"It's like a little hiccup." Rios imitated it, following it with a husky chuckle. "I'll let you in on a secret. I've always thought it was sexy."

Her blasé expression slipped a notch. She kept her mouth closed so she wouldn't make that sound again. No sense giving him a cheap thrill.

His attention turned to the pictures of the chickens. "A new decorator?"

"No," Rayanne said crisply. "An inside joke." One she had no intention of sharing with him.

"So you like working here?" he asked.

"Yes, as a matter of fact, I do. But, of course, I'm extremely busy, which is why I'm afraid I can't spare you any time." Much, much better. Just like a deodorant commercial. Calm, cool, collected.

Catlike, he came to his feet and stepped toward her. The calm, cool and collected went right out the window. Rayanne forced herself not to take a step back, but it was a battle. She firmly reminded herself she was a cop. A tough hostage negotiator. So why did Rios make her feel like a high school girl with toilet paper in her bra?

It had been years since she had stuffed her bra.

"Please tell me why you've come." There was a smidgen of insistence in her voice. She had no doubt that smidgen would increase significantly if he didn't answer her. It was hard to hold back a blush for very long, especially since the images of that night kept creeping into her mind.

"Your aunt sent me."

Rayanne stiffened. "Is something wrong with Aunt Evie?"

"I guess you could say that. She's in the Longhorn jail."

"In jail?" That wasn't her cop's voice, either. It was something like a squawk. "On what charge?"

"Attempted assault with a deadly weapon."

Rayanne let the wall support her weight. A good thing, too. Between the news, her indigestion and Rios's presence, she thought maybe her legs had turned to banana pudding. "Is this some kind of sick joke?"

"No joke. She took aim at Bennie Quinn."

"Mr. Quinn?" The wealthiest, most powerful man in the county? "Mercy, he wasn't hurt, was he?"

Rios fumbled through a candy dish of M&M's and located a half dozen green ones. Cupping his hand, he funneled them into his mouth. "He's fine. Evie didn't even get a shot off. But Bennie still didn't care much for it. I warn you, Rayanne, he'll try to make sure the charges stick. You know how ornery he can be."

Rayanne pushed her hand over her hair. This had been one long day already, and it didn't seem as if it would end any time soon. "So, the first thing I need to do is post bail for her."

"Nope, she doesn't want bail. Believe me, a dozen people have already tried to do that, including me. Evie says she's not leaving the jail until you come for her."

"Why?"

"Heaven only knows. Remember we're talking about Evie Garrett here. The woman doesn't always operate on logic."

Rayanne didn't reprimand him for the insult. It was true. A logical thought would be very lonely in that woman's head. "Aunt Evie wants me to fly to Longhorn just so I can get her out of jail? She's up to something."

"That was my guess, too."

Her gaze met his. His eyes were the color of iced tea, or so all the girls in Longhorn always said. Rayanne didn't think there was anything icy about them. Slow burn was closer to the truth.

"Any idea why Aunt Evie really wants me to come home?" Rayanne asked, getting her mind on the business at hand. And that business didn't include eye color analysis.

"Nope. I gave up asking when she pulled her I'm-having-a-senior-moment routine. You know, sometimes I find it a little annoying when she does that."

Rayanne agreed, silently. And she knew exactly what Rios meant. Her aunt could stonewall a bulldozer just by pretending to be a sweet little old forgetful lady.

"So, why did Evie send you to tell me all of this?" And while she was at it, Rayanne wanted to ask him what he was doing in Longhorn. The last she'd heard, he was riding the rodeo circuit on the west coast. However, she wouldn't ask him anything about that. It might make him think she was interested in what he had to say. She wasn't.

She really wasn't.

He shrugged. It was lazy, like the rest of his movements. "Evie asked me to come. I came. I'd like to think of it as my good deed for the day." His cocky smile returned. "So, are you coming to Longhorn or what?"

Rayanne shook her head. "No, I'll just call her, and—"

"She won't take your call," Rios interrupted.

"She what? Why?"

He fished through his jeans pocket, pulled out a sheet of paper, unfolded it and began to read. "Don't bother calling me, Rayanne. The only way I intend to speak to you is face-to-face. If you can't get away from your busy job, I'll understand. My lawyer, Clyde Mueller, will do his best to see that justice is served. If he's not successful, then maybe you can visit me at Christmas. Right here. In the Longhorn jail. Love, Aunt Evie."

"Great," Rayanne said at the end of a groan. "She's really up to something." She glanced at Rios again. "How long has she been in jail?"

"Two weeks."

"Two weeks!" Rayanne cursed. It was practically whispered, but as close as Rios was standing, he no doubt heard it. "And no one bothered to get in touch with me before now? I should have been notified immediately. This is my aunt we're talking about."

"You know, Rayanne, you really oughta do something about that cursing. It's not very flattering."

"Really?" Well, now. She hadn't wanted to be petty, but that remark seemed to be a pettiness magnet. "I seem to remember you have a mouth like a sewer."

"Nope. Not anymore. I'm a changed man. Cursing's just not a very creative way to express oneself. Take that often misused word that starts with F, for instance. Somebody says that, and they mean it as an insult. But since when is that an insult? It's something people enjoy—"

"Rios." And she couldn't get out anything else until she put a chokehold on her quickly waning composure. "I don't want to talk about your theories of modern communication."

He shrugged. Rayanne wondered how he managed to express so much with a gesture that didn't even require energy. "So, are you coming to Longhorn?" he repeated.

"Well, of course, I will." Especially since it seemed Evie hadn't given her a choice. "I'll have to make some arrangements, but I think I can get there by tomorrow night."

He slipped the cream-colored Stetson on his head and flashed that knee-withering smile again. "Then I guess I'll see you around."

Only if she was incredibly unlucky. Luck had certainly been with her in the past. In the last eleven years on her dozen or so trips to Longhorn, she hadn't set eyes on Rios. Good thing, too. Seeing him only caused her to relive that night she'd been trying to forget.

He stepped into the squad room. "Know what? Not one of these guys look like the characters on TV."

"No? Well, welcome to reality. We're all just a hard-working bunch of cops."

His gaze came to Rayanne again. "Well, at least you lived up to my expectations. You look great."

It wasn't what she'd expected him to say. And it wasn't something she especially wanted to hear since he added a little surveillance to his observation. He looked her over from her head to her sensible walking shoes, but he paid particular attention to the parts in the middle, including but not limited to her breasts.

Rayanne refused to fold her arms in front of her, but she did consider it. Her chest slowly began to tighten, and she could feel the constricted muscles force her breasts against the flimsy lace of her bra. Rayanne didn't have to look down to know that her nipples were prominently displayed against her top. Rios might as well have touched her with his hand instead of his hot, thorough gaze. Fondling by proxy. It was still just as potent.

Rios touched his fingers to the brim of his hat. "Well, I guess I'd better be heading out now." But he didn't head out. He stood there and smiled at her again. "Rayanne?"

"What?" she murmured, her voice small and wishy-washy. Her whole body suddenly felt like a school cafeteria noodle. Why, why, why did he have this effect on her?

"I should have finished what I started that night by Whiskey Creek."

Oh, no. Not that. Anything but that. She hadn't thought in a million years that he'd bring up *the* embarrassing incident. Rayanne quickly ran through her options about how to answer that, and one by one she discarded each response.

"Uh," she finally said. "Okay."

Wait a blasted minute! *Okay.* That wasn't the best she could do. No way. This moment called for a regular belly-laugh zinger, like those she doled out to her fellow officers. There was a problem with that, however. Just like that night at the creek, she couldn't think of anything. Zip. Nada. Not one remotely insulting, score-settling line came to her.

"I've never given that night a moment's thought," she lied, knowing she had to say something. It barely qualified as *something,* but it sure beat standing there with her mouth gaping open.

"Funny, I think about it all the time." With a flick of his wrist, he reached out and caught a copper curl that had slipped from her hair clip. Skimming the hair and his finger along her cheek, he tucked the tress behind her ear. "I should have done better by you, Rayanne. That means I owe you one. You can collect anytime you want."

She quickly stepped away from him. And swallowed hard. Then it hit her. She'd just been zinged. By Rios. Zinged and reminded of a reminder she didn't want to be reminded of. That got her mouth working again. "You are without a doubt the most arrogant—"

"Yeah, I am."

As fast as lightning and as deadly as rattler venom, he brushed his mouth over her temple. Rayanne managed to get out a protesting gasp before he strolled out of the station house. She was vaguely aware of the catcalls and laughter that rippled through the squad room. But Rayanne just stood there. She could only wonder about the color of the truck that had just smashed into her head-on, but she was certain about the license plate.

Rios McKay's name was definitely on it.

CHAPTER TWO

"Talk is cheap until you hire a shrink."
—Bumper Ditties by Evie E. Garrett

RIOS WATCHED FROM beneath the brim of his Stetson. He'd pulled the hat low over his face as if taking a nap, but he didn't think he would get much of a nap in a New York City airport. Too much noise. Too many people. Too many people for him, anyway. And the only person he really wanted to see wouldn't be too happy that he was there.

He spotted Rayanne the moment she walked into the area. She had a sleek black leather bag on one arm and a tall blond-haired man on the other one. Rios remembered Rayanne had called the man Malcolm, and he was a shrink. It was also likely that the guy was Rayanne's, well, boyfriend. It was a term that didn't settle well on his stomach.

Rayanne wore silk. He knew that's what it was by the way it swayed. Moss-green slacks and a top that fluttered and caressed her body every time she moved. It was a far cry from the cutoffs she'd worn as a kid. Yes, a far cry indeed. Rayanne Marie Garrett had grown into one classy woman.

A woman who thought he was one notch below deep-crevice navel lint.

Rios didn't think this trip to Longhorn would improve the situation much. No, not at all.

She had her hair loose, and it fell to her shoulders in a sleek tumble. No fussy curls, nothing overdone, just hair the color of a new penny. It, too, swayed like the silk. Moved with her. And caused heads to turn. But then, Rayanne had always been able to turn heads. Now that she'd filled out, there was just more of her to get those heads turning faster.

"I still don't see why you feel you have to do this," Malcolm said to her as she checked in at the ticket counter. Rios didn't like the sound of his voice. It had a whine to it. "Your aunt's trying to manipulate you."

"Probably," Rayanne answered almost idly. She took her ticket from the attendant and thanked her. She looked around the area, but not in Rios's direction. He slid a little lower in the seat. It wasn't a good idea for her to see him just yet. She might decide to change planes, and for a lot of reasons he didn't want her to do that.

"Then why are you letting her get away with it?"

The whiner again. So, lover boy was trying to talk her out of leaving. Rios didn't think the guy stood a chance. Evie had done her level best to talk Rayanne out of leaving Longhorn eleven years ago, and it hadn't worked. If Evie couldn't talk Rayanne out of doing something, this scrawny fellow didn't have a clue.

Rayanne and the man moved away from the ticket kiosk but didn't take a seat. Instead, she stared out the window. Rios watched her. And listened.

"I'm going because Evie's the only blood relative I have," Rayanne explained. "She'd do the same for me."

"She wouldn't have to do this for you because you wouldn't pull such a juvenile stunt."

Rayanne's mouth went into a flat line. "Malcolm, I know you mean well, but I'm going to Longhorn. End of conversation."

Rios smiled. *Atta girl, Rayanne. Dish out some of that Garrett hardheadedness.* Malcolm shoved his hands in the pockets of his perfectly creased khakis and stared at her. "Does this have anything to do with that cowboy who visited you yesterday?"

That quickly got Rios's attention. Cowboy? He glanced at his jeans and well-worn boots. Yep, the guy probably meant him. Well, at least he hadn't called him Tex.

Rayanne's gaze whipped to her companion. "No, this has nothing to do with that cowboy." She spoke the last word as harshly as a profanity. "He's just some guy who used to work for my aunt, that's all."

Rios's left eyebrow twitched. He hadn't worked for Evie Garrett in eleven years. Rayanne knew it, too. It sure stung to be dismissed like that, but he'd expected to have to endure a few slings and arrows. After all, he hadn't bought Rayanne's line about not ever thinking about what had happened between them that night at the creek. No, she'd probably spent a long while trying to figure out why he had embarrassed her. Heck, it had taken Rios a while to figure it out himself. Maybe one day he would get the chance to explain it to her.

A slow smile curved Malcolm's mouth. Keeping his gaze on Rayanne, he looped his arm around her waist and hugged her. She ended the embrace soon enough, but it didn't matter. Rios had always known he had a jealous bone when it came to Rayanne, and that did a good job of enlarging it. When he'd seen enough of that little display of affection, he cleared his throat.

As if a current of electricity had passed through her body, her gaze lasered across the room. And lit directly on him. Rios put his thumb to the brim of his Stetson and pushed it back so she could see his face. Not that she needed to. Rayanne obviously knew he was there.

Clutching her bag, she stormed toward him, the green silk streaming around her. "What are you doing here, Rios?"

He slowly got to his feet and tipped his head in greeting, first to Rayanne and then to Malcolm. "That's exactly what you asked me yesterday."

"I don't think I'll like the answer any more today than I did then."

"Probably not. It appears we're booked on the same flight."

Her jaw turned to iron, and her Christmas-tree green eyes narrowed to little bitty slits.

Rios glanced at Malcolm. His jaw and eyes were pretty much the same.

"I don't believe we've met," the man said stiffly to Rios. "I'm Dr. Malcolm Keene."

"Rios McKay."

He offered his hand, and Rios shook it. And just like the hug the guy had given Rayanne, the handshake lingered a little too long for Rios's liking. It was clearly a contest. One he'd win. Even if he broke every bone in his hand. Malcolm's eyes widened with surprise.

"Oh, for heaven's sake," Rayanne complained, apparently noticing what was going on. "Stop this now. I mean it."

She quickly dropped the bag by her feet and latched on to both their hands to pry them apart. Malcolm didn't let go, and neither did Rios. Rayanne pulled harder. Rios lapped his left hand over hers, effectively sandwiching it. Malcolm did the same to her other one.

"Stop this now," Rayanne warned. From the sound of her voice, Rios knew she meant business. She might have on silk and smell like Chanel number whatever, but she could be tough as nails. Still, he didn't move his hands first. He waited until Dr. Whine lowered his.

"I'm sorry about that," Malcolm said to her. He caught her arm but kept his stern gaze on Rios. "Rayanne, I won't let you get on the same plane with this cowboy."

"I don't believe I asked you." Rayanne fired the words back.

She reached out and yanked open Rios's jacket. He held up his hands to let her do whatever she wished. Actually, he liked the bewildered expression on the doc's face. And he also liked Rayanne's wild, out-of-control search-and-seizure methods. It was so much better than that ice-princess act she'd put on the day before. Without consideration to buttons, fabric or even his chest hair, she fished through his shirt pocket until she came up with his ticket, which he had tucked inside. She scanned the information on the boarding pass and lifted her annoyed gaze to his.

Rios shrugged.

"You're in the seat next to me," she said. "But, of course, you knew that."

She didn't give Malcolm or Rios a chance to say anything, she marched to the ticket kiosk and began talking to the clerk. To change her seat, Rios figured. The woman could be predictable when she was riled.

"I want you to leave her alone, Tex," Malcolm said, placing a finger in front of Rios's face.

Rios calmly pushed the man's hand away. "The name's McKay," he enunciated.

"Whatever. Rayanne has been under a lot of stress lately, and I don't want you to add to it."

"It seems the source of her stress is right here. Going home might be good for her." Or not. Rios decided to keep that to himself. It was best not to bring up the negative side when trying to make a point.

"Going home could be a disaster. Rayanne might think the world of her aunt, but anyone can see the woman's manipulating her. God knows what she'll put Rayanne through."

"And this is leading where exactly? It seems Evie Garrett is Rayanne's business, not yours."

"I've made it my business. Because I care about Rayanne."

"Oh, you do, do you?" Rios leaned closer and lowered his voice to a secretive, patronizing level. "Well, I wouldn't get my hopes up if I were you. You don't appear to be her type. Personally, I'll bet she doesn't give a flying fig about you." And it didn't matter that it was a petty thing to say or that it might be a flaming lie, Rios just had to get a jealousy-induced jab in there.

Malcolm had already opened his mouth to say something when Rayanne rejoined them. She picked up her bag, her movements jerky and stiff. "Goodbye, Malcolm. I'll see you in a couple of days. Oh, and thanks for bringing me to the airport."

She didn't say anything to Rios. Not that he'd really expected it. But, boy, old Malcolm did.

He aimed a finger in Rios's direction. "You know what he said? He said you didn't care a flying fig about me."

Great day in the blooming morning. Rios hadn't

counted on Mr. Whine being a tattletale, as well. He sure didn't need a crystal ball to know how Rayanne would react to that. She aimed her narrowed eyes in his direction.

"Why would you tell him something like that?" she demanded. "You have absolutely no idea how I feel about him."

There was an old Texas saying—if you really wanted to get out of a big hole, the first thing you had to do was stop digging. It was real good advice, and usually Rios heeded good advice. Not today, though. There was just something about that wussy look in the doc's eyes and the challenging expression on Rayanne's face that made him want to keep on digging.

"If you cared about him," Rios said to her, "then that little hug earlier wouldn't have stayed so little. You got away pretty darn fast, if you ask me." He added a wink, knowing it would enlarge that hole to the size of the Grand Canyon.

It did.

Rayanne grabbed onto a handful of Malcolm's shirt, licked her lips and pressed them right onto the man's mouth. The kiss was long, slow and slightly brutal. She broke away only when the person on the intercom announced it was time to proceed to the gate.

"Bye, Rayanne," Malcolm said somewhat breathlessly. He also had a goofy smile on his face. "Hurry home."

"I will."

Rios got behind her in the line. "So, I guess you showed me. That's really your boyfriend, huh?"

She didn't even look back. "If you must know, no. But that is none of your business."

Too bad it felt like his business. It was also too bad

that her boyfriendless status pleased him immensely. "It's just as well. He seems a little prissy if you ask me." Rios stepped forward when she did. The line of people steadily began to move down the corridor through security.

"I didn't ask you."

He smiled at the sound of her voice. Her normal voice. It reminded him of a rusty gate. Not entirely pleasing, but it brushed against something deep within him. He assured himself it was only because he had gone so long without a woman. A little bit of lust could make even a rusty gate sound arousing.

Yes, indeed. That was all there was to it.

He liked flirting with Rayanne. Loved to tease her. And he cared about her in ways that bothered him at least a dozen times a day. But there was no way he could involve himself with her personally. Not now. There was too much at stake. The woman was definitely hands-off. She could muddy the waters big time.

They boarded, and Rayanne took a seat in first class. His, he knew, was in coach. Way back in coach. So, she'd spent some extra bucks to put some distance between them. She obviously didn't want anything to do with him. Well, he had news for her. If she didn't like being on the same plane with him, she sure wouldn't like what was going to happen when they got to Longhorn.

No, indeed.

RAYANNE LOOKED AT RIOS as if he'd lost his mind—a real possibility considering the source—and she was unerringly certain that she'd misunderstood him. "What did you just say?"

"I said I'm supposed to drive you to Longhorn."

She glanced around the San Antonio airport. It was late, and she was tired. She definitely didn't need offers of rides from ex-boyfriends. She wanted this uncomfortable trip down memory lane to end right here on the swirly patterned carpet in front of gate twelve.

"But I asked Freda to come and get me," Rayanne said. Freda, her aunt's longtime housekeeper and Rayanne's pseudo nanny. Freda had worked for Evie for twenty-five years, and whenever Rayanne made a trip to Longhorn, Freda had been the one who picked her up at the airport. She didn't see any reason for things to change now. Especially when that change involved Rios.

"Evie asked me to do it instead."

Rayanne definitely smelled a rat. A big one. "Why would she ask you to do that?"

"Because Evie didn't want Freda to have to drive at night, especially since we were on the same flight." He motioned toward the exit. "My truck's in the parking lot."

"Great. Just great."

Rayanne stood there for several moments, bag and purse in hand, and rummaged through her options. She could take a taxi, but she had already dropped an extra two hundred and sixty-eight dollars to fly first class so she could avoid sitting near Rios. She was doing okay financially, but that put a dent in her budget, especially since she'd done it to nourish a hissy fit. A rental car was her next choice. Actually, it was her only choice, she decided when she glanced at Rios. That hissy fit feeding apparently wasn't over yet.

"Seems kinda stupid, doesn't it?" he asked.

"What does?"

"You renting a car when it won't cost you a dime to

ride with me. NYPD probably pays pretty good, but I doubt if you have money to burn, especially considering that outfit must have cost you a bundle."

It had cost her a bundle. That was also none of his business. Rayanne gave him her cop's stare. All ice. She knew for a fact it was a good one because she'd practiced it enough in the mirror. It didn't, however, seem to have an effect on Rios. Well, no effect except that he grinned at her.

"I'll understand if you decide not to ride with me," he continued. "After all, I know you don't care much for my company."

She laughed, a single harsh burst of air. "Now, that's the understatement to understate all statements."

Rios calmly set down his bag. "Okay, then let's quit understating and stepping around what we've already stepped in. Let's have a real air clearing. Right here, right now. If we don't, you'll end up spending a small fortune and a lot of time just to keep your distance from me."

Rayanne reminded herself not to be petty. Then she looked at Rios. To heck with it. She felt a real bout of pettiness coming on. "There's nothing you can say that I want to hear."

"How about I'm sorry? I *am* sorry, you know. But have you ever considered how you would have felt if I had made love to you that night at Whiskey Creek? How would you have felt if I'd taken your virginity?"

Rayanne glanced at the people who trickled past them. She could tell from their expressions that a few heard what Rios said. She felt herself blush. She wasn't a prude, but she didn't like her past indiscretions, especially embarrassing ones, blurted out for all to hear.

"Like I said back at the station, I haven't thought of you or that night in years." Well, maybe it hadn't been years since she thought of Rios. But definitely weeks. All right. Days.

Rayanne was sure it had been at least a day.

"Well, I have thought about it," Rios said, "and you know what? You would have regretted it. You would have wanted to kick yourself from here to El Paso and back for letting me have you like that. You were looking for a commitment, Rayanne, and that's something I couldn't—"

"How can you presume to know what I thought?" She glanced around her again. They were starting to attract an audience. A rather tired-looking audience of late-night travelers, but still an audience. "This isn't the place to have this conversation."

"All right, if that's the way you want it."

"It is."

"Well?" he said after another long silence. "Do you want a ride, or are you going to let your pride get in the way of saving some money?"

"I want a ride." Rayanne didn't add anything to it. She couldn't. She had bruised her jaw muscles just to say that. She didn't really want a ride, but to refuse would seem, well, abnormally petty. Plain old petty was okay, but she didn't want to move into the abnormal range just yet.

"Then follow me," he said. "I'll have you home in no time."

"I don't want to go straight home. I want to go by the jail when we get to Longhorn."

Rios glanced at his watch. "It'll be well past midnight. Evie will already be asleep."

He was right. There was no reason to wake up her aunt in the middle of the night. However, she did want to see her first thing in the morning, and she wanted to talk to Sheriff Ryland. Rayanne especially wanted to know why the sheriff, who was a longtime friend of the Garrett family, hadn't already convinced Evie to post bond and go home.

They made their way through the parking lot to his truck. Except the vehicle wasn't just a truck. It was a lifestyle statement. Big. Blue. And budget-draining. Whatever Rios was doing these days, he was apparently successful.

"This truck is yours?" she asked.

He nodded and drove toward Highway 281, which led south to Longhorn. "Why'd you ask?"

"No reason." No reason she'd tell him, anyway. Rayanne wasn't about to point out that things in his life seemed to be good. Good in several areas, actually. He was still in good shape. No beer gut. No sagging bottom. No hair growing out of his nose or ears. He looked well-preserved from his high cheekbones all the way to his cowboy-cut jeans—which were too tight, she finally decided.

"When's the last time you were home?" Rios asked her.

She opened her mouth to answer, but he started playing with the ribbed grooves on the steering wheel. Well, just one groove, actually. And he was definitely playing with it. It distracted her for a moment. "Uh, I'm not sure."

But she was sure about that touching thing. She didn't like it. She didn't like the way he used the tip of his middle finger to trace the nipple-like projection. Slowly. Gently. Thoroughly. Over and over again.

"Too long, huh?" Rios asked.

Rayanne heard him. Somewhere in her brain it even registered, but she didn't have a clue what he meant. "Too long huh what?"

He looked at her, but he didn't stop the touching. His finger was barely grazing the small bulge and yet somehow giving it his complete attention. "Too long huh what?" he repeated. "What does that mean?"

"It means what do you mean?"

"It means I was looking for a simple answer to a simple question. All I wanted to know was how long it'd been since you were in Longhorn."

A simple question, yes, and it could have been a simple answer if she hadn't been so distracted. *Mouth, form words,* she ordered.

"New York," she mumbled.

"Huh? Now, what exactly does that mean?"

All right, not the best effort her mouth had ever put forth, but it was a start. She'd requested that it form words, and it had. *Try harder.* "It means Aunt Evie's been coming to New York so there was no reason for me to return home."

"So it's been a while since you were there?"

It sounded almost like a prompt a lawyer would give a confused witness. Rayanne decided it was best if she nodded. She probably was a little confused at the moment.

"Three years," she finally managed to say.

She took a deep breath and tried to steady her heartbeat. It was so stupid, really—her reacting to something so simple as Rios touching his steering wheel.

After all, it was just a… Mercy. He stroked it! Not just the little bump, either, but he went after the groove beside it. He slipped his big finger right in there. And rubbed. How dare he rub his steering wheel that way? Rayanne's mouth dropped open. Her breasts tightened. She squirmed on the seat.

"You don't miss it?" he asked.

"What? Miss what?"

"Longhorn."

"Oh." Rayanne heard the desperation in her voice and hoped he hadn't.

He had. Rios looked at her, and he had concern written all over his face. "Are you all right? I mean you're not going to get carsick, are you?"

She wished. She'd rather throw up on him than have his finger drive her crazy. "No, I'm fine."

"You don't look fine. You look like you're going to throw up. Should I pull over on the side of the road?"

"I'm fine!" she snapped. Fortunately, the snapping seemed to realign her hormones, and she knew what she had to do to get this madness to stop. With Rios, the direct approach was always best. "I want you to quit touching your steering wheel like that. It bothers me."

He narrowed one eye as if in deep thought. He looked at her. Then he looked at the steering wheel. "You want me to quit touching my steering wheel," he flatly repeated. "What, people in New York don't touch their steering wheels when they drive?"

"They don't rub them and stroke them. They grip them. Real men grip steering wheels."

She thought he might laugh. She thought she might scream. Well, that was one for the record books. *Real men grip steering wheels.* She only hoped Rios would let it pass without making too much of a big deal about it.

No such luck.

"So, let me get this straight," he said in a tone of deep, mock contemplation. "If I want to be a real New York man, I have to grip the steering wheel. I can't touch it." He paused. "Am I allowed to touch the stick shift or would that qualify me as a genuine wimp?"

Rayanne forced herself to breathe normally. Control was the operative word here. She needed to regain control.

"Conversation," she said. "Normal. Try."

He paused again and looked at her funny. "Will. Do. I'm a little afraid to ask after the discussion we've had for the last few minutes, but what exactly constitutes normal conversing for you these days?"

The list was apparently very short. "Longhorn. Let's talk about Longhorn." It seemed safe, on the surface, anyway. As long as Rios didn't touch anything, she thought she might be okay.

"Sure. Longhorn. Let's see. I've already asked you how long it's been since you've been home. I don't really want to go through that again, so let's try this. Um, do you like living in New York better than you did Texas?" He grinned at her. "How's that for normal?"

"It'll do, and the answer is yes. New York suits me."

"You sure about that?"

Slightly bothered, Rayanne puckered her lips. No, she wasn't sure at all, but she didn't want Rios challenging her when they were finally getting around to having a normal conversation. One normal question, and he was already off track.

"I'm positive it suits me," she lied. "I've made a life

for myself there. It's my place in the world, you might say. I would have had a hard time doing that around Longhorn where people still tend to think of me as Evie Garrett's orphaned niece." Or where Rios thought of her as some innocent little kid. "Why do you ask if I'm sure that New York suits me?"

"A couple of reasons. The smell of fruity-flavored antacids on your breath, and you've been acting a little high-strung. Plus your non boyfriend, Dr. Whine, said you were under a lot of stress."

"Malcolm said that?" Rayanne frowned. How dare Malcolm discuss her personal life with anyone, and especially with Rios? Great day, Malcolm was always trying to make something more of their relationship than it was. Of course, that idiotic kiss she'd given him at the airport wouldn't help matters. She would really have to take the time to set him straight, gently, when she returned.

"That riles you a little that Dr. Whine told me that, huh?"

"You're quickly slipping away from the boundaries of a normal conversation, Rios. Let me give it a try. Something normal, I mean." She paused and tried to think of a neutral subject. It wasn't easy. Just talking with Rios was somewhat abnormal. "Okay, I got it. When did you move back to Longhorn?"

"How did you know I'd moved away?"

"Aunt Evie must have mentioned it." Rayanne made it seem as if she didn't know. Actually, she recalled everything her aunt ever mentioned about Rios. For some unexplainable reason those kinds of facts just seemed to stick in her head, no matter how much she tried to unstick them. "She maybe also mentioned something about you being on the rodeo circuit."

"I was. I came back about a year ago."

"Why?"

"Personal reasons."

She hadn't expected a roadblock from Rios, but Rayanne recognized one when she heard it. Well, it didn't matter. She didn't care what personal reasons had brought him back to town. Nope, didn't care one crumb.

Besides, Evie would tell her what she wanted to know.

They rode in silence for a long time, and Rayanne watched the San Antonio city lights give way to the gently sloping countryside. Rios tuned the radio to a country station, and the slow, easy music lulled her into relaxing. Rayanne leaned her head against the seat and nearly fell asleep.

"So, it's really not serious between you and that shrink?" he asked.

Just as quickly her head came off the seat. Apparently, relaxation wasn't in the cards tonight. "I don't want to discuss him with you." But no way was it serious. Malcolm was a friend. Period.

"Discussing the shrink isn't in the realm of a normal conversation, either?" Rios again. But like before, he waited until she'd almost relaxed before he asked it.

"No, it isn't." And it didn't hurt matters that Rios seemed a little jealous about Malcolm. Well, at least curious, anyway. Rayanne decided to let him hold on to that curiosity a little longer.

They passed the Longhorn city limits sign, and Rayanne inched closer to the window to get a better look.

"I guess that means you won't be telling me exactly who you're sleeping with these days?" he asked.

Rayanne was about to glare at him, but she saw something that stopped her attempted glare in mid facial rearrangement. There was a big plastic cow hanging precariously from a cable strung across the main street. On its sagging udders, someone had advertised the dates of the town festival.

"Amazing," she mumbled. She shook her head and kept staring at it. "It really is a plastic cow, and it's hanging over Main Street."

"It's foam rubber, actually. Hal's Hungry Heifer restaurant went out of business over in Floresville, and Evie bought it."

"Aunt Evie bought Hal's Hungry Heifer restaurant?" Rayanne asked in disbelief.

"No, she bought the rubber cow that used to be in the party room. You know, the one that kids climbed on all the time? It was there for going on twenty years. Anyway, Evie decided it was practically a local icon and didn't want to see it thrown away."

"But why is it hanging over Main Street like that?"

"It wouldn't fit in the barn, so Evie donated it to the town."

Amazing. Absolutely amazing. "And the town actually accepted it?"

"The town didn't have much of a choice. You know how persuasive Evie can be when she puts her mind to it."

Rayanne did. In fact, she was living proof of her aunt's persuasiveness. Only Evie could have gotten her to return to Longhorn, and only at Evie's request would she have accepted a ride with Rios. But getting the town to accept a rubber cow? That was quite an accomplishment—even for Evie.

Rayanne kept her attention on the cow as Rios drove beneath it. "That thing won't fall, will it?"

"Already has. A couple of times. Fortunately, it's rubber so it just bounces around until it stops, even though it did mess up Sara Jean Kellerman's new perm. She's thinking about suing."

The ringing interrupted her from thinking another *amazing.* She automatically reached for the phone that was usually clipped to her belt only to remember it wasn't there. She'd put her phone and pager in her bag.

"I think this one's for me," Rios said, answering the phone sandwiched into the console.

Rayanne leaned her head against the window and listened to the sound of his voice. Not exactly comforting, but still so familiar even after all these years.

It was hard to believe she was riding in the same vehicle with Rios. Actually, it was hard to believe she was within twenty miles of him. After that night at Whiskey Creek, she'd sworn she wouldn't give him the time of day. Yet here she was, in his truck, letting the sound of his voice lull her into…not relaxing, exactly.

No, not that at all.

It had lulled her into remembering things that were best forgotten. The lover's things he'd whispered to her that night. The eager caresses, much like the ones he'd given his steering wheel. The kisses. Yes, those hot, wet, brain-numbing kisses. But then he'd blown it, of course, by leaving her high and dry. Despite his apology, she didn't intend to let herself get in that position again. No, sirree. No heated romps on the banks of a creek. Those romping days were over.

"Think we need Doc Keller?" she heard Rios ask. He paused. "Okay, I'll be there in about twenty minutes."

"Trouble?" she asked when he ended the call.

"Just a problem with one of my mares."

"A mare? Are you ranching these days?"

"Some. It's hard not to ranch around Longhorn. Cattle and horses are the lifeblood here."

"You have your own place?"

He nodded and stopped the truck in front of her aunt's house. It looked beautiful in the moonlight. Actually, the moonlight did it a lot of justice. Rayanne knew it was just a two-story house that always needed a coat of paint, the roof fixed or something. Yet she didn't seem to notice those needed repairs when she looked at it. What she saw was home, and as it always did, it made her eyes a little misty.

"Want me to help you with your bag?" Rios asked.

"No, thanks. I can manage."

The front door opened, and Freda came out onto the porch. Cinching her faded chenille robe around her stout waist, she hurriedly made her way across the yard toward the truck.

"Rayanne, honey, it's so good to see you." The woman pulled her into a hard hug and slapped her back. "Always my little ray of sunshine in the middle of a cold spell. Welcome home, honey. Welcome home."

"It's good to see you too, Freda." Rayanne smiled. She always liked the oddball metaphors that Freda came up with. Actually, she liked everything about Freda. Hugging her was like hugging a chocolate-scented teddy bear. "You haven't changed a bit in three years."

"Oh, pshaw, of course I have. I got older, fatter and prettier, in that order. Ain't that right, Rios?"

Still inside the cab of the truck, Rios shook his head. "Nope, only the pretty part's right."

"Oh, pshaw, but so sweet of you to say. Just like hot fudge sauce on homemade ice cream. You've got a real sweet spot in you, Rios."

Rayanne couldn't imagine where he'd been hiding that sweet spot. Even more, she didn't intend to go looking for it. She waved, hoping it would send him on his merry way. "Thanks for the ride. Good night, Rios."

"Same to you, little ray of sunshine in the middle of a cold spell. Get a good night's sleep. I'll see you around."

Yes, but not for long. With luck she'd have all of this mess cleared up tomorrow and be on a plane to New York. Without luck, she'd even do it. Putting some distance between her and Rios was a strong motivator to spur her into action.

"Come on in," Freda said, giving her another hug. "We can have a nice cup of cocoa and some homemade snicker doodles. Then you can tell me all about that chicken that attacked you in New York City. Had to arrest it, I heard."

Rayanne turned toward Rios so quickly she heard her neck pop. "You didn't?"

He shrugged. "There are just some things a real man can't keep to himself."

CHAPTER THREE

"If life's a stage, then I want better lighting."
—Bumper Ditties by Evie E. Garrett

"ARE YOU FINALLY, maybe, almost awake yet?" the small voice asked.

"Huh?" Rayanne grunted and squashed the pillow over her face. Great, now she was hearing voices.

"Are you finally awake yet?" The voice again. "'Cause I've been waiting a long time for you to be awake."

Not just a voice. Not a dream, either. Ugh. Reality. This was probably someone or something she had to deal with if she wanted to get more sleep.

Rayanne pushed the pillow off her face. Her eyelids stirred and finally jarred open. There were streams of piercing bright light coming through the Tinkermouse cartoon curtains on the window. Tinkermouse? Rayanne had been so tired the night before, she hadn't noticed the room, and she hadn't seen those curtains since she was ten. Aunt Evie had obviously decided to try a little retro decor.

The headache-inducing light told Rayanne more than she wanted to know. It was dawn. Or perhaps even later. And she was in her bed. In her room. In Longhorn.

But she wasn't alone.

Her eyes opened wider. Much wider. There, next to

her bed, was a child in pink overalls and a ruffled shirt. She wasn't a dream, either. It was a real little girl with brownie-colored curls tumbling around her face. She smiled at Rayanne.

"Are you finally awake yet?" she repeated, the toothy grin nearly as wide as her face. "I mean, I know you're not dressed yet, but it looks like you're awake."

Dressed? No, she wasn't dressed. But just how undressed was she? Rayanne glanced at her silk teddy. Thankfully, the rose-colored swatch covered vital parts of her so she wasn't giving the child an eyeful. There were plenty of times she went to bed wearing only her nail polish.

"You have a little gown, don't you?" the child asked.

Rayanne quickly pulled the sheet over her. "I guess."

"I think it's even littler than mine. Maybe it's even little enough for my doll. But maybe not. I don't have on my gown 'cause I'm already dressed for school, but I have on my Tuesday panties today."

Rayanne had to think—was it Tuesday? And why did it matter if it was? This didn't seem like a conversation she wanted to have right now. Actually, what she wanted to do was sleep just a little bit longer.

"Who are you?" Rayanne asked.

"Mattie. I made you some tea."

"Mattie," she repeated. The name didn't ring a bell, but the prospect of tea was reason to get moving. Rayanne studied the small tray the child had clasped in her equally small hands. Two delicate, miniature china teacups, a matching teapot and two Twinkies still in their wrappers. "It looks good." Actually, it looked darn good. It had been years since she'd had a Twinkie. "Mattie, why are you here?"

"To bring you some tea. Aunt Freda said I couldn't come up unless you were awake. You're awake. Finally."

"Well, sort of." Rayanne yawned noisily and scrubbed her hands over her face. She probably wouldn't qualify as awake until she had some caffeine mainlined into her arteries.

"Know what Aunt Freda calls me sometimes? Her little spoonful of sugar in her bowl of granola. What do you think that means, exactly?"

"It means she thinks you're sweet." Rayanne tried to smile. "Actually that's one of Freda's better sayings." At least it was one that made sense. There were plenty that didn't. "Where are your parents?"

Mattie sat on the edge of the bed and started to unwrap the Twinkies. "My mother's away on a trip, and Daddy's working this morning. So when he's working I stay with Miss Evie and catch the school bus over here. Well, except Miss Evie's away on a trip to the jail, so now I'm staying with Aunt Freda." She lowered her voice and cupped a dainty hand around her mouth as if telling a secret. "She smells just like chocolate Easter bunnies. I get hungry when I'm around her."

Rayanne got her mouth to cooperate with a smile. And silently agreed with the child's observation. Ah, so Mattie was another of Freda's relatives. Now Rayanne understood. For as long as she could remember, Freda's cousins had been coming to Longhorn to stay with Evie. "So, how long will you be here?"

"Don't know. Nobody tells me much. You know how it is."

She did indeed. After all, her aunt had been in jail for two weeks before anyone bothered to let her know.

Mattie put a Twinkie on one of the small plates and

handed it to Rayanne. When she poured the tea, however, Rayanne saw that it was only water. Still, a Twinkie and water was more than she usually got for breakfast. In New York, breakfast was a half dozen cups of bad coffee and a couple of strawberry-flavored antacids.

She had just taken a huge bite of the smushy pastry when there was a tap on the door. "Come in, Freda. We're having breakfast."

"Breakfast, huh?"

But it wasn't Freda's voice. It was Rios, and as bold as brass he stepped right into her bedroom.

Remembering Mattie's presence, Rayanne clipped off the snippy protest that nearly slid right out. "What are you doing in here?"

But he didn't have time to answer. The child bolted off the bed and rushed into his open arms. Rayanne had to grab the teapot and cups to keep the water from spilling onto the bed.

"Daddy!" Mattie squealed.

Rayanne's jaw went slack. And then she remembered she had the blunt end of a Twinkie poking out of her mouth. It probably wasn't very attractive. Not that she wanted to be attractive for Rios, but she quickly removed it and stuck it on the plate.

"Daddy?" Rayanne questioned. "Daddy?"

Rios shrugged and planted a noisy kiss on the little girl's cheek. "What are you doing up here, Mattie?"

"Bringing Miss Rayanne some breakfast. It's all right. She's awake, and Aunt Freda said it was okay if she was awake, but it took her a real long time to wake up so I had to wait. She doesn't look anything like Miss Evie, and she wears a teeny weensy gown to bed. I'm talking real teeny."

At that, his eyebrow shot up. And he smiled. Rayanne pulled the covers higher until she was sure every inch below her chin was covered. "This is your daughter?"

"Yep."

Rayanne tried to make her brain process that. It couldn't. "But she said Freda was her aunt."

"She is. Well, sort of. Let me see—Freda's great-aunt is married to my second cousin." He kissed Mattie's cheek again. "Better hurry, sugar. The bus will be here any minute."

"Okay, Daddy." She returned the kiss and slid from his arms. The moment her feet touched the floor, she headed for the door. "Bye, Miss Rayanne. I'll see you when I get back from school."

"Bye, Mattie." The cheery expression stayed on Rayanne's face for a millisecond after the child left. She shifted her position on the bed and gave Rios a look that told him he could leave, as well.

"You probably shouldn't have done that." He clasped his hands over his eyes in an exaggerated help-me-I'm-blind gesture.

"Shouldn't have done what?"

"Flashed me. I'm a man, after all, and it's a little disconcerting to my male brain to see parts of you that I shouldn't be seeing. Well, unless you're inviting me to see them."

Her mouth dropped open. "Flashed you? What the devil are you talking about? I'm not offering to show you anything and I most certainly didn't flash you."

With one hand covering his eyes, he pointed in the direction of the dresser on the other side of the bed. Rayanne slowly turned so she could see, and there was a lot to see. The whole front of her was covered, but the whole back of her wasn't. From behind, the silk teddy didn't leave much to the imagination, especially since it had ridden up to new fashion heights. She looked like she was wearing a thong.

Ew, and she'd stuck her elbow in Twinkie cream.

Her gaze fired to Rios, and she was prepared to deliver a scathing sermon about him being in her room. But he was gone. Well, almost. Rayanne could hear the sound of his laughter as he made his way down the hall.

So, Rios was a father? A father. Him? As foreign a notion as it sounded, he seemed good at it. He'd been loving, kind and gentle with Mattie. It sure was a different side of a man whose sides she thought she knew all too well.

But if Rios was a father, then there was also a mother. And that meant he was…married?

Married!

She hurdled out of the bed, wiped the sticky white stuff from her elbow and threw on her clothes. Rayanne only hoped Freda was in a talkative mood. If not, she'd find some way to worm it out of her.

Rios, married!

RIOS HEARD THE screen door slam, and a moment later he saw Rayanne making her way across the yard toward him. At least he saw the bottom half of her body as he peered from beneath Evie's ancient yellow sedan. Rayanne's skirt wasn't exactly short, but from his angle he had a nice view of her shapely legs. Enough of an angle to wish her skirt were longer so he wouldn't be tempted to wish it were shorter.

"Freda?" she called.

"She's at the grocery store," Rios answered. He

checked his watch to time how long it would take her to ask about Mattie. Less than sixty seconds, he figured.

Rayanne leaned down and frowned. She probably would have frowned even more if she'd known he could see right up her slim little skirt. It seemed to be the day for him to get glimpses of her intimate apparel.

"You're flashing me again." He let her know. He forced himself to look away.

Rios heard her gasp. Yanking and tugging at her skirt turned out to be futile, but she apparently wasn't ready to give up her attempt to stay put so she could grill him. She got on her knees and looked under the car at him.

"What are you doing under Aunt Evie's car, anyway?" she asked.

Rios didn't think she'd want to know the truth. It wouldn't seem right for a grown man to admit he was having fantasies about lacy foundation garments. So he decided to give her the other answer instead. "I'm fixing an oil leak."

"Oh." She took a sip of coffee. Rios could smell it. And her. A mingle of everything that was female. It was a strangely enticing blend, even mixed with the scent of motor oil. "And I suppose you do this often?"

"Sometimes." Of course, it had never been quite this interesting. It gave lubrication tuning a whole new meaning.

Rios pushed himself from beneath the car and got to his feet. He took a rag from his back pocket and used it to mop the sweat off his forehead.

Rayanne stood, too, and leaned against the hood. "Mattie sure seems, um, nice."

He checked his watch. One minute and sixteen seconds. All that skirt tugging had obviously slowed her down a bit. If she'd been wearing jeans, this conversation would have already been on its way. "Let me save you a little trouble here. Her mother is Patricia Quinn."

Rayanne's eyes enlarged to the size of dinner plates. "You married Bennie's daughter?"

"I didn't say I married her." Rios kept his attention on the rag he still had in his hand. "She died about a year ago."

"Died? But Mattie said her mother was away on a trip."

"That's what Bennie tells her. Mattie knows the truth, but sometimes she likes to pretend Patricia's coming back."

"Wow." And Rayanne said nothing else for a while. "So, how is it that Bennie didn't force you to marry Patricia?"

"Neither Bennie nor I knew about Mattie. About seven years ago Patricia came out to Denver where I was riding rodeo. We got drunk." He shrugged. "And we slept together. I didn't think much about it until she called last year to ask if I'd raise Mattie."

Rios made the mistake of looking at Rayanne. They were standing close to each other. Probably too close. And she seemed to be taking in every word. It reminded him of those days when she thought he hung the moon. Now she probably wanted to put him on a one-way space shuttle and send him there.

"So what'll happen?" Rayanne asked.

"Until Bennie and I can work out some kind of permanent custody arrangement, Evie and Freda help me out sometimes by looking after Mattie. In turn, I fix oil leaks in the car."

"I see." The words were said so softly that Rios looked at her again.

Evidently his eyes didn't intend to behave this morning because they seemed to be taking in everything Rayanne wasn't offering. Those long tanned legs. The curve of her hips. Her breasts. His eyes seemed especially pleased with those and lingered there for a while before moving to her face. That face. God, that face. The woman was hot.

"You've got the greenest eyes in Texas, you know that, Rayanne?"

She blinked. "That sounds like a bad country music song."

It did, but it was better than comparing her eye color to his favorite flavor of suckers.

Rios had a sudden urge to touch her. Well, maybe not just touch. What he had a sudden ache to do really involved clothing removal. He didn't think he should go that far in broad daylight in front of her aunt's house.

But the barn was pretty close.

Her lipstick was smeared, and Rios doubted she knew it. She'd probably set a world record getting dressed so she could find Freda and ask her about Mattie. But since he couldn't haul her off to the barn, it was that smeared lipstick that would give him his cheap thrill for the day.

"Hold still," he instructed. Before she could figure out what he had in mind, he took her coffee and set it on the car.

She opened her mouth, probably to ask what the heck he was doing, but Rios didn't give her a chance. The moment he put his hand around the back of her neck, she went board stiff. That didn't stop him. Touching her mouth, he slowly inched his thumb over her lip, wiping away the stray color. If he had any sense, he would have left it at that, but apparently he didn't have any sense.

Nope. No sense at all.

He grazed the tip of her tongue. It was hard not to

think trashy thoughts when he had his thumb in her mouth. Keeping his gaze locked with hers, he brought his hand to his own mouth and licked the lipstick off his thumb. Yep. There was no doubt about it. Rayanne tasted as good as she looked.

She gasped. And stared at him. Then gasped again. "Why do you always do crazy things like that?"

"Straightening your lipstick is crazy?" He made sure he sounded like Mr. Innocent. "It was a thoughtful gesture." And a cheap thrill. "Now, kissing you—that'd be crazy."

Rios stared at her. And stared. There was a moment, a split second of time, when he thought he'd talked himself out of what he was about to do. He was so wrong.

"Ah, heck," he grumbled.

He lowered his head and put his mouth to hers. He wanted to feel the lust, and he did. There was lust galore. But he also felt other things. Things that made the kiss go from just plain wonderful to extraordinary. The softness of her mouth. Her taste. *Her.* Especially her. Rayanne was certainly one of a kind.

A quick slam of desire went straight to the nether region of his body. Not a good direction. Rios knew for a fact that part of him rarely made good decisions. He wasn't counting on it to make a good decision this time, either.

Apparently his mouth was thinking along the same erroneous lines.

"More," he heard himself say.

She resisted. But not much. He persisted. A lot. And finally got her mouth open so he could deepen the kiss. She tasted like coffee and cream and more. It was a taste he'd remembered after eleven long years.

His tongue brushed over hers, sipping again at that sweet taste. If he thought it was hard not to have trashy thoughts with his fingers in her mouth, it was even harder now that they were playing tongue footsies.

Rios waited for her to push him away. Rayanne would lecture him for sure. She would give him a long speech about why he shouldn't have kissed her. Maybe she'd even slap him.

But that didn't happen.

She made a low throaty moan of pleasure and slipped her hand around his neck. Her fingers started to play with his hair. Now that he couldn't handle. There was only so much a man could take, and hair playing was definitely heavy-duty foreplay as far as he was concerned. Foreplay could lead to things that couldn't happen between them. Like making love. Making love really, really couldn't happen. This was one time he would have to veto the whining parts of his body.

Rios stopped the kiss and looked at her.

Her eyelids fluttered open. "Let go of me."

He didn't have any part of her to let go of. As if in surrender, his hands were in the air, and he was leaning back. Rayanne, conversely, had the fingers of her left hand clawed into his chest. Her other hand was wound around his neck, and she was still doing that hair-playing thing.

Looking dazed, she removed her hands from him and stepped back. "Swear to me you'll never do that again."

"Nope."

"Nope?"

"You heard me, and I didn't stutter." But Lord, he should have. Rios quickly pushed that negative notion aside. He felt a roll coming on, and he never liked to pass up a roll even if the premise was just plain stupid. "Remember all the heat that used to snap, crackle and pop between us? Well, it's still there, Rayanne. And don't deny it. Your eyes are glazed, and you're breathing like you're asthmatic."

"What—"

"Don't worry, I've got all the signs, too. I don't want to respond to you any more than you want to respond to me. Wanting you could do nothing but complicate my life right now, and I don't need any more complications."

She took a hard look at his face, apparently trying to figure out if he'd just said what she wanted him to say. "Well, good. At least we agree on something."

"You bet we do. That's why I've thought about us just making love and getting it over with. A good long sweaty bout where we get naked and try to kill each other." He continued before she could make her outraged mouth produce words. "But having carnal knowledge of you won't make anything go away. Well, it might temporarily, but I don't think we're talking more than a half hour or so at the most. So, the way I see it, this is just something we have to learn to deal with."

"Deal with? What the heck does that—"

"I have to go." Rios checked his watch but didn't really want to know the time. He already knew. It was time to get out of there before he forgot everything he'd just said. "Evie should be up by now."

Rayanne's gaze fired to her own watch. "Heavens, you're right." She grabbed her cup of coffee and took a large gulp. "I need to get to the jail." But then she stopped and looked at him. "I trust you won't be here when I get back."

"Never can tell. The world's just full of surprises."

"I've already had my surprise quota for the day. The year," she quickly corrected.

Rios begged to differ. The surprises were just beginning.

CHAPTER FOUR

"Don't play stupid with me. I'm better at it."
—Bumper Ditties by Evie E. Garrett

THERE WERE FOAM rubber cow parts in the middle of
Main Street.

Of course, it took Rayanne a couple of minutes to
realize exactly what those parts were. The former Hal's
Hungry Heifer advertisement icon was toast, or more
precisely a mangled heap of manufactured bovine bits.

"Wind," Herman Sheckley, the barber, declared as he
walked by Rayanne. "A big gust of wind."

"Wind did that?" she asked skeptically.

He angled his hands apart as if showing the size of
his latest catch. "Had to be a big gust of wind."

Maybe, or maybe it was someone with an ax to grind.
Those chop marks on the cow's rump looked suspicious.
Still, Rayanne wasn't about to suggest a crime had occurred. If someone in Longhorn wanted to chop up that
rubber cow, then she didn't want to know anything about it.

"You're here to get Evie out of jail?" Herman asked.

"Yes."

"All the way from New York City?"

Since that seemed to be a question, Rayanne nodded.
"How have you been, Mr. Sheckley?"

"Right as rain. Say, Freda mentioned something about you having to arrest a chicken. She said it attacked you."

It was the case that just wouldn't die. Rios told Freda. Freda told Herman. Herman had probably blabbed it over the tristate area.

He chuckled. "Hey, did the chicken squawk when you questioned it? You get it? Chicken, squawk?"

"I get it, but it's not something I like to talk about."

The chuckling continued. In fact, it got so hard, he began to wheeze. "Something you'll tell your grandchildren about, I guess."

No, she wouldn't. No grandchild of hers would ever hear that story. "I'll see you around."

As she stepped around the cow parts and continued down the street, it was easy for her to see that some things never changed. Some things, except for the mutilated cow. The town of Longhorn was pretty much the same as it had always been. Quiet. Laid-back. Even the graffiti on the park bench was spelled correctly and written with good penmanship.

There was Herman Sheckley's barbershop with the poor imitation of a wooden Indian in front of it. A poor imitation because Herman had dressed the statue in his son's old football uniform. Ina Fay's diner still had the Hot Coffee sign in the window. The sign had curled on the edges and offered a steaming cup for a nickel. Or rather an *ickel,* since someone had scratched out the *n.* More often than not, Ina Fay refilled those cups of java for free. It was that kind of hospitality Rayanne missed more than she cared to admit.

She walked down the street until she reached the buttermilk-colored brick building that housed the sheriff's office. It looked exactly as it had for twenty-odd years. There was something comforting about that. Exactly what, she couldn't say.

There was also something else that apparently hadn't changed, and she wasn't the least bit comfortable with it—the way she responded to Rios.

Stupid. Stupid. Stupid.

Stupid.

She'd let him touch her under the guise of repairing her lipstick. That was her first mistake. Then she went from dumb to dumber when she hung around long enough for him to kiss her. Her third mistake, the dumbest, was choosing physical pleasure over common sense.

Kissing Rios had indeed been that—physical pleasure. And maybe it had stirred other areas of her, too. That's why it couldn't happen again. Uh-uh. Thankfully, and miracle of all miracles, he agreed with her. Finally, they were on the same side about something. Now all they had to do was stay away from each other. To make sure that happened, she'd wrap up her business in Longhorn. And wrapping up started with Evie.

Rayanne took a deep breath and went inside the sheriff's office—the place where the buck started.

"Hi, can I help you?" the woman standing behind the desk asked.

Rayanne opened her mouth and closed it just as quickly. The woman was hugely pregnant, her stomach sticking out like a prizewinning watermelon. "Are you—" Rayanne tipped her head to the oversize belly. "All right?"

She smiled and wheezed out a heavy breath. "Not really. I'm due any day now. I wish I could say it looks worse than it feels, but I can't. That's because it feels like I'm carrying a mule." She rubbed her hand over the watermelon. "How are you, Rayanne?"

"Fine." Rayanne studied the woman's face but didn't recognize her. "I'm sorry, but I don't remember your name."

"Arnette Richert. Used to be Arnette Middleton."

"Oh, yes. You were a couple of years behind me in high school."

"Six years, actually," Arnette corrected.

Six years? Something about that didn't set well with Rayanne, and it made her feel more than a little old. Arnette was only twenty-three and already having a baby? Rayanne sincerely hoped it wasn't the ticking of her biological clock that made that information a little hard to swallow.

"I'm the deputy here now," Arnette explained. She waddled to the other side of the room and put a folder in the filing cabinet. That activity apparently exhausted her because she leaned against the wall. "I'm sure it's nothing like what you do. Nothing nearly as important happens around here."

Rayanne wasn't sure of that at all. The kiss Rios had planted on her certainly seemed monumental and illegal. "I'm sure what you do is important to the people of Longhorn." Like cleaning up that rubber cow. The thought of that made Rayanne smile. It might be fun to be a peace officer in a town where the serious crimes roster read like a comedy monologue.

"I suppose you're here to see Evie?" Arnette asked.

"Yes. Is she up?"

"I'm up," her aunt called from the other side of the door. The door marked Sheriff's Office. "Come on in, Rayanne. I've been waiting for you."

Rayanne gave the deputy a questioning glance. "Why is she in there?"

"The jail seemed so dark, and it wasn't big enough for Evie's bed."

"Her bed?"

Arnette nodded. "We couldn't let her sleep on that old cot, so we had somebody bring her bed from home."

Only in a small town could that happen. "Well, thank you." At least they'd tried to make Evie comfortable. That was something, at least.

Rayanne opened the door and peeked inside. She didn't know exactly what she'd expected to see, but this wasn't it. Her aunt was sitting on her giant four-poster bed eating a muffin. A blueberry muffin, to be exact. A cup of steaming coffee was on the bedside table—a table Rayanne recognized as Evie's. Evidently someone had brought that in for her, as well.

There were other little touches that took away any jaillike atmosphere. Fresh flowers next to the coffee. A stack of magazines on the braided country rug. There was even a poster of a winking, grinning, heavily muscled cowboy taped to the wall. He wore boots, his only attire except for a strategically held Stetson.

Evie quickly put her muffin aside and came off the bed. She pulled Rayanne into her arms. "It was so good of you to come."

"As if you gave me much of a choice." Rayanne held the hug a few moments longer, savoring it, then broke away so she could look Evie in the eyes. All in all, her aunt looked healthy. Actually, she looked the picture of health. There were no grayish roots in her sun-gold hair. Her makeup, as usual, was flawless. Even her nails seemed to have enjoyed a recent manicure. In other words, Evie didn't look as if she'd spent the last two weeks in jail.

"I suppose you saw the cow?" Evie asked.

"Cow? Oh, the one on Main Street. Yes, I saw it. Herman Sheckley said the wind blew it down."

"Wind, my fanny. Like Herman Sheckley would know. The man can't see an inch in front of his face. A customer's taking his life into his own hands when he sits down in Herman's barber chair. No, it wasn't the wind that brought down my cow. It was foul play, if you ask me. By the way, speaking of fowl, I heard about the problem you had with that chicken."

"Sheesh. Has Rios told everyone in town?"

"I didn't hear it from Rios. Freda told me when she called this morning. She said it attacked you, huh? Never heard of a chicken doing that, but they can be ornery if you get between them and their chicks."

"Well, it didn't exactly attack me—"

Evie lifted her hands to one of the posters. "What'd you think of him?"

"Of the model?" Rayanne thought she didn't want to talk about him, that's what.

"He's such a hunk. I want to see if I can find some naked pictures of him on the Internet."

Rayanne was about to ask about the shooting, but that stopped her. "You want nude photographs of some model?"

"Oh, but he's more than just a model. He's an actor and he sent me a letter. Well, the president of his fan club did. I'm going to visit him in Hollywood when I'm out of here. Such trying times, these." Evie fanned herself—dramatically so—and walked to the window. "I suppose you're angry because I asked you to come."

"Not angry. Suspicious. And even more suspicious about why you're in jail, uh, or rather why you're in the sheriff's office."

"I'm charged with pulling a gun on Bennie Quinn," Evie said nonchalantly.

"Yes, I heard." Rayanne sat on the edge of the bed. "Tell me exactly what happened."

She dismissed it with a wave of her hand. "I don't want to talk about that now. Tell me about your trip. Did you have a good flight?"

A stall tactic. Evie was awful at disguising them but somehow good at making them work. "The flight was fine. Now—"

"And Rios gave you a ride home from the airport just like I asked him to do. Such a good boy he's turned out to be. Don't you think so?"

"He's not a boy, and I didn't come here to discuss Rios. Or cowboy models. Or the rubber cow or even Herman Sheckley's poor eyesight. I want to discuss your situation, and I'd like to know—"

"Did you meet Mattie?"

Rayanne gritted her teeth. It would be easier to catch a feather in a wind tunnel. "Yes, I met her, and you keep changing the subject."

"I know. It's just the child troubles me so. Such a sad situation. Her mother's dead, you know?"

"Rios told me."

"And Bennie." Evie sighed heavily. "Well, Bennie's being difficult. He's fighting Rios for custody of Mattie."

"No surprise there. I can't imagine he was too happy to learn about Rios and Patricia fooling around. So, did this incident with Bennie have something to do with Rios's custody battle with—"

"I said I didn't want to talk about that."

"Well, I don't see where you have another choice. You're in jail, Aunt Evie, and I want to know what happened."

Evie paused. And fidgeted. And paused again. "Bennie is a cantankerous old fool, and I just wanted him to understand he can't always have what he wants. So, I took your daddy's old beat-up twenty-two rifle and paid Bennie a little visit to try to talk some sense into him."

Heaven help her. "And you thought you could do that by scaring the bejesus out of him?"

"I didn't scare him much," Evie said as if that justified everything. "But the gun was sort of loaded, and even though I aimed it at the knobby hackberry tree near Bennie's barn instead of at Bennie, Rios said that still hadn't been a really good idea on my part."

It wasn't an easy thing for a cop to hear. And not just her aunt's irrational, nincompoopish ideas of intimidation. Rule one of law enforcement was to substantiate the allegation. Well, Evie had just done that in much clearer terms than Rayanne wanted. A loaded gun, even if it happened to be a bent-barreled, sixty-something-year-old rusty rifle, was still a potentially dangerous weapon in the eyes of the law. The fact that Evie had aimed it could be used against her to prove intent to harm. It likely wouldn't matter that the only thing her aunt planned to harm was a knobby hackberry.

"Will you be able to post bond for me today?" Evie asked.

Rayanne pushed out a breath of frustration. "Of course. That's why I'm here. What I want to know is why the sheriff ever locked you up in the first place.

You're not exactly a hardened criminal. He should have forced you to go home by now."

Evie fanned herself again. "He tried."

"Obviously not hard enough. In fact, I intend to speak to him about that as soon as possible." *Speak* wasn't exactly the right word. Rayanne wanted to have it out with Sheriff Ryland.

"How are your headaches?" Evie asked.

"Fine." Now, this was a subject Rayanne didn't want to discuss.

Evie clucked her tongue. "Your stay in Longhorn will be good for you. Next thing you know you'll have ulcers. Or hives maybe. The nerves can only take so much irritating them and they have to flare up. Arncttc's grandmother once got hives on her armpits and had to walk around for a week with her hands in the air. I saw her over at the bank and thought there was a hold-up in progress."

"Aunt—"

"Did you know the sheriff's looking for someone to fill in for Arnette when she has her baby?"

"No, Aunt Evie, don't even think it." Rayanne adamantly shook her head. "I'm not going to work for the Longhorn sheriff's office. I have a job in New York, remember?"

"Well, that place was never the same after Jimmy Smits left."

"Jimmy Smits played a cop on TV, Aunt Evie. I am one."

"An unhappy one, from what I can see. Don't twist your face up so. Causes wrinkles."

Rayanne ignored the wrinkle comment but she did try to relax her face. "And you think I'd be happier in

Longhorn? No, thanks. I have a life in New York. A good life." And she didn't intend to continue this conversation. It felt too much like the one she'd avoided with Rios the night before, and it sounded as if she were trying to convince herself. Which she probably was. "I need to find the sheriff so I can get you out of here."

"He's usually at the diner this time of morning," Evie remarked. "Bring me back a little box of Cocoa Balls cereal, will you? More coffee, too. And maybe a good magazine. You know which ones I like."

Rayanne quickly shut the door between her and her aunt before Evie could add more to her requests. She closed her eyes and leaned against the door to catch her breath. What she saw when she opened her eyes did not please her. Arnette was nowhere in sight, but the place sure wasn't empty.

"Rios, what are you doing here?"

He had his feet propped on the desk and his Stetson tipped back on his head. A sucker stem poked out of the corner of his mouth. "Are you going to ask me that every time you see me?"

"Only when you turn up at places you shouldn't be."

"Well, I gotta tell you, this is one place I should turn up." He opened the middle drawer of the desk, and she watched him fish through it, shoving aside paper clips, rubber bands and at least a dozen lime suckers. He took out a shiny silver badge and pinned it to his crisp white shirt. "This is my office now."

No! This could not be happening. This had to be a dream. Or a weird alternate universe. There was no way Rios could be sheriff. "Since when?"

"Since the people of Longhorn voted me in three months ago, right after Sheriff Ryland retired."

"Mercy." Rayanne sank into the first available chair. "You're the one who arrested Aunt Evie?"

"Had to." He pulled the lime green sucker out of his mouth and pointed it at her. "I told you Bennie made sure the charges were filed, so I had no choice but to do what I did. Oath of office and all that stuff."

"And you're the one who didn't call me to let me know you arrested her?"

"Guess I'm guilty of that, too. I wanted to call, but Evie didn't want you to know."

"That is not good enough. I can't believe you did this."

"Just doing my job, Rayanne. And it's not as if I had a choice. Bennie's the one who pressed this issue."

"So you said. But other than his word, what proof do you have that Evie tried to shoot him, huh?"

"Well, I got Evie's full, freely given, signed confession along with Bennie's statement that verifies everything Evie said."

Oh. She hated to admit it, but it sounded as if Rios had done his job and done it well. Heck. Why couldn't he be incompetent in this one area? "What about the statements of witnesses?"

"There weren't any, but I do have a firearm report that says the twenty-two could have been discharged despite the bent trigger and rusty barrel."

"Firearm report," Rayanne repeated flatly.

"Yeah, you know, a scientific process to determine—"

"I know what a firearm report is, Rios. I just didn't know you had evidence like that."

"Well, we're getting quite progressive here in Longhorn. Women can vote now. No telling how that might affect a man's way of thinking. Might just cause all kinds of changes around here. Which brings me to my next point. Arnette doesn't want to come back to work after the baby's born, so I'll need another deputy. Interested?"

It was an easy question to answer, especially with her suddenly rotten mood. "In no way, shape or form."

"That's what I figured you'd say. I just thought maybe you'd like something to do while you're waiting around for Evie's trial. You could fill in until I find someone permanent."

"Her trial?" That brought Rayanne to her feet. "You expect this thing to go to trial?"

"The DA does. Of course, the DA is Ezra Quinn, Bennie's first cousin, so naturally he'll do just about anything that Bennie wants."

She stopped herself short of banging her head against the wall. "When exactly will this trial be?"

"In two weeks. Hopefully."

"Two weeks!" But that wasn't what bothered her most. It was the *hopefully* part. Two weeks in Longhorn. Two weeks around Rios. Two weeks of staying away from him when he seemed to turn up everywhere she went. Two weeks of the tension. The hot kisses.

"Well, if you change your mind about a job," he calmly offered, "you know where to find me."

Change her mind? She was more likely to lose it first. "I want to take a look at these so-called reports you have regarding the alleged crime. And I need to post bail for Aunt Evie. Will you take a check?"

"Sure, as long as it doesn't bounce."

Rayanne ignored the remark and dug through her purse to find her checkbook. "How much?"

"Five thousand dollars."

She dropped into the chair. "Five thousand dollars! You are out of your flipping mind."

"Not me. Judge Ira Quinn set the bond."

"Another of Bennie's cousins," she said under her breath. It wouldn't do any good to find a bail bondsman, either. There was only one in Longhorn—Bennie Quinn.

"You okay?" Rios asked. "You're looking a little pale there."

"I'm fine." And she forced her teeth to unclench while she wrote out the check. "May I use your phone? I need to call my bank and transfer some funds. Don't worry. It's a toll-free number."

He lifted his hand to his phone in a go-ahead gesture. "Need some financing? If so, I can help you out."

"No, thanks," she said crisply. "You've done quite enough already."

Rios shook his head in a mildly frustrated, halfheartedly rankled sort of way. "Guess you'll hold Evie's arrest against me for a decade or so, huh?"

It was a possibility. Well, except he'd obviously gone to furniture-hauling, poster-hanging lengths to make Evie comfortable during her stay. Heck, Rios had even given up his office. That shaved some time off that grudge she'd likely hold because...well, because it seemed too big a grudge to aim it all at Bennie and Evie.

She picked up the phone, not noticing that the line-in-use button was lit. Rayanne was about to hang up, but she heard Evie's voice. And she heard words she didn't especially want to hear.

"Yes, Freda, we're having a party. A big one," Evie explained. "Tonight. I've already called some people, and they're calling others as we speak."

"Uh, Aunt Evie?" Rayanne interrupted.

"Why, Rayanne, I'm glad you're on the line. You can help. I'm making a list of things that I need you to pick up."

"For the party," Rayanne clarified. "But I don't think a party is a good—"

"Sure it is," Freda and Evie said in unison.

"It's for your homecoming," Evie added.

"But I—"

"It'll be fun," her aunt continued, ignoring what would have been a protest from Rayanne.

"But, Aunt Evie, we have more important things—"

"Pshaw." Freda that time. "Nothing's more important than celebrating your homecoming. And Evie's. It'll be so good to have both pair of my warm fuzzy bear slippers back home again."

She didn't feel like fuzzy bear slippers. Rayanne felt like a blasted Ping-Pong ball. And neither one of them was listening to a word she said. "But we need to get Evie's things moved from the jail—"

"Rios will do that for us," Evie assured her. "Just remember to say pretty please when you ask him. Oh, and invite him to the party while you're at it. Tell him that we won't take no for an answer, that we absolutely insist that he come."

Rayanne huffed. She'd already been roped into doing errands and a request that would guarantee her to spend some time with Rios. And she hadn't yet completed a full sentence. She tried again. "But I need to speak to Bennie Quinn to see if I can get him to drop the—"

Evie took the next round. "Bennie can wait."

As her aunt rattled on about the makings for guacamole dip and her preferred brand of spicy pork rinds, Rayanne's frustrated gaze met Rios's.

"My advice?" He unwrapped a lime sucker and passed it her way. "Surrender. It saves time and breath."

He was right, of course. And there was likely nothing she could do anyway to stop the Texas-size socializing wheels her aunt had already put into motion. Accepting her fate, Rayanne stuck the sucker in her mouth. It appeared she had a party to attend.

CHAPTER FIVE

"Happiness can't buy money."
—Bumper Ditties by Evie E. Garrett

THE PARTY WAS IN FULL swing by the time Rios finished for the day and made it over to Evie's. He caught a whiff of barbecue and more than a whiff of beer. Some people were trying to reassemble the Hal's Hungry Heifer cow in Evie's front yard. Drunk people, obviously. The result looked like a cloning experiment gone bad.

"What ya think, Rios?" Ned Beekers called.

"You might want to move the hoof off of its ear. Just a suggestion."

In true drunken fashion, Ned stood there and scratched his head. Rios decided to let Ned and his inebriated compadres figure it out for themselves. That probably wouldn't happen for a day or two. While he was at it, he'd collect their keys so none of them would do anything foolish such as trying to drive.

Rios climbed out of his truck and slapped a hand on his jeans to get rid of some of the dust. A party certainly wouldn't have been his first choice for a way to spend the evening, but he thought that after a shave and shower he'd be in the mood for one.

Especially since Rayanne would be there.

He didn't really want to sit around and figure out

why that pleased him so. Nothing about his situation had changed. Not really. He still wasn't in any position to start up a full-fledged relationship, even if it would be incredibly satisfying in numerous ways.

Besides, Rayanne would leave town, no doubt soon, and that meant full-fledged would turn into something pathetically temporary. It would be something cheap and tawdry. Cheap and tawdry was all right for some things, but not for a relationship with Rayanne.

"There you are." Evie gave him a beaming smile and held open the front door for him. She had a gallon container of guacamole dip in her hand and an industrial-size bag of corn chips under her arm. "Looks like rain, but I'm hoping the fellas can get the barbecue finished before it starts. Come on in."

"I need to drop by my place and clean up some first. I've been out at the barn with that mare again."

"Oh, is she still not feeling well?"

"She's better, but I wanted to check on her." He stepped onto the porch and gave his jeans another dusting. "Where's Rayanne?"

"I sent her to the store to get a few more things. Don't worry, I made sure the list included some of those green suckers you like so much." She checked her watch and nearly dumped the bowl of guacamole on herself. Rios steadied the dip just in time. "I'm surprised she's not back by now."

He was thankful Rayanne wasn't there yet. He still had some things to settle with Evie. "Did you tell Rayanne about the land yet?"

"No." Evie gave a weary sigh. "I haven't had a chance. Heck, I've had to send her to the store four times because

I keep remembering things we need. And speaking of the party, doesn't the guacamole look good?"

Rios recognized this routine. It was one of Evie's most frequently used stall tactics—changing the subject. "Rayanne has to know," he insisted. "And you can't wait—"

"Mattie just loves Rayanne. That's all the child talked about this afternoon before Freda took her over to Bennie's."

Yep, Rios had learned pretty much the same thing. His daughter was duly impressed with Evie's niece. However, this wasn't at all what he wanted to discuss, and Evie had likely known that when she brought up the subject. "If you don't tell Rayanne about the land—"

"Have you ever thought about asking Rayanne to marry you?" Evie interrupted.

The breath sort of swooshed right out of him. Great day, the woman knew how to take shock and surprise to new heights. Rios put his hands on his hips and stared at her. "No, I haven't."

Well, maybe he'd thought of it a time or two over the years, but that was just some settling-down urges that hit him every now and then. Besides, this was another of Evie's ploys to get him off the subject of the land. He didn't want his brain to have to ponder the notion of marriage.

Well, not at this moment, anyway.

He caught Evie's shoulders, the bulging bowl sandwiched between them. "No more interruptions and no more pretending you can't hold your own in a conversation. Evie Garrett, promise me you'll tell Rayanne tonight."

"Oh, not tonight. Not with the party going on. First thing in the morning." With eyes that seemed to have doubled in size, Evie looked at him pleadingly. "Will you be there with me when I tell her?"

He shook his head as fast and as hard as he could shake it. "Uh-uh. That's not a good idea."

"Of course it is. You have a way with words. Heck, you talked half the young women in this town into going to Whiskey Creek with you, and that was before you owned it. Even Rayanne fell to your charms."

Not exactly, but that was one road he didn't want to go down right now.

"Just help me tell her, please," Evie pleaded. "She'll get upset but then she'll get over it. You'll see. Maybe you can talk her into going up to Whiskey Creek again."

Only if he could convince her it would be a good place to clobber him and hide his body.

He gave Evie's hand a reassuring pat. "This has to come from you. I'll talk to her when you're done, okay?"

She nodded eventually and gave him one of her motherly looks. "For the life of me, I just haven't been able to figure out why you and Rayanne didn't stay together. You seem made for each other."

"Things just didn't work out." It was Rios's standard answer whenever Evie or Freda asked—which was often.

"But now that you have Mattie, don't you think you need to consider marrying and—"

"No." He waved in a don't-go-there gesture. "I'm not getting married just for the sake of giving Mattie a mother."

"But—"

"No," he interrupted, using one of Evie's ploys. "I gotta go wash up." And to make sure the conversation didn't continue, Rios started to walk away.

"You and Rayanne would be so happy together," Evie

called. "Goodness, you're both in law enforcement. Both on the stubborn side. Both single and too old not to be looking harder than you are for something permanent."

"You're talking to the rubber cow." Rios continued to his truck. "Because I'm not listening."

"We'll see about that. I'm wearing you down, Rios McKay. I can see it by the way you slump your shoulders."

He immediately tried to improve his posture but never looked back. The woman could talk Martha Stewart into serving peanut butter and banana sandwiches at a ritzy party, and there was no way he wanted to tangle with Evie tonight.

Too bad she might be right about one thing, though. Well, a little right, anyway. She *was* wearing him down. Or maybe that was Rayanne's doing.

Before Rayanne returned to Longhorn, before that kiss, he'd been almost certain of the direction the wind was blowing between them. Other than asking Evie for information about him, which Evie readily admitted to him, Rayanne hadn't made any attempt to stay in touch. Neither had he. Well, except for the information about her he'd pried out of Evie. Yet it appeared by the way Rayanne responded to the kiss that she still carried a little place for him in her heart.

So, the question was—just how big was that little place? And did he somehow want to make it a whole lot bigger? It'd be a challenge, all right. Like wrangling a longhorn with a broken shoestring.

He grinned.

Heck, he always did like a challenge.

RAYANNE GROANED. The place was already packed. It was just what she didn't need with a headache coming on.

She'd hoped for at least a chance to catch her breath. Apparently, she would have to manage that while she partied with nearly every citizen of Longhorn. Minus the Quinns, of course. None of them would show, even though Evie had no doubt invited them. Evie wouldn't let something like a bitter feud stand in the way of being a good hostess.

She parked her aunt's car in the driveway and with the plastic grocery sack in her hand she started across the yard. A sack that contained lime suckers, one of which she had stuck in her mouth. It was her eleventh one. If she had to face Rios tonight, which she most certainly would, she wanted to do it with a sugar high. It might give her the much-needed edge to resist him.

The rubber cow startled her for a moment. Well, she thought it might be the rubber cow she'd seen hanging over Main Street. The cow, or what was left of it, was near the front steps, like some odd, frightening lawn ornament. It had a hoof glued to its nose and another where its ear should have been. There was some unidentifiable part, perhaps bovine-related, on the tuft of its head. Strange. Very strange.

Rayanne went into the house through the kitchen door. Okay…she managed to get herself *partly* inside the door. The room was jammed with people, all of them sloshing drinks and talking at the same time. Every single one of them welcomed her with a warm hello and some generous hugs. They also gave her some odd looks, but she had no idea what that was about. Maybe her eyes were glazed from the high volume of sugar pumping through her blood.

"Freda?" Rayanne called when she saw her by the

sink. She put aside the sucker and grocery bag. "Where's Aunt Evie? I got the rest of her things."

"Rayanne, there you are." Freda pushed her way through the crowd. When she got closer, she gave Rayanne's cheek a jiggling pinch. "My little case of chocolate éclairs with extra sweet filling and green lips."

It took Rayanne a moment to figure out that the last two words weren't part of the metaphor. Sweet heaven. The suckers. "Are my lips really green?"

Freda nodded and carefully studied Rayanne's mouth as if she were observing some sort of scientific experiment. "Yes, but don't worry about it, they match your eyes."

The greenest eyes in Texas, Rios had said. Well, shoot. She didn't want to walk around all night with color-coordinated facial features.

"What took you so long?" Freda asked.

Rayanne located a napkin and started wiping. So, maybe the attempted sugar high hadn't been such a good idea after all. "I went for a drive."

She looked around but didn't see her aunt or the cause of her drive—Rios. Rayanne could blame the green lips on him, as well, since he was no doubt the reason that particular confection had been on Evie's shopping list in the first place.

Freda gave Rayanne a reassuring pat on the cheek. And pinched it again. "Well, you're here now so why don't you find Rios and talk him into dancing with you? I'm sure he won't mind your green lips at all."

"I don't want to dance with Rios."

"Sure you do. He's a wonderful man—like a big slice of apple pie with ice cream on it—and it doesn't hurt that he puts stars in your eyes, either." And with that absurd but perhaps somewhat truthful observation, Freda winked and headed into the crowd.

Yes, in some ways Rios was wonderful. For example, he could dissolve multiple layers of rust with his kisses. Somehow, Rayanne didn't think Freda meant that as one of Rios's redeeming qualities. The man could certainly fill out a pair of jeans—another noteworthy quality. And he could make her act like a fool—not so redeeming. But it was certainly a knack of his.

Though all those wonderful, knackful aspects, as lust-inducing as they were, hadn't caused her to drive around for the past hour. Nope. It just wasn't easy being around Rios. She'd spent the first eighteen years of her life falling in love with him and the next eleven trying to convince herself that he was toenail fungus.

Great day. Here she was doing it again, whining and lamenting over a man who seemed to be a constant source of whining and lamenting. She grabbed a beer from the fridge and headed straight for the back door. It probably wasn't a good idea for her to hang around a party while she felt like the bearer of gloom and doom. And while she had green lips.

"Don't run into any chickens while you're out there," Philip Ryland, the banker, called. "Squawk, squawk. Planning to feather your nest any time soon?" He cackled with laughter.

Rayanne ignored him and went outside. The first raindrop smacked her in the eye before she made it to the bottom step. More dotted her clothes while she walked to the stables. The droplets didn't deter her. After the day she'd had, a storm was indeed a small thing. Even a belligerent chicken wouldn't have stopped her. Besides, a nice turbulent rainstorm might wash away some of the green sucker discoloration.

Rayanne stepped into the stables, and the familiar smell of horses and hay hit her at once. She gave the roan mare a caress and opened her beer. There were only two horses stalled here, but when she was a kid, the place was always filled to the brim. Evie had probably sold them to cut down on her workload. Too bad. Exercising and cleaning up after the horses had never seemed like work to Rayanne, and it would have been a way to occupy her time while she was in Longhorn.

Her eyes slowly adjusted to the darkness. The only lights came from the house, a good twenty yards away. The darkness suited her mood. Man problems, green lips and a headache. It sounded like a warped Dr. Seuss title.

She wasn't sure what alerted her, but Rayanne suddenly knew she wasn't alone. Shifting her gaze from her beer, she looked at the other end of the stables. There was Rios, leaning against a post. He, too, had a beer in his hand and raised it in a pseudo toast.

"Nice night for a party, huh?" he asked.

Rayanne raised her beer in return and slowly walked toward him. It was a nice night for something, she guessed. She was almost afraid to find out what.

CHAPTER SIX

> "Weather forecast for tonight: dark."
> —Bumper Ditties by Evie E. Garrett

"WHAT ARE YOU DOING HERE?" she asked Rios. Rayanne knew she'd run into him tonight, but she hadn't expected it to happen so soon.

Rios clucked his tongue. "The same question again."

She took a sip of beer, assumed his pose and leaned against the post across from him. "Do you have a logical answer this time?"

"I wanted to get away from the party and that rubber cow for a couple of minutes. Why are you here?"

"Same reasons," she replied. Rios leaned slightly closer, his pinpointed gaze aimed right at her mouth. "Yes, they're green," Rayanne offered before he could make a joke about it.

"Nice color. They match your eyes."

"So I've been told." She drank more beer, hoping the meager amount of alcohol would dissolve the remnants of her lollipop feast. "Where's Mattie?"

"It's her night with Bennie. She spends three days a week and two nights with him. Of course, he'd like nothing more than to have her there all the time. I guess you've heard he's challenging me for custody?"

"Yes, Aunt Evie told me." And it bothered her. Too

much. She'd seen Rios with his daughter and saw the genuine love there. No one, especially Bennie, should be challenging him for custody. "Well, it seems Bennie's trying to cause trouble for both you and Evie. I think I'll drive out there in the morning and see if I can get him to talk to me."

"That's probably not a good idea." He shrugged.

"Well, unless you let me deputize you."

"I'd rather eat that foam rubber cow for breakfast," she joked. But his offer did remind her of a childhood dream she'd left behind. "You know, I always thought I'd grow up to be sheriff of Longhorn."

"Really? I didn't know that."

She nodded. "Yep. I used to see Sheriff Ryland with that shiny badge and that authoritative swagger. He always smelled like starch and shoe polish. I wanted to be like that. Not smell like him," she corrected. "I just wanted to walk around town and have people look at me the way they looked at him." *And the way they now look at you.*

"So, why didn't you stay and become sheriff?"

Rayanne opened her mouth to give him an answer and realized she didn't have one. Her usual response was that she wanted to make her own way in the world, but that seemed sort of a dumb reason, especially since Longhorn would always be her home. The truth was she'd left because she didn't want a daily dose of Rios, because she didn't want to have to face him after the embarrassing incident.

Strange, that it had taken her all this time to figure that out. She'd left the place and family she loved because she was, well, chicken. It was even more ridiculous when she factored in that Rios had left, as well, for years, and she still hadn't bothered to put her pride aside and return home.

Knowing Rios was waiting for an answer, she tried a different approach. "Why are you so anxious to get a badge on me, anyway?"

Rios grinned from ear to ear. "Must be the idea of pinning something to your chest that gets me all excited. That, and I don't like the idea of being without a deputy when Arnette leaves."

"Expecting a crime wave, Sheriff?"

"Well, it's not exactly a high-crime area, but we can have some excitement."

"Oh, yeah? Like what?" she asked.

"The Quik Stop got robbed last month. They got away with a six-pack of nonalcoholic beer and two packages of Ding Dongs. Then someone took an ax to the rubber cow that Evie donated."

"That wasn't exactly a crime," Rayanne retorted. "More like a mercy killing."

"Good point, but Evie wants me to investigate it, so I will. I like being sheriff, but I want to leave some time for Mattie and for my ranch."

Rayanne took another sip of beer. "Exactly where is your ranch anyway?"

"I bought the old Saunders place."

She knew the property well. Too well. It brought back some memories she didn't want to remember. "By Whiskey Creek?"

"Yep, I own it now."

Well, that was appropriate in the cosmic scheme of things. After all, Rios had probably seduced dozens of women at that creek. He could sow oats in the same place he'd sown his oats.

He leaned closer again, his scrutinizing gaze on her lips once more.

"Yes, my tongue is probably green, too," she offered, in case his thoughts were headed in that direction. "And no, I don't need you to verify that for me."

"Well, as interesting as that sort of verification might be to, uh, research, I wasn't thinking about your tongue. You look like you might have a headache."

Great. Now he could read minds, as well. "It's just been a rough day." For a whole host of reasons. Rios was one of those reasons. Actually, he was the main one.

"Anything I can do to help?" he asked.

"Nope." Unless he could somehow change the emotional and hormonal makeup of her body.

"Well, I'm sure you'll work your way through whatever's bothering you. You're one of the smartest people I know."

Confused, she stared at him. "That was, uh, like a compliment. Careful, Rios. You just might make me swoon if you keep that up."

Instead of looking insulted, he smiled. "No swooning allowed tonight. No arguing, either. Let's just stand here and enjoy our beer. And the company."

She didn't frown until he said that last part. Rayanne didn't want to enjoy his company. Well, she did. But she didn't. And it was that *didn't* part that made the *did* part seem all the more interesting. It was no wonder she had a headache.

The rain started in earnest. It tunneled off the stables, making watery curtains in the entryways. Despite the sound of the rain on the tin roof, she could still hear music coming from the house. Patsy Cline was singing about her mental condition. Rayanne could sympathize with her. She had a mental condition big enough for a dozen country music songs.

"Have you thought any more about what I said to you at the airport?" Rios asked.

That entailed a lot of territory, but somehow Rayanne knew exactly what part of their conversation he meant. The part where they discussed *the* incident.

"Let me rephrase that some," Rios continued. "I guess what I'm looking for here is some kind of, well, closure." He shook his head. "Mercy, I hate that word. There's no way for a cowboy to say *closure* and not make him sound wussy. Anyway, wussiness aside, I don't want you going through life thinking I did what I did up there because I didn't want you." He snared her gaze. "Because I did want you. You do know that, don't you?"

Darn it. It was one of those soul-searching questions, and she had to plow through all those years of festering embarrassment so she could make an attempt at being honest with herself.

"I know you wanted me," Rayanne admitted. "I wanted you, too." And she braced herself in case some kind of universal rupture occurred because of what she was about to say. "I should have let you know sooner about my lack of experience."

"And I should have asked."

The fit of orneriness she'd nourished and fed for eleven years landed right on the hay-strewn floor. Confused, stunned, awed, she stood there and stared at him.

He gave a frustrated-sounding sigh. "I just assumed... I mean, you were eighteen. And you were beautiful. *Are* beautiful," he corrected. "Even with those green lips and a headache, you're still beautiful. I just figured your first time had already happened with Trey Jenkins. I mean, not that Trey ever said that you two had, well, you know."

She'd never heard Rios flustered before, and it left her pretty much dumbfounded. That probably wasn't such a bad thing because Rios continued.

"Anyway, I was flattered. More than flattered. I was kind of overwhelmed that you wanted me to be your first." He shook his head. "Sheez, that makes me sound like a wuss, too. Please don't repeat that to anyone. I wouldn't want it to get around that I was ever overwhelmed in a sexual situation. Wouldn't be good for my image."

Her lips twitched, threatening to smile. "Well, I suppose we could strike a bargain here. No more chicken remarks or rehashing chicken stories, and I just might forever put it out of my mind that you were, uh, overwhelmed in a situation where overwhelming would be a definite liability to your stud status."

"That's kind of you." He paused a heartbeat and fought a grin of his own. "But my guess is you'll tattle first chance you get."

"Absolutely. Just like you'll bring up this green lip thing as often as you can work it into conversation."

His grin verified that. "So, have we officially cleared the air?"

Well, considering they were in the stables with the smell of the horses and horse manure, the air was about as clear as it would get.

"We have," she let him know. "I should have told you sooner. You should have asked. And instead of being grossly embarrassed, we would have ended up a little flustered."

"A lot flustered," he corrected.

He was right. For months leading up to that incident, there'd been a veneer covering the fierce attraction between them. That veneer vanished the moment they started kissing and discarding their clothes. Rios had somehow had the wherewithal to get that veneer and their clothes—minus her midnight-blue panties—back on. No easy feat.

Rios set his beer aside. After doing the same to hers, he caught her hand. "Dance with me."

She was shaking her head as fast as it would shake. "Oh, no. I can't dance."

Rios slipped his arm around her waist and pulled her to him. "Sure you can." He laced their fingers together. "The song's doing all the work for us, and all we have to do is move with the music."

That's what Rayanne was afraid of. All she had to do was move to the music with her body touching Rios's. And with her face very close to his neck. That kind of stuff would vaporize her quickly waning resistance, and she wasn't ready for the vaporization process yet.

"This goes here," he said, sticking his foot between her feet. It caused his jeans to rub against the inside of her legs. Slowly, he started to sway to the music. "Now, this is the easy part. Just wander with Patsy."

"Wander?"

"Close your eyes and think about what the music's doing. It's just like taking a walk through the pasture on a Sunday morning. Right after it's started to rain. Think about it. About the taste that's on your tongue when you catch the raindrops. About the smell of the fresh grass. Think about the warm breeze on your face."

Rayanne couldn't think of anything else. Rios's voice was as smoky smooth as the tune. She closed her eyes and let him guide her into the rhythm of the dance. For a moment, she'd allow herself to enjoy it.

A moment passed.

All right, she'd give herself two moments.

"Do you remember I taught you how to saddle a horse right here in this very spot?" His breath was warm, and it caressed her face. "You were all of, what, seven years old, and I was eleven."

"Yes, I remember." In fact, she had a lot of memories of Rios. Good memories. Most of those memories involved watching his various muscles flex while he did sweaty, muscle-flexing chores, but there were some non-lust-related ones, too. Like the time she'd helped him deliver the chestnut mare, Penny, that had become the equine love of her life.

Rios started to caress the small of her back with his fingertips. It tickled, but it felt good, too. It made her feel tingly all over. Rayanne quickly choked back what would have no doubt become a giggle and started to move away from him. But Rios obviously had other ideas. His arm tightened around her waist, and he lowered his head so his cheek rested on her temple.

"We can't do this," she said.

He looked at her. "Are you telling me you don't like this?"

She thought about it, even though she already knew the answer. The answer was right in her face, staring at her green lips. "All right, I do like it," she mumbled. "I just don't want it to lead to anything else."

"It's just a dance. That's all. Well, it could be more. Since this feels kind of warm and fuzzy, how about giving me a kiss?"

"No—"

"You're not chicken, are you?"

"Not the best choice of words, but no."

"Well, I know you're not green with envy. Sorry, that one just sort of slipped out." He tapped the corner of his mouth. "So, kiss me right there. Just a little one."

"This is so stupid. We're not in high school anymore."

"I know that as well as you do. We're two grown-ups with years of mutual attraction between us. That's why I say let's just get it out of our systems."

Kissing him certainly wouldn't do that. Rayanne was about a million percent sure of it. "And if I don't have anything to get out of my system?"

"Then get it out of mine."

"Hardly. About the only thing a kiss would do is heat us both up." And she was talking a really, really hot kind of heat.

His eyebrow rose. "You're admitting that?"

"No reason not to." But she still couldn't understand why she had. It was like handing over secrets to the enemy. He'd figure out a way to use her admission to put another hole in her resistance.

"Then kiss me so you can torture me. Get me so hot, Rayanne, that I'll get on my knees and beg you. Then you can toss your hair the way you like to do and walk away. That'll show me."

Oh, she liked the sound of that. She smiled. But not for long. Rios touched her. He skimmed his hand down her back and edged her closer to him. Now, that was something she hadn't considered. If she could touch and kiss him in the name of torture, then he could possibly do the same to her. If she let him, that is.

But she wouldn't let him. Uh-uh. She could make herself immune to him. It wouldn't be like that kiss he'd sneaked while straightening her lipstick. No way. She was prepared for this one. She could just turn herself off and—

He touched her again and brushed his body against her. Fully against her. In a place that in no way needed such brushing.

"Just one little kiss," he whispered. He put an exclamation mark on that request by lowering his head and placing his mouth solidly on hers.

But it wasn't a little kiss, nor was it one. Well, maybe it was one, but it was a heck of a long one. Rios nudged her lips apart, though it didn't take much effort. Rayanne soon found herself a willing participant. A hesitant willing participant who no longer had a clue what planet she was on.

Warmth radiated within her when his tongue skimmed over hers. Outside, a rumble of thunder and a vein of lightning announced a full-fledged storm. Rayanne hardly noticed it. She was already at a place where rain or storms didn't exist. And Rios was making her feel like a sizzling griddle.

He deepened the kiss, angling her mouth to his. *Yes,* she thought. *Yes, yes, yes!* It was like kissing the heavyweight champion of kissing. Rios was a real pro at this, and he didn't disappoint her. Her lips were damp, and he used that to move over her without restraint. The torture stuff sort of slipped right out of her mind. Every logical thought, every argument went with it.

Her fingertips began to tremble on his chest. While her fingers were there and moving around, she decided to inch them inside the space between his buttons, then inside his shirt. Chest hair. She liked chest hair. There was something virile about it.

She latched on to the front of his shirt, her grip straining the fabric until a couple of buttons gave way. Better. Now she could feel all the chest hair she wanted. Heck, she could get her whole hand in there, and she did.

Rios must have liked her touching him because he grunted, and things started to move a little faster. He moved his mouth to her neck, all the while backing her against the post.

"That's right, Rayanne. Purr for me."

"I'm not purring," she complained.

Oh yes, she was. No matter what she said, she was. The muscles in her body had started to quiver. Her breath was rapid and shallow. It was a language she understood all too well. She wanted him. Her sizzling griddle wanted him.

Rayanne moaned when he shifted his weight into her, again pressing her against the post. He nestled himself into the notch of her thighs. It was a very good place to nestle. He found the exact spot that made her squeak and applied just enough pressure to make her sound like a very vocal mouse.

He didn't stop there, either.

Rios kept on kissing. Kept on nestling. And he kept on pushing and rubbing against her. Squeaking, Rayanne decided she'd let him carry on like this for a while longer. Then she could torture him. Somehow. It was so hard to concentrate on torture plans when he was, well, torturing her.

Rios covered her breast with his palm. Her limp blouse and bra weren't really barriers because they were so thin. He gave a throaty growl of approval and feathered his fingers over her nipples, first one and then the other, bringing them to peaks.

"Rios," she whispered when he kissed her breasts through her blouse.

"It's all right." He moved his mouth next to her ear and kissed her there. "I know what you want."

Yes, he did, Rayanne decided. He apparently knew exactly what she wanted. Better yet, he knew how to give it to her. He, well, bumped her in just the right spot.

Rayanne gasped. "Mercy, you blurred my vision."

"That's good. Want me to do it again?"

"Yes. Oh, yes."

Rios did. He bumped her again. And then he kissed her, stroking her with his tongue in rhythm to those magic bumps. He fisted his hands in her hair and forced her head back so he could take her neck.

"Rios," she said again. She returned the favor and kissed his neck and the surrounding areas.

"Yes?"

Without waiting to hear what she had to say, he slid his hands to her waist and pushed up her top. He dragged the cups of her bra down. He covered one nipple and then the other with his mouth, leaving them shiny wet.

He mumbled something, but the drums were pounding in her head so she couldn't hear him. It didn't matter. His face told her everything she needed to know. He would keep right on going unless she stopped him.

She wouldn't stop him just yet.

In another minute.

Rios slid his hand lower, because he obviously knew that's what she wanted. Oh, yes, that's what she wanted. A soft ache spread through her. He touched her, played with her until her nails dug into his back. Until she was driving herself against him, pleading for more. Heavens, yes, it was what she wanted.

"Yoo-hoo," someone called.

Yoo-hoo? Rayanne knew she was making odd little squeaky sounds, but she didn't think she had said yoo-hoo. Stunned, confused and incredibly frustrated, she untangled herself from Rios's grip. Looking into the rain, she saw Evie walking toward the stables.

"Oh, shoot," Rayanne said. And because she couldn't think of anything better to say, she repeated it.

The torture stuff would have to wait.

RIOS DIDN'T CARE one bit for the yoo-hoo or the person who'd said it. He barely got Rayanne's clothes straightened before Evie came waltzing into the stables.

"What are you doing out here?" he asked the woman. He didn't say it nicely, either. There was a raw edge to his tone. He couldn't help it. Evie's timing was as awful as her taste in foam rubber cows.

Evie was wet. Soaked. And she stood there grinning, rocking on her heels with her hands behind her back. "I came to check on you."

He nearly told her they didn't need checking on, but at the last moment Rios remembered to show some respect. "As you can see, we're fine." He couldn't walk, probably couldn't even move, had possibly permanently harmed his manhood, but he was fine. Now, if only the fabric of his jeans held up. He thought it might rip apart at any moment.

With a sudden look of alarm on her face, Evie leaned closer and stared at Rayanne. "What happened to your mouth?"

"Uh, I ate some of those green suckers."

Her gaze traveled to Rios. "And you must have been

eating them, too," Evie said somewhat smugly. "Because I think I see a tinge of green on your lips, as well."

No doubt. Heck, with all the kissing he'd just done, Rayanne had transferred plenty of color to him.

"You told her, I guess." Evie gave a relieved sigh. "Well, I'm glad you did. Guess those lime-flavored kisses really softened the blow, huh?"

"Softened what blow?" Rayanne asked, sounding as if she'd just woken from a heavy sleep.

"Well, the news about the land, of course."

Rayanne shook her head. "What about the land?"

"Oh, dear. I've said something I shouldn't have." Evie pressed her fingers to her mouth. "I guess he didn't tell you, after all?"

Rios groaned. *Oh, dear,* was right. It was right up there with that blasted yoo-hoo. Rayanne was looking straight at him, and he knew she was about to demand some answers. Worse, he'd have to come up with them.

"What Evie should have told you was—" And here it came. The news that would make Rayanne mad at him for another eleven years. "She sold me some land."

Rayanne stared at him. "What land?"

"Her land. About two hundred acres of it."

Rayanne volleyed glances between her aunt and him, but when she stopped volleying, she narrowed her eyes at him. "She sold you Garrett land? She sold you Garrett land! She sold you—"

"Yes," Rios interrupted.

"She sold you—"

"Yes, she did." He didn't think it was a good idea for Rayanne to keep repeating that thought. She seemed to get madder each time it came out. "But I don't really consider it mine. Evie was just a little short of funds and wouldn't take a loan from me."

Rayanne whirled toward her aunt. "You were short of funds and you went to Rios instead of calling me?"

Evie shrugged. "I didn't want to bother you. It took me a while to get a new bumper sticker contract. Besides, we didn't really need all that land. You're never here, and I got tired of fiddling with it."

"Fiddling with it?" Rayanne repeated. "Aunt Evie, that land has been in our family for over a hundred years."

"Oh, dear. I knew you'd take this hard. Your heart's tied to this place. Well, I'm sorry, but I'm just no good at ranching, Rayanne, and I had a lot more land than I'd ever use. Besides, it's like I said—I needed some cash."

"I could have helped you with the money," Rayanne insisted.

"I didn't want to take your money."

Rayanne hiked her thumb in Rios's direction. "But you'd take his? I cannot believe this. You sold him Garrett land."

Rios stepped toward her, hoping he could soothe her ruffled feathers. Evie looked like she was ready to start bawling, and Rayanne looked ready to implode. He didn't want a bawling implosion happening tonight. Well, unless it involved making love to Rayanne. He was pretty sure that wouldn't happen anytime soon, after what she'd just learned.

"If you have to blame someone, blame me," he told Rayanne.

"Oh, don't worry, I do." She poked him in the chest. "You should have called me the minute Aunt Evie came to you with this stupid idea."

She'd apparently forgotten that she'd ripped his shirt half off him because she looked confused when her poking fingers landed on his chest hair. She looked at the chest hair. Then him. Rayanne made a sound of pure frustration and stormed off.

"You think I should have told her that she's got a pale lime green hickey on the left side of her neck?" Evie asked, her forehead wrinkled in concern.

Rios shook his head. "She'll figure it out soon enough."

Evie shrugged in a suit-yourself gesture. "But maybe you'd like to know that you've got even bigger and darker ones on your..." She leaned closer and had a better look. "Right earlobe. Your collarbone. Your neck, just below your jawline. There's another one on the corner of your mouth. I really hate to be the one to point it out, but I think there's a few in your chest region, as well. It makes you look like you're sort of coming down with some kind of hives."

Well, green spots wouldn't be an easy thing to explain to everyone, especially if Rayanne was sporting them, too. He probably should head home and see if he could scrub them off. If not, then it would add a whole new level of difficulty to the upcoming week. He didn't want that. It appeared the week would be next to impossible as it was.

CHAPTER SEVEN

"Behind every argument is someone else's igno-
rance."

—Bumper Ditties by Evie E. Garrett

THE QUINN RANCH had always reminded Rayanne a little
of South Fork from the old television show *Dallas*. There
was the perfectly painted white house in the middle of
acres of green pastures. Eight hundred and eighty-five
acres, to be exact. There were at least that many cows,
horses and other farm critters. The place had huge stately
oaks, and ponds and barns galore. In the driveway, there
was a big white luxury car with longhorns for a hood
ornament. Yes, South Fork.

Or something.

Rayanne parked her aunt's car in the driveway and
seriously questioned her sanity. Of course, she'd had
reason to question her sanity for a while now. Since her
return, since the lipstick-fixing session by the car and
especially since the wild heated kisses the night before
in the stables. It seemed all her sanity questioning had
one common denominator. Rios.

What could she possibly have been thinking about
when she let him kiss her that way? That was the problem—she hadn't thought. She'd reacted. And, simply

put, she had let him kiss her blind. She had a green hickey to prove it, too.

Worse, he'd been kissing her blind all the while knowing he owned a good chunk of her family's land. He also kissed her when he knew he should have told her all about this long before Evie spilled the proverbial beans. He darn sure should have told her before he started putting his hand up her blouse.

And before he started doing that other stuff to her.

Well, one thing was for sure—she needed to get all this cleared up so she could leave Longhorn. She had to get away from Rios before she did something really stupid. Well, more stupid than she'd already done. Of course, it might be hard to top that kiss-and-grind session in the barn.

She'd stayed awake half the night trying to figure out what she was going to do. She finally decided there was nothing she could do about Rios. He seemed to be one of those green-hickey facts of life she couldn't escape. However, there was a possibility she could do something about her aunt. It was obvious that Evie needed some help managing the ranch. Or at least what was left of the ranch.

Of course, she could always move back to Longhorn so she could personally take control of things. But that would be drastic action. Well, sort of drastic. And she'd need a job if she moved back. A job Rios had offered her. A job she really couldn't consider because her mouth just couldn't seem to stay away from his.

Great day in the morning. Why couldn't this be easier?

And even if she moved back and became a deputy, it wouldn't solve all her problems. She also needed to keep Evie out of jail, and the quickest way to assure that was for her to have a little chat with Bennie Quinn. Hence, the visit that she hoped wouldn't be a complete waste of time.

"Mr. Quinn?" she called from the steps of the porch. She waited for a response but heard nothing. "Mr. Quinn, it's Rayanne Garrett. I need to talk to you."

The front door flew open, but he didn't come out. "I got nothing to talk about, and you're trespassing. Your big-city badge don't mean squat around here."

So this was his attitude? She should have expected it from a sourpuss like Bennie. "Mr. Quinn, I think if we could just sit down and talk, then we could clear all of—"

"Did Rios send you?"

"No." If he'd had a say in it, Rios wouldn't have let her come to the Quinn ranch. Fortunately, he didn't know anything about this little visit. "I read the statement you gave about the incident, and I want to discuss what happened between you and my aunt."

He didn't leave the darkened doorway. "She wanted to kill me, that's what. Nothing to discuss. So you can just turn around and leave the way you came."

Rayanne had no intention of giving up that easily. "Please, Mr. Quinn, I just need a moment of your time. This is about Mattie, too. You must know how much she cares for Evie—"

"You leave my granddaughter out of this."

"That's hard to do when it affects her."

A few seconds later Bennie walked onto the porch. Rayanne tried not to stare, but it was hard not to. The years certainly hadn't been kind to him at all. The man's jowls had jowls. His wrinkles had wrinkles. And he had more hair in his eyebrows than he did on his head.

"Mattie told me you'd come back to town." Bennie didn't say anything else for a while. It seemed as if he was sizing her up. "She likes you, you know."

Since that seemed to be a semi-friendly remark, Rayanne offered him a smile. "Well, that's good. I like her, too. She's a sweet child."

And now that Rayanne had gotten a good look at the man challenging Rios for custody, she was more than a little concerned. How could such an old man keep up with an active little girl? It didn't seem right, especially when Mattie had a loving father who seemed more than willing to take care of her.

Rayanne quickly put that observation aside. It wasn't her business. Even though it sort of felt like it was. Rios was a friend, despite all the kissing and embarrassing moments they'd had. And despite that land-buying incident. She certainly didn't want him to lose Mattie. Too bad she didn't know what to do to keep that from happening. Maybe she could somehow work that into her conversation with Bennie, especially since it was the custody battle that had provoked Evie into doing something stupid.

"It doesn't matter how Mattie feels about you," Bennie continued. "I'm not gonna drop those charges against Evie. You don't expect me to forget she tried to kill me, do you?"

"I'm not sure she actually tried to do that. Could we just sit down and talk about this like adults?"

He stared at her hard. And continued to do so for a long time. "Evie wasn't acting like an adult when she came out here that day, now was she? She acted like a dingbat."

Rayanne made a sound of agreement. "But what sense

does it make to send Evie to jail? The woman is sixty-one years old."

His response shocked her. He smiled. Bennie parted those wrinkly lips and practically grinned. "From where I'm standing, sending Evie to the pokey makes a whole heck of a lot of sense. That or the nuthouse, which is where she probably belongs. This conversation is over, little lady. It's time for you to leave."

"But Mr. Quinn—"

"I meant what I said." His voice dropped some serious notches. "You are trespassing, and on top of it, you're making things worse for Evie."

That significantly improved her posture. "How?"

"Because you've riled me, that's why. Now, you've got five seconds to get back in that car and get the devil out of here, or I'll call Arnette and have her come out here and arrest you for trespassing."

Great. Just great. Rayanne kicked a rock as she headed to the car. She wanted to kick herself. She'd known Bennie Quinn all her life and knew it would have been easier to bargain with a tree knot than with him. She truly hoped she hadn't made things worse.

She climbed into the car, turned the key in the ignition and heard an odd little clicking sound. That's all. Just that sound.

"You got two seconds left," Bennie called.

Rayanne tried again. More clicks. She stepped out of the car. "It won't start."

"You got one second to get off my land," Bennie offered. And, apparently to prove his point, he pulled a tiny phone from his pocket. "It's sure not gonna look good on your big city police record when you get arrested for trespassing."

Well, this was a fine how do you do. She grabbed her purse and went to take out her own phone so she could call Freda to come and pick her up. There was just one problem—her phone wasn't there. She remembered Evie had borrowed it earlier.

"I don't suppose you'd let me use your phone to call Freda?" she asked.

"Nope." Bennie kept his gaze on her while he punched in some numbers. "You'd best get to walking, little lady, because Arnette's gonna have no choice but to come out here and arrest you. Might go easier on you if you were actually off my property by the time she gets here."

Rayanne stood for a moment to weigh her options. She didn't have any. She didn't know how to fix clicking sounds in a car engine and she didn't have time or the resources to send out smoke signals to Freda.

Rayanne slammed the car door and started walking. Behind her, she heard Bennie continue to make his call. A call that might lead to a potentially embarrassing situation for her.

Rayanne prayed Arnette would come alone. While she was at it, she added something pretty significant to that prayer. Maybe, just maybe, Arnette wouldn't tell her boss. Maybe Rios wouldn't find out anything at all about this.

She was fairly sure she heard the angels in heaven snicker when she added that last part.

RIOS FOUND HER WALKING up the dirt road that led to the highway. Rayanne had covered some distance, about a mile, but she was still a long way from home. She was also a long way from being happy. Her shoulders were hunched. She kicked at rocks. And she was mumbling under her breath. Well, at least this time he wasn't the cause of her unhappiness. Maybe that was progress.

He pulled up beside her and lowered the window of his truck. "Get in. I'll drive you back."

She gave him one of those I'm-having-a-real-bad-day looks. "Are you going to arrest me for trespassing?"

"No, but Bennie will probably file a complaint."

"Great." And she did more of that mumbling under her breath.

"Don't worry. I'll figure out a way to talk him out of it."

"You can't talk that man out of anything." Looking dejected, she climbed inside the truck.

Probably not, but talking him out of it was a figure of speech. Rios would likely pay Rayanne's fine on the sly and never bring up the incident again. It was the least he could do for her after seeing that pale green hickey he'd left on her neck. Fortunately, his had scrubbed off, but apparently he had better suction or more intense color-embedding techniques than she did.

"I can't believe Bennie called you," she commented.

"He said he was calling Arnette."

"He did, but she couldn't come. She had the baby this morning. A boy. Eight pounds and a couple of ounces."

"Please tell her I'm happy for her."

But there was nothing congratulatory about her tone. Not that Rios expected there to be. He could guess what had gone on between Bennie and her. She'd tried to fix things, and Bennie hadn't been receptive. Now she felt lower than hoof grit. Well, it was obviously time to try to cheer her up. But how? There weren't a lot of subjects they could discuss that wouldn't lead them right to Evie's dilemma.

Ah, it finally came to him. The perfect subject. "I was lying in bed last night thinking about sex."

She made a face and folded her arms over her chest. "Rios, I don't think I want to hear this. This sounds kind of personal."

"Not that kind of sex. What I had in mind was something more along the lines of making love. To you. I want you, Rayanne. But it's more than just that. I care for you more than I've ever cared for any other woman. I thought it was about time I told you that, and that's why I was thinking about us doing something about it."

She stared as if he'd truly turned to hoof grit right in front of her eyes. "That wouldn't be a smart idea, and that's the mildest way I know how to say it."

True, but this was the really good part Rios thought she might like to hear. "That's the same conclusion I came to last night. If I started fooling around with you and Bennie found out about it, he'd use that against me in the custody hearing. I've got enough going against me as it is. So, the way I see it, we'll just have to stick with being friends."

Bingo. It was something she wanted to hear. Well, maybe. At first, she looked ready to agree with him. Then her eyebrow slowly came up. "You mean that?" she asked.

"Sure." And he did. But underneath all that logical thought, Rios knew he could never be just plain old friends with Rayanne. Still, he'd keep that to himself. No need to muddy the waters between them when they were just starting to clear up.

"Then..." She paused as if still giving that some thought. "All we have to do is just not kiss or anything."

Yes, that was it. Well, it was except for the *anything*

part. That was giving him the most trouble. "That's right. No kissing or anything. I mean, it's for the best and all, since you'll be leaving town as soon as you settle Evie's problems. Uh, you will be leaving, I suppose?"

"Yes. Of course. Except I haven't figured out exactly how to settle Evie's problems yet. One way or another, I need to make Bennie understand how things really are."

"The best way to do that is to let me deputize you." And because he knew she'd put up a fuss, he continued. "Just hear me out. Bennie will have to talk to you if you're wearing a badge. It'll give you a license, a legal one, to get those answers you think you stand a chance of getting from him."

It seemed she was about to smile or laugh hysterically, but she didn't. There was a split second of satisfaction in her eyes before they narrowed. Obviously, she considered both sides of this coin.

"Sweet heaven." She huffed out a breath. "I can't believe I'm going to agree to this."

He didn't dare smile. Didn't dare. Didn't dare even let his mouth quiver. But inside he was doing some line dancing. She was going to do it. Rayanne was going to allow him to deputize her. Why that made him so happy, he didn't know. After all, this probably wasn't the best idea he'd ever come up with.

"I'll have to call New York and arrange for a leave of absence," she added.

By now the mental line dancing had stopped completely, and Rios was starting to think about the implications of what he'd done. He'd offered Rayanne a job, and she'd accepted. She'd be working for him, no less. In Longhorn.

Now what was wrong with this picture?

Remembering he was in the middle of a conversation, Rios asked, "Will getting a leave of absence be a problem?"

"No. I'm sure Malcolm can push it through for me."

So, it seemed Dr. Whine was good for something, after all. "All right. We can go by the office, pick up your badge, and I can swear you in."

She held up her hand. "Wait a minute. I have a couple of conditions before I accept this."

Of course. Conditions. Rios hadn't thought she'd give in without some of those. Maybe she would condition herself right out of accepting the job. "What?"

"Well, first of all, you can't boss me around."

"But I'll be your boss," he replied.

"But no bossing, got that?"

Unfortunately, he understood exactly what she meant. "No bossing unless the situation dictates it."

Rayanne didn't answer right away. She gave that some thought. Apparently plenty of thought. She finally nodded. "But even then, you can't gloat."

"Deal. No gloating." He could live with—

"Another condition," she continued. "I notice you don't carry a gun, but I'd want to."

That he could live with, too. "Suit yourself. I don't think you'll find that necessary, though."

"Indulge me. I like the idea of carrying a weapon if I'm also wearing a badge. And that brings me to the third condition—I don't want you to tell anyone about this unless it's absolutely necessary."

"Beg your pardon?"

"I don't want you to tell a lot of people about this like you did about that chicken."

"I only told Freda. She told everyone else."

"Okay, then don't tell Freda. Or Aunt Evie." Rayanne paused. "Or Arnette."

"Then how are you supposed to exert your authority if nobody knows you're my deputy?"

"I'll manage. And another thing—I'm not your deputy. I'll be a temporary law enforcement assistant in the Longhorn Police Department."

Rios hitched a thumb to his chest. "A department that I just happen to run because I'm the sheriff."

She frowned. "That's awfully close to gloating, and we already agreed you wouldn't do that, right?"

"Right." That didn't mean he couldn't gloat later. In private. "So, let me get this straight. You'll become a deputy, but you don't want anyone to know and you won't take orders from me. Oh, and you want to carry a gun even though I don't."

"That's right. Do we have a deal then?"

"Not just yet." Rios had some conditions of his own. "I have no doubt that you're a good cop up in New York City, but I don't really want you running this particular investigation. That means I don't want you going off half-cocked the next time you talk to Bennie."

"I've never gone off half-cocked in my entire life."

"That's debatable," he corrected. "When you talk to Bennie, you've got to leave the emotional stuff out of it."

"Emotional stuff?" She made it sound like some kind of disease. "I assure you, Rios, I can handle an interrogation."

"A New York interrogation, yes, but you need a little advice about handling Bennie. It's best to let him think he's in control. If not, he's just going to pull rank and call in one of his cousins. Another thing, when you're interrogating someone in New York, I'm sure it's not personal like it'll be when you talk to Bennie. You have to remember that and stay calm."

"Thanks for the advice, but I know what I'm doing. Just as soon as you swear me in, I'll go right back out and have a nice long talk with Bennie Quinn."

Rios tried to keep the groan down to a low volume. "Then I suppose I'll go with you."

"Not necessary."

"Oh, yes it is," he assured her.

"That sounds a little like bossing, and we agreed you wouldn't do that."

"We also agreed I could boss you around if the situation dictates. Believe me, this dictates."

RAYANNE COULD SEE Bennie's jaw tighten considerably when Rios and she approached him. Rayanne smiled inside. She had a badge pinned to her shirt and was carrying a holstered .38 that she prayed was in working order. She was ready for anything he might try. In fact, she hoped he pulled something, because the idea of arresting him appealed to her.

"That's far enough," Bennie yelled from his porch. He tipped his head to Rios, who was standing next to Rayanne. "What are you doing here?"

"My deputy and I are here to question you about your statement regarding the alleged incident with Evie."

He made a rough sound of disapproval. "Your deputy? Since when?"

"Since about an hour ago."

Another sound, louder and more disapproving than the first. "Well, well, this is an unholy pact if there ever was one. But don't either one of you come a step farther.

Any questions you ask me, you can do it when Buck's around."

"Buck?" Rayanne softly questioned Rios.

"Buchanan Quinn, his lawyer. And his second cousin. More professional incest."

Rayanne made a sound of disapproval. "All right, if you insist that your lawyer be present, then I—uh, we expect you at the sheriff's office in one hour. Be prepared for a long interrogation." Rayanne paused. "Or you can answer one or two questions now and get it over with. It's up to you."

She could tell he was thinking about it, and finally he nodded. "Ask your questions and then get off my land."

Rayanne didn't dare show any signs of relief, but she was very much relieved. Her first challenge, and she'd succeeded. Well, partially. "I'm glad you decided to cooperate. What I want to know is did you provoke Evie in any way before she allegedly aimed a weapon at you?"

"There's nothing alleged about it."

"Maybe, but did you provoke her?" she repeated.

"No. That crazy woman just drove up, parked her car at the end of the road and aimed a gun at my hackberry tree."

"At your tree? Then she wasn't aiming at you," Rayanne said.

Bennie screwed up his face. The saggy skin was seemingly twisted around his bulbous red nose. "If she was aiming at my tree, then she was aiming at me. And she wanted to shoot me."

"Not necessarily. Perhaps she saw some sort of wild animal or something in your yard. Maybe a bear—"

"There weren't any wild animals!" Bennie yelled.

"Just one crazy woman with an old bent-up twenty-two aimed at me and my tree."

Rayanne latched on to that. "Bent-up, huh? So, let me get this straight—a sixty-one-year-old woman aims an old bent-up twenty-two, and you automatically assume she wants to shoot you? Mr. Quinn, had Evie ever shown any overt hostility to you before?"

"Overt?" He looked at Rios. "What the heck does that mean?"

"It means obvious. What Rayanne wants to know is did Evie ever threaten you before that day?"

"You know darn well she didn't. I already told you this when you asked me. Now, by my way of figuring it, I've answered enough questions today."

"Not just yet." Rayanne didn't give him time to object. "I want you to go back over what happened that day, and I think you'll see that Evie had no intentions of harming you."

"No intentions? The woman aimed at me."

"Not at you. By your own admission, you said she was aiming at your tree."

Bennie's face twisted up even more, and though Rayanne hadn't thought it possible, his nose got redder. "Now you're turning my words around. I know what happened. That crazy old bat was mad because I wouldn't hand over my granddaughter to Rios, and so she came here and tried to shoot me."

Rayanne put a check on her temper. She didn't like anyone calling Evie a crazy old bat even if there were times when Evie acted like one. "I'll use your own words again—she was aiming at your hackberry. Therefore, she couldn't have been trying to hurt you. Isn't that right, Mr. Quinn?"

"No. Evie was mad. Now, maybe she didn't actually threaten me in that, uh, overt kind of way you were talking about, but she came here to try to force me into giving up what's mine."

"What's *yours?*" Rios and Rayanne said in unison.

"Are you talking about Mattie?" Rayanne questioned.

"You're darn right I am. She's mine, and I'm not gonna just hand her over to some bar-brawling, skirt-chasing rodeo rider who happened to sweet-talk my daughter into bed."

"So that's what this is really all about?" Rayanne asked, tapping her foot. "It's about custody of Mattie."

"I never said it wasn't." He aimed a finger at them. "I'll even tell you both something else. If Rios will drop his claim on my granddaughter, then I'll drop the charges against Evie."

In Rayanne's opinion, that was the wrong thing to say. Not just the wrong thing, but the most wrong thing that could have ever come out of his wrong-saying mouth. "Why, you old geezer. You miserable, grouchy old geezer."

Rios caught onto her arm. "Rayanne, I think—"

Rayanne quickly shook him off. "How dare you use that sweet child or my aunt to get your way. You're being petty and selfish. Mattie is Rios's daughter, and he has a right to raise her. Patricia wanted that, and you darn well know it. That's what galls you about this. You want something you can't have. And as for Evie, I can see why she took aim at you—your tree."

"Uh, Rayanne—"

She didn't let Rios finish what he had to say. She was so mad she couldn't see straight, and she aimed that anger at the red-nosed old geezer on the porch. "Just what makes you think you're good enough to raise Mattie, huh? You're old and you're grouchy. Mattie doesn't need that. She needs a family and she can have that with Rios."

"And how do you figure that, little lady? Rios is just Rios."

"Rios is a fine man and a respected peace officer in this town. And he won't have to raise Mattie alone. Evie and Freda will help, and I'll help, too, when I'm here." She hadn't intended to say that, but it sort of flew out along with the other things she was yelling. "What could you possibly offer her except a bunch of ingrate cousins who have their noses stuck so far up your rear end that they can't see their own noses on their own faces?"

She heard Rios groan at that bad analogy. She groaned a little, too. Some people could come up with great lines while under pressure, but Rayanne had to admit she wasn't one of them. Under the circumstances, it was the best she could do.

Bennie's voice rose a considerable notch. "I've taken all the guff I plan to take from you, little lady. That badge doesn't give you a right to call me names. Now, get off my land before I phone one of my ingrate cousins. Go home to that crazy old bat of an aunt and tell her I'll see her in court." He turned, went inside and slammed the door.

Rayanne had to bite her lip to keep from screaming.

"Pardon me if this sounds a little like bossing," Rios said calmly. "But didn't I tell you not to come in here half-cocked?"

She made an angry shivering sound. "He just got me so mad. He's using Evie to try to get custody of Mattie. Doesn't that make you furious?"

"Yes, it does, but that's something we'll work out in court, not here in Bennie's front yard." He caught her arm and started toward the truck. "Believe me, I'll let the judge know exactly what Bennie's trying to pull. I have to believe it'll end up helping my case. In fact, the judge might dismiss Bennie's petition entirely."

"But in the meantime, how can you be so calm?"

"What choice do I have? If I get mad and bad-mouth Bennie, it'll only end up hurting Mattie. He's her grandfather, and she loves him."

Lord, Rayanne had forgotten that. She'd apparently also forgotten everything that centered on logic and standard police procedures. She'd screamed at the alleged victim of the alleged crime. Worse, she'd majorly ticked off Bennie, and that couldn't be good for Evie or for Rios.

"Oh, Rios, I'm so sorry. I probably hurt your chances with the custody. Bennie will probably call his cousin Judge Ira—"

"Ira's not deciding this custody case. I had the petition moved to the judge in Floresville. I was about a hundred percent sure I wouldn't get a fair shake with Bennie's cousin."

"Well, good. That's something, at least. Maybe I didn't mess that up."

"No, but you do need to work on your interrogation skills." He held up his hand. "I know, that sounds a little like bossing."

It sounded a lot like it, but he was right. She'd blown it. And it wasn't as if she didn't know how to interrogate someone. She did. She'd let emotion get the better part of her. "I'm not used to questioning anyone when there's something personal at stake," she mumbled.

And in this case there was a lot personal at stake.

However, at the moment Rayanne didn't want to think long and hard about who or what that *personal at stake* involved. It wasn't just Evie or Bennie. Somehow, Mattie had gotten mixed up in this, too. And Rios, of course. But then, he'd been part of the mix for years now. Heck, he was the main reason the mix was confusing.

Rios hooked his arm around her neck. "Don't worry, little lady," he teased, imitating Bennie's croaky voice. "You'll get the hang of this deputy stuff soon enough."

Rayanne had to tell him what he could do with that suggestion—that was a given.

But she smiled when she did it.

CHAPTER EIGHT

"Time heals, but everybody else wants a fee."
                    —Bumper Ditties by Evie E. Garrett

"I FIXED YOU some breakfast."

Rayanne forced her eyelids open at the sound of Mattie's voice. It was early. Very early. After working the swing shift for four years, Rayanne didn't think her body could function before ten o'clock. Still, this was Mattie. Even if she couldn't function, she intended to get up, or rather sit up.

"That was nice of you to fix me breakfast." Rayanne looked at the tray, hoping she'd see a Twinkie there. She didn't. There was some very dark crusty toast and a Granny Smith apple. She smiled anyway. This was one of those situations where the company outweighed the menu.

"I wanted you to eat something healthy before you went to work today," Mattie explained.

"Thanks." Rayanne picked up the apple. So, Rios had told Mattie about making her a deputy. Well, of course, he had. There wouldn't have been a way for him to keep it from her.

"Because I wouldn't want you to have to arrest any bad guys or anything if you hadn't had a good breakfast," Mattie continued. She sat on the edge of the bed and helped herself to a piece of toast. It crunched like a potato chip when she took a bite. "Do you get to wear a badge?"

"Yes. Your daddy gave it to me yesterday."

"And you'll get to work with Daddy?"

"Yes, I'll work with him. Not for him."

Mattie nodded, apparently grasping that right away. Rayanne only hoped Rios caught on soon enough. "I have on my Friday panties today. Which day do you have on?"

It took Rayanne a moment to switch subjects. "Mine don't have days, just colors. I'm wearing—" She had to look under the covers to make sure. "My peach ones. They have little polka dots on them."

"Polka dots are nice. Stripes, too." Mattie stood and started to play with the fringe on the bedspread.

Rayanne could tell the child wasn't her bubbly self today. "Is something wrong, Mattie?"

She shrugged, a gesture that reminded Rayanne so much of Rios. Actually, there was a lot of Rios in Mattie. The dark chocolate hair. Those amber-colored eyes. But Rayanne could see some of Patricia Quinn there, too. The shape of Mattie's face and the graceful ease with which she moved. Rayanne had always thought Patricia moved liked a dancer, and her daughter had definitely inherited that.

"You know, you could tell me if anything was wrong," Rayanne added when Mattie stayed silent. "I'm a good listener."

Mattie sat on the bed and folded her hands in her lap. "Will you say yes if I ask you to do something?"

"That depends on what it is."

"So you wouldn't say yes without hearing what it is first?"

A little concerned, Rayanne put the apple aside. "I'd have to hear it first, but then I'd try very hard to find a way to say yes. What is it, Mattie?"

She took a deep breath. "Okay, here's the deal. I need a mother day after tomorrow. I was wondering if you could do it because Aunt Evie's real nice, but she's too old and nobody in town would believe she's my mother. Miss Freda's nice, too, but she can't be my mother, either. When I asked her, she said something about me being a bright and shining blessing for her but it wouldn't be a bright shining blessing if she had to pretend it was so when it wasn't." She paused and looked at Rayanne. "What does that mean exactly?"

Rayanne frowned. "I'm not sure." It would have been easy to blame the sleepy fog in her head, but quite often she wasn't able to decipher Freda's analogies.

"Anyway, that's when Freda gave me a glass of chocolate milk and told me to come and talk to you."

"Well, I'm, uh, glad she did." At least Rayanne thought she might be glad. She definitely didn't like the idea of Mattie wandering around with something on her mind. "Why do you need a mother?"

"For Grandpa Bennie. I'm staying with him day after tomorrow, and he's always saying how nice it'd be if I had a mother and how sorry and sad he is that I don't. Well, I figured if I had one then he wouldn't keep wishing that, and then him and Daddy wouldn't get in arguments about me anymore."

Oh, my. A major problem. Rayanne had hoped it was something simple—like the elastic being shot in her Sunday panties. This didn't sound like a one-minute solution. No wonder Freda had spouted something incomprehensible and told Mattie to talk to someone else.

For better or worse, she was that someone else.

Rayanne put her arm around the child's shoulder. "I'd love to be your mother, honey, but your grandpa Bennie knows that I'm not." Rayanne had to replay what she'd said. Had she really told Mattie she'd love to be her mother? Yep, she had.

Was it true?

Rayanne thought about it.

Yes, it seemed that it was.

But this didn't have anything to do with Rios. No, indeed. This was about Mattie's big brown eyes looking pleadingly at her. Mattie could have been anyone's child, and Rayanne would have felt the same.

She would have.

Honestly.

So, why did she feel an extra little place in her heart when she thought about how happy Mattie seemed to make Rios? And vice versa. And why did that little place feel more right than anything had felt in a long, long time?

"I'll tell you what I can do, though," Rayanne continued, forcing herself away from little places and other confusing things. She owed Mattie this much, especially after the way she'd botched things with Bennie. "Maybe I can figure out a way to talk to your grandpa and your daddy. Maybe I can convince them not to argue about you anymore." And this time she wouldn't go in there half-cocked, either. She'd do it the sensible way.

"You think that'll make it better?" Mattie asked.

"I can certainly try. You know the only reason they argue is because they both love you so much?"

"Yes, I know." The voice of experience. Too much

experience for one so young. And there was a twinge of pout added to the tone. "That's what everybody says. I don't think it's all the way true, though."

Rayanne hauled the child into her lap. "You're lucky. I mean, you've got two people who love you—your daddy and your grandpa. Plus, you've got Aunt Evie, Miss Freda and me."

"I like that last part best." As if it were the most natural thing in the world, Mattie slipped her arms around Rayanne's neck and snuggled against her. "I heard Miss Freda say your mother died when you were a little girl."

"Yes, she did. My dad, too. When I was just a couple of years older than you are now."

"So you know what it's like?"

Rayanne nodded, not trusting her voice. She knew exactly what it was like. She'd been fortunate to have Evie. Her aunt had taken her in and raised her, but Rayanne would never get over the ache of losing her parents.

Mattie's voice stayed soft, and she wiggled closer. "And that makes us like friends, then."

"You bet." The knock at the door spared Rayanne's eyes from watering, but it was close. "Come in," she called.

With his hands shoved in his pockets, Rios walked in and eyed them with concern. "Is everything all right in here?"

"Just some girl talk," Rayanne assured him.

Mattie unraveled her arms from Rayanne and looked at Rios. "Did you used to be Miss Rayanne's boyfriend a long time ago? That's what I heard Miss Freda say. Miss Freda said you were like Miss Rayanne's honey-glazed ham and cheese in her mustard and rye sandwich of life."

Rayanne flexed her eyebrows. Freda seemed to be a wellspring of information this morning. First she mentioned Rayanne's mother to Mattie, and now this? She'd have a talk with Freda later. She could certainly do without a wellspring before she'd gotten out of bed.

"Rayanne and I dated," Rios said after a long hesitation. He sat on the bed next to his daughter.

Dated and almost became lovers. Well, that was behind them now. Since he'd deputized her, Rios hadn't made one single sexual comment. And he hadn't given her any of those long, steamy looks, either. So maybe that meant he'd be able to think of her as a friend.

A friend.

That didn't create an oozy feeling in her heart. Instead, much to Rayanne's dismay, it caused a knot in her stomach. Not good. Nope, not good at all. She didn't want knots, and a friendship with Rios was the ideal solution to their occasionally stormy relationship. Well, maybe not ideal. If it were ideal, she wouldn't be dwelling on it, would she? She wouldn't be wondering what it would be like to try to latch on to what was sitting right in front of her.

A horn blared, and Mattie barreled off the bed. "Gotta go. That's the bus. Daddy, remember to get that saddle for me today. Don't forget." She kissed Rayanne and Rios before she hurried out the door.

Rayanne picked up the apple and took a bite. She was still in such deep thought about Mattie it took her a while to realize she was alone with Rios. And he was on her bed.

He lifted the apple out of her hand and took a big, crunching bite.

"So, is this where you tell me what a rotten father I am?" Rios passed her the apple and braced himself for the answer. If anyone would give him the truth, it was Rayanne. She wouldn't pull any punches, either. If the truth didn't hurt too much, he thought he might be able to take it.

"You won't hear that from me. From what I can tell, you're not a rotten father at all. You're a good one."

"Really?" That was a surprise. "Then what were you and Mattie talking about?"

"She's just concerned about you and Bennie arguing over her. She wanted me to pretend to be her mother so it'd make Bennie happy. She thought that would solve everything."

Rios shook his head. He should have known Mattie would say something like that. "She's been asking about a mother for days. Well, since you came back to town. I'm sorry she tried to bring you into this."

"Don't worry about it. I like Mattie and I like our morning talks."

Another surprise. He hadn't thought of Rayanne as very motherly. Of course, that probably had something to do with all those steamy fantasies he had about her. Nope. There wasn't a motherly image in that whole repertoire of smutty thoughts.

Still, it pleased him that she'd made this kind of connection with his daughter. There weren't a lot of women in Mattie's life, and with the exception of Rayanne, none under the age of fifty.

That was just one of the problems with the present custody situation. He wasn't sure he was giving Mattie the right role models. Heck, he wasn't even sure he was a good father, despite what Rayanne had said.

His father had left before Rios was born, and he'd never met the man, leaving some serious gaps in his fatherly role models. His mother had passed away the year before Rios learned about Mattie, and that meant he no longer had any family of his own. Well, except for Mattie. And he could lose her in this stupid custody battle with Bennie.

"Don't worry about your daughter, Rios," Rayanne said softly. "She's a well-adjusted kid, and she'll turn out just fine."

Then she did something that surprised him. She leaned closer and kissed him on the cheek. Not a hot, I-want-your-body kind of kiss. A friendly kiss. It was, well, nice. But even *nice* while he was sitting in bed with Rayanne could get him into trouble. Rios had to do something about it before parts of his body starting making foolhardy suggestions that would ruin their renewed friendship.

He caught her hand. "Come on, Deputy Garrett, get dressed. It's time we did patrol together."

Since Rayanne didn't seem to object to that suggestion, Rios left so she could dress. A while later she came downstairs squeezed into a pair of jeans that made him wish he hadn't been so accommodating about the nice part. He'd have liked to have seen exactly how she managed to get herself into those jeans. Margarine was his guess. That and maybe a good shoe horn.

"Patrol duty?" she reminded him.

Rios needed that reminder, too. After all, he'd been standing at the bottom of the stairs looking at her. His mouth was open a bit. But what did she expect when she looked like that? It gave a whole new meaning to the expression armed and dangerous.

"Patrol duty," he repeated, sounding moronic. "We'll take my truck."

"Fine."

"What would you be doing on a typical day at NYPD?" he asked as he drove toward town. Best to keep his mind on things that didn't involve smutty thoughts or her jeans.

"There really isn't a typical day. There's always paperwork, and sometimes I have to testify in court."

"So the chicken thing was a fluke?"

She chuckled. "That was just a little bit of excitement in the middle of a sea of boredom."

"Sea of boredom, huh? Well, I can't promise you much better than…" His words trailed off. "Now, I wonder who did that?"

The rubber cow was back, hanging over Main Street, but it was clear to anyone not legally blind that returning it to that very visible spot was a big mistake.

"Sweet heaven," Rayanne mumbled. "It looks like an ad for *The Texas Chainsaw Massacre*."

On a frustrated sigh, Rios agreed. "Evie must have talked somebody into putting it up there. Well, it can't stay, that's for sure. It'll scare little kids."

She eyed it, then him. "Please don't tell me it's part of my job description to take that thing down?"

Well. For a minute he considered it, but he didn't want Rayanne climbing up a ladder in those tight little jeans. It would probably cause a couple of traffic accidents. It would certainly cause him to trip over his tongue, anyway. "No, I'll take care of it later."

"Did you see the cow?" Herman Sheckley, the barber, asked when Rios parked in front of the sheriff's office.

"Yeah, we saw it, Herman. How did it get up there?"

"Evie talked the boys on the high school basketball team into putting it back up." Herman tattled. "The sign advertising the dates of the festival is missing. You reckon those boys did something with it?"

Rios didn't want to speculate what teenage boys would do with a rubber cow and a sticky vinyl sign, but anything was possible. "I'll look into it."

Herman bobbed his eyebrows. "Or maybe your deputy will look into it?"

Rios saw Rayanne stiffen. "I didn't tell him," he quickly assured her. "I only told Mattie."

"Bennie Quinn told me," Herman proudly volunteered. "He's not real happy about it, but Evie's about to bust a gut she's so proud. She's planning a big party this weekend to celebrate."

Rayanne groaned. "Not another party. We haven't finished cleaning after the last one."

Since Rios didn't think any part of this conversation would please her, he took her by the arm and led her into the office. He fixed them both a cup of coffee and sat down for a much-needed little talk.

"Rayanne, I don't think it's realistic for you to believe people won't find out that you're my deputy. That kind of thing tends to get around."

She nodded. Then shrugged. "You're right, but that's not what's bothering me. It's Evie. I wish I could get her to understand that she can't keep having these parties. I worked up a budget for her, but I know she won't stick to it." Rayanne looked at him again. "I suppose I should thank you for helping her out when she was short of funds."

Rios nearly choked on his coffee. "Beg your pardon? I thought you were madder than a hornet at me for buying Garrett land that's been in your family for over a hundred years."

"I guess I wasn't really mad at you. I was just mad at the situation. I know you were just trying to help out like you always do. Heck, Evie was right. She does own more acreage than she'll ever use. Besides, in a lot of ways, you deserve to own that land. You're the son that Evie never had."

Like the kiss on his cheek she'd given him earlier, that sounded nice. Nice in a friendly sort of way. That probably meant Rayanne had somehow come to grips with the physical attraction between them. Come to grips with it and squelched it.

Oh.

Rios wasn't sure he liked anything being squelched when it came to her attraction for him. Because in their case, that attraction might be just the...what? The first thought that came to mind was icing on the cake. They had a good friendship. Years of companionship. A whole history together. But mixed with all that history had always been something smoldering. Lust. Well, lust and a few more feelings drizzled in with it. Truth was—and he was finally beginning to see this—just as he was the son Evie never had, Rayanne was the wife he had never had.

Or something like that.

Lordy, it was confusing. Rios was still trying to sort through things when the phone rang. He picked up the extension on the front desk and listened to Jessie Herring tell him what was going on with his neighbors, the Beekers family. The sorting out of his feelings would have to wait. Duty called.

Rios hung up and caught her hand. "This might be right up your alley, Deputy Garrett. It appears we have a hostage situation."

CHAPTER NINE

"Lead me not into temptation. I can find it all by myself, thank you."
—Bumper Ditties by Evie E. Garrett

THE HOSTAGE WAS A COW.

It was a longhorn, to be specific, and to Rayanne it looked like a bag of bones with antlers. An equally skinny bag-of-bones man was in front of the cow, a baseball bat aimed right between the poor animal's eyes. A rather large woman was standing behind the man, and she had another bat raised high in the air lined up directly with the bald spot on the skinny man's head.

Rios had parked his truck down the road, and they'd walked to the scene, but nowhere along the way had he told her the hostage wouldn't be human. Probably for a good reason. Rayanne wasn't sure she would have come. This looked more like a case for men in white coats than the sheriff's office.

"Don't let them see you," Rios whispered. He caught her hand and pulled her behind a sprawling oak. The limbs grew low and thick, but they could still see the pasture where the situation was going on. Or rather where the situation was stationary. No one was moving. "I don't want anyone to get hurt."

Rayanne hadn't been especially alarmed until Rios made that last remark. "Will they come after us?"

"No, but I don't want to force anyone to play a hand they don't really want to play. They do this about once a month."

This? This happened once a month? Amazing. She hadn't thought a cop would run into a situation like this in an entire career, and here Rios got a monthly dose of it. "So, what exactly is going on, anyway?"

He kept his voice so low Rayanne had to lean closer to hear him. "Well, you probably remember Ned Beekers and his wife, Alice?"

Yes, she remembered them and had seen them at Evie's party. However, Rayanne hadn't heard anything about the persistent problem of taking a longhorn hostage, and Evie had been particularly good at passing on those kinds of juicy tidbits.

"Why is Ned holding a bat on that cow?" Rayanne asked, almost afraid to hear the answer.

"Because it belongs to Alice. She had an affair with a man over in Kerrville about five, maybe six years ago. Anyway, Ned thinks the man gave Alice the cow as a sort of present, something to rub in Ned's face, so to speak. Alice says it wasn't a present at all, that she bought it with her own money because she liked the looks of it. So now, whenever they argue, Ned always seems to bring the cow into it. He threatens to bash it. Then Alice gets mad and threatens to bash him."

"Do they ever bash anything?"

"No," he whispered. He was so close she felt his warm breath on her ear. "But they like to make a big fuss about it. With all that experience you have with chickens, a cow should be a piece of cake."

"Don't go there, Rios. No chicken remarks." But Rayanne smiled. And she shivered because his breath tickled her ear. "So, how do you usually talk Ned and Alice into surrendering their bats?"

"That depends. They both still look pretty mad, so it probably won't do much good to try to talk them into anything right now. Let's give them a couple more minutes and see if they start yelling. Yelling in this case would be a good sign."

Rayanne figured that yelling, angry people would be the last thing Rios would want on his hands. "And why would that be a good sign?"

"Because it gets them talking to each other again. Then we can sort of turn the tables on them."

It happened again. His breath brushed her ear. And her cheek. It felt like a caress, and Rayanne didn't like the way it sent her heart racing. She tried to inch away from him so it wouldn't happen again. The problem was, she couldn't inch too far without the Beekers seeing her.

Rios craned his neck so he could look between the tree limbs. The adjustment caused him to shift his posture. So much for her inching away from him. Now his chest was against her back.

Ned Beekers said something to his wife, something Rayanne couldn't hear, but she hoped it was good they were talking. Ending this hostage situation took on a new urgency for her. An urgent urgency. The close contact with Rios was starting to make her a little itchy.

"I'll do it! Don't you think I won't, either," Ned yelled. "I'll bop this miserable excuse for a cow right between the eyes."

"And you'll regret it if you do, you miserable excuse

for a buzzard!" Alice shouted. "I'll bash your head in just like an overripe watermelon."

Rayanne grimaced at that gruesome image. She leaned back slightly so she could talk to Rios. "This kind of yelling is good, right?"

He nodded. Rayanne knew immediately that he shouldn't have done that. Of course, she shouldn't have leaned back in the first place. The nod brushed his mouth against her cheek. His lips brushed against her ear. And his middle brushed against the back of her middle. All that brushing had an effect on her.

She stiffened.

So did Rios.

Well, at least Rayanne thought he'd stiffened, but then she realized the stiffening was somewhat localized. Extremely localized. Just below his belt and right in the center of his jeans.

Rios mumbled something indistinguishable under his breath. Rayanne didn't dare ask what. She didn't want to know what. It definitely wasn't a good time for this. That localized stiffening seemed to send a weird primal signal for her body to start softening. This wasn't good. Not good at all.

"Please tell me what's happening here really isn't what I think is happening," Rios mumbled.

"No." Which was a stupid answer, because his question didn't make sense. Well, it wouldn't have made sense to anyone but her. Rios wasn't a fool. He could tell she was breathing hard. Besides, she was probably giving off some primal female scent that his primal male nose picked up right away. "I mean yes, it might be happening, but I don't want to talk about it."

"Well, neither do I, but—"

"No buts, and no talking about it," Rayanne insisted. "Maybe it'll just go away if we don't say anything else."

"Doubtful."

"Shh. I said don't say anything else about it. Besides, it's probably all just some kind of adrenaline reaction to the hostage situation."

Rios glanced at her. "I thought you didn't want to say anything else about it?"

"I don't." Rayanne rubbed her hand over her face. "I was just giving you a reasonable explanation for it, that's all."

"There's a reasonable explanation, all right, and it has nothing to do with an adrenaline reaction. Or cake icing."

Rayanne glanced at him over her shoulder. "Cake icing? What does that have to do with anything?"

"It's a metaphor." Rios leaned into her. Well, he didn't actually lean. He pushed his body against her, and she had no trouble figuring out that the mysterious stiffening wasn't her imagination. Unless Rios had taken to carrying a weapon or a flashlight, she could also guess exactly what it was.

"I can't walk now," he told her. "Satisfied?"

Why would he think something like that would satisfy her? This was exactly what she'd been trying to avoid. Rayanne hadn't done a very good job of avoiding it, but that gave him no reason to think she'd be satisfied that she'd heated him up. Well, maybe she was, a little…

Don't go there.

"You make it sound like it's my fault you can't walk," she complained. "I can't help if you have these stupid reactions to—"

He put his hand over her mouth, but since Rayanne

didn't like him doing that she kept right on talking. He kept his hand there until he got an odd look on his face. "Did you tongue my fingers?" he asked.

"Huh?"

"Your tongue. Did you just stick it in between my fingers?"

"Maybe." Except it came out garbled since he was still trying to muzzle her. Maybe she had, but it hadn't been intentional. She'd never intentionally stuck her tongue between anyone's fingers. "Why?" That came out garbled, too.

"Because you can't do it, that's why," Rios insisted in an obstinate whisper. "That spot between my fingers is very sensitive, and it's especially sensitive to a woman's tongue."

"Well, if you would move your hand, my tongue wouldn't get caught between your sensitive little fingers." Her protest sounded like a speech delivered in muffled pig Latin. Rayanne shoved his hand away. "I think it's time to add another rule to our working arrangement—no putting your hand over my mouth."

"I won't put my hand on your mouth if you'll stop breathing hard right in my ear. Deal?"

They stared at each other, both looking pleased that they'd managed to accomplish something. Exactly what, Rayanne didn't know, but she was sure she'd gained something from that tongue-in-finger altercation.

Rios gave her a firm nod. "Let's just get this over with, so we can get out of here. Can you shoot that limb?"

She followed the direction of Rios's gaze and spotted the limb that was hanging directly over Ned's arm. "Sure."

"Then do it."

Rayanne withdrew her .38, slipped off the safety and aimed at the leafy projection. With one shot, she clipped the branch, sending it down on Ned. The man quickly jumped out of the way.

"Drop your bat, Ned," Rios called. "And, Alice, you do the same."

Rayanne wished like the devil that Rios hadn't shouted those demands until he got his mouth away from her ear, but his orders seemed to work. Ned dropped his. Alice dropped hers. And the longhorn stood there chewing its cud as if this were the most boring part of its entire day.

"Well, it seems our hostage situation is over," Rios announced, moving from behind the tree.

It was. It was really over. Rayanne couldn't believe what she'd just experienced. Rios's plan had worked. The laid-back, wait—'em-out, shoot-a-tree-limb approach had worked. The hostage situation seemed to be defused, and no one was threatening each other or the cow.

"But what would you have done if I hadn't had a gun?" Rayanne asked with some smugness. After all, she was the one who had ended the whole thing with her expert marksmanship.

Rios reached down and picked up a small rock. With very accurate aim, he pitched it and hit Ned right on the shoulder.

"Hey!" Ned hollered. "Why'd you do that, Rios? I already put down my bat like you told me to."

"I was just proving a point to Rayanne, that's all, Ned. Nothing personal."

That would have worked, too. Again, Rayanne couldn't believe it. Rios could have solved a hostage situation with a rock and a warning. The man was darn good at his job.

"Now what?" Rayanne asked, trying to keep her mouth from gaping. "Do you arrest them?"

"No sense in it. I'll just talk to them a little bit and try to make them see the error of their ways."

"And you can do that?" It seemed like a tall order, but Rayanne didn't doubt him after what had just happened.

"Yep. I can do that." It seemed to her he had a swagger to his walk when he started across the pasture toward the Beekerses. Or maybe it was just that little stiffening problem he'd made her aware of when he bumped into her.

"Well, you're a regular Sheriff Andy Taylor from Longhorn RFD, aren't you?" Rayanne said mockingly.

The swagger turned into a full strut. "Careful, Rayanne, that would make you Deputy Barney Fife, now, wouldn't it?"

She tried not to. She really did. But she couldn't help it. She laughed at his ridiculous attempt at humor.

She watched him stop in front of the cow and give it an affectionate rub between the eyes. He murmured a few words into the longhorn's ear then turned his attention to the Beekerses. All the while he spoke to them, he continued those gentle strokes on the cow. It was such a simple gesture and not unusual for Rios. He always did have a gentle way with animals. And people.

Especially her.

As she stood there in the warm Texas sun and watched Rios work, she could almost smell the starch on his shirt and the saddle soap he'd used to polish his boots. He was the sheriff, all right. A good one. Along with being a good father. And a good man.

Then it hit her. Rios was more than a soft spot in her heart. Much more than a friend. More than someone to be admired. He was the only man she'd ever loved.

Shoot.

Now that she'd finally worked out that little soul-rocking revelation, it left her with one question. What the devil was she going to do about it?

CHAPTER TEN

"A penny for your thoughts, twenty dollars if you
act it out."

—Bumper Ditties by Evie E. Garrett

"WHY ARE WE COMING to the Saunders's old barn?" Rayanne asked when Rios stopped the truck in front of the
outbuilding.

Rios glanced at her, thankful she'd finally said something. Since they left the Beekerses, she had clammed
up. Why, he didn't know, but he figured it had something to do with that little whisper-and-nudge session
that had gone on earlier.

"I promised Mattie I'd get a saddle for her," he answered.

"Oh, that's right. This is your barn now." She pointed
to the house that was snuggled in the middle of some tall
pecan trees. "You gave the place a fresh coat of paint. It
looks better than it ever did when the Saunderses owned
it."

"Thanks." It was a compliment that pleased him far
more than he'd thought it would. For some reason he
wanted Rayanne to approve of what he'd accomplished.
Odd, he hadn't wanted or needed that approval from
anyone else other than Mattie.

Rios glanced around his property, trying to see it

through Rayanne's eyes. The place wasn't modern by anyone's standards, but it looked lived-in and cared for. That's because it was. He'd worked plenty of hours clearing away old brush, repairing fences and fixing the house and outbuildings. Now the place was truly his, and he'd done his level best to make it a home for Mattie.

"But isn't Bennie your nearest neighbor?" she asked.

"Yes. A downside to living here, I guess. If we got along better, it'd be good for Mattie, though. All she has to do is walk through that peach grove to get to his house."

Rios pulled open the creaking barn doors and went inside. Tiny threads of sunlight seeped through the gaps in the old wood, but it was still pretty dark. Actually, it was pitch dark. He reached for the flashlight that was usually on a hook by the door, but it wasn't there. Only then did he remember he'd seen Mattie playing with it the night before. She'd probably forgotten to put it back.

"How good can you see in the dark?" he asked Rayanne.

"All right, I guess. Why?"

"The saddle's all the way at the back, and I don't want to trip over anything."

"Here." She picked up an old lantern and shook it. "It still has some kerosene in it. Got a match?"

"In the truck." While she waited, he went to the glove compartment and fished out a box of matches. Once he'd lit the wick, he pocketed the matches and they went inside.

Rayanne fell in step behind him. "Say, this place is huge."

"It is. I use it for storage now, but I'll have to clear it out when I bring in more horses."

"You're planning to do that?"

He nodded. "If I add some more breed stock, I figure I'm only ten years or so away from having one of the biggest operations around Longhorn."

"Really? Bigger than Bennie Quinn's place?"

Another nod.

"You've done well for yourself," she told him.

"That surprises you, huh?" Rios spotted the saddle on a rack on the back wall. He stepped around some bales of hay and made his way toward it.

"Not really. I'd heard you were successful riding rodeo. It figures you could carry that success into ranching."

"Careful with those compliments, Rayanne. They just might go straight to my head." Or his heart. But the caution was too little, too late. It seemed just about everything Rayanne said or did went to his heart. It wasn't easy for him to accept that she had that much power over him.

Rios handed her the lantern and hauled the saddle onto his shoulder. Rayanne walked ahead of him, and when she got closer to the door, she blew out the lantern. Obviously, she blew it out a little too soon. Rios didn't see the last bale of hay, and he tripped over it, sending him and the saddle sprawling. His head collided with the pommel, his shoulder with a post. The rest of him collided with the ground.

"Heavens, are you all right?" Rayanne hurried to him and dropped on her knees beside him.

He rubbed his head, groaned and sat up. "I'm fine, I think. Maybe next time, though, you shouldn't get in such a hurry to blow out that lantern. I wasn't kidding when I said I really can't see much in the dark."

"Sorry. I thought you were right behind me."

"No, I was a couple of steps behind those hay bales."

"Well, don't move until we've made sure nothing is broken." Rayanne retrieved the lamp and used his matches to light it. She set it on a hay bale a few yards away, and the golden light sprayed all around them.

"Okay, where do you hurt?" she asked, kneeling beside him again.

Rios intended to answer her, he really did, but the words didn't make it out of his mouth. That's because he made the mistake of looking at her.

Their gazes locked. His heart slammed against his chest. And it just kept on slamming. Maybe he was still in a lather about that whispering session, and maybe he'd been in a lather since he'd seen Rayanne in New York. Rios suddenly didn't care.

She was here.

He was here.

They were alone.

And he wanted her mouth for supper.

Before he could talk himself out of it, Rios leaned over and put his mouth right next to hers.

"What do you think you're doing?" But she didn't sound puzzled. Or even shocked. There was a lot of breath in her voice, whispery, sexy breath, and she darn sure didn't move away.

"I'm stirring a pot that probably shouldn't be stirred." Rios brushed his lips against her earlobe. "And this time, I won't leave any green hickeys."

Rayanne shivered, and a tiny sound came from deep within her throat. An unconscious invitation for him to give her more. It was the only invitation he needed.

"It doesn't feel like you're stirring a pot," she said. "It feels like you're kissing my ear."

He gave it some thought. "That, too."

She grabbed his shirt with both hands and locked him in a fierce grip. To stop him, was Rios's first thought. But she sure didn't do that. She grabbed him. That was another invitation, as far as he was concerned.

He nuzzled the little area just below her ear, dampening it slightly with the tip of his tongue, then whispered a hot, soft breath over the same spot.

Rayanne whimpered.

The seductive dance with his mouth continued. Rios went from her ear to her cheek, making the journey one long, slow kiss.

"Don't worry," he said, in case she planned to protest. "We'll just play around for a while. No one will ever have to know but us. How long has it been since someone played with you, Rayanne?"

She whimpered again when he kissed her neck. "About three years ago, and I didn't have, uh, much fun."

Three years? And he thought his love life had been sluggish. Hers had obviously come to a screeching halt. "And you didn't have much fun, you say?"

She shook her head. "A very disappointing encounter."

"Well, heck, I'm surprised you didn't give up on men altogether." He slipped one hand behind her neck and eased her to the ground.

"I have given up on them."

No, she hadn't. She was here with him, and whether she knew it or not, her body was still issuing a lot of invitations. Rios leaned over her and placed a forearm on each side of her head. "Tell you what, Rayanne. Let's see if we can have some fun."

"All right," she said dreamily. "Will you kiss me again?"

His gaze moved to her mouth. And stayed there. With the ease of a man who had all the time in the world, he visually traced her lips. "I was giving that some thought, yes."

"And?"

"And I decided…"

But he paused. Obviously for too long. So Rayanne did something he hadn't counted on. She kissed him. With her hands still filled with his shirt, she wrenched him closer until she forced their mouths to meet. And they met, all right. There were no preliminaries, no yearning looks, no soft caressing breaths, no gentleness. Just them. Two people kissing each other as if they'd never have the chance to, ever again.

"I got tired of waiting for you to decide," she said when they had to break apart to breathe.

"Yeah, I figured that out for myself."

He drew in a gulp of air through his mouth, taking in her taste and scent at once. The sensations raced through him and stirred every drop of his blood.

Rios kissed her again, twisting and knotting his fingers through her hair so he completely controlled the movement of her head. The soft hay shifted, rolling him on top of her. Rayanne didn't resist him. She automatically adjusted her body to accommodate his weight.

The stretchy top didn't give him much resistance when he caught the scooped neck and pulled it down to expose her breasts. He lowered his head and brushed the tip of his tongue over her peaked nipple. She moaned,

and her back bowed, thrusting her breasts higher so he
could easily take her nipple into his mouth.

When his lips closed around the hard bud and his
tongue circled it, drawing it deeply into his mouth, she
bucked beneath him. And, Lord, could the woman buck.
Rios was suddenly very glad he'd been so good at bronc
riding. Of course, that kind of riding had never been
quite this exciting.

"I want more," he informed her, fingering the clasp
of her bra. He whispered his words directly against her
wet skin.

"Yes. Yes. More sounds good."

Very encouraged by her agreement, he decided to
give things a little shove. Well, actually a well-placed
shove. He shoved his knee between hers, pushing his
hard thigh up against a place he thought would please
her. It must have because she started making little
squeaky noises. Rios kept up that pressure until the
squeaky noises turned to moans, and she was bearing
down as hard as he was.

Rayanne's breath hitched in her throat. "I'll die if you
keep doing that."

It didn't slow him down. This kind of dying was exactly what he wanted her to do. Three years was a long
time to go without dying.

He added a new dimension to the torture session. He
slid his hand down her stomach and lower, drawing back
his leg slightly so he could caress her. Not with fingertips. Not gently, either. He fit his hand to her intimately.
As if the fabric of her jeans didn't exist, he touched her.

"Do you like the way I play, Rayanne?"

"Yes," she mindlessly agreed. She ripped open his
shirt and ran her hands over his chest. "Play harder."

That wouldn't be a problem. Things were getting pretty hard.

She went after his zipper, shoving it down. "Harder, I said."

Well, now, as if he could turn down a request like that. If the woman wanted harder, that's exactly what she would get. He went after her zipper. Stretching his hand into her jeans, he found a snug little place that made her say things Rios was sure she didn't mean—something about him being a sex god and that she would love and cherish him for the rest of her life.

Well, maybe in her eyes he was a sex god. At the moment, anyway. The woman was certainly entitled to her opinion, even if Rios figured she didn't really have a clue what she was saying.

"More," she demanded.

More was about to mean stripping off her clothes and sinking hard and deep into her. Rios didn't really see a problem with that. Well, it wouldn't have been a problem if he hadn't detected something.

"Do you smell smoke?" he asked.

"Not yet, but keep trying."

That wasn't what he meant, but he liked her attitude. For a moment that attitude distracted him until he caught another whiff of smoke. "Rayanne, I think there's a fire somewhere."

She lifted her head slightly and sniffed. She sniffed again, and Rios saw the alarm come over her face. They both snapped their heads toward the lantern she'd left on the hay bale. It was on its side, and yes, there were flames dancing all around it.

Rios thought they probably broke speed records coming off the floor. Rayanne grabbed a saddle blanket and started slapping at the fire. He peeled off his shirt and began to do the same. Since that didn't seem to be doing a lot of good, he pulled her out of the barn and went for the hose.

"Here!" He handed her the end of the hose while he ran around the side of the barn to turn on the water.

The water pressure seemed to be at a trickle, so Rios decided to try to beat down the flames with the saddle blanket while Rayanne handled the hose. He lost track of how long they worked, but by the time the last ember went cold, they had saved every part of the barn but the door and some hay. He'd even gotten out Mattie's saddle. He was also exhausted. That exhaustion was probably the reason he didn't see the approaching car until it was right in front of the barn.

Rios looked at his visitor and could only shake his head. Mercy, he didn't need this now.

"Yoo-hoo," Evie called. "Is everything all right here?"

Rios looked at Rayanne, at the smeared soot on her face, at her state of undress. With the fire, he'd forgotten that the neckline of her top was below her breasts. He quickly dropped the saddle blanket and tried to fix her clothes. That's when he noticed their jeans were unzipped. He also noticed something else.

Evie wasn't alone.

Dr. Malcolm Keene stepped out of the driver's side of his rental car. Putting his hands on his classically cut khakis, Dr. Whine stood there and looked at them. Evie did the same, except it seemed she was trying to figure out what was going on. Rios supposed Dr. Whine already had a good guess. That in itself would have been uncomfortable enough if a truck hadn't come barreling up the road toward them. A truck Rios unfortunately recognized.

"I saw the smoke," Bennie yelled, throwing open his truck door. "Mattie's not up here, is she?"

"No." And thank heaven, she wasn't. All in all, it was the only redeeming thing Rios could see about this predicament. This was probably what people meant when they said there'd be the devil to pay.

The devil was most certainly demanding payment, and he wondered how much of his butt it was going to cost him.

RAYANNE LOOKED AT the three people who'd arrived at the barn but couldn't decide which of them she dreaded most. It was a toss-up.

There was Aunt Evie, appearing troubled and a little confused. Then Bennie, who was probably ready to explode. His Rudolph nose looked like a sunburned baby's butt. Then there was Malcolm. He looked like all those other things put together—troubled, confused and ready to explode. No sunburned baby-butt nose, but in his case she could add horrified to the things she saw in his expression.

Rayanne hoped Malcolm had brought his anxiety meds. He'd need them for sure, and maybe he'd let her borrow some. She suddenly felt a panic attack coming on.

Since the silence seemed more unbearable than the inevitable, Rayanne fluttered her fingers toward the barn. "Uh, there was a fire," she told everyone. Now, exactly what part of the predicament that would clarify, she didn't know, but it seemed the safest remark she could make. Everything after it would clearly go downhill.

"Is that what happened to your clothes?" Evie asked, wrinkling her nose.

Yes, her clothes. Dreading what she might see, Rayanne finally got enough courage to look down. Nothing exactly vital was showing, but her bra was around her waist, and her jeans were unzipped. It would be hard to explain that. Even harder to explain it in combination with Rios's unzipped jeans and ripped shirt.

"Uh, there was a fire," Rayanne repeated. She hoped they'd think the fire had caused the displaced bra, the unzipped jeans and her somewhat limited vocabulary.

"Did you try to pee on the fire?" Evie asked. "Is that why your jeans are all unzipped?"

Rayanne had to bite her lip to keep from laughing hysterically. She wished she'd come up with that herself. If she agreed now, it would seem too obvious a lie.

"Rayanne." That from Malcolm. But then he just stood there and stared at her. It seemed as if he were trying to figure out what to say, too.

As discreetly as possible, considering three people had their eyes trained on her, Rayanne shoved her bra under her top and zipped up her jeans. "Malcolm, uh, there was a fire."

"Yes, I can see that. Are you all right?"

"Fine." It was a Texas lady's answer to everything. Even if her hair had been in flames, the answer was *fine*. Of course, any moron could see that things were far from fine. "What are you doing here, anyway?"

Malcolm walked closer. "I was worried about you. When you asked for a leave of absence, I thought they were holding you against your will so I decided to fly down and check on you."

She shook her head. Holding her against her will?

Rayanne would have told Malcolm just how far off the mark he was if Bennie hadn't interrupted.

"Oh, I get it now. I can see what's going on here."

Rayanne didn't think that took any intelligence on Bennie's part. She didn't dare repeat the line about there being a fire or Evie's suggestion. There were some things that didn't bear repeating.

"I see it all now," Bennie said. "Rios brought you here so it would improve his chances of getting custody of Mattie."

"What?" Rayanne had obviously missed a step in Bennie's reasoning process. Anyone with half a brain could see that Rios and she had been fooling around. And that was fooling around in the most extreme way. "What happened in that barn has nothing to do with the custody disagreement between you and Rios."

"Sure it does." Bennie's ragged voice boomed. "Rios brought you here so you two could get married—"

"Married?" Rayanne howled.

Rios repeated it. Except he howled even louder than she had. "Married? You've lost your mind, Bennie. I didn't—"

"Don't deny it, Rios. It won't do any good. I heard your lawyer tell you the case would go better for you if you got married."

Rayanne looked at Rios for verification. He verified it with a frustrated shrug. She responded with a frown. Why hadn't he mentioned this sooner? She thought they'd discussed every aspect of the custody dispute. Obviously not. Not once had the subject of marriage come up.

"Then you heard me tell my lawyer that I wasn't going

to get married any time soon." Rios fired the words at Bennie.

"Yeah, but you musta changed your mind because a couple weeks later you flew off to New York and brought Rayanne back with you. This is low-down dirty pool, Rios, even for you. Well, I won't let you get away with it. No, I won't." He stomped to his truck, got in and drove away.

Rayanne figured that was one down, two to go. Make that three. She didn't like the fact that Rios might have had marriage on his mind when he brought her to Longhorn. She intended to question him about it, and he better have the right answers.

"Well, that didn't go so good," Evie said on a huff. "There's only one thing you can do now, Rayanne. You'll just have to marry Rios."

"Marry him?" It had finally happened. Evie had completely exited the real world. "Aunt Evie, this isn't the Dark Ages. I can darn sure make out with a man in a barn without having to marry him."

"Oh, it's not about making out." Evie paused. "Was that what you were doing?" She smiled. Beamed, really.

"Oh, for heaven's sake. What I was doing with Rios is my business. I'm a grown woman—"

Evie latched on to Rayanne's shoulders and used her motherly tone, something Rayanne hadn't heard her use in years. Not since that night Rayanne's midnight-blue lace panties had fallen from her hair clip onto the living-room floor. "Do you want Rios to lose custody of Mattie to that old man?"

"No, of course not."

"Then you should be doing something to stop it, that's what. This is all your fault, you know."

"My fault? How do you figure that?"

Evie's grip tightened. "Because Bennie will go straight to the judge and tell him that you and Rios were fooling around in broad daylight."

"We weren't in broad daylight. We were in a barn." Rayanne was so angry it took her a while to add anything to that. "And even if we weren't, that doesn't mean I've hurt Rios's chances of getting custody of Mattie, and it darn sure doesn't mean I'd marry him. Great day, Aunt Evie, I can't believe you'd suggest such a thing. I wouldn't marry him if—"

Rayanne put the pause button on her hissy fit when she remembered Rios was standing right next to her. Practically arm-to-arm next to her. One glance into his eyes, and she remembered they were indeed the color of iced tea. Heavy emphasis on the iced. She'd obviously hurt his feelings.

"I'm sorry," she said softly. "It's just that I can't marry you to help you with your custody battle."

His voice was low and cold when he spoke. "I don't remember asking you to." He turned, and much like Bennie, he went to his truck, got in and drove away.

Rayanne had only one thought—what the heck had she done?

"Oh, dear." Evie fanned herself. "This didn't turn out at all like I planned. I never thought everyone would get so mad."

In frustration, Rayanne scrubbed her hands over her face. "What does that mean?"

"Well, I have a teeny little confession to make."

Rayanne didn't like the sound of that. There was no such thing as a teeny confession when it came to Evie.

The woman only made whopper mistakes. "Spill it, Aunt Evie."

"Well, you see, I sort of came up with this plan to bring you here. Now, before you get all mad, hear me out. I knew you'd make a good mother for Mattie, and it's true you really like her, don't you?"

"I do, but right now I'm far more interested in hearing about this plan of yours." Rayanne hadn't thought it was possible to produce sound from such a tightly clenched jaw, but she proved it could be done.

Evie hemmed and hawed a moment. "I took aim at Bennie's hackberry knowing Rios would have to arrest me. I knew that would bring you back to Longhorn. And then, because you wouldn't be able to keep hiding your feelings, you and Rios, well, I figured you two would do what comes naturally to two people who are attracted to each other. I figured nature would take its course. Then you two would get married, and Bennie would give up this stupid custody fight. I know in my heart all he wants is a family for Mattie."

Rayanne squeezed her hands against her head. "I cannot believe you did something like this."

"I know. Can you forgive me?"

Maybe in a couple of decades, but right then Rayanne couldn't talk anymore about it. Another word about marriage, plans and motherhood would send her screaming through the woods like a crazy woman. She might do it anyway, even if no one mentioned those things. She didn't have a lot of options, and going off the deep end definitely appealed to her.

"Come on, Rayanne." Malcolm hooked his arm through hers. "I'm taking you back to New York."

Finally, a voice of reason. Rayanne took the first step

with him before she realized what she was doing. What she was doing was something stupid. This wasn't the voice of reason. It was Malcolm, and he rarely made sense.

Rayanne stopped so quickly he nearly tripped. While he was trying to stop himself from falling face-first into some questionable brown droppings, Rayanne had a revelation. Practically a divine manifestation. She'd come to the proverbial crossroads, and suddenly everything became crystal clear.

"I don't want to go back to New York," she said firmly.

Malcolm shook his head. "You can't mean that."

She did mean that. "I do too mean it."

"But there's no reason for you to stay here."

"Oh, yes, there is. There are more reasons for me to stay than there are for me to go back."

Malcolm obviously didn't agree. He was looking at her as if she'd sprouted feathers and left those questionable droppings. "But what about your job? You're a police officer, not some hayseed hick who belongs here in this cow-patty town."

Okay. She had to give him a little slack here. Malcolm was obviously perturbed and hadn't fully thought out what he'd said, much as she'd done earlier to Rios.

"You're right about the first part—I am a police officer," Rayanne said calmly. "But I don't have to live in New York to be a good cop. And you're wrong about me not being some hayseed hick. That's who I am, that's where I came from, and it'll always be part of me."

"That's not you." He begged to differ. "That *was* you. But you've shaken all that off and made something of yourself."

"I was something long before I ever went to New

York. I just forgot that for a while. And I'm tired of living someplace I don't want to live simply so I can say I've made my way in the world. Well, I've made my way, and it's brought me right back here, and here is exactly where I want to be."

Evie started clapping and saying how happy she was. Rayanne tried to concentrate on finishing the conversation with Malcolm.

He didn't seem ready to finish a conversation at all. He looked more confused than ever. "And what about us?"

Oh, Rayanne didn't like this part. She obviously needed to restate something she'd been telling Malcolm for ages. "There never was an us, and I think in your heart you know that. We've known each other three years, and the only time we've kissed was that day at the airport. That says it all, doesn't it?"

"I thought you just liked to take things slow."

Only with him. She hadn't had a problem going full speed ahead with Rios. Now, that said it all. Eleven years the man had been out of her life, and they'd picked up a couple of steps ahead of where they'd left off.

"Go back to New York, Malcolm, and find a woman who'll appreciate you for what you are."

He swallowed hard. "You're going after that cowboy, aren't you?"

She nodded. You bet she was. Rios was the best thing that had ever happened to her, and she was in love with him. The problem was, she didn't know if Rios would even speak to her after the way she'd treated him.

Groveling was a distinct possibility. She only hoped she didn't have to do it in any questionable brown droppings.

IT TOOK THE BETTER PART of the afternoon, but Rayanne finally found Rios. Well, she found his horse first. The roan stallion was grazing in the pasture near Whiskey Creek. Rios was nearby, and she watched as he hauled a calf out of the boggy ground near the water.

Since he didn't notice she was there, Rayanne stood for a while and watched. It gave her some time to try to figure out what she was going to say to him. Or to try to figure out if there was anything she could say that would make him listen. If their positions were reversed, she probably wouldn't listen to him. Heck, it had taken her eleven years to get over him turning her down.

Thankfully, she had finally seen the light.

And speaking of seeing things, she noticed what Rios was wearing. Brown leather chaps over his dusty working jeans. And spurs. When he turned the calf loose, she heard the silver spurs jingle against the thick heels of his boots.

Interesting.

She had seen him as a cop and a daddy, and when he was younger, he'd been into his biker-leather James Dean phase. But this was another side of Rios.

The real cowboy.

Rayanne decided she liked it as much as the other sides of him. Well, maybe more. Maybe even a lot more.

The chaps were a definite plus. They were old and well worn. The leather was pliant. Instead of being shapeless and baggy, Rios had fastened them snugly over his hips and thighs. The opening outlined the front of his jeans. And other things. Manly things.

Rayanne couldn't help thinking of ancient maps she had seen in books where there was a large X placed to denote an area of importance. Or valuable treasure. Yes, the chaps were indeed a definite plus, but they were... cake icing.

She smiled, remembering Rios's odd comment. All the outside of him, as positively tantalizing as it was, was merely icing. The man beneath was far more and far better than the sum total of his looks. She tested one of Freda's metaphors. Rios was her little ray of bright warm sunshine in the middle of a winter storm, and she was disgustingly in love with him.

And finally, she knew exactly what she wanted to do with Rios McKay.

She only hoped he'd cooperate.

CHAPTER ELEVEN

"Oink, Flap, Oink, Flap...well, I'll be darned."
—Bumper Ditties by Evie E. Garrett

RIOS SAW RAYANNE by the tree and scowled. This was just what he didn't need. Her, anywhere near him. He wasn't in the mood for dealing with anybody right now, but especially her.

"What are you doing here?" he snarled.

"That's my line." She walked closer. Slowly, though, as if she was a little afraid of him. Good! If she had any sense, she'd run in the other direction.

"I came to apologize, Rios. I'm sorry about what I said back there at the barn."

He didn't answer her. Couldn't. He was still steaming over the way she'd spoken about him. How dare she think he'd come up with a plan to trick her into marrying him? And how could she possibly say she wouldn't ever marry him? Just who the heck did she think she was? Huh?

"Aunt Evie confessed to everything," she continued. "She pretended to take aim at Bennie so I'd have to come back to town and get her out of jail. She thought once I was here that nature would take its course. Those are her words, not mine."

He bent and washed the mud off his hands. "So?"

"So, I sent Malcolm back to New York and I told Aunt Evie that I was coming to find you." She stepped even closer. "And it appears I've found you."

"I'm not in the mood for playing games." Rios started toward his stallion, but she caught his arm.

"Well, actually, neither am I." Rayanne looked at his clothes. "You're wearing chaps."

"Yeah, so?"

"Spurs, too."

Was she writing a fashion column or something? "Rayanne, is this conversation actually leading somewhere?"

"Hopefully."

"Then could you speed it up a little bit? I'm in kind of a hurry here."

"Okay." She moistened her lips. "I've decided to stay in Longhorn, and I want to make sure I can keep working for you."

It sounded like a trick question. Or the answer to his prayers. Still, that didn't mean everything was settled between them. She hadn't said a darn thing about staying in Longhorn because of him.

"You can keep your job," he said none too enthusiastically.

"Good. We'll discuss raises and such later on. You don't pay me nearly enough." She shook her head. "But I'm getting off track. I want you to think back to the conversation we had in New York. The one we had about that night at Whiskey Creek. Specifically, the part where you said you owed me one and that I could collect any time."

"What about it?"

"Well, that's why I'm here—to collect."

It took him a few seconds to recall the conversation and to realize that Rayanne was talking about making love. With him.

That confused Rios. A lot.

"I…" Rios couldn't figure out what to say. He was still mad at her, yes. Furious, really. And hurt over her comments. But she was offering something he really wanted—her.

"What's the matter? Is the offer no longer good?"

"It's still good, after we get a few things straight." There. Rios had to applaud himself. There probably wasn't a functioning red-blooded male on earth who'd insist on putting off lovemaking just to talk, but this conversation was important. "I would have never tried to trick you into marrying me."

She nodded. "I know."

That confused him, too. He'd expected a little argument from her. Or at least a little hesitation. But her nod had been a firm nod, and her *I know* had been a genuine *I know*. Okay. The only thing he could do was go on to his next point of contention.

"And I didn't appreciate you getting mad at me before you even asked if I had anything to do with it."

Rayanne gave another nod. "I know. I was wrong."

He squinted one eye and looked at her. "You mean that?"

"I wouldn't be here if I didn't mean it."

True. Rayanne wasn't the kind of woman to offer herself to a man she was still at odds with. Well, then. That solved the bulk of his major issues. Later, much later, they'd work out the other things.

He reached out, caught a handful of her hair and roughly pulled her closer. She did some pulling of her own. She grabbed his shirt, knotted it in her hands and dragged him against her. Not that she had to drag much. He'd already started in that direction.

Rios kissed her. Hard. Long. And then kissed her again and caught her shirt. "If you're really taking me up on my offer, then I want this off now." He pulled her to the ground.

She bit his earlobe. "I want yours off, too."

He figured she meant his clothes. Well, maybe not, judging from the way she started kissing his chest. It was entirely possible she was talking about getting something else off. For that to happen, the clothes had to go.

Getting out of chaps, spurs, boots and jeans was no easy feat. It especially wasn't easy with Rayanne's hot little mouth moving all over the place. She had a wild look in her eyes when she wrestled with the chaps. There was definitely something exciting about this sudden urgency she had to strip off his clothes, and he loved it almost as much as he loved her. Rios hurriedly shucked off his leather vest and shirt, slinging them aside.

But he stopped when he realized the notion that had just raced through his mind. *Almost as much as he loved her.* He gave his head a hard shake. No, he didn't mean that, did he? Well, heck, it seemed the answer was—

Rayanne didn't give him time to finish that thought. She caught his ears and pulled him on top of her.

"I wanted you to be my first, but it was that stupid jerk in college," she mumbled through the French kissing.

"I'd rather be your last than your first, anyway."

She went completely still. With a hearty grip on his ears, she looked at him. "Do you mean that?"

Did he mean what? Rios had already forgotten what he'd said. Oh, yeah. He'd said something about wanting to be her last lover, and now she wanted to know if he meant it. Did he? Since the only thing separating his overly aroused body from hers was her pink panties and about a millimeter of his self-control, he was inclined to agree to anything she wanted him to agree to. But he wanted to make sure he was telling her the truth.

"Did you mean it?" she repeated, her voice breathy and hot.

He looked into her eyes, then at her face. Then at her body. Looking at her body distracted him, though. Mercy, but the woman had filled out nicely. He was thinking C-cup here.

"Rios? Did you hear me?"

Yes, he'd heard her all right. Mercy, a C-cup. She had a body better than most pinups he'd seen, and here she was, lying beneath him waiting for him to…answer her.

Again, he nearly forgot the question. Oh, yeah—did he mean the part about wanting to be her last lover? This time, he didn't let her body distract him. This time, he looked at her and let his heart do his answering for him.

"There's no way I want you to be with another man after this. Just me and you, Rayanne. Got that?"

She smiled, all dreamylike, and sighed. "I think that's the most romantic thing you could have said."

Romantic? He'd actually said something romantic, without rehearsing it or anything. Rios had a hard time concentrating on the conversation but was glad he said the right thing at the right time. The fact that it was true made it a first for him.

Her breasts distracted him again. He used his tongue to wet his fingertips and slipped them over her nipples. First one and then the other. They tightened into rose-colored buds.

Rayanne moaned his name, adding that breathy little hitch to it. "Yes," she said. "Yes."

Since it was obvious that she was enjoying it as much as he was, Rios lingered for a while, making sure her nipples became familiar with his mouth and letting his mouth become familiar with them. He would have lingered even longer if Rayanne hadn't slid her hand between their bodies. She latched on to the only part of him that could get his complete, undivided attention.

His eyes crossed.

"Don't make me wait any longer, Rios."

He completely understood the urgency. He couldn't wait any longer, either, but he didn't want to act like a brute. He ripped off her panties and threw them in the creek. Okay. Since that probably could be construed as brutelike, he slowed down as much as he could.

Capturing her mouth in a deep, wet kiss, he positioned himself, intending to take her slowly. He offered her an inch, but she took a great deal more than that. She took about nine times more than that. All right, only seven times more. Rayanne wrapped her legs around his waist, shoved her body forward and completed the snug, wet, mind-boggling union in one gasp-generating collision.

After the gasp, she gave a moan of relief. After his gasp, Rios grunted. All things considered, he thought he was doing good to get out that grunt. He was deep-seated right in the portal of paradise, and he wouldn't let anything get in the way of making them both crazed thrill seekers.

There was nothing graceful about the rhythm they found. But nothing that happened was ordinary. Rios knew that, and he figured Rayanne knew it, too. That's why he said her name in that last moment, so she would look at him, so he could look into her eyes. Somehow, that was more intimate, more important, more urgent than what they were doing. And he watched her as he pushed her right over the edge.

Yes, indeed. He learned Rayanne could be quite persuasive in those last mindless, thrill-seeking moments. She didn't go through that portal of paradise alone. Oh, no. She latched on to him and took him right along with her.

Rios decided he'd thank her for it later. Right after he let her know that he was head over heels in love with her.

RAYANNE SAW STARS. Big ones. Rios had, too. It was hard for a woman not to be aware of something like that.

At first, she thought she'd killed him. About the same time they had seen those stars together, Rios had gutted out some fairly creative profanity and collapsed in a dead heap on top of her. But he wasn't dead. Every now and then she felt a special kind of stirring—slight, but in the right area to indicate he was not only alive but might be ready for seconds.

"Rios?" she whispered.

He made a groaning sound.

Well, he might not have the breath yet to talk, but she sure did. She wanted to shout it from the treetops that she'd finally made love with the man she loved. What could possibly be better than that? She mentally shrugged. A commitment, maybe. But she wouldn't push things. Not right away, at least.

Rayanne thought the ringing sound was in her head until she heard Rios groan. Not a moaning groan but one of aggravation.

"Phone," he clarified. "Don't you dare go anywhere. I'm not done with you yet." He rolled off her, sat up and began to rake through the heap of clothes they'd discarded.

A phone. Great. They were naked in the middle of nowhere and had been interrupted by a phone call. He finally located the ringing annoyance in his vest pocket, turned it on and pushed it against his ear.

"Sheriff McKay. And it'd better be important."

Rayanne silently agreed. It had better be a matter of life and death. But after seeing the frustrated, aggravated expression on Rios's face, she realized it was probably important on at least a nonpersonal level. That meant they likely had to get dressed and leave. It also meant they might not get to have a second try at finding paradise.

"Now?" Rios asked. He mumbled something under his breath and shoved his hand through his hair. "Give us an hour." His gaze landed on Rayanne. "Make that two hours."

Well, maybe she would get around to those seconds, after all. "Who was that?"

"Evie. She wants us to meet her at my place. She said it's important."

"Is Mattie with her?" Rayanne asked.

"No, she's with Freda. Evie wants to talk to us alone."

"She probably just wants to make sure we're not furious with her. Which we are, aren't we?"

"Well, I'm not happy that she plotted to get us married, but I'm glad she got you back here." Rios grinned, causing his dimples to show. "If she hadn't done that, we wouldn't be where we are right now."

True. So, maybe she wasn't mad at Evie, after all.

He smiled at her and circled her nipple with his finger. "C-cup, right?"

It took her a moment to realize he was talking about her breasts. She nodded and leaned over so she could kiss him.

"No!" he yelled.

Confused, she stared at him. "No, what?"

"No to the moving part. Not yet, anyway. I want you to stay right there so I can just look at you. If you start touching or kissing me, I won't be able to think, much less appreciate the view. Your kisses turn my brain to stump water."

Rayanne felt a little uncomfortable under his intense scrutiny. After all, she was buck naked and probably had a dozen hickeys. There was probably some mud and grass in places she didn't want to think about.

"You're so beautiful, Rayanne." He gently slid his hands down her back, caressing her along the way. "You're perfect. Your body, your face. *You.* I'm the luckiest man alive."

She smiled. Mercy, but he was romantic. The truth was, they were both lucky. And if she was right about that gleam in Rios's eye, she was about to get lucky in a whole different way.

Rios winked at her. "Now, you can distract me," he said.

Rayanne did her best.

"Do you see my underwear around anywhere?" Rios asked when they were getting dressed.

An alarmed expression came over her face. "No. You can't find them? Quick, look in my hair."

"For my Jockey shorts?"

"Just do it."

He looked in her hair. No shorts. But Rios certainly hadn't expected to find them there.

"I just wanted to make sure," she said, as if that clarified everything.

He sifted through his clothes and shook off some dirt and a few roly-polies. "After we talk to Evie, I think you and I need to sit down and discuss some things." Now that she'd agreed to stay in Longhorn, he had to find some way to keep her in his life, as well.

Rayanne grinned at him. And winked. "Maybe you can take me for a, uh, ride somewhere later."

He grinned back. Rios really liked her insatiable appetite, but then he remembered this was serious. They could still do the ride and other things, but he wanted a lot more than that from her. He was looking for some kind of permanent relationship here, and from the romantic look in Rayanne's eyes, she seemed ready to spell out the kind of commitment she wanted. Rios was ready to hear it.

"A penny for your thoughts," he said, kissing her cheek.

"Really?" Her face brightened. "Well, how about you put on those chaps later. No jeans, no shorts. Oh, and maybe the leather vest with your badge on it. Then maybe we could go to the barn and get on one of those bales of hay." She stopped and blushed. "Well, you get the idea."

Yes, and as ideas went, it was a darn good one. Except he wanted Rayanne to wear the vest and badge. Maybe even a pair of cowboy boots, but certainly no underwear, unless they were those little lacy high-cut things. Rios swore and shook his head. If he kept thinking about that, they'd never get out of these woods.

"We'll do that," he finally said. "Later. After we talk to Evie."

And after they talked to Evie, he'd figure out a way to talk Rayanne into giving him a commitment. He hadn't ruled out using sex. And he certainly hadn't ruled out using those chaps. Or begging.

But one thing was for sure—Rayanne Garrett was staying with him.

CHAPTER TWELVE

"Oh, what the heck—go ahead and put all your
eggs in one basket."
—Bumper Ditties by Evie E. Garrett

RAYANNE BLINKED TO make sure she wasn't seeing things.
No, she wasn't. Evie was sitting in a rocking chair on
Rios's porch. Bennie was in the chair beside her. And
Evie was holding a double-barreled shotgun on him.

"Well, this should be fun," Rayanne said under her
breath. Together, Rios and she got out of his truck and
walked to the porch steps.

"We've been waiting for you." Evie's voice was
weather-discussion calm.

That calmness scared Rayanne a little. She knew from
experience this was the kind of situation that could get
quickly out of hand.

"Why don't you put down that gun, Evie?" Rios
asked. His voice was calm, too.

"I will in just a minute. Bennie has something to tell
you first."

Bennie's nose was redder than usual, and he was
chewing on the stub of an unlit cigar. "I'm supposed to
say that I won't oppose Rios's custody of Mattie."

Evie gave a satisfied nod. "There, you heard it from
the horse's mouth. All your problems are solved."

Rayanne groaned. "Aunt Evie, this won't work."

"Of course, it will. You heard what he said, didn't you?"

"I did, but you can't force Bennie into doing this. He has to feel it's right for Mattie."

Bennie looked at her as if she'd found a cure for every disease known to man. "That's right, little lady. I have to do what I feel is right for my granddaughter. I didn't think you of all people would see my side of it."

"Well, of course, I see your side. You want what's best for Mattie. Rios wants the same thing, and so do I. Aunt Evie does, too, but she just has an odd way of showing it. A *very* odd way."

"But Rios wants to cut me out of Mattie's life," Bennie objected.

"No, I don't," Rios disagreed. "But you have to let me be her father, because that's what I am."

Evie came to her feet. "That's what I've been telling the old geezer—"

Rayanne gave her aunt a look that pleaded with her to keep quiet. Name calling wouldn't get them anywhere. Rayanne knew that firsthand. When she was certain she'd silenced Evie for the moment, Rayanne turned to Bennie.

"I'm sure Mattie has told you how much she loves her father. Mattie and I were talking about this just this morning. She also told me how much she loves you, and she doesn't want you and Rios arguing over her." Rayanne slowly walked up the steps.

"She said that?" There was a softness in Bennie's voice she hadn't heard earlier. Progress, maybe.

"Well, of course, she did, you old geezer." Evie again.

Rayanne had had just about all she could tolerate

from her aunt. She snatched the gun from Evie's grip and handed it to Rios. Rayanne tried to remember to speak respectfully to her aunt, but it was rather hard to do. "Aunt Evie, it's a good time for you just to sit back and listen, okay?"

Evie gave an uncertain nod and dropped into the rocker. Bennie, on the other hand, rose from his chair. Rayanne didn't know what he'd do, but she was thankful Rios was with her.

"I talked to Mattie myself, just a little while ago," Bennie continued. "She said she wanted to live with her, uh, father. And that she wanted you to live with him, too."

"Oh," Rayanne muttered somewhat uncomfortably. She glanced at Rios, and he didn't look comfortable with that remark, either. "Well, I suppose that's something we'll have to discuss."

Evie stood again. "Let's just cut to the chase, shall we? You're in love with Rios, aren't you?"

The discomfort went up a notch, not because Rayanne wasn't sure of her answer, but because she hadn't expected to make such a first-time profession in front of anyone but Rios. "Yes, I love him. Very much."

No one said anything for several snail-crawling moments. "Very much?" Rios questioned. "How much is very much?"

She gave a few awkward-looking bobs of her head. "A lot. More than, well, air and other vital necessities."

Traffic-cop style, Evie held up her hand before Rios could speak. "And Rios, don't you love her?"

"Yes, I do. Very much."

Rayanne looked at him. "Very much?"

"Loads. Big giant buckets full."

She caught her bottom lip between her teeth to keep from smiling. It didn't seem a good time for that. Not yet, anyway. She fully intended to do some smiling later.

"Loads," Evie repeated. "Buckets full. And more than air. That sounds like a marriage proposal, if you ask me."

"I don't think they asked you," Bennie grumbled.

"Well, they darn well should have. Mattie can still spend some weekends with you, but she needs a family. A mother and a father. We're not old, Bennie, but we're not young enough to be raising a little girl. That's a father and a mother's job."

Bennie looked at his feet for a while. Then he looked at the trees. Then the yard. Finally, he looked at Rios. "You two would be getting married, you say?"

Rios caught Rayanne's hand and brought it to his mouth to kiss. "If I have anything to say about it, we will."

"You have a lot to say about it," Rayanne assured him.

"Is that a yes then?" Rios asked her.

"It's a yes." She wanted to celebrate. Well, actually, she wanted to haul Rios off to bed, repeat in thorough detail how much she loved him and whisper sweet nothings in his ear. However, they first needed to finish business with Bennie. "Well, Bennie?"

He shrugged. "I guess we can give this arrangement a try."

Rayanne looked hard at him. "No custody battle?"

"No custody battle."

She looked harder still at him. "And what about the charges against Evie?"

Rios stepped slightly closer. "I think he'll drop those,

since I won't be charging him with malicious and intentional damage to municipal property."

"Huh?" That from Rayanne.

"He's the one who chopped up Hal's Hungry Heifer," Rios explained. "Since Evie donated it to the city, it's municipal property and protected under the law."

"You chopped up the rubber cow?" Evie gasped. "Of all the sick things you could have come up with."

"Well?" Rios quizzed. "What'll it be, Bennie? If you charge Evie, then I'll have to charge you."

"I'll drop the charges," Bennie said with effort. "If Evie will swear to me she'll give up these stupid plans of hers. The woman's just not very good at this sort of thing."

"I won't ever do anything like this again," Evie declared.

Rayanne didn't believe her, and she was fairly sure Bennie and Rios didn't, either. But since the plan had seemed to, heaven forbid, work, then Rayanne didn't see any reason to criticize her aunt.

Evie latched on to Bennie's arm and quickly hauled him down the steps. "Well, now that that's settled, we'll just be going so you two can have some privacy. By the way, Rayanne, you got a pair of men's underwear hanging out of the leg of your blue jeans. I don't suppose you want to try to explain that, huh?"

Rayanne looked at the top of her shoe and groaned. Why did she have this penchant for underwear attaching itself to her at the most inopportune time? Rayanne did what had worked for her the last time it happened—she mumbled.

Evie gave a firm nod. "That's what I figured you'd say. Bennie and I will just be on our way."

Rayanne had never seen two people move so fast. They looked like cartoon characters hurrying to the car. The aging sedan kicked up gravel as her aunt peeled away.

She looped her arm through Rios's. "How did you know Bennie had chopped up the rubber cow?"

"Lucky guess."

"You guessed?" she asked in disbelief.

"That, and Mattie mentioned there was some sticky paper on Bennie's ax. Paper that advertised the dates of the town festival."

"Well, that's not much of a guess. That's evidence."

"I guess." Rios slid his arm around her waist. "So, I figure you must have conditions before you'll marry me, huh?"

"Nope. No conditions. I'm just looking for what every woman wants. A devoted husband, a tender father, an adventurous lover and joint custody of the remote control. I think you'll do nicely on all accounts."

His grip tightened around her waist. "And you said something earlier about loving me?"

"Oh, that. Yep, I'm in love with you all right. Crazy, madly, deeply in love with you. It's the forever-after kind, too. The kind that'll make me act really sappy and totally nuts for years on end. You should have fun with that."

That earned her a kiss. A long, wet one that had her breathing hard when he pulled away and looked at her. "You're the only woman I've ever loved, you know that?"

That earned him a kiss. A long, wet one that had him breathing hard when Rayanne pulled away. "We're going to be good together, Rios. Mattie, you and me."

He grinned. "You really do like her, don't you?"

Rayanne shook her head. "Nope. I love her." She shrugged and blinked back some tears of happiness that were trying to sneak into her eyes. "The way I have it figured, I get to have this wonderful daughter without having to go through all the labor pains and stretch marks. It's a great deal for me. And if we play our cards right, we can eventually give her a brother or a sister."

A tear escaped, after all, and Rios wiped it away with his thumb. "It's a great deal for all of us. Come on." He caught her hand. "Before we go to Evie's and tell Mattie, I want you to take a little walk with me to the barn."

"But the fire—"

"Not that barn. The one in the back of the house."

It wasn't hard to tell what he had on his mind. Funny, she suddenly had the same thing on hers. What better way to celebrate being in love? "Why can't we just go to your bedroom?"

"The barn's more interesting. Hay bales."

"Good point," Rayanne agreed. Really good point. "Oh, yes. I suppose I should let you know I intend to run for sheriff in the next election."

"Oh, will you?" Rios asked calmly.

"Definitely."

"It should be interesting, because I plan to run for reelection."

"Then you're right." Rayanne gave a firm nod. "It should be interesting. Don't worry, if I'm elected, I'll keep you on as my deputy. I'm sure you'd do the same for me."

"Of course. Wait a minute, I forgot something." He led her to the truck and pulled out his chaps and vest from the back. "I'll need these to reenact that little adventure you told me about at the creek."

"Will this adventure involve seeing stars?"

"Absolutely," Rios assured her, adding another of those famous cowboy kisses that made her glad she was on the receiving end of them. "Big ones, darling. Really big ones."

* * * * *

We hope you enjoyed reading

Courageous

by *New York Times* bestselling author
DIANA PALMER

and

The Deputy Gets Her Man

by *USA TODAY* bestselling author
DELORES FOSSEN

Both were originally HQN and
Harlequin® series stories!

From passionate, suspenseful and dramatic
love stories to inspirational or historical,
Harlequin offers different lines to
satisfy every romance reader.

New books in each line
are available every month.

Harlequin.com

"Who's in the house?" he asked.

Another head shake from Laney. "A man. I didn't see
his face."

Not that he needed it, but Owen had more confirmation
of the danger. He saw that Laney had a gun, a small
snub-nosed .38. It didn't belong to him, nor was it one
that he'd ever seen in the guesthouse where Laney was
staying. Later, he'd ask her about it, about why she hadn't
mentioned that she had a weapon, but for now they
obviously had a much bigger problem.

Owen texted his brother again, to warn him about the
intruder so that Kellan didn't walk into a situation that
could turn deadly. He also asked Kellan to call in more
backup. If the person upstairs started shooting, Owen
wanted all the help he could get.

"What happened?" Owen whispered to Laney.

She opened her mouth, paused and then closed it as
if she'd changed her mind about what to say. "About

ten minutes ago, I was in the kitchen with Addie when the power went off. A few seconds later, a man came in through the front door and I hid in the pantry with her until he went upstairs."

Smart thinking on Laney's part to hide instead of panicking or confronting the guy. But it gave Owen an uneasy feeling that Laney could think that fast under such pressure. And then there was the gun again. Where had she got it? The guesthouse was on the other side of the backyard, much farther away than the barn. If she'd gone to the guesthouse to get the gun, why hadn't she just stayed there with Addie? It would have been safer than running across the yard with the baby.

"Did you get a good look at the man?" Owen prompted.

Laney again shook her head. "But I heard him. When he stepped into the house, I knew it wasn't you, so I guessed it must be trouble."

Again, quick thinking on her part. He wasn't sure why, though, that gave him a very uneasy feeling.

"I didn't hear or see a vehicle," Laney added.

Owen hadn't seen one, either, which meant the guy must have come on foot. Not impossible, but Owen's ranch was a good half mile from the main road. If this was a thief, he wasn't going to get away with much. Plus, it would be damn brazen of some idiot to break into a cop's home just to commit a robbery.

So what was really going on?

Don't miss
A Threat to His Family *by Delores Fossen,*
available January 2020 wherever
Harlequin® Intrigue books and ebooks are sold.

www.Harlequin.com

INTRIGUE

EDGE-OF-YOUR-SEAT INTRIGUE, FEARLESS ROMANCE.

Save **$1.00**
on the purchase of ANY
Harlequin® Intrigue book.

Available wherever books are sold,
including most bookstores, supermarkets,
drugstores and discount stores.

- ✂

Save **$1.00**

on the purchase of any Harlequin® Intrigue book.

Coupon valid until April 30, 2020.
Redeemable at participating outlets in the U.S. and Canada only.
Not redeemable at Barnes & Noble stores. Limit one coupon per customer.

52616554

® and ™ are trademarks owned and used by the trademark owner and/or its licensee.

© 2019 Harlequin Enterprises ULC

BACCOUP01567

ROMANTIC suspense

*Navy SEAL Brett Morgan has come home to
Sunny Creek to recover after a disastrous deployment,
desperate to remember what happened. Anna Larkin
returned home, determined to forget what happened.
Together, Anna and Brett must fight to live and love
as their pasts threaten them both.*

Read on for a sneak preview of
Navy SEAL's Deadly Secret, *the first book in*
New York Times *bestselling author Cindy Dees's
brand-new Runaway Ranch miniseries.*

The memories flooded back so fast and hard, slamming
into him like a physical blow, that he stumbled behind
Anna, and had to catch himself with a hand against the
wall.

How could he have forgotten all of that stuff?

Anna stopped abruptly in what looked like a dining
room and turned to face him, tipping up her face
expectantly to the light. The curve of her cheek was
worthy of a Rembrandt painting, plump like a child's and
angular like a woman's. How was that possible?

"Well?" she demanded.

"Uh, well what?" he mumbled.

"Are my pupils all right?"

He frowned and looked into her eyes. They were
cinnamon-hued, the color of a chestnut horse in sunshine,

with streaks of gold running through them. Her lashes were dark and long, fanning across her cheeks as lightly as strands of silk.

Pupils. Compare diameters. Even or uneven. Cripes. His entire brain had just melted and drained out his ear. One look into her big innocent eyes, and he was toast. Belatedly, he held up a hand in front of her face, blocking the direct light.

She froze at the abrupt movement of his hand, and he did the same. Where was the threat? When one of his teammates went completely still like that, it meant a dire threat was far too close to all of them. Without moving his head, he let his gaze range around the room. Everything was still, and only the sounds of a vintage disco dance tune broke the silence.

He looked back at her questioningly. What had her so on edge? Only peripherally did he register that, on cue, the black disks of her pupils had grown to encompass the lighter brown of her irises. He took his hand away, and her pupils contracted quickly.

"Um, yeah. Your eyes look okay," he murmured. "Do you have a headache?"

"Yes, but it's from all the sanding I have to do and not from my tumble off your porch."

Don't miss
Navy SEAL's Deadly Secret *by Cindy Dees,*
available January 2020 wherever
Harlequin® Romantic Suspense
books and ebooks are sold.

Harlequin.com

HRSEXP1219

Love Harlequin romance?

DISCOVER.

Be the first to find out about promotions, news and exclusive content!

f Facebook.com/HarlequinBooks

t Twitter.com/HarlequinBooks

O Instagram.com/HarlequinBooks

P Pinterest.com/HarlequinBooks

ReaderService.com

EXPLORE.

Sign up for the Harlequin e-newsletter and download a free book from any series at **TryHarlequin.com.**

CONNECT.

Join our Harlequin community to share your thoughts and connect with other romance readers!
Facebook.com/groups/HarlequinConnection

HARLEQUIN®

**ROMANCE WHEN
YOU NEED IT**